# THE BANG-BANG BANG SISTERS

## ALSO BY RIO YOUERS

# THE BANG-BANG SISTERS

# A NOVEL

# RIO YOUERS

*WM*

WILLIAM MORROW

*An Imprint of HarperCollinsPublishers*

THE BANG-BANG SISTERS. Copyright © 2024 by Rio Youers. All rights reserved. Printed in the United States of America. No part of this book may be used or reproduced in any manner whatsoever without written permission except in the case of brief quotations embodied in critical articles and reviews. For information, address HarperCollins Publishers, 195 Broadway, New York, NY 10007.

HarperCollins books may be purchased for educational, business, or sales promotional use. For information, please email the Special Markets Department at SPsales@harpercollins.com.

FIRST EDITION

*Designed by Nancy Singer*
*Title page type and art designed by Philip Pascuzzo*

Library of Congress Cataloging-in-Publication Data has been applied for.

ISBN 978-0-06-331180-0

24 25 26 27 28  LBC  5 4 3 2 1

*For Lily Youers,*
*who always inspires me*

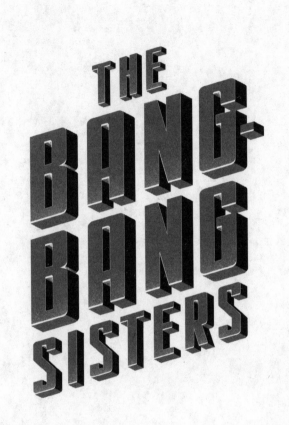

# PROLOGUE

A stream of purified oxygen ran from the concentrator, through the nasal cannula, down his trachea, and into his lungs. The man—known far and wide as the wren—paused for several seconds and stared at the sky. It called to him, but he wouldn't take flight until he saw the first drops of blood.

The garish digital clock on the Kotter-Bryce Tower (664 feet of glass-and-steel ugliness) read 8:37. Through the haze of pollutants, the sunset dressed itself in purples and golds. A spectacle anywhere else, but here it was wasted—here being Reedsville, Alabama, population 56,700, with an M16-toting mayor and a violent crime rate of 27.8 per 1,000 people. Regarding this grim statistic, the wren had played his part.

He skirted the noise and crowds of Waterloo Square, keeping to the quieter side streets. Even at this distance he felt the tug on his skin, the *unraveling*, not a complete deterioration, but enough to quicken his heartbeat. He kept walking—frequently touching the cannula to make sure the nasal prongs were secure—and within twenty minutes had made it to Pine Vista, the middle-class neighborhood where Susan Orringer lived.

The wren didn't know her. Not personally. They'd had some interaction on Facebook, insomuch as she'd liked and commented on one of his comments. She was forty-two years old, a recent divorcée (her ex was a former MLB player turned civil engineer), with a twenty-year-old daughter at UA. She worked as a business manager at a local Harley-Davidson dealership. Her favorite cuisine was Vietnamese and her favorite movie was *Titanic* (for the longest time Susan's Facebook cover photo was Jack and Rose "flying" on the bow of the doomed ocean liner). She had changed her hair recently—cut it shorter, dyed it darker—and had lost twenty-four pounds since separating from her husband, due in part to the spin classes she attended every Monday and Wednesday evening.

She lived alone.

**IT WAS LIGHT ENOUGH TO** see, but shadowy enough to not be seen.

The wren entered Susan's property via a neighboring garden. No fences here. The owners of these mature lots frowned on fences, favoring strategically placed trees and bushes for their privacy. More shadow, more cover, all to the good. The wren removed leather gloves from his pocket and worked his hands into them. He crossed the garden swiftly, using his ears as well as his eyes. Above the low, electric whir of his concentrator, he heard teenagers splashing in a nearby pool, a freight train ripping through the crossing on Confederation Avenue, a radio tuned to one of the local country music stations. He edged from the shadows and hunkered low next to one of Susan's basement windows.

It was Wednesday evening. Susan was still spinning. He imagined her briefly, straddling her bike, her cropped tank glued to her back with sweat. The wren tried the window, but it was locked. He tore through the screen and thumped the glass with the fleshy side of his fist until it cracked, then removed large, jagged pieces quietly. He reached inside, flipped the catch, and pulled the window open. It was narrow, but the wren was a small bird, and he slipped inside easily.

**HE DROPPED DOWN INTO A** laundry room, gloomy, smelling thickly of Tide, but infinitely more comfortable than the chaos of the outside world. The walls were solid, dependable. The wren touched them and closed his eyes, acclimating to this new environment, soon feeling confident enough to shut off his concentrator. There were still a few tight bands around his chest, however, so he turned the machine back on and decreased the flow rate instead. He breathed for a moment and touched the walls again.

It was a split-level house with the main bedroom above the garage. Here, working in the dimness, the wren removed a bag of feathers from his backpack and scattered them across the floor and bed. A framed print of the New York City skyline adorned the wall opposite the door. He lifted it off its hooks, leaned it against the dresser, then reached into his backpack again and took out a pot of black paint and a brush. For a moment, in the nervous rush of everything, he forgot the haiku. It had taken him an hour to compose, and he'd recited it over and over. The wren closed his eyes and imagined a perch in some high, clear space.

"Ascends," he said. The haiku clicked into place. He unscrewed the lid of the pot, dipped the brush in, and wrote in the pale rectangle where the print had lived:

> the night in my wings
> her blood in my brown feathers
> my heart ascends too
> —*wren*

The haiku was his calling card. He'd usually type it on a sheet of pink or yellow paper and place it in the victim's hand. One time he wrote it on the victim's body with a fountain pen. It had looked like a messy tattoo. Whatever the canvas, it was his mark, and the one detail that the police withheld from the public to rule out bogus confessions and better identify the actual killer.

A fragile smile touched the wren's lips. He returned the paint pot and brush to his backpack and took out a paring knife wrapped in sackcloth. It had a curved three-inch blade—small, like a wren's beak. *Peck-peck-peck.* Susan Orringer would return home from her spin class in twenty minutes, give or take. (He knew her routine; it wasn't splashed all over her socials, but he'd been watching her awhile.) She'd probably putter around the kitchen and living room for several minutes—kick off her heels, grab a drink, check her phone—but would make her way to the bedroom in due course. The displaced air from the opening door would lift a cloud of feathers off the floor, prompting an instant of surprise and confusion—this followed, as her eyes tracked to the name beneath the haiku, by nightmarish realization.

HE WAITED BEHIND THE DOOR with the knife clutched in his right hand. Darkness fell, absorbing the haiku and the feathers, until a car swung into the driveway and its headlights scrolled across the walls, revitalizing the scene for one bright second. The garage door rattled up, then rattled down again. Susan entered the house a moment later. He heard the distinct jangle of her keys, her heels on the hardwood floor.

"*The night in my wings,*" the wren whispered. He considered the day-to-day stranglehold of his other life, constantly battling disorderliness, tethered to the ground.

He cranked up the flow rate on his oxygen concentrator. He felt it in his lungs and in his feathers.

The sky beckoned.

# ONE

Jessie Steen. Thirty-one years old. Guitar and vocals.

She had a playing style that aligned with her character and with everything else she did in life: vivacious, fearless, but with a precision that could raise the roof. Jessie rarely missed a note *or* a shot.

It didn't hurt, of course, that she looked good doing it—whatever *it* happened to be. Not just her image (".40-caliber goth," she called it), but the way she moved. She had a catlike grace, a heightened awareness of her environment, and a showperson's instincts. Some of it was natural, but most came the hard way: through a daily regimen of yoga, meditation, and training. Jessie had spent endless hours shredding her instrument, unloading shots at the range, and sparring with a succession of steroid-fueled men—all to good effect. Watching her perform was like standing at the edge of a waterfall.

She'd been taught guitar by an aging British glam rocker (dead now, RIP Gene Topaz), and a friend of the family—Uncle Dog—had taught her how to fight. From an early age, Jessie knew that neutralizing an opponent, no matter their size, wasn't all about strength. Technique played a vital part, and technique was the product of posture, timing, and repetition. It was the same with music. The best singers didn't always have the biggest voices. The best guitar players didn't have the busiest fingers. To be effective, you just had to hit your mark cleanly. You had to do the small things right.

FLORENCE "FLO" BELLA. THIRTY-ONE YEARS old. Bass, backing vocals.

Flo had once dated a Hollywood A-lister who presented to the media as a good, clean, all-American boy, charitable and politically aware, but away from the cameras was—like many Hollywood A-listers—a vain, self-interested piece of shit. When they left a restaurant or party, he would position himself to take both barrels of the paparazzi shotgun, not because he was trying to protect Flo's privacy, but because he liked being photographed. When they had sex, he would angle the mirrors to better see himself. ("Look at my fucking abs!" he once shrieked, mid-orgasm, which had killed the moment for Flo.) It was the *Him Show* 95 percent of the time, which, despite the red-carpet lifestyle and Hollywood parties, wore thin quickly.

He'd learned *some* things about Flo during the short span of their relationship. He knew that she'd lived in China for five years, but not that she'd spent the majority of that time at a secluded mountain temple learning Shaolin kung fu. He knew that she "dabbled" in music (his expression), but not that she was an accomplished multi-instrumentalist who'd once shared a stage with John Legend. He knew that Flo's mother had been killed in a car accident, but not that the accident had been caused by a drunk driver who, because of his connections, subsequently ducked all charges.

Flo had packed a lot into her thirty-one years, but Mr. Hollywood was not interested. He was with her because—Black, strong, and beautiful— she made him look good. Flo had tried, she really had, but after six weeks of being little more than an accessory, she ended their relationship over text.

Because fuck that guy.

**BREA STEEN. THIRTY-FOUR YEARS OLD. DRUMS.**

Like any good drummer, Brea laid down the groove—a creative, dependable foundation that her bandmates built upon. She had impeccable timing, controlled power, and an innate *feel* for any situation. She'd been this way since she was young. Balanced, intuitive, with enviable rhythm. No surprise that the drums were Brea's weapon of choice, although she was partial to anything that went boom.

Brea and Jessie's father had left home when Brea was three (and Jessie, a newborn), to deepen his worldly understanding and to experience things inappropriate for the family dynamic. "I don't know if I'll ever come back," he'd said to the girls' mother. "Don't wait for me." He'd walked away with a single change of clothes and $270 in his wallet, and was shot to death two years later by Tuareg guerrillas in Mali.

He wasn't mourned, and their mother hadn't waited. She'd remarried within eighteen months of Mickey Steen walking out the door. Her new husband was a better man—a big-time record company exec, wealthier in the heart as well as the pocket—and they all lived together on a thirty-acre ranch in the northwestern corner of the San Fernando Valley. Brea's childhood memories included cross-country trips on private jets, yachting on the Sea of Cortez, and birthday gifts from Michael Jackson. It was a blessed upbringing.

Their stepfather's best friend also lived with them on the ranch, in a converted loft above the barn. Joe Collie (affectionately nicknamed Uncle Dog) was a Hollywood stuntman and stage combat instructor who'd studied martial arts in eight different countries and had developed his own fighting style—a combination of *pencak silat*, Brazilian jiujitsu, and close-quarters combat. He called it *hujan badai*, meaning "thunderstorm" in Indonesian. His students were primarily movie stars who wanted to back up what they did on film. As a favor to his best friend—but also because he was particularly fond of them—he also taught the girls.

Brea had little interest in fighting, at least to begin with. She did it only to keep up with Jessie, who trained an hour every day with Uncle Dog. Brea didn't want her little sister to be better than her at anything—a sibling rivalry that had fueled all their ventures and interests. With *hujan badai*, they were effective in different ways: Jessie was lithe and precise, and focused on striking pressure points to incapacitate her opponents. Brea had rhythm and power. She focused on breaking bones.

Brea realized the full benefit of her training at the age of twenty-one, when she was set upon by a broad, bullish man in the parking lot outside a Chinese restaurant in Santa Clarita. It was dark. The man had stepped out from behind his cargo van and grabbed Brea's upper arm. She dropped her order of kung pao chicken, swiveled on one heel—calculating his mass, posture, and exposed vulnerabilities in the half second it took her to turn—and punched her attacker in the throat. Or rather, she punched him *through* the throat. She felt his whiskery skin, then the fragile pipe-work of his trachea, which collapsed easily beneath her fist. She even felt the blunt nubs of his cervical spine. The man squeaked like a dog toy and hit the asphalt with a crippled thud. Brea picked up her kung pao chicken and left him spasming on the ground.

Brea and Jessie were similar in many ways, and equal, but they had their differences, especially when it came to relationships. Jessie was straight. Brea identified as pansexual, attracted to personality with no emphasis on gender. It was, in fact, the same with her vigilante work. She responded only to a person's character, and from this arrived at her own unscientific conclusion: that of all primal urges, killing and fucking were the most closely aligned.

**THEY PLAYED BARS AND CLUBS** across the Lower 48, no distance too big, no venue too small. As a hard-rockin' three-piece, they went by several different names, including L.A. County Breakout, the Sweetcakes, and Crash the Moon. For their other engagements—the vigilante gigs—they were known as the Bang-Bang Sisters.

# TWO

Banjo McCoy's. Clear River, New York. A Thursday night in late August.

The first set was slow, the tables occupied by patrons who were more interested in ingesting calories than listening to a live band. A ripple of polite applause followed each song. The dance floor, such as it was, remained empty. By ten P.M., most of the diners had vacated, and the bar started to fill with a rowdier clientele: the drinkers, the revelers, a couple of truckloads of upstate rednecks and their tattooed, big-haired lady-friends. Tables were removed to make more space for dancing.

The sisters started the second set strong and built from there, a succession of rock anthems that turned Banjo McCoy's from a small-town bar into a ruckus of light, motion, and sound. There was dancing on the tables, fighting in the parking lot. Some drunk, sweaty dude jumped onstage and tried to grab the mic, but Jessie planted her boot up his ass and put an end to that. Security skulked like mastiffs in a junkyard. They helped several disruptive customers find the exit, usually face-first. The sisters stoked the flames with every new song, every thumping chord change.

They played until 12:20, but the crowd was still hungry. It stomped and swelled, crying for an encore. Jessie's voice was cracked, but her adrenaline was amped. She huddled with Brea and Flo.

"We got time for one more?" she asked.

Brea, flexing her tape-wrapped fingers: "We're, what, thirty minutes from Barrel Lake?"

"Give or take," Jessie said.

"We can do under-the-radar later, but this . . ." Flo slapped the E string on her bass, generating a couple of deep thumping notes. "*This* is our moment to be loud."

"I'm down with that." Brea twirled her drumstick and smiled.

The crowd continued its demand, spilling beer, the air above filled with pumping fists. Jessie swept her gaze across the room, nodding her head appreciatively. She turned back to her bandmates.

"Okay, one more song," she said. "Another thirty minutes to get paid, pack up, and load the van. Keeping to the speed limit, we'll be at the target's location . . . no later than one forty."

"That'll work," Brea said.

Jessie flicked hair out of her eyes. "Let's see if we can tip this joint on its side." She wheeled toward the mic, counting her sisters in, and they ripped into a cover of Joan Jett's "Bad Reputation." The crowd responded—a mesh of wild bodies, dancing, pushing, electrified. Three minutes of beautiful chaos.

They didn't tip the joint entirely on its side, but they left it at a skewed angle.

THEY WERE EN ROUTE TO Barrel Lake fifty minutes later. It took longer than they'd hoped to pack up because a larger-than-usual number of patrons insisted on extolling their enthusiasm for the band. They wanted selfies and contact info, and to reveal their thinly veiled misogyny ("You gals can actually *rock!*"). The sisters were courteous in return but didn't wallow in the love. It was important to keep moving—to ride their post-performance high all the way to their next gig.

South on NY 26, the needle dead on fifty-five. Their tour van was a 2017 Chevy Express with blacked-out rear windows and nearly two hundred thousand miles on the clock. They'd covered a lot of country in their three and a half years as a touring band. Brea sat behind the wheel, her eyes on the road. Flo rode shotgun, with Jessie sprawled on the second-row bench seat and their gear in the cargo space behind her.

They drove with their windows halfway down. It was a humid night, and the van's air con had given up the ghost when the odometer was still at five digits. The wind rush was cool and loud. The stereo played at a rhythmic thud. Flo had one hand in her hair to keep it from whipping around her face. Brea had tied hers back. The glow of the GPS on her phone placed little rectangles in her eyes.

"ETA one forty-eight," she said.

"Any luck, he's sleeping," Jessie said.

"And alone," Flo added.

"Drug dealers tend to burn the midnight oil." Brea touched the brake and steered around a dead deer splashed colorfully across the south-bound lane. "He's probably bingeing TikToks or playing *Fortnite* with his homies. Whatever he's doing, I guarantee he's within arm's reach of a semiautomatic."

Spencer Zaal, aka Smally-Z, was white trash wrapped in gold. He'd been in and out of juvie as a teenager and had spent three years at Fishkill Correctional for a Class D felony assault as an adult. Now his jam was street drugs, mainly heroin, operating with impunity out of his Barrel Lake home. The Trace—an underground network of gray-hat hackers and cybersecurity experts—had uncovered communication between Smally-Z and Barrel Lake's chief of police, Roland Hyatt, and it appeared the drug dealer had leverage: a number of compromising photographs of Hyatt's eighteen-year-old daughter (the sisters had seen these photographs, and "compromising" was an understated description). All Smally-Z asked in return for not sharing these photographs with the world was indemnity from the law, and Chief Hyatt appeared willing to oblige.

This alone would not have been enough for the Trace to post the job to its virtual bulletin board, but within the past six months Smally-Z had expanded his customer base. He had his teenage nephew working for him, slinging dope at Barrel Lake High. At the beginning of the summer, a fourteen-year-old girl had OD'd on Smally-Z's product while partying with friends at the lake. The Trace had hacked the BLPD mainframe and determined that Smally-Z hadn't even been questioned. If he had, it was off the record.

Smally-Z, meanwhile, covered himself in Gucci bling and drove around in his pimped-out Camaro.

It was time to stomp on this dirtbag.

Brea followed the GPS prompts, turning off 26 onto Fringe Road. Minutes later, they passed the sign welcoming them to Barrel Lake, population 4,300. WE'RE ALL FRIENDS HERE! There were not enough "friends" for Smally-Z to make serious bank. Most of his customers were in Syracuse and Utica. His product came up from Poughkeepsie, which in turn came from Queens.

"We're a mile from his door," Brea said.

"Recon time," Jessie said.

Brea turned the stereo down. She navigated the van to an empty parking lot behind a thrift store. Jessie reached beneath the bench seat, pulled out a black plastic case, and opened it. Inside was an ÜberFlyte Series 2 drone with GPS, a three-mile control range, and a thermal camera. Jessie powered the system up. Within a minute she'd set the speed, altitude, and destination. She rolled open the van's side door and launched.

The drone climbed to a height of 180 feet, then zipped off in the direction of Smally-Z's residence. The sisters gathered around the controller's screen, watching Barrel Lake pass below them by way of the aircraft's thermal cam. There wasn't much hot color at this time of night. The town was cool and sleeping. They saw a single person walking unevenly along the sidewalk on Main, probably on their way home from the local watering hole. Several deer crossed Sycamore Park at a blazing orange gallop. A bobtail truck idled at a stoplight downtown. In the three minutes it took the drone to travel the mile to Smally-Z's house, this was the only activity they saw.

"I love these small-town jobs," Jessie said.

The drone stopped and hovered above a shabby Craftsman home on a quiet, crescent-shaped street. Jessie took over the controls. She descended to sixty feet and circled the house meticulously, checking out the lay of the land.

"It's a junkyard in back," Flo pointed out. "That'll be tricky to navigate in the dark."

"We go in here." Brea indicated a side door, accessed by a cement path shot through with weeds but otherwise clear. "It might even be unlocked."

As much as the drone helped the sisters plan their approach and exit, they chiefly used it to gauge conflict scenarios. On past jobs, they had detected the fluorescent heat signatures of attack dogs and armed guards. They had spotted potential witnesses on adjacent blocks and police cruisers doing their nightly rounds. On a job in Baton Rouge, a swampy backyard filled with malnourished gators informed them that going in through the front door was a wiser course of action.

They saw no activity around Smally-Z's house, although lights burned both upstairs and down, indicating that multiple rooms were occupied. Reinforcing this logic, there were three vehicles in the double-wide driveway, the pimped-out Camaro among them.

Jessie elevated the drone twenty feet and zoomed out, surveilling the neighboring streets and properties. It didn't take long to find what she was looking for.

"We can park here. It's farther away than we'd like, but look . . ." Jessie ran her fingernail across the screen. "Cut across this backyard, hop this fence, and we're there. It's a direct line to Smally-Z's side door. We avoid the lights out front and the junk in back."

Brea nodded. "Yeah . . . good. If the door's locked, we shoot it open. You two take the ground floor, I'll take upstairs."

Jessie tapped the home icon in the corner of the screen, and the drone started back toward them. Empty streets scrolled beneath the cam.

"Sixty seconds," Brea added. "In and out."

The van was unremarkably white, except for a skin of road dust and twin bows of rust above the rear wheel arches. There was no band name emblazoned across the side, no bumper stickers or signage of any kind. It could blend in anywhere, a typical workperson's van. The tools of the trade were far from typical, though. Two-thirds of the cargo area was loaded with their musical equipment. The remaining space housed weaponry and ammunition: knives, daggers, nunchakus, various explosives, AR-15s, semiautomatic pistols, concealed-carry handguns, a Savage 10FP sniper rifle. Something for every occasion, all of it disguised in customized Fender and Gibson guitar cases.

The sisters armed up in the three minutes it took for the drone to return. They chose semiautomatic pistols with suppressors attached (which wouldn't completely silence the shots but would at least keep them from waking up the neighbors). Flo strapped a fighting knife to her hip. Jessie tucked a seven-hundred-gram nunchaku into the back of her jeans. They all wore black gloves and ski masks.

The drone landed three feet from the van. Jessie packed it away while Brea got behind the wheel. They drove the mile to Smally-Z's house and didn't see another vehicle on the road.

FLO POWERED UP HER LAPTOP, connected to the Trace, and clicked on a recent photograph of their heroin-dealing target. The guy was a walking piss stain: peroxide-blond spikes, a hard, angular face, Americana tattoos spilling out from beneath his Aeropostale tank top. Another distinguishing feature: different-colored eyes, one brown, one blue. His expression was as welcoming as a piece of broken glass.

The sisters studied the photograph for several seconds, logging every small detail, then looked at one another. Brea was the oldest, so had naturally assumed the leader's role. She booked their music gigs (keeping their cover intact), managed the finances, and called the shots on contracts. She didn't need to say anything in that moment, though. They all understood—they'd done this before. It didn't matter how many lowlifes and criminals were in that house, they had one target. Everything else had to be nonlethal. They'd go in, take care of business, and keep shots fired to a minimum.

"Ready?" Brea said.

Jessie and Flo nodded. They rolled down their ski masks and exited the van into a deep, rich night that smelled of cut grass and heat. They followed the short, direct route they'd marked out via the drone, through a neighboring backyard, over a shoulder-high wooden fence, and onto the southwest side of Smally-Z's property. The sisters paused for ten seconds, listening for footsteps, voices, breathing. They heard only the low rumble of music from inside the house, so advanced to the side door, expecting to have to unlock it with a .40-caliber key. This wasn't necessary. Brea twisted the knob, and the door opened without so much as a creak. A touch of good fortune. Maybe everything would be so easy.

They entered the house, pistols ready.

It was on.

# THREE

Always in these moments, before the hit, Flo remembered her mother: the softness of her skin, the melodic, Bajan lilt to her voice, and the feeling, as a child, of being lifted in her arms, how the sky had seemed so much closer. Esther Bella was a woman of God who'd shone through and through and found joy in every instant. She had not a sour drop in her entire heart.

Johnny Rudd had killed her. A 0.16 blood alcohol content had turned his Cadillac Escalade into a weapon every bit as devastating as a high-powered rifle or a brick of C-4. But Johnny was a privileged punk with connections, and had found a way to stay out of prison. Flo had thought that popping a bullet between his eyes would alleviate her grief, and it *had*, for a while, but the nation was filled with Johnny Rudds—as evidenced by the Trace's extensive shit list—and for every Johnny Rudd there was an Esther Bella, a beautiful life destroyed.

And so, in those moments before the hit, when Flo was most apt to second-guess her life choices, she thought of her mother.

They crouched behind their weapons, edging through a darkened hallway toward the light and noise. Brea, as planned, took upstairs. Flo and Jessie took the open-plan kitchen and living room, separating once they got there to herd the occupants from both sides and guard the exits. This was a critical moment. Were they dealing with gangsters or pretenders? The smoothness of this contract would be decided within the next five seconds.

Flo curled her finger around the trigger. She extended to her full height and swept into the kitchen. Her adrenaline—still up from the gig at Banjo McCoy's—ran through her like water. She tasted it in the back of her throat and it was good.

There were two men in the kitchen. One was Latino, early twenties, a boyish fuzz of hair on his upper lip. The other was a scrawny white guy, drinking from a bottle of Bud. His chin was wet and his eyes were gone. High on something. They flinched at the sight of Flo's vigilante persona—the black jacket and ski mask (Jessie sometimes called it their "superhero outfit"). The gun in Flo's hands was double the length, and more dangerous looking, with the suppressor attached.

The Latino guy raised his hands slowly. His strung-out friend stared at her, the beer bottle lifted halfway to his lips. He wasn't so high that he hadn't registered the threat. His mouth dropped open, showing a row of nicotine-stained teeth.

"Put the bottle down," Flo said to him. A bottle could quickly be turned into a weapon, and she wasn't taking any chances. The guy complied. Flo scanned for other threats—a handgun, maybe, tucked into the waistband, partially concealed. She saw nothing to indicate that either man was carrying. Her eyes darted across a junk-cluttered countertop to where Jessie had rounded up three people in the living room. Flo flicked the tip of the suppressor in that direction.

"Move it."

Mr. High nodded and took the lead. The Latino guy spat at her feet before following. "*Puta*," he said. Flo flared one eyebrow in response. She'd pop a bullet in his shoulder if she had to.

BREA SCALED THE STAIRS TWO at a time, placing her feet in a way to limit noise. She ghosted down the landing, cleared the first room—nothing in there but stained walls and a mattress on the floor. She cleared the bathroom next. Aromas of shaving foam and designer cologne took the edge off the piss stink. The shower curtain was dotted with mold spores. Brea edged back onto the landing and took a moment to breathe. It didn't matter how many times they'd done this—how many drug dealers, rapists, and killers they'd taken out—Brea always felt a wave of nervous energy. Like being onstage, they depended on talent and timing . . . but an amp could blow at any time, a snare head could break. This was a live performance.

There was a strip of light beneath the next door she reached and voices on the other side. Two people, Brea thought, but the thump of music coming up through the floor made it difficult to be certain. She removed her nondominant hand from the pistol, threw the door open, and surged inside. Brea was six feet tall with broad shoulders and muscular legs. She looked like a force of nature in her superhero outfit, and had become accustomed to a specific reaction: fear.

On this occasion, Brea got exactly 50 percent of what she expected. There were two people in the room. The man was walleyed and bearded, his naked upper half adorned with tribal ink. He had a rubber strap cinched around his left biceps, one end of it clamped between his teeth. The woman had a drapery of worn skin over her bones and a headful of dirty dreads. She cooked heroin in a bent spoon.

The man shrieked and fell off the bed, and there it was: the fear, as reliable as ever. The woman hadn't read the script, however. The flame on her disposable lighter went out. She looked at Brea with bubbling venom. It was obviously not the first time she'd had a gun pointed at her.

"What the fuck?" she hissed. "Get the fuck out of here. This is a business meeting."

"Where's Smally-Z?" Brea growled.

"I dunno. In your mama's ass. Get the fuck"—she threw her lighter at Brea—"*out* of here!"

Brea touched the trigger. She was tempted to shoot a round into the mattress, an inch from the woman's knee, but remembered their rule about keeping shots fired to a minimum. She *wanted* to, though, and hesitated for several seconds—exactly as long as it took for the man to find his balls and drag a .357 Magnum from beneath the bed. He swung the barrel toward her, holding the revolver in one trembling hand.

Had Brea's finger not already been on the trigger, she might have been a split second too late. As it was, she got her shot off first—*barely*. She aimed and fired in one fluid motion, blasting a hole in the man's left flank at the exact moment he squeezed his trigger. The report was wall-shaking. Brea flinched, feeling the high-caliber round pass within inches of her skull. It went through the door behind her, leaving a huge hole. The man fell back against the wall, his arm pulled sideways by the Magnum's recoil. Brea squeezed off a second shot, removing the gun from his hand and taking three fingers with it.

He squealed and dropped and that should have been that, except the woman jumped up off the bed and ran at Brea, gnashing her teeth, a dirty needle and syringe raised over her head like a dagger.

Brea put a bullet in the woman's shoulder. It slowed her down but didn't stop her.

JESSIE AND FLO STOOD BEHIND their pistols at either end of the living room, guarding the exits and keeping a close eye on the five individuals clustered between them: four guys—including the two Flo had herded in from the kitchen—and one woman. The room stank of weed and old food. There was a python in a cage and a box of live rats next to it. The snake was as long as a car. A film of dust coated everything.

"Whachoo wahhn?" one of the guys asked. He was a skinny white dude with short black hair and bad teeth. Jessie thought he might be Smally-Z but wasn't certain enough to pull the trigger. His hair was different from the man in the photograph's, but black dye was easy to apply. His most distinguishing features—different-colored eyes and Americana tattoos—were hidden behind dark sunglasses and a Knicks hoodie.

One look at those eyes and Jessie could end this.

"No green here, bruh," the guy who might be Smally-Z said, and spread his hands. "You shit outta luck, bruh."

Jessie sneered. She was about to demand that he remove his sunglasses, hoping she'd see mismatched eyes—she really wanted to shoot this prick—when a gunshot sounded from upstairs, a goddamn *cannon* blast, definitely *not* Brea's silenced Smith & Wesson. The ceiling shuddered, sending little vibrations through the walls. The woman screamed, and one of the guys dropped to his knees. Jessie and Flo exchanged concerned glances but kept their guns leveled.

"That weren't no baby gat," the guy who might be Smally-Z noted, pointing at Jessie's and Flo's suppressed weapons. "You got a friend up there, bruh, Imma say he got a hole through him the size of the Lincoln Tunnel."

The two sisters glanced at each other again. "I'll go," Flo said. She wheeled away, back through the kitchen, gone in a moment. There were more noises from upstairs, thuds and shouts. Jessie focused on the living room and its occupants, switching the sights of her semiauto from one to the other, keeping them in line. She said nothing but didn't have to; her aim was steady.

"Whachoo wahhn?" the guy who might be Smally-Z asked again. The light from the TV flashed off his sunglasses. "Ain't nuthin for you here, bruh. Nuthin."

"Ain't no brother," the man standing to his left said, a husky guy with a spider tattoo on his throat. "That's a *girl*, man. Can't you tell?"

"Shit. *Shit.* Huh?" The guy who might be Smally-Z whistled through his bad teeth. "Bitch play like a gangsta. *Shit.* Whachoo wahhn? Whachoo wahhn, bitch?"

Another volley of thumps and cries from upstairs, but Jessie barely noticed. She lunged forward, kicking a small coffee table onto its side, spilling crap all over, disregarding the other four to center her aim on the skinny little dick-seed who was probably (and *damn*, she hoped he was) Smally-Z.

Jessie didn't see him, though. Her vision was obscured by a ghost from her past, a kid from high school, too stupid for his own good, who habitually used the word "bitch" in place of nouns and pronouns. When Jessie had got all up in his face and suggested he adopt a less offensive vocabulary, the kid had flashed an ugly grin and said, "Bitch, I will knock your bitch ass down," and the *crack-crack-crack* sound of his jaw breaking in three places was a high moment in Jessie's young life.

Now there was this guy, wearing sunglasses indoors, as toxic as he was dumb. He shrugged his bony shoulders and cocked his head to one side.

"Whachoo wahhn, bitch?"

Jessie looped her forefinger around the trigger and said, "I want to see your eyes."

MOST OF THEIR JOBS WERE uncomplicated: one target, one bullet, and out. They were often playing a gig in a different time zone before the body was even found. Every now and then, though, the sisters had to deal with more advanced challenges: open spaces, witnesses, escape routes. These required a different approach. Greater firepower, perhaps (that Savage 10FP sniper rifle had been called into action on more than one occasion), or undercover work. Sometimes they had to split up. It was never ideal—there was safety in numbers—but they did what they had to in order to get the job done.

On paper, this small-town, dead-of-night job appeared uncompli-cated, but as Flo raced up the stairs and onto the landing, she wondered if they should have waited for a better time to strike. That thundering gunshot unsettled her deeply. Had someone gotten the jump on Brea? Had her laser focus dimmed for just a second? Flo had taken only a few steps when she saw something encouraging: a fist-sized hole in the door at the end of the landing and another in the drywall opposite, clearly made by a high-caliber round that had not been slowed down by any part of the human anatomy. Whoever had fired that cannon had missed.

Flo reached the door and heard pained grunts on the other side, along with the thumps and thuds of a struggle. She glanced briefly through the hole but at this angle saw nothing but an unmade bed speckled with fresh blood. Flo pushed the door open but took cover to one side before entering, just in case that cannon was waiting to greet her. She counted to three, then went in.

The first thing she saw was Brea in close quarters with an older, un-kempt woman with dirty dreadlocks spilling down her back and a bullet hole in her shoulder. As Flo watched, this woman leapt clumsily at Brea, bringing her right hand down in a stabbing motion. Brea was too close to get off an accurate shot. She avoided the attack by twisting her upper body, then countered with a hard straight punch to the woman's chest.

Flo aimed for the back of the woman's leg and was about to drop her when she noticed the man to her left. He was on one knee beside the bed, his maimed right hand clutched to his chest. Blood darkened the left side of his sweatpants from an entry wound just above his hip. The cannon was in his other hand, a .357 Magnum, its barrel pointed in Flo's direction, oscillating from side to side. That shot would miss nine times out of ten, but at this range, Flo wasn't about to leave it to chance.

She swiveled, aimed, beat him to the trigger. Her shot hit him in the stomach, *maybe* nonlethal, depending on how quickly he received medical attention, but her primary objective in that moment was to eliminate the threat, and in this she succeeded. The man was driven backward into the corner, between the wall and the bedside cabinet. The revolver flew out of his hand and landed on the bed. Flo picked it up and tucked it barrel-first into the back of her jeans.

Brea, meanwhile, had taken care of *her* threat. She'd grabbed the unkempt woman's wrist and twisted her arm up behind her back, going beyond the point where a person's arm is naturally designed to twist. There was a solid, gristly *crack* as her shoulder dislocated. The woman howled, both of her shoulders out of commission now. Flo saw a loaded syringe topple out of her hand. It hit the floor and rolled beneath the bed.

"Crazy bitch," Brea said.

The woman wasn't quite ready to give it up. She thrashed her upper body from side to side and lunged at Brea with her jaw snapping. Brea took her down with a leg sweep. The woman hit the floor hard, thumping the back of her head on the dresser on the way down. She continued to flop and howl.

"She's a fighter," Flo said.

"She's an animal." Brea grabbed the back of the dresser and tipped it over. It fell with a crash, landing across the woman's body. The attached mirror shattered and filled her dreadlocks with glimmering shards.

**THE GUY WHO MIGHT BE** Smally-Z refused to take off his sunglasses, so Jessie cracked him in the jaw with the butt of her handgun. His head whipped to one side and his shades flew off. Problem solved, and in a most satisfactory way. As he straightened up, cupping his jaw, Jessie got a good look at his eyes. One brown, one blue. This was all the confirmation she needed. She took a couple of steps back and locked her sights on the center of Smally-Z's chest.

This should've been the end of it. A single, lethal shot, then the Bang-Bang Sisters would put Barrel Lake in the rearview, and the Trace could cross one more name off its virtual shit list. This contract was determined to prove difficult, though. In the chaos that followed, Jessie—not unlike

Flo only moments before—would wonder how a relatively straightforward job could go sideways so quickly.

Rats poured across the living room floor, *dozens* of them, sleek and brown, with sharp little claws and tiny rat larynxes full of sound. The Latino guy with the fuzz of hair on his upper lip had upended the box of python food at the same moment that Jessie had pistol-whipped Smally-Z in the jaw. By the time she'd confirmed her target and locked him in her sights, the rats were flowing around her ankles and crawling over her boots. She glanced down for half a second, but that was all the distraction Smally-Z needed. He threw out his right hand and slapped aside the pistol's long suppressor, then lunged forward with his shoulder and barged Jessie off-balance. She stepped on several rats. They squirmed beneath her boots. The brawny guy with the spider tattoo ran at Jessie. He wrapped his arms around her and slammed her up against the wall. She groaned, feeling the impact in her rib cage and along the length of her spine. Her head filled with fluorescent beats of light.

Smally-Z—clearly as big a chickenshit as he was a degenerate scumbag—didn't stick around to see how this played out. He hightailed it into the entranceway and then out into the night, leaving the front door open behind him. Jessie struggled to break free and give chase, but the big guy held her tight, pinning her gun arm to her side. She couldn't even get the angle to put one in his foot.

Jessie's left hand was free, though, and both her legs. She planted the sole of her left boot against the wall and pushed off, sending her and the guy into a clumsy spin. The rats scampered beneath them. Mr. Spider Tattoo stumbled but held on.

"Help me out," he cried to his lowlife compadres. "Chrissake, help me the *fuck* out here."

The scrawny high dude was in no position to help anyone, including himself. He stood on the sofa, pointing at the rats zipping this way and that across the floor, shrieking, "What the fuck, man? What the *fuuuuck?*" The woman wasn't doing much better. She was rooted to the spot, the collar of her Sex Pistols T-shirt lifted up over her face.

Jessie twisted her body, creating enough room to direct her knee into Spider's solar plexus. It was a good, firm attack. She followed it with another, chopping the side of her left hand into his neck, striking his carotid artery. Spider groaned and wobbled at the knees.

"Help me," he shouted again. "Get the gun off her. *Alonso.* Move your fucking ass."

Alonso, the Latino guy, leapt forward at the sound of his name. At the same moment, Jessie thrust upward with her head, cracking Spider beneath the jaw. He stumbled backward, finally letting go. With her right arm free, Jessie lifted her handgun into the ready position. She was about to shoot Spider in the leg—his thighs were wide enough that she hardly had to aim—when Alonso hit her hard and low, throwing his shoulder into her side. Jessie folded in the middle and slumped to her knees. The gun popped out of her hands, landing inches from Spider's sneakers.

He went for it, but he was still dizzy from that strike to his carotid artery, and on his first attempt he stumbled a little. Alonso, meanwhile, had advanced for another attack. He aimed a kick at Jessie's head, but it was slow and awkward. Jessie blocked it easily. A rat scampered across the floor to her right. She grabbed it and tossed it in Alonso's direction—a distraction, not an attack. Alonso jerked backward, batting the rat away mid-flight, which gave Jessie the time she needed to regain her feet. As she rose, she pulled the nunchaku from the back of her jeans.

She could whip the branches around her body like Bruce Lee, but that flashy shit achieved nothing. For Jessie, the weapon served one purpose: to inflict quick and devastating damage. She had mastered torque and velocity through hundreds of hours of training, striking wooden boards and cinder blocks until she could break straight through them. For accuracy, she used to practice with Ping-Pong balls balanced on lengths of bamboo, arranged around her like attackers. If the bamboo so much as quivered after she knocked the ball off, Uncle Dog made her do fifty push-ups and start over. *Hujan badai* was not for the faint of heart.

Spider had grabbed the gun, raised his arm high enough to stare along the sights, and curled his finger around the trigger. Jessie turned on one heel, twisting her body while drawing power up through her hip and along her arm. The nunchaku painted a blurred circle in the air. Jessie flicked her wrist at the last moment, giving the weapon a little more snap. The extended branch smashed into the back of Spider's hand, shattering bones and knocking the gun off target. His finger jerked against the trigger and a shot zipped across the room, hitting the scrawny, high dude in the foot.

All this happened in half a second. Spider dropped the gun and fell to his knees, holding his damaged hand. Jessie got the nunchaku back under control. She twirled the branches over one shoulder and around her waist, not for show but to build up momentum. Her next strike impacted Spider's cheekbone, making a sound like a rock hitting a windshield. He remained on his knees for a moment, his head back, his eyes flickering. Then he toppled forward, broken but still breathing.

Jessie turned, twisting the nunchaku and catching the branch beneath her right armpit. She advanced on Alonso, who backed away with both hands raised, wanting no part of her.

"Oh fuck," he said.

The rats scurried. The high dude screamed, clutching his bloody sneaker. The woman had dropped onto the sofa, curled into a ball with her face still buried inside her T-shirt. Jessie took it all in, gauging the threat level. She was debating whether to incapacitate Alonso when the decision was taken out of her hands. Her sisters returned, surging back through the kitchen and into the living room. Flo didn't break stride. Acting on pure instinct, she delivered a savage roundhouse kick to Alonso's temple. He flew backward over the armchair and crumpled in the corner.

Brea took three seconds to survey the chaos. A rat darted over her boot. She looked questioningly at Jessie.

"Smally-Z?" she asked.

"He took off, but he can't have gone far." Jessie slotted her nunchaku into the back of her jeans, retrieved her pistol from the floor, and jumped over Spider on her way to the door.

Brea and Flo were right behind her.

IF THEIR TARGET ESCAPED, THE sisters would notify the Trace and the contract would go into cooldown—a three-month waiting period to let the dust settle. Then, assuming Smally-Z hadn't been neutralized in the meantime, the bounty would be reposted, and the Bang-Bang Sisters (or any of the other vigilante squads out there) could try again. This was not an acceptable outcome for the sisters, mainly because they wanted this dangerous drug dealer off the streets ASAP, but also because they wanted to get paid.

Speed over stealth, they returned to the van via the same backyard route. Smally-Z could have run in any direction, and he had a three-minute head start on them. In a highly populated environment, he would have disappeared already, blended into the masses. But this was Lake Podunk at night, and the sisters still had one card left to play.

Brea jumped behind the wheel. She started the engine, engaged the transmission, but waited before taking off. Jessie worked quickly. Within forty-five seconds she had the drone powered up and launched. It climbed quickly into the night, displaying an owl's-eye view of the surrounding streets.

"Anything?" Brea asked.

"We only just got airborne," Jessie said. "Be cool. We'll find him."

Flo joined Jessie at the screen, both of them huddled intently, looking for a flash of body heat. Smally-Z could be running. He could be hiding behind a car or in someone's backyard. He might already have made it to the safety of a friend's house. The drone climbed higher, tracking southwest toward downtown. Still nothing. A few nocturnal animals, and a single car driving along Main that disappeared beyond the edge of the screen. Jessie navigated the drone east, then north again. Brea made a tight, throaty sound and drummed the wheel impatiently.

"There!" Flo said. She pointed at the bottom corner of the screen. A fiercely glowing man shape crossed a street on the outskirts of downtown and ran at speed along the sidewalk.

"That has to be him," Jessie said. She rolled the side door closed and gave directions to Brea, who was already moving. "Go, *go*! Turn right at the end of this street. Head back toward town."

The van's tires screeched. It wasn't capable of much in the way of top speed, but Brea was going to push it. Streetlights streaked past on both sides, leaving long trails. They blew through a radar speed display at thirty over the limit, and it blinked indignantly at them.

Jessie dropped the drone lower, hovering eighty feet above Smally-Z. She followed him through someone's backyard, then across another street.

He slowed down for a moment and looked behind him, then got moving again.

"Next right," Jessie said. "Then second left."

"We're closing in," Flo said.

Brea barely slowed for the turns. The van lurched and swayed. The equipment in the back shifted with dull, echoing knocks and dissonant gongs.

"Through the lights," Jessie said. "Next left."

The light was red, but Brea didn't stop and the silent, sleeping town didn't notice. She took the left turn at the same reckless speed. More sound from the tires, working hard to stay on the road. Jessie braced herself with both legs, pressing back into the seat. She continued to operate the drone with both hands. On screen, she saw their van blaze into view, less than fifty yards behind the drug dealer.

"He's just ahead of us," Jessie said. "You should see him any moment. Left-hand side of the street."

"I see him," Brea said.

Jessie looked up as they closed in. They were on a residential street, narrow enough for the trees to reach over and meet in the middle. She saw the man tearing along the sidewalk, skinny limbs flapping. The headlights picked out his cropped black hair and orange Knicks hoodie.

"That's him," Jessie said. "Target confirmed."

"I got this," Flo said. She rose from her seat and clambered over Jessie with one hand to steady herself, the other clasping her semiautomatic. With the van still moving, she yanked the side door open, grabbed the "oh shit" handle, and leaned out with her gun hand extended. She found the target and took aim, waiting for enough of a gap between the parked cars and trees. Smally-Z—no doubt feeling the glare of the van's headlights— glanced over his shoulder. His face was a cartoonish scrawl.

He tried leaping over a fence but wasn't fast enough. Flo pulled the trigger. On screen, Jessie saw a brief spark of light as the drone's thermal cam registered the heat of the pistol's discharge. She looked up through the windshield in time to see Smally-Z hit the sidewalk.

Brea stepped on the brakes but kept the engine running. The sisters jumped out of the van in a fluid rush, three guns drawn. They stepped over to the sidewalk. Smally-Z crawled away from them on his elbows, dragging his legs behind him. Flo's bullet had caught him mid-spine. He was weeping.

"Oh Jesus, bruh, naah . . . *naaaah.*"

In these moments, it was always tempting to address the target, to let him (or, very occasionally, her) know why he was in the crosshairs and who was pulling the trigger. It would achieve nothing, though. What good was an education if it lasted only as long as it took a bullet to exit a chamber?

The sisters made their noise onstage. When it came to killing, they favored silence.

"Nah, bruh . . . fuck . . . *fuuu—*"

Jessie finished it. One trigger pull. One .40-caliber round in the back of Smally-Z's skull.

One more name crossed off the shit list.

**JESSIE BROUGHT THE DRONE HOME** and returned it to its case. Smally-Z's blood hadn't even reached the gutter by the time the van pulled away.

They drove south and didn't stop until the gas light pinged on.

# FOUR

The story broke at 5:10 A.M., with updates coming through on the hour: two dead following a "violent incident" in Upstate New York. Spencer Zaal, twenty-nine, was found shot to death half a mile from his Barrel Lake home. A second man, Lucian Bright, died en route to the hospital. He was forty-one.

Witness accounts were inconsistent (the correspondent hinted at various levels of intoxication), but early reports indicated that three armed assailants broke into Zaal's property at approximately 2:00 A.M. Things went from bad to worse when the occupants of the house put up a fight.

"We didn't see their faces," Mr. Alonso Peña told reporters at the scene. "They were wearing masks . . . uhh, ski masks, you know? But one of them was a woman. I know that for *sure*. Maybe even *two* were women."

Barrel Lake police found an unlicensed .357 Magnum in an upstairs toilet and seven kilos of a heroin-fentanyl mixture in a bedroom closet.

"We've just started putting the pieces together," Police Chief Roland Hyatt said in a brief statement. "But Mr. Zaal had history, he was known to us, and everything points to this being a drug-related crime."

Chief Hyatt answered a few more questions. The sisters thought his tone was surprisingly upbeat, considering he'd been yanked from his bed in the small hours of the morning and now had a double homicide on his hands.

In fact, he looked like a man with a great weight removed from his shoulders.

**THE TRACE WOULD ACCESS POLICE** files and photos, confirm the kill, and close the contract. This process could take up to seventy-two hours. The bounty would then be paid, always in cryptocurrency, which the sisters would convert to US dollars and deposit into a bank account they'd opened under the bogus name of Jane Morrison. Depending on the demand for crypto, the Smally-Z contract should net them close to $8,300 each, which they would withdraw from ATMs over the course of several weeks and deposit into their legit accounts. Good money for a few hours' work. It always was.

**THE SISTERS TOOK TURNS DRIVING** and made the Jersey Shore by 7:30 A.M. They had a gig that night at the Stone Pony in Asbury Park but needed a serious reset before then—to get out of their stinking clothes, shower hard, and fall into a deep bed for at least eight hours.

"There's a place called the Dynamite Motel just outside Asbury," Jessie said, scrolling through her phone. "Sounds like our kind of place."

"Just point the way." Flo stifled a yawn with the back of one hand. She'd been driving for two hours.

Barrel Lake was nearly three hundred miles in the rearview, and they'd driven most of that in exhausted silence, catching glimpses of sleep between shifts at the wheel. Outside of commenting on the news coverage, they didn't mention the job at all. Now, eight minutes away from the Dynamite Motel, Brea raised her seat and lifted her boots off the dash.

"It was messy," she said, "but we got it done."

"Messy?" Jessie clicked her tongue—something she did when she couldn't think of what to say. "That's . . . I mean, yeah . . ."

"We can do better," Flo said.

"There were seven people in that house. Two or three, we take care of business easily. Seven?" Brea shook her head, letting the number hang in the air for dramatic emphasis. "I'm not saying it was a flawless performance, but we did okay, under the circumstances."

"Two dead," Jessie said simply.

"We try for nonlethal. Doesn't always work out." Brea turned in her seat to look at Jessie. "And besides, the other victim—"

"Lucian Bright."

"Right, yeah, if it's the guy I think it is . . . he was a fucking junkie asshole, and he nearly took my head off with a .357 Magnum. Excuse me if I don't mourn for him too deeply."

They drove south out of Asbury Park, passing gas stations and auto-body shops and car washes, everything looking like the blueprint for a Springsteen song. A passenger train ran parallel to them, its windows flashing rhythmically in the early-morning sunlight.

"This is the job," Brea said. She nodded, as if to reaffirm this to herself, then added, "It's a tough business, but it's what we do."

Jessie said, "I don't know how much longer I can keep doing it."

FLO SOMETIMES JOKED THAT IT was a wonder they hadn't killed one another, not because they didn't get along—they did, though like any sisters, they had their moments—but because they spent so much time together. They traveled hundreds of miles every week, locked in a cramped white box, seeing the same stretch of interstate unfurl through the windshield. They shared the same small stages in the same bars and clubs, feeding off one another's energy like lovers. And with yet greater intimacy, they killed together.

"It sometimes feels like we're the same person," Flo had interpreted after a year or so on the road. This had been during a meditation work-shop at a woodland retreat in Vermont, with spirituality and oneness at an all-time high. "No, not person. *Entity*. The same entity. A force of nature divided into three parts."

"A typhoon has three parts," Jessie had said. "The eye, the eye wall, and the rainbands. We roll in, cause chaos, then leave."

"There's no separation," Flo had added. "We're going to burn ourselves out."

After arriving at this enlightened conclusion, the sisters decided they needed distance whenever possible. They achieved this in a couple of ways. First, they spent less time on the road—three months max—with longer stretches at home in between. Second, when they *were* on the road, they each had their own hotel room. This wasn't the most cost-effective approach, but it gave them valuable alone time, which in turn kept them intact and agreeable. They spent these hours sleeping, working out, watching movies, sexting lovers, training, beautifying themselves, surfing their socials, shopping, meditating, *healing*. They were not sisters during this time, they were individuals. Then, when it was time to go to work, they put on their rock garb and the typhoon came together again.

THE DYNAMITE MOTEL. NO SURPRISES. A strip of serviceable rooms behind eggplant-colored doors, a pool with a foot of green water in the deep end, a vending machine with OUT OF ORDER behind the glass. A beautiful, storied elm with hundreds of pairs of initials carved into its trunk cast a tangled shadow across the parking lot. Twenty feet of scrub and a chain-link fence separated the property from a working rail yard, busy with motion and noise.

Brea and Jessie checked in while Flo grabbed a screwdriver and switched from fake Pennsylvania plates to their real California ones, choosing the deepest part of the elm's shadow, away from other vehicles. She'd just finished tightening the second screw when her sisters returned. Brea held up two key cards.

"You want nearest the rail yard or the pervy owner's office?" she asked.

"Rail yard," Flo responded immediately.

Brea curled her lip, handed Flo the card in her left hand. "Room thirty-three."

"Thanks."

"I'm in room two." Brea pointed. "If you need me."

"Nineteen." Jessie flashed her own card.

The sisters dragged luggage from the back of the van, grunting with the effort. They stood in a disheveled triangle looking at one another with eyes as heavy as thunderheads.

"We go on at ten tonight," Brea said, "which means getting to the Pony no later than nine. We're the support act. Fifty minutes and out. Easy money."

"Sounds good to me," Flo said.

"You want to meet out here at, say . . . eight thirty?" Brea shrugged one shoulder. "Or should we grab dinner first? You know, together?"

"That'd be good," Jessie said. "No Bang-Bang Sisters work tonight. Let's just have a good time."

"Yeah," Flo said.

"Okay. Six thirty, at the van. Dinner, a couple of cocktails." Brea shifted her luggage to her other hand. "Then we rock and roll."

Murmurs of agreement. The sisters turned away from one another and started toward their respective motel rooms, then Jessie stopped them.

"Hey!" She put down her luggage and ushered them close. "Bring it in, bring it in."

They came together again, a tight three-way embrace, their bodies linked and their foreheads touching. For just a second, their weariness lifted. Even the shunting, hissing sounds from the rail yard faded. It was just the three of them—their dependable shape, each side supporting the others.

"I love you both," Jessie said.

Brea echoed this, then Flo. They stood that way for a moment longer, saying nothing, each absorbing the others' constancy and devotion. Only two were biological sisters, but the bond shared by all three went beyond that, as deep and firmly rooted as the tree at the edge of the lot.

FLO CLOSED THE DOOR BEHIND her. The room was dim even with the curtains open, and everything she expected it to be: the threadbare carpet, the lemon sheets, the blue-tile bathroom. A black-and-white photo of the Asbury Park Boardwalk hung askew on the wall over the bed. In this light, Flo distinguished a vague face print on the glass.

She checked her phone. Emails from her insurance company, Spotify, and Fender. A text from Imani, her sister—*her* biological sister—back home in Panorama City: Couldn't sleep last night, watched the suicide squad. OMG IDRIS!!! he wouldn't want me now my ankles r swelled up like beachballs. hahaha!!! xoxox. Flo smiled and texted back: his loss. miss u sis xoxox. She shut down her phone, found an outlet to charge it, then drew the curtains. Seconds later, she was in the shower, leaving a trail of dark, grimy clothes on the floor behind her. The water was hot, the flow underwhelming. She stood beneath it and rubbed soap across her body, into every crease and fold. She washed her hair until her scalp tingled. The gig at Banjo McCoy's and everything that happened in Barrel Lake gurgled down the drain, and Flo stepped out of the shower several degrees separated from the woman who had stepped in. She toweled off, brushed her teeth, and fell into bed like a fighter hitting the canvas.

The rail yard woke her a touch shy of four P.M., an aggressive, steaming sound. She opened her eyes. Her dreams whispered against her lashes, as light as leaves, then gone. Flo reached for her phone and turned it on. She had numerous emails and messages, but only one she had any interest in reading: a reply from Imani.

miss u 2. when u coming home???

Flo started to type a reply, then decided to video call instead. It had been a few days since she'd seen her little sister's glowing face. She flicked on a side light, slipped into shorts and a T-shirt, and brought Imani up on Skype. The sound of the jingle seemed overly vivid against the clangs and clanks from the rail yard. Imani answered quickly. Her voice came through first, stuttering through the initial seconds of connection.

"Hey, girl . . . just thinking . . . rock-star sister."

"Rock star? Pfft, yeah, right." Flo sat cross-legged on the bed and waited for the video to catch up. "I can hear you, but I can't see—" Then the connection was completed. Imani's sunshine face popped up on Flo's screen, staring back at her from 2,500 miles away. "There you are."

"Here I am."

They looked at each other for a sweet moment, both smiling, Flo wishing she could reach through the screen and touch Imani's beaming face. They were four years apart in age, with each believing the other had won the genetic lottery. Flo had their father's natural athleticism; Imani had their mother's Bajan skin tone and endless smile. There was no doubt they were sisters, though. It was in the slope of their jawlines and upturned eyes, and in the depth of their emotions. They could love and rage with an equal ferocity.

"You look incredible," Flo said, and she meant it.

"Stop it. I'm a walking watermelon." Imani puffed out her cheeks and crossed her eyes. "Where *are* you?"

"The Mark, New York City," Flo said straight-faced. "We're playing the Garden tonight."

"It's about time."

Flo laughed. It surprised her, and she loved the sound of it, so sudden and clear. "No, no, I'm in a two-bit motel on the Jersey Shore. That's the *real* rock and roll lifestyle."

Imani's turn to laugh. She adjusted her position, moving somewhat awkwardly, and Flo caught a glimpse of the blue sky over Panorama City, then Imani's backyard—the worn patio furniture, the willow drooping full and heavy. A wave of homesickness washed over Flo. She blinked at tears and subdued the emotion with a deep and steady breath.

"What I'm *really* asking," Imani said, her face appearing on-screen again, "is when are you coming home? I mean, you can't get much farther away than Jersey and still be in the same country. You feel me?"

"I feel you," Flo said. "And trust me, Im, I cannot wait to get home. Rub your big fat swollen feet, plump your pillows, sing to your bump."

"Oh, you mean this bump?" Imani tilted the phone to show the mountainous swell of her pregnant belly. "*This* bump? Is this the bump you're talking about?"

"Yeah, that's the one."

"Hmm, I barely even noticed it."

They shared identical smiles, perfectly aligned, despite the miles. Flo held her phone in one hand and clutched her sweetly aching chest in the other.

"You're beautiful," she said.

"Seven months," Imani said. "Third trimester. This bun is just about done, hon. If this were a sports game, the coach would be calling time-outs. But I can't stop the clock. I'm weeks away. *Weeks.* And I would really love to have my big sister here beside me."

Imani had people close to her—friends, a few cousins on their daddy's side—but nothing could compare with immediate family, and here the roster was notably lacking. A brain tumor took their daddy away in 2006, at the unthinkable age of thirty-nine. Their mom, Esther, had moved back to Alabama in 2019 to take care of *her* sister, who had stage 4 cancer, and who ended up outliving Esther by three weeks, courtesy of Johnny Rudd and his alcohol-fueled SUV. Lamonte Wood—the bump's father—was a mostly vacant man-child who three months ago had confessed to Imani that he wasn't ready for the pressure and responsibility of fatherhood, so Imani had kicked his useless ass to the curb. "This is an all-or-nothing commitment," she had said to him. "And you got nothing!" Lamonte had recently relocated to San Francisco, where he was trying to get his cannabis business off the ground.

"I'll be there in time, I *promise*," Flo said, with as much sincerity in her expression as in her voice. "Listen, we're in Asbury Park tonight, Atlantic City tomorrow, then we're heading west. Cincinnati . . . St. Louis. I'm not sure of our exact itinerary, but we're on our way. We'll be back in California in two weeks—three at the most, if we pick up a couple of big bookings along the way."

By "big bookings," Flo meant Bang-Bang Sisters work. They would check the Trace's bulletin board. If there was a contract near where they were playing, and if the money was right . . .

"It's far in terms of distance, but not time. I'll be home before you know it. But hey, listen, our gig last night . . . it went well." Flo remembered the last bullet Jessie fired, splashing Smally-Z's brains across the sidewalk. "We made a little extra money, so I'm going to wire some over to you. It won't be much—maybe just enough to pamper yourself for an afternoon somewhere. I don't know, a body scrub, a mani-pedi, then beef ramen from that Japanese place you like."

"Aw, Flo, that's so sweet, but you don't—"

"Yes, I *do*. It's happening." Flo angled her head and raised one finger to the screen, her big-sister-laying-down-the-law look. "I want to do it. You deserve it. And besides, it'll make me feel less guilty about not being there."

"Well, when you put it like *that* . . ." Imani smiled, a chink of radiance within her already glowing face. "But I'm going to be honest, while a body scrub sounds nice, I'll probably spend that money on maternity pants and stretch mark cream."

"You spend it however you like."

"Okay, well, thank you. Really. And the bump thanks you, too." Imani angled the phone to her beautiful round belly, then back to her face, applying one of her novelty filters as she did so. Her eyes expanded to cartoon size and huge white bunny ears sprouted from the top of her head, flopping this way and that as she moved.

"I *wuvvv* you," Imani said. Little pink hearts cascaded from the top of the screen.

"I love you, too."

Imani twitched her cute bunny nose. Flo laughed from deep in her soul and the tears came again, not just pricking at her eyes but rolling down her cheeks.

"Silly rabbit," she said.

**JESSIE WOKE FROM A NIGHTMARE** midmorning, and although it faded the moment she opened her eyes, she still found it difficult getting back to sleep. She tossed and turned for close to an hour, then got out of bed, put on sweatpants and a tee, and walked to room two.

Four strident knocks. Nothing. Four more, and Brea opened the door, pouchy-eyed, her blond hair in chaos. She had sleep lines across her brow and a thread of dry saliva on one cheek.

"Last night . . . the .357." Jessie's voice was blank, but her eyes brimmed with expression. "How close was it?"

Brea held her thumb and forefinger three inches apart.

"Jesus." Jessie shook her head and swallowed hard. "I can't sleep."

"C'mon." Brea took Jessie by the hand and led her into the room, toward the bed. They climbed into it and cuddled up, so close that they shared the same pillow. They could have been four and seven again, stronger together, bonded against the monsters under the bed.

Despite her restlessness, Jessie was asleep within minutes.

**THERE WAS NOTHING SAGE ABOUT** Uncle Dog. He was too schooled in reality, too damn jaded. "Knock your opponent down first, *then* quote Sun Tzu," he'd once said to Brea and Jessie. "Actually, forget that. *Never* quote Sun Tzu. Just put your opponent on his ass." He instructed through action, not words, with one exception.

They were at Zuma Beach, throwing kicks in chest-high water, boosting core strength and endurance. Uncle Dog—fifty-six and fit as hell—had taken off his shirt, revealing a body more in line with a thirty-year-old's, along with a thick scar that ran diagonally across his chest.

"I'd hate to see what you did to the other guy," Brea said, gesturing at the scar.

"I'll tell you what I did," Uncle Dog replied. "I ran away."

Brea and Jessie looked at each other, frowning. The idea of this man, who'd only ever shown uncompromising power and lethality, running away from *anything* did not align with the hero-like vision they had of him.

"Some rare wisdom from a guy who's been around the block a few thousand times," Uncle Dog had said, reading their expressions. "There's always someone better out there, someone smarter and stronger. Of all the lessons I'll teach you, the most important by far, and the one that will keep you alive, is that you have to know when to back down."

The light coming through the gap in the curtains was as bright as neon. Jessie woke first. She checked the time on Brea's phone: 4:53. She got out of bed and peed and splashed cold water on her face. Brea was awake by the time she returned to the room, propped against the headboard, wiping sleep out of her eyes.

"You tinkle loud," she said.

Jessie cracked a smile. "I think the water's lower in these Jersey toilets. It creates deeper acoustics."

Brea nodded, as if this outlandish statement had some scientific merit. Both women stretched and yawned. Brea scanned her phone, flicking through the usual apps, mostly out of habit. She put it down after a minute and turned on the side light.

"Did you mean what you said earlier?" she said, and there was a serious note in her voice, despite the just-woken-up drawl. "That you don't know how much longer you can do this?"

Jessie sat on the edge of the bed and made a vague gesture, somewhere between a shrug and a nod. Elsewhere, they heard voices in the parking lot—two guys with thick Jersey accents—and the unmelodic bangs and shunting sounds from the rail yard.

"Is this a new thing?" Brea asked. "Or have you been thinking it for a while?"

"In some ways, since the first job," Jessie replied.

"Johnny Rudd?" Brea looked surprised. Her eyes, still tired, were suddenly a lot wider.

"No, that was different. We did that for Flo." Jessie plucked a loose thread from the sleeve of her Pearl Jam tee. It was getting old now—the print across the front was mostly faded—but it was still a favorite. "I'm talking about the farmer."

They'd been friends with Flo since they'd met at a battle of the bands in 2004, but the Johnny Rudd job made them sisters. Less than a month later, a friend of Brea's—a former government cryptanalyst—gave them an in at the Trace, and they were soon granted access to the anonymous server. Their first contract was a livestock farmer from the San Joaquin Valley, who'd promised undocumented immigrants fourteen dollars per hour but instead slit their throats, trafficked their organs on the black market, and fed the remains to his pigs. It seemed only fitting that he should meet the same fate.

The Bang-Bang Sisters were in business, and judging from the volume of names on the Trace's bulletin board—murderers, drug dealers, domestic terrorists, traffickers, pedophiles, and rapists, all of whom had evaded justice—they would have work for a long time to come.

"I didn't think we'd still be doing this three and a half years later," Jessie said. "Maybe on occasion . . . you know, if we came across a real dirtbag—"

"They're *all* real dirtbags."

Jessie nodded and let out a deep sigh. "It's been constant, is all."

"This is what we do, Jess. It's what we're good at." Brea shuffled along the bed, closer to Jessie. The strip of light through the curtains fell neatly between them. "When our bodies begin to slow down and our minds are not as sharp . . . then, yeah, I get it. But we're not there yet. Not even close."

"You want to talk about close?" Like Brea had earlier, Jessie held her thumb and forefinger three inches apart. "That's how *close* you were to leaving Barrel Lake in a body bag."

"An occupational hazard." Brea curled her lip. "Police get shot at in the line of duty. Soldiers drive over land mines. Do they quit?"

"Sometimes, yeah." Jessie gave Brea a moment to challenge this, but she didn't. Both women looked away from each other, staring at the water stains on the ceiling, the motes of dust swirling in that fine blade of light, then Jessie dragged a hand through her hair and said, "Besides, I'm not quitting. I'm just . . . considering the future."

The voices in the parking lot faded. Even the rail yard fell quiet. For a long stretch, the only sounds were the rattle and thrum of the air-conditioning unit and the bedsprings creaking as the sisters shifted their weight.

"These months on the road, living out of a suitcase, bouncing from laundromat to motel to dive bar . . ." Jessie drew her legs up onto the bed, angling her body to look at Brea earnestly. "There's something to be said for the stability of a normal life. And a *boyfriend*. Jesus, I haven't had a steady boyfriend since I was twenty-four years old."

"It's tough, Jess. I get it."

"I'm worried about Mom, too."

"Mom's fine."

"She *says* she's fine, but we both know better."

Their stepfather, Bryan, had been diagnosed with ALS two years ago. In a matter of months, he'd gone from being one of the top names in the music industry to not being able to brush his own teeth or chew food. Their mom took care of him to begin with, and did so without complaint or self-pity. Aubree Vernier, like her daughters, was built tough, and she had a love that never stopped. As Bryan's condition worsened, though, she brought in full-time help, not because she didn't want to do it anymore, but because she wanted her husband to have the best possible care. These days, Bryan buzzed around their huge Chatsworth home in his electric wheelchair and communicated via a computer with eye-tracking software. Aubree read novels to him. They watched movies, played chess, and went on dates. When she wanted time alone, she went for long walks in the Santa Susana Mountains. The last time Brea and Jessie spoke to her, she was sunburned and tearful.

"Mom needs a vacation," Brea said. She drifted for a second or two, then snapped her fingers. "She was talking about visiting her girlfriend in Florida. Let's make that happen, push her to do it."

"Yeah." Jessie nodded.

"And you. You need a break, too."

"That'd be a good place to start."

"We'll get home, chill for a while. No work, no gigs. Just downtime." A breezy plan, for sure, somewhat undermined by Brea's heavy sigh. "But trust me, Jess—a month of that, and you'll be ready to roll again."

"Maybe, yeah. I don't know. It's just . . ." Jessie clicked her tongue. Brea waited, nostrils flaring. Finally, Jessie said, "What about you?"

"Me?"

"How long can you keep doing this?"

Brea opened her mouth to respond, then shook her head and grabbed her phone from the nightstand. With a few deft taps, she brought up a news story with the ominous headline: THE WREN CLAIMS ANOTHER VICTIM. Jessie read through four bleak columns with coldness leaking into her bones. Susan Orringer, forty-two, from Reedsville, Alabama, was found stabbed to death in her home. Everything matched the wren's MO: the arrangement of the victim's corpse, the puncture wounds stuffed with feathers.

"I'm nowhere close to throwing in the towel," Brea snapped. "Not while there are crazy motherfuckers like this out there."

Jessie set the phone aside. She found another loose thread on her T-shirt and looped it around the tip of her forefinger. "The police will catch up to him. They're bound to. Eventually."

"In *Reedsville?*" Brea all but spat the name of the city. The sisters had experienced the delights of that particular Alabaman shithole. It was Johnny Rudd's hometown, where the local cops had admitted to using a defective breathalyzer and justice had *not* been served—at least not until the sisters stepped in. "Forgive me if I don't share your optimism."

Jessie shrugged. A fair point.

Brea got up from the bed. She crossed to the window and peered through the gap in the curtains, more to collect her thoughts than to see what was going on.

"Your contact at the Trace." She turned back to Jessie. The light softened her countenance, but the emotion was still in her voice. "Eight-Ball, or whatever their alias is—"

"Nine-Star."

"Have they been in touch lately?"

"Not for . . . I don't know, four or five weeks, maybe."

It was not common practice to be in contact with anyone at the Trace, but an operative called 9-$tar had obviously taken a shine to the sisters—to Jessie in particular. He/she/they had revealed that the Trace had accessed Reedsville Police Department files and uncovered a key detail withheld from the general public: that the serial killer known as "the wren" left a haiku at every murder scene. In a DM sent to Jessie on the Trace's platform, 9-$tar wrote that the team was using this information to refine the search—hacking into the personal computers of poets, English teachers, and writers across the Black Belt, beginning with those on the sex offender registry.

**We'll go deeper as necessary,** 9-$tar had written, **but I'm confident we'll have a name soon. Be ready!**

Several weeks later and still no name, only another dead woman on the wren's résumé.

"This latest kill," Brea said. "More evidence, maybe more clues. We could get a heads-up from Nine-Star at any time."

"It's possible," Jessie said. She unwound the loose thread. The tip of her finger tingled.

"I need you in the right headspace if the job comes up."

"Yeah, I . . . I . . ." Jessie clicked her tongue.

"What we do, Jess . . . it makes a difference. For every depraved piece of shit we take out, we make the world a little safer." Brea placed her hands on her hips and stepped away from the window. "It's also our primary source of income. What else are we going to do? Play rinky-dink bars for three hundred bucks a night?"

"I don't know," Jessie said, and shook her head. "What *do* normal people do?"

"They sit in traffic and wait for the weekend," Brea replied sternly. That muscle in her jaw twitched again. "Fuck that. Not me."

"We can't do this forever, though," Jessie said, hoping the softness in her voice would blunt her big sister's edges. "You know that, right? We need to think about the future."

"This *is* my future," Brea said, still with the edges—even more, in fact. "And mark my words, Jess, I'll do this alone, if I have to."

"Brea, I—"

"I don't need you. I don't need Flo, either."

Brea took off her T-shirt, threw it on the floor, and stood in front of Jessie. Her upper body was a tapestry of aggressive tattoos: a king cobra coiled around her right biceps, a semiautomatic pistol on each flank, a grim reaper on her left breast, a fiery skull on her right. Chinese characters laddered the length of her spine, translating as DEATH, REVENGE, and HONOR. The tattoos were complemented by the scars that Brea had picked up over the years, mainly knife wounds. Some were self-inflicted.

She spread her arms and pirouetted slowly, an exhibit of hurt and anger.

"This is who I am," she said.

# FIVE

The black SUV cruised through downtown, myriad lights bouncing off its buffed paintwork and chrome. Like its owner, it was big, beautiful, and American made. It was recently off the production line, only 2,300 miles on the clock, with custom twenty-four-inch rims and a jacked suspension. There were two stickers adhered to its back glass. The one in the bottom right corner read PRO-GOD, PRO-GUN, PRO-LIFE, ANTI-BIDEN. The one in the bottom left was of the Stars and Stripes flying brightly over the missive DOES THIS FLAG OFFEND YOU? CALL 1-800-LEAVE-THE-USA.

"Did you have a good evening, sir?" the driver asked. He was tall with thick arms and a creased, bald head. Chance Kotter, sitting in the passenger seat, couldn't remember if his name was Scott or Steve. He *was* new to the payroll, in Chance's defense.

"Remind me," Chance said, and flicked a finger at the driver. "Scott or Steve?"

"Neither, sir," the driver said. "It's Shaun, but everyone calls me Goose, on account of—back when I had hair—I looked like that actor from *Top Gun*."

"Goose," Chance said with a smile. "Shit, I like that. *Top Gun*, huh?"

"Yes, sir."

"Well, listen up, Goose, I got three things to say." They stopped at a red, and the person crossing the street there—Prudence Wallis, owner of Sunrise Retail Management—recognized Chance and waved. Chance's opinion of Prude was that she was a shitbird of the very highest cali-ber. Nevertheless, he mustered a diplomatic smile and waved right back. "Thing one: I apologize for forgetting your name. That was remiss of me, and I will do better."

"That's fine, sir," Goose said. "I'm sure you have a lot of people work-ing for you."

"That I do," Chance agreed. "It's no excuse, though."

The light turned green, and Goose got them rolling again.

"Thing two: don't call me 'sir.' When it's just the two of us, you can call me Chance. When I have company, it's Mr. Kotter." There was a cruiser outside Fat Fanny's Ale House, its lightbar signaling brightly. Chance craned his neck as they drove past, but there was nothing worth seeing. "You copy that, Goose?"

"Loud and clear," Goose said.

"Thing three: yes, I *did* have a good evening, thank you for asking."

"I'm glad to hear that."

"Lost some money at the wrestling match"—Chance pronounced it *rasslin'*—"but that's okay. If you can't afford to lose, you shouldn't play."

"Couldn't agree more," Goose said.

"And we had ourselves a time, regardless." Chance chuckled. His big pale belly, straining at the buttons of his XXXL dress shirt, wobbled grandly. "Hey, Goose, hang a right on Harper and pause at the top of the hill. I sure like the view from there."

Goose checked the mirrors and edged into the right-hand lane. Harper Avenue ran east-west through the center of Reedsville, crossing the Waynesboro-Conecuh Southern Line, Main Street, and the Mary River—a slow-moving tributary of the Alabama. It was a lively strip, for the most part, shadier west of Main (safer not to venture too far in that direction after dark, or even before), but notably scaling up in class as it headed east toward Waterloo Square and the business district beyond. Goose signaled, made a rolling right, and found a spot to pull over farther along. From here, they could see the lights and bustle of some of Reedsville's more upmarket establishments, sloping downhill toward the Wishbone Bridge, so named on account of its design. Best of all, on the other side of the river, the Kotter-Bryce Tower rose sheer and handsome into the sky, standing sentinel over not just the other buildings in the business district (the next tallest was a paltry twenty-four stories) but the whole damn town.

"Quite the view," Goose observed.

Chance nodded in reply. He took a deep breath and exhaled slowly. The sound of it rumbled from his chest like the purr of a kingly, well-fed lion.

IT REALLY HAD BEEN A good evening, despite the fact that Chance had lost $10,000 on the rasslin' match. It had been hosted by Dylan Cobb, who farmed thirty acres of soybeans just north of Reedsville and turned a less honest buck running illegal fights out of his barn. Chance had seen all kinds there—bare-knuckle thugs, cocks, dogs, little Mexican fellas with knives, half-naked gals flopping in the mud with their panties wedged all the way into the cracks of their asses. Chance used to work a dog there, back in the day. Dolly. All muscle and bite. She'd made him a pretty penny, too. Then one day she just lay down in the pit and let the other animal have at her. A god-awful sadness. Chance just hadn't been able to recognize how tired Dolly had become.

Cobb had hoisted a couple of speakers onto poles and had the music playing. A boar turned on the spit, black and fatty. There was beer in the keg, but Chance wasn't a big drinker—maybe a shot of his own bourbon or a glass of Chandon Brut on special occasions, but that was all. His doctor had advised him less alcohol and more exercise, and Chance figured he'd give one of those things a try. Some fifty folks had gathered for the event, including Mayor Austin Hasse and Chance's sister, Bethany Kotter, who just happened to be Reedsville's chief of police. Chance talked a little business, ate a lot of boar, and wiped black grease out of his white Kenny Rogers beard. Bethany invited him to dance, but he declined. His belly was too full of boar for him to be jigging around like a goddamn teenager. But then—wouldn't you know it—Alan Jackson came on singing "Chattahoochee," and Chance buckled. He danced, just to that one song (he was a sucker for "Chattahoochee"), feeling top-heavy and somewhat self-conscious on his disproportionately thin legs. He flapped a hand and bailed before the song had even finished.

"Christ Jesus," he puffed to Mason Nurll, who operated a peanut farm farther north still. "That got me sweatin' like a glassblower's ass."

"It's the heat," Mason said kindly.

"That it is."

The party then moved inside Cobb's barn for the featured attraction: a rasslin' contest between Cajun Dan, a tough-as-nails farmhand from bayou country, and "Death-Roll" Gus, an 830-pound alligator from the Everglades. Now, Gus was an ornery sumbitch and particular of his personal space. Cajun Dan had an empty look in his eyes but claimed to have rassled gators before.

There was the usual hum of prefight chatter, with bets being made every which way. Chance didn't know where to put his money, so he did what any self-respecting gambler would do. He flipped a coin. Heads for Cajun Dan. Tails for Gus.

It came down heads, and he put ten large on the Cajun.

"Now, the thing with rasslin' gators," Cobb said, taking a ringside seat beside Chance, "even big ol' whores like thissun, is you gotta take their jaws outta the equation."

"You don't say," Chance returned dryly.

"This is best done by jumpin' on their backs Tarzan-like, pushin' down on the top of their heads so their lower jaw is flat to the ground, then takin' hold of the snout and liftin' that sumbitch back. Once the head is at ninety degrees, all the fight goes outta 'em."

"Sounds easy enough," Chance said, perhaps forgetting that he'd nearly blown a gasket dancing to two minutes of a country song. "I'd say Cajun Dan has this one in the bag."

"Well, maybe so, but the two most important things: he's gotta keep his wits about him, and he's gotta respect the animal."

Cajun Dan did neither. He stepped into a ring twenty feet in diameter, with "Death Roll" Gus—fourteen feet long—taking up a good portion of that real estate. This clearly wasn't Gus's first stint in the limelight. He appeared unaffected by all the hooting and hollering and kept his focus on the Cajun. It was much of nothing to begin with. Cajun Dan would make a half-assed lunge, and Gus would open his mouth and hiss. This happened six or seven times—the sum total of the action in the opening ten minutes. Mostly they circled the ring counterclockwise, each keeping the other in their sight line.

"Kinda slow," Chance observed.

"It can turn quickly," Cobb said.

There were a few boos from the crowd, who'd clearly figured a man wrestling an alligator would be more entertaining. Cajun Dan heard those boos and tried to increase the thrill factor by flashing his bare ass to Gus and giving it a couple of "come get it" slaps. Gus snarled but didn't bite. This was the point at which Chance realized Gus was an old pro, and Cajun Dan was just plumb stupid.

"I think I'm out ten large," he said under his breath.

Man and beast circled half a dozen more times. The boos started up again. The Cajun flashed his ass in another weak effort to keep everyone engaged, then got *real* ballsy and started to kick the big gator—first in the tip of the tail, then farther up. This didn't please Gus at all, and it pleased Chance even less, not because he didn't appreciate Cajun Dan's willingness to up the ante, but because kicking wasn't part of the sport.

"What's he doing?" Chance asked Cobb.

"He's kickin' that gator," Cobb replied.

"I can see that, you dumbass, but why—*why* is he kicking that gator?"

"I don't rightly know," Cobb admitted.

The kicks got a little firmer and a little higher up the gator's body, until Cajun Dan's confidence got the better of him and he aimed his boot at Gus's belly. Now, Chance was new to the particulars of gator wrestling, but even he could see what was going to happen. Everybody in attendance could see, with the exception, perhaps, of the one person who *should* have seen.

An old saying occurred to Chance—the one about a wise man knowing where courage ends and stupidity begins. He'd had occasion, over the years, to ponder this logic and found it usually proved true. Such was the case now.

Gus was the weight of a small car but as quick as a cat. He twisted, lunged, and snapped all in a blink, his mighty jaws closing around his opponent's leg as it swept forward in its kicking motion. With the same vicious power, Gus dragged the Cajun toward him, then rolled three times on the packed dirt of Cobb's barn floor. The Cajun rolled with him, different bones breaking on every go-round. Several in the audience averted their eyes, while others exclaimed in shrill voices, uncomfortable with this turn of events.

Gus's handlers entered the ring: four ropy men wearing cargo shorts and boonie hats. Three of them grabbed Gus by the tail. The other grabbed Cajun Dan. They pulled in opposite directions, separating man and beast. *Most* of the man, leastways. His left leg remained with the gator.

"My luh-luh-leg!" Cajun Dan blubbered, all bloodied up and broken. "My *laaaaahhhhgggg*!"

Gus didn't look set to relinquish his prize. Chance watched as the big old gator rolled the Cajun's leg between his teeth like a hayseed chewing on a blade of wheat.

Cobb jumped to his feet and started flapping his arms, signaling the end of the fight and indeed the evening. Chance smiled and placed both hands on the magnificent dome of his belly. He had been entertained. Yessir, he'd lost a chunk of change, and nossir, losing money was never good. But the Cajun had crossed the line—he'd played a dirty game—and it was worth every cent just to see that whoreson bleed.

"WHERE YOU FROM, GOOSE?"

"Hmm, a straightforward question like that deserves a straightforward answer. Truth is, I don't rightly know. I was born in Lubbock, Texas, just like Buddy Holly, but my old man's job took us just about everywhere, including overseas. Europe, Saudi Arabia, Japan—"

"He a military man?"

"US Air Force. Lieutenant colonel, retired. He lives in New Mexico now. Plays golf and shoots tin cans in his garden."

"God bless him," Chance said.

"I backpacked around Europe until I was twenty-six, then returned Stateside and went to college. That didn't last. I dropped out my freshman year—chased a woman to Florida. That didn't last, either. It's been a steady run of jobs and cities since then, but I've been in Reedsville for three years now and, dare I say, it's beginning to feel like home."

Chance nodded and raked fingers through his beard. The lights of Harper Avenue, from where they were sitting all the way down to the Wishbone Bridge, flashed in his eyes. He had a framed photograph of Harper Avenue on the wall in his study, taken in 1969—the year he was born—and looking wholly different from how it did now. Not one of the dusty old stores that used to line this street remained. JoJo's Toys, Tip-Top Records, the Reedsville Mercantile, Franco's Barbershop, A Stitch in Time—all gone, bought out by bright, capital-minded businesspeople with solid ambitions. Chance was one such businessperson. At the tender age of twenty-four, with his faith in God (not to mention a sizable start-up loan from Enterprise Bank and Trust), he had purchased Old Jay's Flea Market (an unruly shithole), razed it to the ground, and constructed in its place the Mary River Distillery, which, within the space of five years, became one of the largest producers of high-rye bourbon in the South. Chance didn't stop there. He removed the Big Train Motel and the Del Mar Theater from the town's geography, and on the newly freed-up land, he built two sports bars, a bowling alley, a gun shop, and four office buildings. Not long after, Franco's Barbershop gave way to Kotter Fine Wines & Tobacco and Tip-Top Records became an upmarket cocktail bar called the Glass Garden. As of this day, Chance owned or part-owned twenty-three businesses in Reedsville. He was also heavily involved with the local food bank and firemen's association, and was cochair of the cultural roundtable.

There was a reason his tower was bigger than everyone else's.

"We got our share of problems, heaven knows," Chance said, looking solemnly at his driver. "But overall, it ain't such a bad place to call home."

"Not bad at all," Goose agreed.

Chance turned his gaze back to Harper Avenue. That photograph from 1969 was still in his mind. He loved it, not only because it was taken the year he was born, but because it reminded him how far he had come—how much of a difference he'd made. On any given day, Chance would stare at it for minutes at a time, often with tears in his eyes.

"Some people say that moving from city to city, state to state, will broaden your horizons. I don't doubt that to be true, and you'd know better than me, but there's something to be said for staying in the same place your whole life." Chance lifted both hands, gesturing not just at

Harper Avenue but at the entire city, from the bleakest part of the ghetto to the top of the Kotter-Bryce Tower. "I *know* this town. Every street, every building, every crack in every sidewalk. I know its people, its history, and its secrets."

Goose said nothing and that was okay. He knew when to speak—a fine quality, Chance thought. One of the benefits of having a lieutenant colonel for a daddy.

A cruiser—perhaps the same one that had been outside Fat Fanny's—rolled down Harper, lights dark. Elsewhere, sirens wailed, three or four in harmony. The clock on the Kotter-Bryce Tower ticked over to 10:08.

"I *am* this town," Chance said.

His cell phone lit up and purred. He hooked it out of the narrow slot in the center console. There were dozens of unread messages, but the one that just came through was from Burl Rowan, his head of security. Chance opened it and read:

We found Lucky Pinder. He's here.

Chance cracked something like a smile and responded right away. His pudgy thumbs worked the screen with care.

Punch him square in the eye and lock him in the garage.

He returned his phone to the narrow slot and sighed. Goose looked dead ahead, one hand on the wheel.

"I'm all over this town, everywhere you look," Chance said, continuing his line of dialogue. "And I ain't just talking about that tower. I built, helped build, or had a say in just about every successful business that has come to Reedsville these past thirty years. I got the right people on my side, and I keep them close."

Again, Goose said nothing.

"You don't need to broaden your horizons when you got everything in the palm of your hand." Chance nodded contentedly at this—you could put that shit on a bumper sticker—and folded his hands over his belly. "Take me home, Goose."

"You got it."

LUCKY PINDER HAD A SWOLLEN eye and a busted mouth. Burl must've punched him twice. That wasn't what Chance had asked for, but he was fine with it on this occasion. Lucky was a lying, thieving, sneaky, cheating, underhanded, dirty-dealing, no-good son of a buck. For some folks, one punch just wasn't enough.

You could put *that* on a bumper sticker, too.

"I'm sorry, Chance. Really, I am. I know . . . Lord, I *know* I did you wrong, but if you've a mind to listen, I can tell you exactly—"

"I've not a mind to listen," Chance said. His voice was steady. A slow-burning flame. "Only reason you're sorry is because you got caught. I've a notion you wouldn't be nearly as apologetic if you were running free and spending my money."

"It was just a *loan*," Lucky said. Fluid leaked from his puffy eye. "I was gonna pay you back."

"A loan is an agreement between two or more parties," Chance said. He linked his fingers. The chunky ring on his pinkie flashed in the bare light. "Did I agree to let you steal from my cash registers?"

"What? No, I—"

"Did I agree to let you steal from my gals?"

"No, but—"

"Then there *was* no agreement." Chance smiled—little white teeth in the snugness of his beard. "Therefore, it was not a loan."

"No, I guess not. But . . . but . . ." Lucky licked blood from his lower lip. "I was still gonna pay you back."

"Your mouth is full of lies," Chance said with a touch more emotion in his voice. "Lies and dogshit."

"Dogshit?"

Lucky Pinder was a slick-haired, boy-faced fortysomething with buckteeth and a scowl. He'd rode his thumb into town a couple of years ago, got a job washing cars, and stuck around. A few months later, he was working for Chance, first as his driver, then as a bartender at Fourth and Inches, then as the manager at the Devil's Own, a strip joint on the "other" side of town. This was a swift ascent by any reasonable standard, and Lucky should have felt blessed beyond measure, only fellas like Lucky didn't always appreciate when good fortune fell their way, and got it into their cotton-brained heads that they were owed a little bit more. The reason he was in his current predicament—said predicament being duct-taped to a chair in Chance's four-car garage—was because he'd decided to take that little bit for himself.

Stealing from the Devil's Own did not require substantial wile, given the volume of cash flowing through the place (most patrons elected not to swipe their debit or credit cards) and the arbitrary cost of some of the services on offer. Lucky saw this as too good an opportunity to pass up. He started out small. Twenty bucks here and there, maybe a hundred on a busy night. But when nobody noticed that money going missing, he got more daring. He'd peel two or three hundred off the day's take and disappear it into his pocket. And if stealing from Chance wasn't bad enough, Lucky also took from the girls. As a rule, general tips were split among all the dancers, and many of them depended on that extra chunk of change. When Venus—a fine gal and a good mother—approached Chance and told him that she'd noticed a drop in her share of the gratuities, Chance decided to investigate. He had Burl set up a hidden camera, and sure enough, there was Lucky with his hand in the cookie jar.

Lucky must've gotten wind that Chance was onto him because he took off in an awful hurry. That was two months ago. Burl found him in Sable Point, forty-three miles south, balls-deep in some crack whore at the Punchout Motel.

"I brought you into my employ," Chance said now, slowly circling the chair to which Lucky had been secured. "That means I brought you into my family, a position of great trust. And what did you do, Lucky?"

"I did you dirty, Chance."

"You spit in my eye."

"Yessir, I did. I surely did."

Chance circled the chair again, momentarily lost in thought. It occurred to him that Lucky was a lot like Cajun Dan, a man whose overconfidence and cocksureness had tumbled into plain stupidity. Chance remembered "Death Roll" Gus with the Cajun's leg poking out from between his jaws. Maybe Lucky would be . . . well, *luckier.*

"As it happens," Chance said. He stopped in front of Lucky and leaned over, hands planted on his thighs. "I believe in second chances. Bible says that God's mercies are never-ending, that they are new every morning. That's the reason Jonah found himself on the road to Nineveh, spat from the belly of the whale."

Lucky nodded enthusiastically. His mouth was bleeding good.

"Now, I don't pretend to have God's mercy," Chance said, "nor His tolerance for fools, but I *am* gonna give you a shot at freedom."

"Oh shit, thank you. Thank you, Chance." Lucky tried a smile, but it was an ugly thing. "*Thank* you. I won't . . . I won't ever . . ." He whimpered with gratitude, the sound echoing around the garage.

They were in bay two. Chance's 1977 Trans Am was parked on one side, his Caddy and Lincoln Navigator on the other—all fine American automobiles, and that Trans Am looked so much like the one in *Smokey and the Bandit* that, every time Chance looked at it, he expected to see a young Burt Reynolds sitting behind the wheel. Similarly handsome and mustachioed (and *named*, come to think of it), Burl stood in the background, awaiting orders.

Chance straightened to his full height—six-three in his boots—and said to Burl, "Go get Errol. A clean rag, too."

Burl nodded and exited the garage by way of a side door. Lucky watched him leave, then scrolled his good eye back to Chance. He gasped another thank-you. A thread of snot burst from his nostril and hung heavy on his upper lip.

"Don't thank me yet. I said a *shot* at freedom." Chance stepped to a console on the wall. He pushed a button labeled 2, and the door in front of Lucky rumbled open, revealing the garage's concrete apron and the night beyond. Except for a few lights twinkling between the trees, it was dark indeed.

Lucky looked longingly outside, straining at the duct tape. He'd be free and running soon enough.

"It won't surprise you to learn," Chance said, strolling gradually back to bay two, "that mine is the longest driveway in all of Reedsville. Two hundred and eighty yards from here to the main gate. A fast man—your average wide receiver, say—can cover that distance in about thirty seconds. I don't expect you to be *that* fast, Lucky. You're an elite asshole, but not an elite athlete. Even so, you're gonna hafta pick up your heels."

At that point, Burl returned to the garage with Errol on a leash. Chance greeted man and dog with a wide smile. Lucky, not so much.

"Jesus," he said. "That's a Dracula dog! I seen it in movies. You ain't . . . I mean, you *wouldn't*—"

"Your average human male," Chance interrupted, running his hand lovingly over the dog's sleek head, "can sprint one hundred yards in about fourteen seconds. Which means, Lucky, assuming you're an average human male, it'll take you about forty seconds to reach the main gate."

Errol sat tall and still, a regal beast, his coat shimmering softly in the overhead light. He cast a single dark look at Lucky, then stared straight ahead.

"Aw, shit." Lucky squirmed in his seat. His open eye was as round and bright as a silver dollar. "I can see where this is going, and I hafta say, I don't much like it."

"This beautiful boy is Errol, a purebred Doberman pinscher." Chance scratched beneath Errol's chin and Errol cocked his head higher. He appeared to enjoy that. "Say hello, Lucky."

Lucky shook his head and bled from the mouth and squeaked a wretched hello.

"Had me a greyhound once," Chance said. "A good dog." Then he frowned and looked at his head of security. "Hey, Burl, what did we call that greyhound?"

"Stevie Wonderdog," Burl replied.

"Right, of course. Stevie Wonderdog." Chance snapped his fingers. "Now, Stevie was fast—made me some money, back in the day—but he didn't have a mean bone in his body. Had me a fighting dog, too. Dolly. A pit bull terrier. That dog was as mean as the day is long, but she wasn't fast."

"Please, Chance," Lucky implored. His damaged eye leaked slow tears. "*Please.*"

"Errol here is the best of all dogs." Chance patted Errol between his pointy ears. "He's mean *and* fast. He'll go from zero to thirty in a blink and can make it to the main gate in about eighteen seconds."

Lucky groaned and looked up at the ceiling. Chance spared him a pitiful glance, then held his hand out to Burl and said, "Rag." Burl dug into his pocket and pulled out a square piece of cloth, gray as a raincloud and perfect for the job.

"I said you had a shot, Lucky, and I mean that." Chance folded the rag into a smaller piece and used it on Lucky's face, first to wipe away his tears, then to smear the blood from his mouth and chin. He worked tenderly, like a nurse or a mother, cradling the back of Lucky's head in one hand. "Here's how it's going down: I'm gonna cut you out of that chair, and on my go, you're gonna start running."

"*Please*, Chance," Lucky said again, blinking his bright eye. More tears spilled out. "I know . . . let me . . . let me *work* off what I took from you. That's a good idea, right? I . . . I'll do anything you want."

"Now, you in a straight race against Errol . . . you wouldn't stand a chance, so I'm gonna give you a fair and sizable head start." Chance refolded the cloth and used the fresh side to clean the snot from Lucky's nose. "How much of a head start should we give him, Burl?"

"Twenty seconds," Burl said.

"Oh, Burl, you are a *hard* son of a bitch." Chance chuckled and held up the rag, made heavier with bodily fluids. "I'm gonna say twenty-*five* seconds."

Lucky nodded his head yes, then shook his head no. The poor terrified bastard.

Chance took two steps toward Errol and held out the rag. The dog sniffed at it hungrily, his lip curled, showing teeth. A dreadful growling sound reverberated from his chest. He looked at Lucky and strained at the leash. Burl had to steady his feet to keep from being pulled forward.

"On the count of twenty-five," Chance said, dropping the rag into Lucky's lap, "Burl is gonna let Errol off his leash. By my calculation— again, assuming you're an average human male—you should reach the main gate with three or four seconds to spare, which'll give you time to hop over it."

"I ain't sure you've accounted for certain variables," Lucky said desperately. "Wind resistance and such. Also, I'm wearing these."

He thrust out his legs, on the ends of which were a pair of Laredo western boots with fancy embroidery and three-inch heels.

"Yeah," Chance said. "I'd take them off if I were you."

Errol growled and jerked at his leash. Chance walked over to a tool rack on the back wall and selected a pair of heavy-duty scissors. He returned to Lucky, stood behind him, and started to snip away the duct tape binding him to the chair.

"I'm a fair man, and I play by the rules," Chance said. His voice had remained that steady, slow-burning flame, barely a hint of emotion this whole time. "If you make it over that gate, you are free and clear, and you can keep every cent you stole from me. On that you have my word."

Chance cut through the last of the duct tape and pulled it off Lucky's chest and arms. Lucky stared at the dog, who stared back harder.

"However, if Errol reaches you before you reach the gate . . ." Chance rolled the tape into a silvery ball and tossed it away. He stepped in front of Lucky and spread his hands. "Word of advice: let him at your throat. It'll be over quicker."

"Oh shit," Lucky said miserably, then thrust out his chin. "Nope. Fuck you, Chance Kotter. I ain't playing your crazy fucking game. I'm staying right in this seat."

"You can stay where you are," Chance said, "or you can take to your heels. Either way, on twenty-five, Errol gets sprung."

"Shit." Lucky bared his teeth, large and pink with blood. "Shit . . . shit . . . *shit* . . ." He said it half a dozen more times, such was his disposition.

"You fucked with the wrong man, Lucky Pinder." Chance stepped aside and gestured at the open garage door. "You ready?"

"Shit . . . *shit*." Lucky reached down, grabbed the heel of his right boot, and started to pull. "Gimme a second to get my goddamn boots off."

Chance did. More than a second, in fact. (He really *was* a fair man.) Lucky rose shakily from his seat, standing in stocking feet with his big toe poking through a hole.

"Go," Chance said coolly.

Lucky took off with a fire under his skinny little ass, and Chance began counting.

HE COUNTED ALL THE WAY to twenty-five, as promised, with a clearly pronounced "Mississippi" between each number, then Burl thumbed the catch on the leash and Errol was gone. The black-and-tan dog shot through the open door and disappeared into the darkness. Chance and Burl looked at each other.

"I got a hundred dollars on Errol," Chance said.

"I'm not taking that bet."

The two men stepped out through the open door and started along the driveway. They'd taken only a few sauntering steps when they heard a series of pained cries—brutal, defenseless sounds, blessedly silenced after several seconds. Chance and Burl kept walking, following the little lights posted along the driveway, and at length came upon Lucky and Errol. To Chance's great surprise, Lucky was still alive. His mouth gaped in the red mess of his face. His good eye stared at the limitless sky. As Chance watched, Errol tore a strip out of Lucky's throat and shook it like a plaything. He was maybe twenty yards from the main gate.

"He got close," Burl noted.

"Not close enough," Chance said. "Must not be an average human male."

There was a time when Chance could stand like a cowboy, thumbs tucked into the belt loops of his jeans, but he hadn't been able to reach that far beneath his belly for many a year. These days, to achieve a similar stance of manly repose, he would pull his shoulders back, cock one boot on its heel, and place his hands on his bulging sides. He did so now and remained in that position until Errol's work was done.

"I can leave this with you," Chance said, gesturing at Lucky (dead now) and the puddle of blood around him.

"Absolutely."

"You're a good man, Burl." Chance looked at him earnestly and smiled. "Will I see you tomorrow?"

"Nossir. I'm taking a day with the family. We're driving up to Alabama Adventure in Bessemer. I'm going to ride the Rampage." His face illuminated at the prospect.

"Well, that sure sounds like fun, and you give that lovely wife of yours a squeeze from me." Chance clapped Burl on the shoulder. "I'll see you Tuesday."

With that, Chance turned on his heel and walked back to the house.

NOT THAT TUESDAY BUT THE one after, Burl came bursting into Chance's study with some kind of look on his face. Chance, who just happened to be staring at that old photo of Harper Avenue at the time, couldn't place its source at first. Excitement? Adrenaline? Fear? It might have been the same look Burl had right before the Rampage plunged him one hundred feet.

"What is it?" Chance asked.

"We found them," Burl replied.

Chance knew exactly whom Burl was referring to. He took an involuntary step backward, feeling an odd sensation inside, cold at first, then heating to a ravenous glow. It lifted him. He crossed smoothly to Burl—the quickest and daintiest he'd moved for a long time. Burl removed a folded piece of paper from his pocket and opened it up. On it were the photographs of three young women, one Black, two white.

"Shit," Chance said. Anger crackled behind his rib cage. He clenched his fists. "A buncha gals."

Burl said, "They call themselves the Bang-Bang Sisters."

# SIX

He stuffed her mouth with sparrow and crow and, yes, wren feathers, working them deep, all the way to the back of the throat, then he ran a strip of duct tape over her lips, sealing the feathers in. Across the tape, in shaky lowercase, he wrote:

> sky, promise, calling
> blue god, my birdbody aches
> she will take me there
> —*wren*

He rubbed his knuckle across "promise" and "god" and "birdbody," smearing the letters, just enough to keep them legible (and keep the graphologists guessing). There were sixty-three knife wounds across her body, most of them in her torso but some in her throat and thighs, and he stuffed these with feathers, too.

HER NAME WAS RACHEL GRODIN. She was twenty-seven years old, had a boyfriend nicknamed Blaze (because of his fiery red hair), and lived with her two roommates in a rented house in Colton—a small town six miles west of Reedsville, famous for its annual Sacred Harp Festival. Rachel enjoyed country music, kayaking, and college football. She *loved* horses. Her earliest memory was of riding a sweet-natured Morgan named Fortune's Boy, and she had a bumper sticker on her Acura that read THIS GIRL RUNS ON JESUS AND HORSES.

This passion led her to the job at Guthrie's Ranch. Yates Guthrie himself was dead of a heart attack. Lynn, his widow, at seventy-seven, was too bone-weary to do much of anything, so Rachel showed up at six thirty every morning (including Sundays) to feed and water the horses, then clean out their stalls while they took in some exercise in the arena. The wren knew this. He knew everything about Rachel. He'd been monitoring her for some time.

That morning, he'd waited for her in one of the empty stalls, perched on a stack of hay bales so his feet wouldn't show in the gap beneath. He didn't care for the environment. It was too stifling, too *rumbly*. The horses unsettled him. They whinnied and jostled, bumping their heavy flanks against the sides of their stalls. The wren increased the flow rate on his concentrator until 100 percent oxygen seeped into his lungs. He covered his ears, closed his eyes, and imagined the sky. In a moment, the horses settled and so did he.

Rachel arrived at 6:27. She went directly to the stable and greeted the horses, giving each of their noses a good scratch over the stall doors. "Hey there, Piper . . . Good morning, Mr. Chestnut . . . Oh my, Gigi, ain't you pleased to see me!" By this time, the wren had the paring knife, recently sharpened, in his gloved right hand. His concentrator hissed quietly beneath the horses' snorts and grunts. As Rachel passed his stall, he slipped off the hay bales, opened the door, and approached her from behind.

His first strike was to the side of her throat. She went down, and he climbed on top of her, pinning her arms to the ground with his knees, covering her mouth with his free hand. The horses, restless once again, neighed and stomped their hooves. They didn't bother the wren now. He brought the knife down quickly. Rachel's body was as soft as butter. He breathed his purified oxygen and brought the knife down again. Soon, his wings unfurled. He fluttered around the stable for a minute or so, then exited through the open door and took to the sky. His body expanded immediately. His lungs were as large as barrels. He flew higher, where the clouds were silk threads, then circled broadly. The ranch was beneath him, looking exactly like it had when he reconnoitered it on Google Earth, except for Rachel's silver Acura, parked close to the stable.

The sky was freedom and calm. There was no clamor up here. No anxiety or pain. The wren flew for a long time and sang beautiful songs.

CONFINED SPACES. CROWDED PLACES. CARS, buses, trains: these were all triggers. Antidepressants took the edge off but weren't enough by themselves. Medical-grade oxygen, which the wren had discovered by accident, allowed him to function. He could tolerate public places and even ride in a bus, if it wasn't too crowded.

Mostly, though, he stayed home.

His therapist (one of the many he'd had in the course of his thirty-eight years) explained that his agoraphobia stemmed from his PTSD, which in turn stemmed from the car crash that had killed his parents.

"That feeling of being trapped . . . helpless," the doctor had said. "It's overwhelming, I know. It makes you feel small."

The wren, nineteen years old, had nodded.

"You can rise above it, though." The doctor had nodded encouragingly. "You need to take control, find something that elevates you."

"Like . . . a hobby?"

"More like a passion. Something you can't live without. And the gratification—the feeling—this brings . . . let *that* define you."

THE WREN LEFT THE STABLE via a back door. He walked for a time, clinging to those dawn shadows, then crawled beneath a wire fence onto a neighboring farm. No doubt Mr. Farmer was wide-awake and tending to his animals, but the wren steered well clear of the farm proper. He cut along the eastern edge of a swaying, rustling cornfield. The corn wasn't as high as an elephant's eye, but it was close, and it concealed him, although he had to open his concentrator all the way to cope with the density of the plants. From here, he passed into a gently sloping patch of woodland, which led down to White Park, where the Colton Sacred Harp Festival was held the first weekend of every June. The wren walked through the park, quiet at this time of the morning—just a few joggers and dog walkers, was all. He was even comfortable enough to remove his cannula, although he inserted it again walking through downtown Colton on his way to the bus stop. The wren rejected the 7:40 bus to Reedsville (*way* too crowded), but the 8:20 was much better. He sat close to the doors, though, in case the iron bands around his chest squeezed too tightly and he had to make a quick exit.

He returned to his apartment and slept until early afternoon, then rolled out of bed and hopped over to his computer. Rachel Grodin was everywhere, as he knew she would be. There were pictures of her freckled face and shots of the crime scene. Lots of shots of horses, too—Mr. Chestnut and Gigi among them, looking quite sad.

It wasn't the killing that defined him, but the heights it lifted him to.

# SEVEN

Three hundred miles from home and you want to turn around?"

"I think it's something we should discuss," Jessie replied. She wanted to go home, too—they'd been on the road for eleven exhausting weeks—but this was big and objectively worth turning around for. "We have an exclusive window. If we decline, then it's somebody else's scalp."

Flo shrugged: *And?*

Brea joined them, carrying three cans of Red Bull. They were due onstage in eight minutes. Not one of them felt like performing, but sometimes you had to energize and get the job done. Brea handed a can to each sister, popped the top on her own, and took a swig.

"So serious," she said. "Are we discussing Alabama?"

Flo nodded. Jessie blew foam from the lip of her can.

"There's nothing to discuss," Brea said firmly. "This job is ours. You don't want any part of it, that's fine. I'll drive you to the nearest bus depot. I'll even drive you home. But make no mistake, with or without you, I'm taking that van and I'm going to Reedsville."

THEY WERE IN NUEVA VIDA, California, a dusty desert burg a stone's throw from the Nevada state line. There wasn't much to it: a couple of eateries, a snake farm, and this Wild West–themed rock club called Stray Bullets on the outskirts of town. The sisters sat on a boulder at the edge of the parking lot. Van Halen thumped from external speakers at a volume that would carry for miles, and a steady stream of greaseballs shuffled through the front door. This was supposed to be their last stop before heading home. They all needed to recalibrate, to sleep in their own beds, to be around other friends and family members.

But forty minutes from the small desert town, Jessie's phone lit up with a message from 9-$tar: **WE FOUND HIM.** It was followed by a link. The sisters pulled off to the side of the road and huddled around Jessie's phone.

"Do we really want to open this?" Flo had asked.

Brea, impatient, had tapped the link.

It took them to a page on a private server loaded with information. The sisters read through it quickly. By the time they'd finished, the air inside the tour van—already stifling in the desert heat—had a different feel, as if an electric current were running through the steel frame.

There was a photograph of a thirtysomething male with blond hair and doll-like eyes. He had a thin neck, narrow shoulders, and toothpick arms. He might be described as scrawny, frail, nonthreatening, except the name beneath the photo proved otherwise. **Mitchell Spahn (Childs), aka "the wren."** This bantamweight piece of shit was the epitome of danger.

"It's him," Brea said.

The wren had slipped up, and the Trace had caught him. On his most recent kill, he'd left a haiku with the line *blue god, my birdbody aches*, which bore a distinct similarity to the sentence "Mother Sky, my birdbody sings for you," from the 1988 novel *A Heart Full of Robins*, by the late William T. Baugh. It was a tenuous lead but worth pursuing. It helped that Mr. Baugh's novel had been out of print since the early nineties. "Out of print" didn't mean unavailable, and BookScan numbers revealed that sixty-two copies had sold through retail outlets across North America in the last ten years. The Trace checked the buyers and got a couple of maybes: a fifty-seven-year-old lawyer from Mississippi who'd self-published a poetry collection in 2019, and Mitchell Spahn, a thirty-eight-year-old web designer from Galesburg, Illinois, whose Amazon purchase history also included Jack Kerouac's *Book of Haikus*.

The lawyer was a dead end. The Trace had dived into his computer, his browsing history, and his cell phone. No red flags, other than the usual roster of porn sites and several "after-hours" text messages to his former secretary.

Mitchell Spahn was a different story.

While still in his early twenties, Mitchell had served two and a half years for rape and another year for assault. He was diagnosed with social anxiety disorder in 2016 and had spent nine weeks at a psychiatric care facility in Peoria. Four years later, Mitchell changed his surname to Childs (his mother's maiden name) and moved to his aunt's house in Reedsville, Alabama. He set up his work-from-home web design business and faded into an unremarkable life. Or so it appeared.

The Trace went deeper. It discovered that Mitchell wasn't on the Alabama Sex Offender Registry because he hadn't *officially* changed his name or address. He'd adopted "Childs" for his business (no doubt to distance himself from his sullied past) and online persona. His banking details and legal documents were still linked to his mother's address in Illinois.

These were damning signs, but breaking into Mitchell's computer gave the Trace's meticulous gray hatters all the evidence they needed. To begin with, they found that Mitchell had created multiple fake social media accounts that he used to "follow" his victims. They pulled Google Maps data that corresponded with the victims' home addresses and places of work. The coup de grâce, though, was a rough draft of the haiku that the wren had left at the scene of Susan Orringer's murder—information never released to the general public.

"Jesus Christ," Jessie had said. She turned off her phone and looked at her sisters. "That's him. They really found him."

The bounty was twelve hundred Xuko: approximately $48,000.

9-$tar must have been notified as soon as the link was opened; they sent another DM to Jessie several minutes later:

You have an exclusive window. This contract will go live in 72hrs.

The edginess among the sisters had started then and intensified as they approached Nueva Vida. Brea clearly wanted to turn their van around. That was obvious from the tightness of her shoulders and the way she clenched her jaw. Flo's only concern was getting home to Imani. Jessie was caught between the two.

Now, sitting outside Stray Bullets, moments from hitting the stage, the tension had reached an unpleasant high. They sat on the boulder, drinking their Red Bulls and shooting challenging glances at one another. Van Halen gave way to something louder and more aggressive, which didn't help the mood.

"I want to do this together," Brea said. She wiped a fleck of grit from beneath her eye. "But I'll do it alone if I have to."

Flo didn't look at her. She stood up, slapped dust from the seat of her pants, and started across the parking lot toward the club.

"It's showtime," she said. "Let's get this over with."

BREA BANGED THE DRUMS TOO hard, Flo overcompensated with the bass, and Jessie messed up some of the lyrics. The audience was unaffected by these lapses. It surged and cheered. It jostled and rocked. The sisters, at least, finished strongly. Their last four songs found the groove they'd been lacking, and they ended the night with a twelve-minute version of "Helter Skelter," incorporating a drum solo that encouraged all of Brea's aggression. The sisters left the stage to window-rattling applause. Moreover, they each felt that they'd burned off their frustrations and were better placed, emotionally, to talk about the wren.

FORTY MINUTES LATER, THEY SAT on the same boulder at the edge of the parking lot.

"I can't turn my back on this," Brea said. There was no tightness in her voice or posture. She glowed with spent energy. "Not this job. Not this scumbag. I can't just drive away and hope that somebody else gets it done."

"I understand," Flo said. "But this doesn't have to be our responsibility. There are other crews out there."

A tumbleweed bounced dramatically across the lot. Only their tour van and an old Dodge Ram remained, this belonging to whichever Stray Bullets staff member was closing up. A few lights burned inside the club, but the neon outside was cold and dark. Somewhere across the desert, coyotes howled.

"Maybe we should sleep on this," Jessie said.

"Seventy-two hours," Brea responded. She glanced at her phone, then put it away. "Actually, sixty-six hours now. The window is closing. I've made my mind up. I don't need to sleep on it. The only question is, are you going to make me drive you home, or can I drop you at the bus depot in Vegas so that I don't lose too much time?"

"Brea, hey . . ." Jessie clicked her tongue. The exact words weren't there, but she came up with something close: "I don't think you should do this by yourself."

"I don't think I should, either," Brea said. She swallowed hard and stared across the desert. Its breadth and darkness were mirrored in her eyes. "The wren's latest victim, Rachel Grodin . . . there's a video doing the rounds on social media of her bouncing her twin nieces on her knees, up and down, like they're riding horses. The girls are, I don't know, maybe three, four years old. They're laughing their little asses off, and Rachel has a smile on her face that could melt snow."

Flo looked at her boot tops. Jessie sighed and curled her shoulders inward.

"That video keeps playing in my head," Brea continued. "I can't stop thinking about those little girls—how they're too young to know what really happened, and how confused and sad they must be."

The coyotes howled again. They sounded closer. Brea stood up and stretched, getting a percussion of pops out of her spine and hips. She looked tired. They all did. They all *were*.

"We're not the justice system," Flo said, speaking to them both but looking at Brea. "That's not our role. We put things right when the system fails. If you really want a hand in bringing the wren down, maybe think about turning this information over to the Feds."

"The Trace would *not* like that," Jessie said. "All their hard work, for the Feds to swoop in and take the glory? No, we'd be excommunicated. Access revoked."

"We'd do it anonymously," Flo countered.

"They'd still know."

"Even if they didn't, and the FBI gets the collar, what do you think happens next?" Brea waited exactly one second for a response, then provided it herself. "I'll tell you what happens: there's a long, drawn-out trial, during which the wren pleads insanity. Then he gets to spend the rest of his life in a high-security hospital, popping benzos and watching flowers grow."

"He'll get the needle," Flo said.

"Right," Jessie said. "After ten years on death row."

"Except the average time between sentencing and execution is closer to twenty years," Brea said, and sneered. "What kind of justice is that?"

The lights inside Stray Bullets were shut off. Moments later, the staff member on closing duty exited the property and locked up. Her name was Savannah. She still wore her novelty Stray Bullets cowboy hat, except now she had a Smith & Wesson revolver holstered to her side—a little extra security on this lonely desert night—making her look even more the part. Savannah popped a smoke between her lips, struck a light, and walked toward her Ram. She was taillights twenty seconds later.

The sound of the truck's engine faded, leaving only the night song: the breeze stirring the greasewood, grit skimming across the terrain, the coyotes again. The sisters sat in their own deep silence, until Flo sighed and said:

"How long will it take to get to Reedsville?"

"If we take turns at the wheel, about twenty-eight hours." Brea dropped to her haunches and leaned close to Jessie and Flo. "That includes gas stops and short breaks to stretch our legs."

"Better to stop halfway and get some real sleep. Even then, we should be in Reedsville by Sunday evening. The window closes Monday, ten P.M. central time." Jessie blew over her upper lip, looking at her sisters with tired eyes. "That gives us at least twenty-four hours to recon the target and get the job done."

"Then I'll drive you both to the nearest major airport," Brea said. "You fly home to L.A. I'll follow in the van. I'll be a few days behind you."

Flo pressed her lips together and dipped her chin. "I miss Imani. I promised her I'd be home today."

"We promised our mom the same thing," Jessie said.

"This won't be a long delay. It *can't* be, because we're against the clock." Brea tried to keep her tone measured, but she was too charged, too determined. "If you fly, you'll be home Monday. Just a couple of days late."

"And the wren will be history," Jessie said. She exhaled, releasing the tightness in her chest and shoulders. "I've got to admit, that's a pretty good way to close out the tour."

The sisters exchanged small, tired smiles. Brea stood up straight. Jessie hopped off the boulder and stood next to her, then Flo joined them.

"Together?" Brea asked.

Jessie nodded. Both she and Brea turned to Flo, who—fighter that she was—cricked her neck and shook the fatigue out of her arms.

"Let's go get this son of a bitch," she said.

# EIGHT

Interstate 40, where for long stretches the landscape didn't change, and Brea didn't see another vehicle in either direction. She followed the van's headlights in a trancelike state.

Flo had reclined the passenger seat and slept with her head on a bundled hoodie. Jessie was curled up on the seat behind them. Neither sister slept deeply, but Brea envied every second they managed to get. She'd been the driving force behind this change of direction, though, so it was only fair that she took the first shift at the wheel.

An hour west of Flagstaff—150 miles into their journey—a mighty storm rolled across the plains. It brought savage rain and a wind filled with muscle. Lightning strobed within the thunderheads, illuminating miles of blanched desertscape. At one point, Brea saw a wild horse, reared high and terrified. Its tail and mane flailed in the wind, and its eyes were mad circles.

Thunder rang. Rain slapped the van from all directions. Flo and Jessie woke from their disjointed sleep. They peered through the blurred windshield with an almost childlike awe.

"Think this is a sign?" Jessie asked, trying for humor. "What's the word? An omen?"

"Only if the omen is us," Brea said.

"Okay," Flo said with a hint of derision. "But maybe we should pull over. Wait this out."

Brea shook her head. She enjoyed the heavy way her heart was banging and the dull ache in her hands from gripping the wheel so hard. The *real* sign here was that she wasn't backing down. She pushed harder, in fact, increasing her speed from forty to fifty, proving to the fates—or perhaps just to herself—how determined she was to see this through.

They were diverted off the interstate by a jackknifed semi and took a narrower road through a small town made up mostly of trailers, all without power, some rolled onto their sides. An old school bus painted rainbow colors had caught fire, maybe hit by lightning. The road was littered with debris, and now Brea had to slow down, steering around the larger pieces: a splintered branch, a motorcycle gas tank, a baby's stroller (thankfully empty). A mangy dog left to fend for itself ran scared lengths behind a fence and barked voicelessly.

"Poor thing," Flo said.

"Looks like it's survived worse," Brea said.

The storm began to run itself dry after another three miles. They rejoined the interstate. Five miles after that it was just the wind buffeting the van. It was like driving through a shaft walled with shoulders and elbows. Jessie curled up again and slipped back into something like sleep. Flo didn't. She brought her seat upright and covered her lap with the hoodie she'd been using for a pillow.

"Need me to take over driving?" she asked.

"I'm okay for now," Brea replied. "That storm got my blood pumping. We need to stop and gas up soon, so maybe then."

It was just shy of 6:00 A.M. (they'd lost an hour to the mountain time zone) and still dark, not even a wrinkle of light on the horizon. Brea had been driving for three hours, but it felt longer. By 6:10, the wind abated. The interstate reverted to ordinariness, every mile a carbon copy of the last.

"The road is identical in both directions," Flo said, picking up a similar vibe. "There's no real indication which way we're heading, but I can feel deep down that we're moving farther from home."

"I know what you mean," Brea said.

"It feels like we're driving against the grain."

THEY STOPPED TO REFUEL IN the town of Holbrook. By this time the sun had climbed over the horizon and dressed the road ahead in fierce color.

Flo and Jessie bought gas station food and gas station coffee. Brea opted for yogurt and bottled water. She had designs on sleeping for the next couple hundred miles and didn't want anything to upset that.

Flo took the wheel, and they got rolling. Brea was on the backseat, curled more awkwardly than Jessie, being taller. Jessie sat up front, wide-awake, sunglasses on.

"GPS says we're twenty-one hours away," Flo said, and exhaled so deeply that she fogged the windshield. "Imani's going to be so upset when I tell her that I won't be home today."

"Try not to dwell on that," Jessie said. "Focus on the good we're doing."

"I am. I'm trying, at least."

"You'll be home Monday."

Flo unwrapped her breakfast sandwich. "You flying back with me?"

"Haven't decided yet," Jessie said. "I might take the slow road home. Partly to keep Brea company. Mainly to stop her from doing anything crazy."

"Crazy?" Brea mumbled from the backseat. "Me?"

The sameness of the landscape continued for as long as Flo drove. Everything south of the sky was beige and gray. Even the billboards were coated with a dull skin of sand. Flo and Jessie diverted their boredom by playing Fuck, Marry, Kill, which was fun to begin with, but they soon ran out of viable spouses, so changed it to Fuck, Kill, Kill. This version aligned more closely with their temperaments and was therefore less engaging.

They stopped for gas. The van's tank was still half full, but it broke up the monotony. East of Albuquerque, Brea started snoring, so Flo turned on the radio, just loud enough to hear. She hummed or sang along to the songs she was somewhat familiar with. Jessie chimed in sporadically. They giggled when they got the lyrics wrong, which was often.

Jessie burned up a chunk of time scrolling through her phone. She updated their socials, posting photos of the Stray Bullets gig. The differences between their musician and vigilante personas never failed to resonate with Jessie. She zoomed in on the faces in the audience—alight, alive, caught up in the moment—not one of them knowing who they were *really* applauding.

"You okay?" Flo asked.

"Yeah. Why?"

"You look like I feel."

Jessie cracked a smile, then turned off her phone and dropped it into her lap. "Tiredness, I guess."

"It's more than that," Flo said, and glanced over her shoulder at Brea on the backseat. She was still sawing wood, out for the count. Even so, Flo lowered her voice to a whisper. "I know you, Jessie, and this whole thing—driving east, the wren . . . you don't like it any more than I do."

"Maybe," Jessie said, gesturing at the backseat with a flick of the head. "But she would have gone alone, and if anything happened to her, neither of us would be able to live with ourselves."

"It was unfair of her to put us in that position," Flo said, unable to keep the resentment from her voice. "I don't blame *you*, though. She's your sister. You'll do whatever it takes to protect her."

"She's your sister, too."

"It's different. You and Brea are blood. It's an unbreakable bond."

Jessie nodded. "True. Imagine if Imani was in the band."

"Never." Flo's voice changed again. It went from resentful to stony. "That'll never happen."

Jessie lifted her sunglasses and wiped her eyes. Again, she reflected on the audiences they'd played for and how they had no idea whom they were applauding. This was true of everyone in their lives: friends, family members, ex-partners. Nobody knew they were the Bang-Bang Sisters. Even the Trace didn't know their real names.

They were silent for several miles, watching the dusty road unfold. The radio signal faded. Jessie tuned through numerous country and evangelical stations and finally found something to their liking. She tapped her boot in time, then turned to Flo and asked:

"Do you think you'll ever tell Imani what we do?"

"No," Flo replied without hesitation. "There are some things she doesn't need to know."

"I get it," Jessie said. "But you're so close, and there's this whole side to you that she knows nothing about."

"And it's going to stay that way." Flo's voice was stony again.

"It's a burden, is all," Jessie said. Not for the first time in recent days—*years*, even—she wondered what an ordinary life would look like. "It's hard."

"I know," Flo agreed, her gaze flicking between Jessie and the road. "What about you? Would you ever tell anyone?"

Jessie had friends—people she'd known for years—but they were a world away from guns, fighting, and rock and roll, and that was exactly where she wanted to keep them. They were her balance, her link to a routine existence. Maybe, one day, she could share her secret with a significant other, if one ever came along, but that would require a level of trust she hadn't found in any partner so far.

"I've got no one to tell," Jessie said.

"Your mom?"

Jessie shrugged, unsure how to answer. In truth, she'd briefly considered telling her mom about the Bang-Bang Sisters a couple of years ago, because they were friends as much as they were mother and daughter, and it hurt Jessie to keep anything from her. Aubree Vernier had been a long-time advocate for the marginalized and had raised Brea and Jessie not to tolerate injustice. She would not be pleased to learn about their vigilante side gig, but she would at least *understand* it. Jessie had approached Brea to get her take, and Brea had fiercely objected. "Don't you *dare* tell her," she'd hissed, pinning Jessie against the wall. "Not now. Not ever."

"It's Brea's secret, too," Jessie said. She leaned closer to Flo and lowered her voice another notch. "She's always worked so hard to impress our mom, constantly trying to one-up me."

"Why am I not surprised?"

"It's flattering, in a strange kind of way," Jessie said. "But I wouldn't want to damage Mom's perception of Brea. That would be a worse burden to carry."

"I hear that," Flo said. Her lips crinkled—a sympathetic smile. She held up her right fist and Jessie bumped it, and they drove on without saying anything for a long time.

FLO RACKED UP 430 MILES, cutting a horizontal line across most of New Mexico, then it was Jessie's turn to drive. She'd barely set off when another DM came via the Trace. 9-$tar again: **55 hrs.**

Brea, awake now, read the screen over Jessie's shoulder.

"Tell them we're on it," she said.

Jessie tapped the reply in with her thumb, her eyes flicking between the screen and the road. She clicked send, then slotted her phone into the cupholder.

"You going back to sleep?" she asked, looking at Brea in the rearview.

"Nope." Brea rolled the stiffness out of her shoulders.

"Good," Jessie said. She cranked the radio up.

OKLAHOMA CITY. GOOD FOR COWBOYS, college ball, and tornadoes. The sisters had played a club there—the Spike—a couple of years before. It was a mean, whiskey-smelling den of a place, with Stetson-wearing ranch hands lining one wall and jocks in Sooners gear lining the other. The testosterone could have fueled a freighter, and the sisters kept amping it up. They played one rage-filled song after another. It was like adding air to a tire that was apt to go bang—and go bang it did. Both sides of the club came together, chests pumped and fists swinging. Tables, chairs, bottles, and bones were broken. The police arrived in riot gear, and the sisters stopped playing only when the manager cut the power to their amps.

It was their first time stopping in Oklahoma City since that loud, bruising night. They weren't here to perform this time but to eat a good meal and sleep in a real bed—and not some crummy motel bed. Given the sizable payday on their horizon, the sisters decided to opt for something with at least four stars over the door.

"The window closes in fifty hours," Jessie said, swinging the van into the Sheraton's parking garage (with the range of equipment in the back, they weren't comfortable handing the key to a valet attendant). "GPS has us eleven and a half hours from the target. Time is on our side, girls. We can recharge here."

"Good," Flo grumbled. She had pouches under her eyes.

They checked into separate rooms, where they showered and changed into fresh clothes—routine by any reasonable standard, but it felt like an extravagance. Brea took a short but satisfying nap. Flo Skyped with Imani, who was still upset that Flo wasn't home to rub her big fat swollen feet as promised, but totally understood the need to play two super-high-paying gigs in Reno.

"It's not like I'm having the baby tomorrow," Imani said. "At least I *hope* not."

Jessie checked in with her mom, then called a friend in Reseda and arranged a girls' night in West Hollywood the following Friday. Even taking the slow road with Brea, she'd easily be home by then.

At some point, Jessie noticed, 9-$tar had DM'd an update. She read it quickly and shared it with her sisters over dinner.

"We know that the wren lives with his aunt," she said, placing her phone down on the table and angling the screen so that Brea and Flo could see. She'd logged in to the Trace and brought up the contract page—the modern equivalent of a WANTED: DEAD OR ALIVE poster, or in this case, WANTED: DEAD. VERY DEAD. NOTHING BUT DEAD WILL DO. The face of their target stared up at them, sallow and weak-chinned.

"Mitchell Spahn," Brea said stonily. She sipped from her glass of water, raising her eyes to Jessie. "Let's not call him 'the wren.' His name is Mitchell, and he's just a man. A sick, scared little man."

They were at a seafood restaurant in Bricktown, part of a refurbished warehouse, with nets and mounted fish on the walls and country pop playing through speakers hidden inside lobster traps. It was Saturday night and busy. Folks circled the bar, eating noisily, watching baseball on one of the many flat-screen TVs. The main floor was jammed, but the sisters managed to score a table in the corner, where it was quieter. Even so, they spoke with lowered voices.

"Okay, so *Mitchell* lives with his aunt in Cedar Mills," Jessie said. "That's one of the few well-to-do neighborhoods in Reedsville."

"Middle-class white boy turns serial killer," Flo said. "Why am I not surprised?"

Jessie nodded. She scrolled down the contract page to the latest update, which amounted to two bullet points. "The aunt, Olivia Childs, has a basement apartment that she rented out until three years ago—"

"When Mitchell moved to town," Brea said.

"So he's living in the basement," Flo said. "And if it's a former rental property, it probably has a separate entrance."

"We won't even have to disturb the aunt," Brea added. Her eyes shimmered.

"That's assuming we take care of business quickly and quietly. We know it doesn't always work out that way, but there is another option." Jessie took a drink of water and tapped the second bullet point on the phone's screen. "Mitchell is a web designer. He works from home. Likely doesn't get his nose out of his ass until eleven A.M. But Aunt Olivia is an administrator at the local hospital. She leaves the house at five forty every morning to be at her desk by six."

"What time's sunup?" Brea asked.

"Six thirty, or thereabouts," Jessie replied. "That gives us fifty minutes under the cover of darkness with the target alone in the house."

The server came over with a tray of drinks. Nothing alcoholic. A lemon ginger cooler for Brea. Virgin mimosas for Jessie and Flo. They wanted their bodies and minds completely clear for the task ahead of them.

"We can't assume the target is alone," Flo said a few moments later, their drinks in front of them and the server out of earshot. "There could be a dog. Or maybe the aunt—or Mitchell—has a partner."

"There are always risks . . . curveballs," Brea said. "We'll be ready for whatever is thrown at us. But that's our play. We wait for the aunt to leave for work, then move in."

They each picked up their glass, raised them toward one another in silent acknowledgment, and drank. The restaurant buzzed around them, an orchestra of conversation and clinking cutlery. Florida Georgia Line filtered through the speakers at a nonintrusive volume, keeping the atmosphere upbeat. The old fella at the table next to theirs brought his crab mallet down like a judge with a gavel.

There was no chance that the sisters would be overheard, but still . . .

"This is the house," Jessie whispered. She placed her phone between them again, zoomed in on a Google Maps view of a midsized rambler on a good splash of land, backing onto six acres of cemetery. "108 Montgomery Avenue. You see the enclosed area in back? I could be wrong, but I'm guessing that's where we'll find the separate entrance."

"Mm-hmm, and we can cut through the cemetery." Brea took a big swallow from her glass and winked again. "Hop the fence and we're there. Easy money."

Brea and Jessie fist-bumped across the table. Flo sat back in her seat, one hand on her jaw, a crease in the middle of her brow.

"Is it just me," she said, "or does this all seem . . . I don't know, just a little *too* easy?"

"And that's a problem how?" Brea asked.

"Hey, I'm not complaining. But given the significance of the job, the payday . . ." Flo shrugged, brought her mimosa to her lips, and put it down again without drinking. "It feels like this is being handed to us on a silver platter."

Jessie angled her head as if considering Flo's words, but Brea displayed no such pretense. She ran her tongue over her teeth and inhaled sharply.

"You're overthinking it," she said. "The bottom line is most serial killers are broken, cowardly men. This was never going to be difficult."

"That's true," Jessie said. "Besides, we've had easier jobs."

"I guess." Flo sipped her drink. That crease still occupied the middle of her forehead. "I just can't remember ever being spoon-fed this much information."

"No? How about Thad Nieto, that child-killing motherfucker?" Brea said this with just a touch too much volume. She recognized this, pulled an awkward face, then leaned closer to her sisters and whispered, "The Trace told us *everything* about him—gave us his itinerary to the minute."

"And the code for his security alarm," Jessie added.

"True," Flo conceded. "But we've *never* been given an exclusive window. I mean . . . why us?"

"Probably because I've established a communication with 9-$tar— someone on the inside." Jessie swished her glass, making the ice cubes rattle and spin. "They know how much we want the wren. Call it . . . preferential treatment."

"Or maybe it's because we're the best at what we do," Brea said. "The Trace trusts us to get the job done."

"Right. This is big for them, too." Jessie finished her drink in a single, throat-bobbing hit. "This is the kind of scalp that keeps their donors very happy."

"And if they're happy," Brea said, "they'll keep throwing the money down."

A colorful exclamation rang out from the bar as the opposing team ended the game on TV with a walk-off double. One turtle-faced man whipped his ball cap away in disgust and it came down perfectly on the tail of a mounted catfish. (This seemed to cheer everybody up.) Elsewhere, crab and lobster claws cracked under persuasion, while the music switched to something soft but melodic.

"Listen," Jessie said, speaking to both sisters but looking mainly at Flo. "Law enforcement in Reedsville leaves a lot to be desired. We know that. But chances are the Feds are following all the right leads and closing in fast. Everything about this speaks to the Trace's sense of urgency, from the exclusive window to the big payday."

"I know," Flo said on the back of a sigh. "I'm just—"

"Overthinking it," Brea said again.

Their food arrived shortly after, and the sisters switched up the conversation. They talked briefly about what they planned to do once they got home, which bands they wanted to see live, and what to buy Imani for her baby shower. Mostly, though, they ate, making contented little noises, pulling delighted faces, emptying their plates until only shells and crumbs remained. They ordered another round of drinks and a slice of raspberry cheesecake, which they attacked with three spoons.

Their bellies full and happy, the sisters walked back to their hotel. They didn't speak much. They said their good nights in the elevator, on their respective floors, then collapsed into their big, clean beds. Only Flo had bad dreams. At one point, she woke up and threw her pillow across the room, certain that it was stuffed with dead birds. She'd heard their small bones breaking every time she moved her head.

RECHARGED, THEY WERE ON THE road by eight A.M., 750 miles from Reedsville. They each took four hours at the wheel, stopping between changes to gas up and refresh. In Memphis, they switched from California to Missouri plates—the only disguise their nondescript van needed.

The energy was buoyant, for the most part. They shared anecdotes, laughed, and sang along to the radio. They shed their bandmate and vigilante skins and were simply friends. But as they motored through Mississippi toward the Alabama state line, the silences grew longer and deeper.

It was 7:20 and mostly dark by the time they crossed into Alabama. Their arrival was signaled by a vehicle fire at the side of the road, nobody in sight: no police, no fire trucks, just a blazing Durango.

"Another omen?" Brea asked.

The miles ticked by. The darkness deepened. They passed flourishing cotton fields and dusky restaurants and trailer parks where rebel flags waved. Finally, city lights smoldered on the horizon, somewhere between the blacktop and the moon.

"Reedsville," Jessie said.

The Kotter-Bryce Tower stood straight and high like a shovel in the dirt.

THE SIGN WAS RED AND silver. It read: ROLL TIDE! YOU ARE IN REEDS-VILLE, THE JEWEL IN ALABAMA'S CROWN. POPULATION 56,700. STAY AWHILE! They passed through a small business district dominated by that tall glass tower, then crossed a bridge shaped like a wishbone. The Mary River rolled eighty feet beneath, deep and lazy.

"It's good to be back," Brea said, sneering.

"Wouldn't want to be anywhere else," Jessie offered with equal scorn.

Downtown began on the other side of the bridge, rising steadily uphill toward Main Street. The Sunday night traffic was light, but there were people on the sidewalks and outside restaurants. The sisters didn't see a single woman alone. Two police cruisers flew south on Main with their blues and reds whirling. A stray dog patrolled one corner, barking at everything.

The mood inside the van had reached an uncomfortable low. Brea and Jessie couldn't pinpoint why they felt the way they did. They'd visited hundreds of shady towns and neighborhoods. They'd experienced, and often eliminated, the worst that these places had to offer. Why should Reedsville be any different? Brea thought it was because they were so close to the wren. Jessie wondered if perhaps the streets transmitted a certain energy—one of destitution and fear—that was impossible not to tune in to.

Flo's reason was clear-cut. This was where her mother had been killed. In any other place, Flo could remember the best of her. Here, though, in Reedsville, those sweet memories were eclipsed by the sound of breaking glass and bone. Flo struggled to even recall her mother's face, only dark thoughts of her corpse being extricated from the wreckage and zipped up in a long black bag.

Brea looked over her shoulder and saw Flo with one hand over her eyes, her shoulders trembling. She reached back and clasped Flo's knee.

"Hey, girl. We're here for you."

"I hate this town," Flo said.

JESSIE PUNCHED "108 MONTGOMERY AVENUE" into the GPS. It took them north on Main, past a Winn-Dixie and a string of fast-food joints, then east on Franklin Boulevard. There was an outreach center and needle exchange on the corner, its front steps populated by the homeless, most dressed in rags, some wrapped in blankets. The firehouse and Reedsville police headquarters were farther along, flanked on one side by a strip mall and on the other by a gas station and auto shop. Beyond this, the properties got notably grander. The paint was cleaner, the lawns were greener, and the cars in the driveways were only two or three years out of the showroom. Pine Vista—where Susan Orringer had been killed in her home—was to the south, merging into Waterloo Square and the more upmarket areas of downtown. Franklin Boulevard doglegged north. The sisters followed it, passing Fit4U Gym and Mustang Guns & Ammo (TRY OUR RANGE! TEACHERS 35% OFF! THURS. LADIES' NITE!), and arrived in Cedar Mills—the wren's neighborhood—several minutes later.

Montgomery Avenue was horseshoe shaped, occupied by old maples and 1970s-era homes on generous lots. They approached 108. Jessie touched the brake but did not stop. There was a RAV4 in the driveway. TV light flickered through the blinds in a front window. The sisters saw nothing else of note on this pass. No ADT Home Security or BEWARE OF DOG signs posted in the yard.

It was 9:17. The street was quiet but not empty. An elderly man walked his spaniel along the strip of grass between the sidewalk and the road. There were neighbors on every fifth porch or so, watching the day's end while sipping something cold. A couple of twentysomething dudes in matching tank tops unloaded fishing gear from the back of a Ford pickup. By midnight, Montgomery Avenue would be dark and sleeping, maybe a raccoon or two busy in the trash.

"Are we doing this tonight?" Jessie asked. "Or do we stick to the plan, wait until the aunt leaves for work?"

"Stick to the plan," Brea replied. "Let's find a motel out of town, get some rest."

They drove to Selma, twenty-six miles away, and found a cheapish motel on the Alabama River. Flo checked them in, gave a false name, paid cash. She got a single room with two beds. The sisters showered, then turned out the lights. Flo and Jessie were in one bed, Brea in the other.

The alarm on Brea's phone woke them at 4:30.

BACK IN REEDSVILLE BY 5:20. The miserable feeling the city gave them had been replaced by adrenaline and anticipation. They parked on Montgomery Avenue, a good distance from 108 but with an unbroken view of the house. The RAV4 was still in the driveway. Lights burned on the main floor—Aunt Olivia going about her morning routine, getting ready for work. All good so far. The sisters sat low in their seats and waited. They didn't speak much, but when they did it related to the mission.

"One of us should secure the main floor," Brea said. "Make sure there are no surprises."

"I'll do it," Flo said.

"We'll take care of Mr. Spahn, or Childs, whatever his fucking name is." Brea curled her lip. "I want to be the one to put the bullet in his skull."

"I don't care," Jessie said. "Let's just get the job done."

At 5:42, the front door of 108 Montgomery Avenue opened and Aunt Olivia stepped out, closing and locking the door behind her. She was captured in an exterior light for a second or two—portly, but with a thin face not unlike her nephew's—then merged with the shadows as she proceeded to her vehicle. In the stillness of the hour, the sisters heard the

RAV4's engine come to life. Lights flared front and back. Moments later, the aunt drove along Montgomery and turned left on Jelks Street, in the direction of the hospital.

Forty-five minutes until sunup.

FLO REFRESHED THREE MAGAZINES, LOCKED them into the grips of their respective pistols, then attached suppressors. Jessie prepped the drone. They parked behind a used car dealership a hundred yards from the cemetery that neighbored the property Olivia Childs shared with her evil-incarnate nephew. If it all went to plan, Mitchell Spahn would be taking up residence in that boneyard very soon.

Jessie rolled the side door open and launched the drone. It ascended to 180 feet, then buzzed over the quiet streets, over the quieter cemetery, and positioned itself directly above 108 Montgomery Avenue. Jessie switched to manual, lowered the aircraft, scanned the property on all sides. The sisters huddled around the screen, studying the thermal image.

"Separate entrance?" Flo asked, pointing at the door off the enclosed area in back.

"Maybe," Brea said. "Doesn't matter, though. That's where we're going in."

Jessie summoned the drone home, then took out her phone. She accessed the link that 9-$tar had sent and brought up the photo of Mitchell Spahn. The sisters studied it for a full minute, branding every detail into their minds. He stared back at them, dark-hearted and skewed, venomous as a rattlesnake's bite.

# NINE

As planned, Brea and Jessie took the basement apartment while Flo checked the main floor.

She knew something was wrong the moment she opened the door to the living area. It was the smells first: aftershave and sweat and reheated pizza. *Man* smells. She wondered if Mitchell shared the upstairs space. Or maybe Aunt Olivia's boyfriend—assuming now that she had one—had returned home from a late shift, thrown a slice under the broiler, and fallen asleep on the sofa.

These thoughts dashed through Flo's mind in seconds, issuing warnings. But it was the *absence* of smells, too. No coffee, toast, or freshly run shower—the aromas Flo associated with early mornings before work.

Something was definitely amiss here.

She edged down a short hallway, holding her pistol and flashlight Harries style: wrists crossed, the backs of her hands pressed against and supporting each other. The cone of light danced over featureless walls and a hardwood floor scuffed with grime. Flo passed a small powder room and nudged the door open with her boot. The toilet seat was up. A damp towel sagged from a hook. She continued to the living room. There was no sweaty boyfriend sleeping on the sofa, but she found the pizza. Three large boxes crowded the coffee table, with only a couple of slices left. Flo directed the flashlight's beam around the room, viewing everything along the barrel of her pistol. It was a large space. The fixtures and fittings were good quality, but everything was a mess. The rug was rucked up. There were a few magazines scattered across the floor—*Fur-Fish-Game* and *Hot Rod* and *Sports Illustrated*—along with an assortment of dirty plates and glasses. A Crimson Tide hoodie, large enough for all three sisters to climb into, was thrown over the back of an armchair.

Flo became aware of her heartbeat working a touch too eagerly. A thread of sweat trickled between her shoulder blades. She wasn't one for gender stereotypes, but the obvious couldn't be refuted: this place hadn't known a woman's touch for a long time.

"We've got the wrong house," she said under her breath, and with some confusion. They'd seen the aunt leave for work, after all.

A sound from outside claimed all of Flo's attention. She lowered the flashlight and stepped to the window in time to see two pickup trucks pull up hard, tires squealing. The doors popped open and a crew of bulky men—five of them, at least—marched toward the house.

Flo retreated to the hallway and the door she'd come through. *Trap*, she said, except she only mouthed the word, a breathless gasp. She was about to try again when something—some*one*—came up from behind and hit her hard.

BREA REALIZED MUCH SOONER THAT they'd been set up. She and Jessie had separated when they reached the bottom of the basement stairs. Jessie covered the kitchen and living room. Brea continued down the hallway to the bedrooms. She opened the first door and there was a middle-aged man with a receding hairline and a thick black mustache sitting on the bed. It was difficult to tell from his posture, but he looked to be six-five and all of 230. He might have been a linebacker in days gone by.

Brea lowered her flashlight—there was no need for it; a lamp on the nightstand glowed softly—but kept her .45 on the man.

"Where's Mitchell?" she hissed. "Mitchell Spahn?"

"I know that ski mask is supposed to hide your identity," the man replied, pointing a steady finger at Brea. His teeth flashed neatly beneath his mustache. "But I can see you're tall and I can see you're white, so I'm hazarding you must be Brea Steen."

Brea's body flushed cold. She took a step forward and looked more intently through the sights of her semiauto.

"You a cop?"

"One of two ways this goes down," Mr. Mustache said, cool as you like. "You can either drop that shooter and come quietly, or my boys can bring on the hurting . . . and you come anyway."

That wasn't cop talk, although, Brea understood, it might be *Reedsville* cop talk. The standards were different here.

"I don't see any *boys*," she said, moving her finger from the trigger guard to the trigger itself. "Just you."

Right on cue, she heard sounds from upstairs: the front door banging open, followed by the thump of footfalls—*many* footfalls. Brea's gaze tracked to the ceiling. There had to be half a dozen of Mr. Mustache's goons up there. His *boys*. And Flo.

"So," Mr. Mustache said, getting to his feet. "How are we playing this?"

The rules that the sisters endeavored to follow—to keep shots fired to a minimum, and to go nonlethal on everyone except the target—did not apply here. This was no longer a job. It was a dangerous and potentially deadly situation. Brea squeezed the trigger and put a bullet in Mr. Mustache's chest. He flew backward over the bed and slumped to the floor.

She whipped from the room, staying behind her handgun and flashlight. The thudding footfalls continued upstairs, the sound carrying through the ceiling and along the walls. Within moments they'd be down here, but there was only one entrance into the basement apartment, as far as Brea knew, which gave her every advantage. She could cover the door and pick the goons off as they poured through—hopefully take three of them out before they realized what was happening. Then it would be a more even fight.

BEFORE COVERING THE DOOR, SHE had to help Jessie, who had her hands full in the living room. She'd been disarmed, likely ambushed. How many of these thugs had been waiting in the dark? One guy—easily as big as Mr. Mustache—held Jessie from behind, his forearm wrapped around her throat. A second goon with a wagon-red goatee was winding up with a strip of two-by-four. That red wasn't natural, though, and it didn't come from a bottle of dye. It was blood, Brea realized. Jessie had gotten at least one hard shot in.

Red swung the two-by-four. Brea wasn't quick enough to stop him. The length of timber met Jessie in the middle, and she writhed in pain. Brea lined up her target and pulled the trigger twice. The first shot hit Red in the shoulder. The second found center mass and threw him limp against the wall.

The big guy holding Jessie pulled an alarmed face. "I'll snap her fuckin' neck," he warned. Brea adjusted her aim, pulled the trigger, and shot him in the foot. He screamed and went slack. Jessie slipped out of his stranglehold but kept a firm grip on his wrist, twisting it backward, lowering him to his knees. He screamed even louder as she broke his forearm in two. Brea was about to pull the trigger a fifth time—if only to silence the big guy's screams—but Jessie had it in hand. She picked up the two-by-four, swung it pickax style, and caved the top of his skull.

FOOTSTEPS ON THE BASEMENT STAIRS, a torrent of them, then the door crashed open and the reinforcements appeared. Brea shot the first guy in the throat. She triggered again and missed the second thug by a whisper. He'd stumbled over his fallen comrade, then dived for cover behind an ottoman. The dome of his back was visible, and Brea was about to target it when two more of Mr. Mustache's boys appeared, one with a chain looped around his fist, the other with a tranq pistol in the ready position.

A length of two-by-four, a steel chain, a tranquilizer gun. Nothing lethal, but Brea had surmised from her brief conversation with Mr. Mustache that this was a grab job. Whoever had set them up wanted them alive. Knowing this didn't make her feel any better.

Mr. Chain swung his weapon wildly, throwing Brea off-balance. Mr. Tranq took his shot, and it was dead-on. Brea felt the dart pierce her throat. She groaned and snatched it away. It could take up to a minute— sometimes longer—for the anesthetic to do its thing, which was why these goons came with other blunt-force weapons. Either way, Brea had time.

She reset behind her .45, established her target—Mr. Tranq's brightly tattooed skull—and pulled the trigger. Her shot was dead-on, too. Tranq fell backward through the door and crumpled in the darkness beyond.

Seven shots fired, one round in the chamber, two in the mag.

Jessie lurched forward, clearly in discomfort from having taken a strip of lumber to the midsection. Mr. Chain took a swing at her. She held up the two-by-four—spattered with the big guy's blood—and the chain wrapped itself around the top half. They both pulled at the same time and met in the middle. Jessie threw an elbow. Mr. Chain threw a left hook. They circled awkwardly, exchanging blows.

Brea turned her gun toward them, looking for the shot. She moved smoothly but slowly. Her left eyelid dipped. The edges of her vision faded. She took a stumbling step to her right, then another thug appeared, armed with a Taser. Brea switched targets, slumping to her knees as she did. She pulled the trigger, but her shot was nowhere close.

Eight rounds fired now. Or was it seven? Or nine? How many in the . . .

"No," Brea said, slurring even this one syllable. *Nuurrr*. Her flashlight tumbled to the floor. She tried aiming her pistol again, but it had turned to lead, dragging her hand down.

FLO WAS LIFTED TO HER feet. She had a man on either side. That sweat and pizza smell was stronger. One of them yanked the ski mask off her face. The back of it was wet with blood, and Flo felt more of it soaking her neck and the collar of her shirt. She'd been walloped good.

"Got us the Black one," the goon to her left said. He was Black himself but spoke like he'd been raised in a trailer park. He had offset eyes and a scar in the middle of his forehead. "And *hawt*, too. Wouldn't mind a slice of her pie."

"You wish," the other man said. He had Flo's Glock 23 down the front of his pants and a golf club in his free hand—doubtless what he'd coldcocked her with. "Go grab the duct tape. We'll tie her at the wrists and slap a piece over that mouth, too."

Mr. Scar left Flo's side. She heard him whistling in the gloom as he went about his chore. Now it was just her and Golf Club. He stepped in front of her, pressed the business end of the club beneath her chin, and tilted her head backward.

"Can you walk?" he asked.

Flo nodded as well as she could.

"Can you *behave*, or am I gonna hafta tee off on you again and drag yer Black ass outta here?"

Another nod. Her bottom lip trembled.

Mr. Scar came back with a roll of duct tape in his hand, picking at the end with his fingernail. He got it lifted and—*rrrriiiiiiiiipppp*—yanked off a strip.

"Turn yerself around," Golf Club said to Flo. He took his eyes off her, lowering his guard, as Mr. Scar handed him the tape.

They should have tied her up when she was still on the ground, but they were obviously counting on her being woozy. And woozy she *was*. She still had her hands free, though, and that was enough. With artful quickness, Flo reached inside Golf Club's pants, pulled the trigger on her semiauto, and blew both balls down the inside of his leg. He stumbled backward with his crotch flooding red. Flo relieved him of the golf club, swiveled at the waist, and whapped the iron face off Mr. Scar's jaw. She felt the impact through the shaft of the club—felt his jawbone crumble. He hit the floor like the proverbial sack of shit, and his teeth followed a second or two after.

Flo dropped the club and retrieved her flashlight. Golf Club squirmed on the floor, making a shocked, blubbering sound. She extracted her gun from his pants and switched her attention to whatever was happening in the basement apartment. She heard grunts and cries, the occasional burst of a suppressed pistol shot. Those two pickup trucks had been full of muscle, and most of it had rushed downstairs. Brea and Jessie needed help.

She proceeded along the hallway with her gun and flashlight extended. Her steps were unsteady. She fell against the wall, pushed herself off with one shoulder. The door to the basement was open. She shone her flashlight down and saw a dead body at the bottom of the stairs. Flo descended carefully and, stepping between the corpse's splayed limbs, entered the apartment. Her vision wavered as she tried to make sense of the scene. A living room. Furniture toppled. Bodies positioned unevenly. Brea lying unconscious, her eyes fluttering. There was a tranq dart with a hot-pink stabilizer on the floor next to her. A goon with a salt-and-pepper crew cut huddled behind an ottoman.

Of more immediate concern, another goon had his Taser aimed at

Jessie, who was locked in battle with a chain-wielding guy twice her size. Flo took aim, but Mr. Taser beat her to the trigger. The darts extended across the room, latched on to Jessie, and administered their voltage. Jessie folded instantly. She hit the floor and twitched.

Flo squeezed the trigger. If she hadn't been concussed, her .40-caliber round would have punched a hole through Mr. Taser's chest. As it was, she shot him in the shoulder. Nonlethal, but it dropped him anyway. Flo turned her attention to the guy with the chain. She was about to drop him, too—he was a *big* target—but at that point Crew Cut decided to join the fight. He leapt out from behind the ottoman and tackled Flo from the side. She was thrown off her feet and went backward over the sofa. Her gun and flashlight were knocked from her hands. She got groggily to her knees, saw her gun nearby, and crawled toward it, but Mr. Chain stepped around the sofa and kicked it across the floor. His nose was broken and blood trickled from his mouth—courtesy of Jessie, who would've done more damage if that Taser hadn't intervened. The chain still drooped from one hand. He had a tranq gun in the other.

"Hey there, sweet stuff," he said. He blew Flo a bloody kiss and pulled the trigger.

BREA'S VISION FADED IN AND out. Her body felt as heavy as a truck. From her angle, she saw Jessie on the floor. She'd fallen in an awkward position. The Taser's barbed electrodes were still attached to her clothing. Brea could see Flo, too—or Flo's leg, at least. It was very still.

Everything went black, and Brea thought this time she would stay down, but a seam of light appeared only seconds later and slowly expanded. She heard muffled voices, then footsteps on the hardwood. A shadow fell over her. With colossal effort, Brea turned her head three inches and rolled the iron ball bearings that were her eyes. Mr. Mustache stood above her. He was as tall as the Empire State Building. As she watched, he pulled open his shirt, revealing the ballistic vest beneath.

"You should've taken the less painful option," he said. He removed a bullet fragment from his vest, digging and wiggling to work it loose, then crouched and pushed it into Brea's mouth. She didn't have the energy to spit it out.

# TEN

Some of the injured were able to walk away. Others—Golf Club, for instance, with his balls blown off—had to be carried out. The dead were left for now, although the body at the bottom of the stairs was dragged out of the way to make egress easier. Of the ten men who either had been lying in wait or had shown up in pickup trucks, only three could function without *too* much pain: Mr. Mustache, Mr. Chain, and Crew Cut. They took care of the sisters. They bound their wrists, ankles, and mouths with duct tape and carried them out to a waiting SUV. Jessie woke up while she was being moved and struggled viciously. Mr. Chain dropped her. He got down on his knees, ran his fat, warm tongue over her eyes, then cracked the back of her head off the sidewalk.

It was still dark outside.

A MAN NAMED GOOSE DROVE. Mr. Mustache rode shotgun.

"We were warned these bitches were something wild, but Jesus H. Christ." Mr. Mustache whistled through his teeth. "How was your night, Goose?"

"Fair, I'd say."

Brea was propped uncomfortably in the backseat between Crew Cut and Mr. Chain. She stirred awake and looked out the window at the passing city streets. The sun had edged up, and regular folk went about the beginning of their workweek. Storefront shutters were rolled up. A line had formed at a bus stop and another out the door of Coffee Karma.

Some of the people standing in line looked at the SUV as it drove past. They couldn't see in, of course, because the windows had a limousine tint—likely not legal in the state of Alabama, but Brea had a feeling the owner of this vehicle didn't concern themselves with laws.

Jessie and Flo had been tossed luggage-like into the back, and Brea heard them both moaning. She grunted behind the duct tape and tried twisting in her seat to look over her shoulder at them, but Crew Cut grabbed her by the jaw and turned her face forward.

"Quit squirming," he said, "or I'll pop you right in the fucking jaw."

"She's a handful, Nash," Mr. Mustache noted. "A real sour peach."

Brea looked forward, blinking her eyes. She felt an unfamiliar combination of fear and anger, each throwing its shoulder against the other, fighting for control. The altercation filled her brain with noise. She couldn't think. Finding focus and calm was like trying to isolate a single sweet voice in a crowd.

THEY LEFT DOWNTOWN AND TOOK a road that snaked into greener country. Dilapidated houses flashed by on both sides. They passed a church that looked like a barn and an old schoolhouse with a crumbled bell tower, then it was farms: cotton, broilers, and sorghum. Brea saw a field of horses, most grazing, others running free, and an image pounced into her mind: the wild horse she'd seen during the storm, captured in a flash of lightning, reared and terrified. She wondered now if it had even been real or some kind of premonition—a warning. Either way, she felt a sudden and overwhelming affinity for the creature.

Three or four miles from the city proper, they arrived at a high iron gate that opened onto a long driveway. This led to a grand house with a four-car garage and a fountain that caught the morning light, pink as cotton candy. Goose stopped in front of the garage doors. They all got out. Mr. Chain dragged Brea out with him and threw her to the asphalt. She rolled and settled on her side. Crew Cut—real name Nash—opened the SUV's liftgate, then he and Mr. Chain grabbed Jessie and Flo and flung them down next to Brea. They writhed together like three worms, and Brea forced herself to think of the horse.

"The Bang-Bang Sisters," Mr. Mustache said, looking at them. He had a brown leatherette case in his hand with a zipper along three sides. "You'll mostly be making small noises from here out. Maybe the occasional scream."

He tugged the zipper and opened the case like a book. There was a needle and syringe kit inside and a bottle of some kind of knockout drug. Ketamine, maybe. He injected Jessie first, turning her head to get to her throat. Her eyes closed and she softened immediately.

"Can't trust you not to turn alley cat," Mr. Mustache said to Brea, drawing another dose of anesthetic into the barrel. "God knows, you've got it in you."

Brea arched her back and kicked with both legs, but it was a fruitless effort. Comical, even. The men looked at one another and chuckled, then Mr. Mustache planted his knee on Brea's chest, turned her head sharply, and plunged the needle into her throat.

She felt the sting. Her head flopped to the other side, and she found herself looking into Flo's eyes. The last thing she noticed before fading away was the cold and accusatory anger in them.

JESSIE CAME TO, HUNGRY AND hurting. She wondered if a couple of her ribs had been cracked by the thug with the two-by-four, but there was an all-over pain that started in the balls of her feet and traveled north from there. She blinked and looked around, assessing her situation.

"Not good," she groaned. She was in a cement room, a pale light shining down, no windows. It measured about twelve feet square. The only furniture was a bucket to shit in and the steel pipe she was handcuffed to. There was a narrow wooden door in the opposite wall, out of reach. The ductwork and exposed wiring overhead indicated it was an unfinished basement room.

Jessie closed her eyes and breathed as deeply as her injured ribs would allow. This was far from the perfect meditative space, but the fact that she *could* breathe—that she was still alive—was something to be thankful for. Before long, the chaos in her body and mind began to ease. It didn't fade away, but it separated enough for her to navigate through. She found a shred of calm and carried it with her.

The duct tape had been removed and she was fully clothed. These were not things to be grateful for, but they were something to build on. Jessie opened her eyes and looked around the room with a marginally calmer mindset. Nothing had changed. The bucket in the corner suggested she wasn't leaving any time soon. She inspected the handcuffs. They were police issue, solid steel loops. The pipe she'd been cuffed to was equally unyielding. There was no hope of escape. Whatever this was, she had to wait it out.

Jessie closed her eyes again and meditated—or *tried* to—a moment longer, in and out with her breaths, inhaling musty air. She stood up and stretched as well as she could. The cuff slid up and down the pipe with little taps and clangs. Even after she sat down again, those clanging sounds continued. Jessie looked at her motionless cuff, then realized the sounds were coming from a nearby room.

"Brea," she said. Her voice was cracked and quiet. She swallowed, cleared her throat, and tried again. "Brea." A little louder this time. Then again. "Brea . . . Brea . . . Flo . . . that you?"

The tap-clang sound stopped. There was a stretch of awful silence, then Flo's voice replied gruffly: "Jess . . . Jessie . . . It's me, Flo."

"Flo." Tears spilled unexpectedly from Jessie's eyes. "Thank God you're alive."

Flo said, "If they wanted us dead, they'd have killed us already."

It was too soon to know whether that was a good or bad thing.

THERE WERE ONLY TWO ROOMS in the basement suitable for holding a person for any length of time, so they put Brea in an empty shed outside, cuffed to a ringbolt in the floor. Whenever she attained a scrap of energy, she expended it trying to escape. She kicked the walls, which boomed but did not give. She yanked at the ringbolt and scoured the concrete floor for something—an old nail, a piece of wire—that she could use to pick the handcuffs' lock. Sometimes she screamed. It was the only thing that felt good.

The beatings certainly didn't. Mr. Mustache—real name Burl—came, usually with backup, and one of them held her down while the others went to work. The longer she was in that shed, the heavier their fists and boots became.

"A hurting, see?" Burl had said. He had a habit of grooming his mustache every time he'd finished with her. "You should know that your sisters are eating grilled chicken and drinking ice-cold Pepsis, and haven't asked after you once."

"Bullshit."

Not that Brea went without. On day two, or thereabouts, Mr. Chain— real name Carson, with a strip of tape over his busted nose—brought her a dog's bowl filled with water. He set it down on the floor and used his boot to nudge it close.

"You expect me to drink from that?" Brea asked.

"Act like an animal," Carson said, "and get treated like one."

"YOU THINK BREA IS STILL alive?" Jessie asked, her voice barely audible through the solid wall.

Flo sighed and repressed the urge to respond that she didn't care either way, which wasn't true, or not *quite* true. Brea had cajoled them into taking the wren contract, but whoever had set them up would likely have gotten to them anyway, somewhere down the line, so maybe this wasn't entirely her fault.

"Flo. You awake?"

"Yeah."

"You think Brea is still alive?"

"Like I said, if they wanted us dead, they'd have killed us back at the house." Flo wiped grit from her cheek, then gingerly touched the goose egg—although it felt more like an emu egg—at the back of her head. "So yeah, I think she's still alive."

"Her blood runs hot, though. Maybe she pushed them."

"Maybe."

Since waking up in this small cement room, Flo had spent many hours pondering the reason they were here. Was it revenge? Had somebody turned the tables and put a bounty on them? And why were they being kept alive? Every question prompted ten more. Flo had no answers, only hunches—like her initial hunch that this so-called wren contract had been too easy, too *enticing*. Was Mitchell Spahn even a real person? Had the Trace double-crossed the sisters, or had it been fed the wrong information?

Her mind ached, and her anger was never far away. Unlike Brea, she kept it beneath the surface. There was no screaming. No futile escape attempts. No raging. Other emotions leaked through. Fear, of course (Flo was strong, but she wasn't inhuman), and grief. She thought all too often about Imani and her unborn baby, all that beauty and sweetness, all that comfort and kindness.

They'd traveled the breadth of the country and back. They'd been three hundred miles from home. Three *hundred*, then they'd turned around.

What she would give to see Imani again and hug her close—as close as her big, beautiful belly would allow. What she would *do* for even one brief conversation with her sister.

Her *real* sister.

Flo heard Jessie's cuff jangle against the pipe as she edged closer to the wall that separated them.

"I was thinking," she said, just loud enough to be heard. "What if the wren is more than one man? What if there's a whole bunch of men working together, and we stumbled into their nest? You think that's what this is about?"

"No," Flo replied. She'd also been remembering her mother, trying for happy thoughts, but always coming back to the sound of screeching brakes and crumpling steel . . . which again led to pondering the reason they'd been brought here. "I think this is about Johnny Rudd."

NO WINDOWS. NO CLOCKS. IT was impossible to gauge time. They slept and stretched and meditated. Brea screamed and tried to break out, although her efforts waned as the days dragged along. Three days? Five? Jessie thought it might have been a week. Every so often the door opened and someone appeared with food and drink, usually fruit and water. Brea's was always served in a dog bowl. They'd stopped beating her, at least. One time, Flo was served steak and eggs and a cold glass of milk. Burl set it down in front of her, pressed a finger to his lips, and winked.

THEY STANK. THEIR SHIT BUCKETS had been changed once. They were given one bowlful of lukewarm water to wash with. Brea recognized the thug who brought hers. She'd put a bullet in his shoulder and another in his chest. He'd obviously been wearing a ballistic vest, too, because here he was, still upright. He had a sling on, though, and had washed the blood out of his goatee.

"Clean yerself up, if you've a mind," Red said, throwing a washcloth into the bowl. "I don't care much either way."

"You want to watch?" Brea asked. She flared her eyes and chewed her lower lip. "I can get fully naked if you take this cuff off."

Red lingered for a moment. He appeared to consider Brea's offer, then a gap-toothed grin spread across his face. "Might've taken you up on that, Blondie, only my whacking-off arm is temporarily out of commission." He gestured at the sling. "Besides, I see nekkid gals every day down at the Devil's Own, and not one of 'em stinks of shit like you."

Red turned and was almost out the door when Brea stopped him.

"Whatever you're doing, you won't get away with it." She shook her head. Tiny fireworks sizzled across her vision. "We know people, and they're far more dangerous than you."

Red barked an ugly laugh, then winced and held his chest. No doubt he'd picked up a decent-sized bruise where her bullet had impacted the ballistic vest. If only she'd gone for a head shot.

"Ain't nobody knows where you are, Blondie," he said. He lifted his good arm and pointed at her. "That's what happens when you play in the dark."

THEY WERE LIBERATED FROM THEIR prisons some hours later. Burl, Carson, and yet another goon packed with muscle had visited each sister in turn. Brea wasn't given a choice. Carson juiced her with a 50,000-volt stun baton, then they cuffed her hands behind her back and dragged her from the room. Jessie and Flo opted to come quietly, although they were cuffed, too.

"Where are you taking me?" Flo asked.

Burl peeled hair off her forehead and looped it behind one ear. Flo—shuddering, disgusted—angled away from him and clenched her jaw.

"It's time to meet Mr. Kotter," he said.

# ELEVEN

**B**rea was led across a patch of gravel, dragging her feet, a guy on each arm to keep her moving. There was someone behind her, too. She didn't know who. Her brain worked in confused bursts. Fighting was out of the question. They passed a line of pickup trucks, most sporting patriotic decals: a stylized Stars and Stripes, a swooping eagle. One had a sticker on the back glass that read TESTED POSITIVE FOR FREEDOM. This struck Brea as funny, given her current predicament. She threw her head back and laughed. The movement caused her to stumble, and the guy on her right—it was Burl—hefted her up roughly.

"Move your ass," he snarled.

They walked across a patio. Surveillance cameras tracked their every step. Brea saw the broad back of the main house, the edge of a swimming pool, an arena beyond, probably for horses. She got a sense of the property's size, trying to configure the layout. As bruised and beaten as she was, Brea imagined returning here six months from now with a .45 strapped to her thigh and a katana on her back. She would shoot and slice her way through the entire operation, leaving corpses and severed limbs everywhere. It was a ridiculous notion, of course—this place was teeming with security—but a girl could dream, couldn't she?

They entered the house via a back door and walked along a wood-paneled hallway lined with oil paintings of white-haired Alabamans in nineteenth-century garb. Politicians, Brea guessed. Or slavers. Or both. From here, they passed through a lounge filled with comfortable leather chairs and bookcases. There was another painting above the fireplace of a white-haired man, this more recent. He had a fantastic stomach and a revolver on each hip and stood like a cowboy. Brea regarded it hatefully—everything about that painting set her teeth on edge—before she was moved down another hallway and into an opulent study. The décor was rich polished wood and leather. Elk, deer, and cougar heads were mounted to the walls, along with an arrangement of ornamental rifles. The desk was Cadillac-sized and looked to have been finished from a single slab of walnut. Another mean-looking goon stood to the right of the desk, and next to him was a Doberman pinscher on a leash. The dog sat eyes forward, its back straight.

There were three wooden chairs in front of the desk. Brea was pushed down into the leftmost one. Burl produced a second set of cuffs and secured her to one of the wooden spindles.

"What? You don't trust me to sit still?" she asked.

"Shut your goddamn mouth," Burl replied. He, Carson, and the third thug left the room, heels clipping across the hardwood. Now it was just Brea, the dog, and the man holding the leash.

Brea shifted in the seat, trying to find a comfortable position. She looked at the man. "What's your name?"

"You don't need to know." Nothing but the South in his voice. Brea thought he'd probably get a nosebleed if he crossed the Mason-Dixon Line.

"What's his name?" She nodded at the Doberman pinscher.

"Errol."

"Earl?"

"*Er-rull.*" The goon leaned forward slightly, his nose wrinkled. "And one snap of the fingers from me, he'll take that purdy face right off your skull."

Brea shifted again. She looked around the room. There wasn't much on the desk: some papers, a laptop computer, a photograph of a redheaded policewoman in dress uniform. A second photograph caught Brea's eye. It was of the white-haired man in the painting—he with the barrel-shaped stomach—standing above a dead grizzly, shoulder to shoulder with 1970s rock idol and Republican blowhard Ned Sargent. Both men wore shit-eating grins and had their rifles hoisted. Sargent had blood on his shirt.

JESSIE WALKED STIFFLY BUT DIDN'T drag her feet. She was taken through a large basement room with a pool table, a bar, and a mechanical bull.

The ultimate man cave. Pictures of NASCAR drivers and movie cowboys adorned the walls. A vintage jukebox flashed blue and pink. They went from here into a kite-shaped room with a green marble floor and a huge aquarium built into one wall. Smooth-hound sharks prowled the clear water.

Burl thrust his chin at a stairway at the far end.

"Go," he commanded. "Quickly. Let's move."

Jessie took the stairs as swiftly as she was able. At the top, she was directed through more rooms and hallways until they came to the study. She saw Brea sitting in one of the seats in front of a large, rustic desk. Jessie tried saying her name, but only a fractured breath came out. Burl parked her in the middle seat and double-cuffed her in the same way, then he and his colleagues left the room. Jessie glanced at the dog and the bruiser holding its leash, then turned to her sister.

"How you doing, Jess?" Brea's face was bruised, her lip split. Her hair was full of dirt, and she looked to have lost at least ten pounds.

"Brea . . . Jesus, I'm . . . I . . ." It was easy to imagine Brea getting smart with their captors, maybe fighting back, and they'd dealt with her the only way dull men knew how. "Brea, you . . . you—"

"I'm okay," Brea said. "A little knocked around, is all."

"Did they feed you?"

Brea shrugged: *Sorta.*

Jessie sighed and, like Brea, tried to make herself more comfortable on the hard wooden seat. She gritted her teeth as pain flared in her rib cage. The cuffs clanked against the spindle, earning the dog's attention. It looked at her for a moment, then faced forward again. There was a machinelike coldness in its eyes that Jessie had only ever seen in attack dogs, as if all the natural warmth and companionship had been trained out of it.

"We'll get through this," Brea whispered. "Whatever it is."

Jessie wasn't so sure. They'd run into the devil here in Reedsville, and not the devil they'd expected. This was organized and powerful and more than three women—as skilled and determined as they were—could hope to overcome.

She looked at Brea, angling her head so the bruiser couldn't see, and mouthed, *Johnny Rudd?* Brea shrugged again.

The door opened a few minutes later and Flo came in with her three-man escort. She looked pale and tired, but she hadn't been knocked around like Brea. Burl dropped her into the rightmost seat and cuffed her to the spindle. This time, he and his entourage remained in the room.

Jessie turned to Flo, but Flo could only look at Brea. The atmosphere crackled.

"You can't blame me for this," Brea said. Blood leaked from her split lip. "This is a vendetta. They'd have gotten to us anyway."

"Don't talk to me," Flo sneered, and looked away.

Jessie lowered her head. The pain in her heart was worse than anywhere else. "I don't know what's happening," she said.

Burl stepped forward. He placed one hand beneath the dog's snout and scratched. "You'll find out soon enough."

WITHIN MINUTES, THE DOOR OPENED yet again, and in stepped a man dressed in simple clothes—a white button-down shirt and Levi's—but who looked like a boss nonetheless. It was in the broad-shouldered way he carried himself, in his manicured beard and the roundness of his belly. Rings bejeweled his sausage-like fingers, and a thick gold chain circled one wrist. Brea recognized him immediately as the man in the painting and in the photograph on the desk. Sargent's hunting buddy.

"I'd say nice to meet you, but that'd be a lie. I'm grateful you're here, though." The boss man stood for a moment, hands perched on his protuberant sides. "I've thought too long about looking each of you in the eye."

He took a seat behind his desk. His big leather chair creaked beneath his weight. Brea thought for sure that he would produce a humidor from one of the drawers, light a long, fat cigar, maybe rest his boots up on the desk. He didn't, though. He just linked his hands across his belly and stared at them, full of ice.

"You're from Los Angeles, right? The City of Angels, and don't that ring true. Look at 'em, Burl." He flicked his gaze to Burl and grinned. "Three busted-up little angels."

The sisters said nothing. They stared at the man, trying to show fortitude. Brea recalled something Uncle Dog had told her: *You don't always need your hands; you can disarm your opponent with the look in your eye.*

"I don't care for L.A. myself. Too big. Too many people. And that *traffic.* No thank you." The boss man pulled a face, then placed his knuckles on the desk and leaned forward. "Do you know who I am?"

"Mr. Kotter," Flo said. "That's all I know and all I want to know."

"Chance Kotter." He settled back in his seat and a smirk touched his lips. "I'm what you might call a preeminent figure in this city. I ain't the mayor. I ain't even a councilman. I'm a businessman. A captain of industry."

"A person of influence," the goon holding Errol's leash offered.

"Thank you, Wilder. That sounds about right," Chance said with a museful nod. "But a *man* of influence, none of this 'person' horseshit. I'm a *man*, goddammit. That's how the good Lord made me."

"So you're a mobster," Jessie said.

"A mobster is a criminal, and criminals take what isn't theirs. They *steal.*" Chance stroked his beard. His clunky gold jewelry winked in the ambient lighting. "I'm a fair man—a hardworking American who enjoys the fruits of his labors. Anybody who stands in the way of that will pay the price."

He leaned forward again, looking at each sister in turn. There was an avuncular aspect to his appearance—his cotton-white beard, those sparkling eyes—but his energy had a serrated edge.

"To put it another way: stay on the level with me and everything'll be fine." He pointed at the sisters, first Brea, then Jessie, then Flo. "Mess with my money, my family, or my friends, and we got a problem."

Errol flicked his cropped ears. The quick movement caught Chance's attention. He looked at the dog with great fondness, then got out of his seat with a grunt and walked over to him. "Attaboy. Yeah, who's a beautiful boy?" Chance crouched, looking distinctly top-heavy—it wouldn't take much to knock him on his ass, Brea thought—and scratched Errol's nape.

"We got 'em, didn't we, boy? We got those bitches."

Errol whined contentedly.

"We sure did. It took some time, but we tracked 'em down." Chance crouched yet lower and planted a kiss on Errol's nose. "Yeah. That's my boy." He straightened, pressing one hand to the small of his back and puffing out his cheeks. "I was sure it was a professional hit. It was all too clean, too goddamn slick, and God knows that nephew of mine had enemies."

Flo closed her eyes and rolled her head back. Maybe she was trying to find calm, but a muscle in her jaw ticced once a second.

"I know people who do that kind of work. Killing work," Chance said. "I pulled a few favors, asked around, but kept drawing blanks. We got a witness says he saw three masked individuals exit the alleyway where the hit took place. No descriptions, though. No names. It was like looking for shadows."

Chance stepped behind the sisters, walking slowly. Jessie kept him in her sight line, but Brea looked straight ahead. She saw his reflection in the window, as full and white as a sloop's sail. He completed most of a lap, then propped his ass against the edge of his desk and looked down at them.

"Know how we finally gotcha? The *internet*." He curled his lip in a self-satisfied way. "Now, I confess to an absence of knowledge when it comes to the World Wide Web, but I *do* have deep pockets, and it turns out that's all that matters. We hired the best, didn't we, Burl?"

"We did," Burl said.

"Hackers and such. The best. Even so, it took 'em a while, but eventually, they uncovered . . ." Chance screwed one eye shut, using a circling hand gesture to illustrate how hard his brain was working. "Aw, shoot, what's it called, Burl? The computer thing? The . . . the wire?"

"The Trace."

"The *Trace*. Yeah, that's it." Chance snapped his fingers, then looked at Brea and grinned. "My computer fellas hacked the hackers. How'd you like them turnip greens, little lady?"

Brea returned Chance's stare. She spoke in a monotone. "I don't know what you're talking about. This is clearly a case of mistaken identity."

"*NOOO!*" Chance lunged forward and screamed into Brea's face. The sound rumbled up from his chest and through his throat, like a Mack truck out of a tunnel. "No! *No!* You *don't* get to deny what you did. That's *not* how this works."

Brea leaned back in her seat but didn't turn away. Chance burned his eyes into her for five long seconds, then pulled back. He ran his hands through his hair and took a moment to catch his breath.

"Can you believe this shit, Burl? These dumbass gals think this is a hearing. Well, it *ain't*. It's a sentencing." He pointed a fat finger at the sisters, not any one in particular. "*You* killed my sweet nephew. *You* killed Johnny Rudd. This is where the bill comes due."

Brea and Jessie were silent. They showed nothing in their expressions. Flo still had her head rolled back and her eyes closed. Brea noted the tension in her body. She was like a string pulled tight. Finally, Flo lowered her head and turned her remorseless gaze in Chance's direction.

"It was me. I killed him," she said. "I put a bullet right between his fucking eyes, and I'd do it again."

The silence that followed was leaden. It slowed time and lowered the room's temperature. Brea wondered if Chance would end it by pulling a semiautomatic pistol from his top drawer—he no doubt had a gun of some description in there—and blowing a hole through the middle of Flo's chest. Instead, he stepped toward her, propped his hands on his thighs, and leaned almost to the point of tipping over.

"I ain't gonna lie. Hearing you say those words out loud makes me wanna cut those pretty brown eyes right out of your skull." Chance lifted a curlicue of hair from Flo's shoulder and twirled it between his fingers. "But I respect your honesty. You got some guts."

She pulled away from him, as much as her restraints would allow. The bottoms of her chair legs squeaked across the hardwood floor.

"And it makes sense, you being the triggerwoman, seeing as it was your mama who died in that tragic accident. But let me remind you: my witness saw three people leave the scene of the crime. One. Two. Three." Chance pointed at each of them as he counted. "You play together, you *pay* together."

From the moment she'd seen Burl sitting on the edge of the bed to when Chance Kotter had strolled emperor-like into the room, Brea had believed they would find a way out of this situation. She'd even said as much to Jessie. But now, knowing for certain that this was about Johnny Rudd, she wasn't so sure. This redneck prick had gone to a lot of trouble to trap them and bring them here. He'd put his men's lives on the line. Whatever twisted revenge he had planned, the sisters were destined to suffer it.

The fighter in her would not submit, though. Even cuffed to the chair, Brea surveyed the room for escape scenarios and weaknesses she could exploit. Was there a way to use the chair as a weapon? Could she break it—freeing up her lower body—and kick her way to safety? Could she dislocate her thumb and slip her right hand through the cuff, then grab whatever gun Chance kept in that top drawer and shoot these bad motherfuckers before they knew what was happening?

No, of course she couldn't. These were desperate fantasies, and although Brea let them play out in her mind, the blood she saw spilled was always hers.

JESSIE KNEW THAT FIGHTING WASN'T an option but wondered if she could negotiate a less sinister outcome. The idea of offering these men *anything* made her feel sick inside, but she'd do it if it kept her sisters alive.

Something gnawed at her, though, like a mouse making holes in her train of thought. Jessie focused on her breathing, employing the 4-7-8 technique, ushering her mind into a more balanced place. On her fifth cycle, she flicked out a mental hand and snagged the mouse—held it by the tail. If she hadn't been so hurt and scared, she'd have caught it sooner.

"You're a liar," she said, looking at Chance, who'd dropped back into his big leather chair. "Johnny Rudd was a personal job. The Trace had nothing to do with it, so you couldn't have found us through them."

Chance pressed his lips together, looking momentarily perplexed. "You wanna field this one, Burl?"

"Sure," Burl said, and stroked his mustache. His voice had the assuredness of a hammer. "As soon as our team learned that the Trace was a dark-net resource for vigilantes, they started investigating their operatives. There's a whole roster of them, apparently, but they narrowed their search by looking for connections to Johnny. Loan sharks, gang members, debt collectors. Johnny didn't always keep the best company."

He let this hang in the air, watching Jessie, Brea, and Flo exchange glances. A long smile brightened his face, then he stepped toward Flo, clasped her chin in his large hand, and tilted her head so that she looked up at him.

"Florence Bella. One-third of the Bang-Bang Sisters." He inhaled. His chest filled. "How long do you think it took our little band of geeks to figure out that you are Esther Bella's daughter?"

"God rest her soul," Chance said dryly.

"Wait. We don't use our *real* names at the Trace." Jessie looked at Burl, daring him to challenge her. "They only know us as the Bang-Bang Sisters."

"It's completely anonymous," Brea added. "Which is why we don't gig under that name."

Burl removed his hand from beneath Flo's chin but remained standing over her for an uncomfortable amount of time. She lowered her head and shriveled—something Jessie, in the nineteen years she had known Flo, had never seen. It broke her heart.

"All I know is what my number one geek told me: that all your information is right there in the Trace's database. Names, addresses, cell phone numbers. Everything." Still smiling, Burl took a couple of backward steps and turned his attention to Jessie. "What? You don't think a bunch of cyber criminals would want to know who they're working with? It couldn't have been hard for them to find out. You gave them payment details, didn't you?"

"Our crypto wallets are noncustodial," Brea said. "No personal information is shared."

"Yeah, well, I guess everything can be tracked."

Chance Kotter shifted position and his seat gave a mighty creak. Jessie looked at him, then glanced at the other bruisers in the room. They hadn't moved. Wilder stood soldierlike next to Errol, still holding on to his leash. Carson and the other goon—sorely dumb-looking—were over by the door. Once again, Jessie's mind touched briefly on the idea of negotiation, but this redneck militia wanted blood. Outside of that, nothing she could offer would be enough.

"The family connection was significant, but we wanted to be absolutely certain, so we dug deeper." Burl stroked his mustache again. "The markings on the .40-caliber slug dug out of Johnny's brain were consistent with those on a .40-caliber slug recovered from the body of Jeremy Kemper, a convicted sex offender from Grand Rapids, Michigan."

"In other words, they were fired by the same gun," Chance explained unnecessarily. He picked up the framed photograph of the policewoman and turned it for all to see. "That information was verified by my own dear sister, who just happens to be chief of police here in Reedsville."

Burl said, "Mr. Kemper was, I believe, your second contract with the Trace."

Jessie sighed. She remembered Kemper, a former soccer coach who'd raped six high school girls. Prison time hadn't rehabilitated him, judging by the content the Trace had found on his computer. Flo had pulled the trigger on that contract, and yes, she'd used her Glock 23, the same gun she'd used to end Johnny Rudd.

These fuckers knew everything.

"See? We did our homework." Chance put the photograph of his sister back on the desk and spread his hands. "Well, not *me*. I don't know my U-R-L from my I-B-S. Ain't that right, Burl?"

Burl just chuckled.

"Point is, we got you for Johnny. We got a motive, and we got hard, ballistic evidence. Now, I was all set to round up a posse, drive out to Los Angeles, and take care of business." Chance made a pistol shape with his right hand and pressed it to his temple. "But then one of our fellas hit on the idea to set a trap that might bring you here, to my backyard, where *I* set the rules."

"You blackmailed the Trace," Jessie conjectured. "You threatened to expose them, then used them to set us up."

"Blackmail? Shoot, that sounds like a good way to add my name to their most wanted list." Chance whistled through his teeth. "I don't think so."

"We *baited* them," Burl said. He had the smug air of a hunter who'd downed an apex predator. "We knew from certain correspondence how desperate you were to get your hands on the wren. And I can hardly blame you. He is a blight on our town—"

"I'd kill him myself," Chance interjected, "if I knew who he was."

"We all would," Wilder chipped in.

"Our team of hackers left a trail of digital breadcrumbs," Burl continued. "Some were legit, to boost credibility: crime scene photos, witness statements, forensic analyses—all courtesy of our very own chief of police—"

"Ain't she a button?" Chance tapped the top of the photo frame.

"Most were fabricated. The wren's name, for instance. We got that from an old Barrett Lorne movie. And that whole thing with the aunt . . ."

"Now *that* was a nice touch." Chance laughed once at the cleverness of it all. His belly wobbled. "By the way, the woman who left the house Monday morning was Carson's old lady."

"Yeah," Carson said. "Ain't nothing she won't do for a bottle of bourbon."

All the fellas laughed at that. Even Errol flicked his ears again. Jessie had been trying to keep her cool, meditate, *think* her way through this, but now she circled back to wanting to fight. On some level, she was relieved to learn that the Trace hadn't double-crossed them. It had merely acted on the evidence it found. Mostly, though, she was furious about being duped by these fucking rednecks.

"It was a ballsy scheme." Burl peeled a long black hair—probably Flo's—from the sleeve of his suit jacket and let it fall to the floor. "Hand to God, I didn't think it would work, but the Trace pounced on that fake info like sharks on blood. They gave you the scoop, as we figured they would . . . you know, with you being so desperate for the kill."

Chance's eyes shone. He licked his lips, wolflike. "And here you are."

"DIDN'T ONE OF YOU STOP to think how convenient all this was? How easy?"

It was Burl who asked this question, but Flo only had eyes for Brea. Her anger was depthless. She recalled snippets of their conversation in Oklahoma City, when she'd expressed her concern about the wren contract being handed to them on a silver platter. *You're overthinking it*, Brea had replied. *The bottom line is most serial killers are broken, cowardly men. This was never going to be difficult.* Now, Brea looked straight ahead. She couldn't meet Flo's fiery stare.

"Too horny for the kill, I guess," Chance opined, shaking his head. "Bloodlust can blind a man. Or a woman."

"If you know all about us," Jessie snarled, jerking forward in her seat so that her cuffs pulled tight against the wooden spindle, "then you know that we only kill people who deserve to be killed. Rapists. Murderers. Pedophiles. That's what the Trace is all about—exacting justice when the system fails."

"Like it failed with your nephew," Brea said, and sneered. "A defective breathalyzer? Really?"

"Johnny had his faults, but to include him with the likes of pedos and rapists . . ." Chance flashed his teeth, clearly bristling. He took a deep breath and cooled a touch. "He was a decent kid at heart. Sometimes you had to look deep, but it was there. He loved his mama. Loved his dogs."

"That doesn't mean shit," Brea said. "Adolf Hitler loved dogs."

Chance gave her a withering look but didn't retort. He stood up from his desk, walked grandly over to Errol, and rubbed that place on his nape again. Errol's eyes glazed. If he had a tail, he'd have thumped it.

"Johnny lost his daddy when he was fourteen. A mining accident out in Pike County. It hit Johnny hard, and he went off the rails." Chance shook his head with a raincloud-like sadness. "He got mixed up with the wrong crowd—started doing stupid shit around town, getting into fights, stealing cars, that kind of thing. I got him a part-time job humping crates at the distillery. Good manual work. It righted him some, but he was never quite the same. I'll say this, though: he gave half of every paycheck to his mama to help with the bills, not knowing that *I* was helping out in that regard, too. But that's what I'm talking about. Johnny was a good kid at heart."

"Spare us the sob story," Brea said. "Let's just get to why you haven't killed us yet."

"Don't worry, we'll get there," Chance assured her. "I know your motive. Now you'll know mine."

He gave Errol a final, hearty scratch, then walked over to Burl and whispered in his ear. Flo was certain she heard the words "feed" and "ready," and her stomach turned. That didn't sound good at all. Burl nodded. He took out his phone and started texting. Chance gave him a brotherly clap on the shoulder, then stepped behind his desk and looked at the sisters.

"Heather Rudd—Johnny's mama, my kid sister—took his death very hard." Chance lowered himself into his seat and pooched out his lower lip. "Johnny was her baby, a living reminder of her husband, the one thing they made together in love. That boy meant everything to her. He meant everything to me, too. He was my only nephew, and I loved him so."

Still with that poochy lip, and an altogether reflective expression, perhaps recalling family barbecues and Thanksgivings and other such happier times. He appeared kindly for a beat or two—or as close to kindly as it was possible for a man like Chance Kotter to get—then blinked and snapped out of it.

"Two weeks after putting Johnny into a hole in the ground, right next to her young husband, Heather slipped the barrel of a Colt 1911 into her mouth and pulled the trigger. It was me who found her body. I went to her house to see if she needed anything, and there she was, her brains splashed all over the goddamn walls." Chance leaned forward. His gaze flicked over Brea and Jessie and settled hard on Flo. "So you didn't just kill one person. You killed *two*. Now talk to me about justice."

Flo returned that hard stare and doubled down. "Like I said, I'd do it again."

Chance slammed his fists on the desk—that photo of him and Ned Sargent toppled over—and gestured impatiently at his laptop computer. "It's time, goddammit. Burl, help me out with this." He waved a hand over the keyboard as if hoping to unlock its magic. "Get the screen up. The *feed*. The video feed."

Burl hastened over to take care of that. The sisters looked at one another, switching up expressions, everything from anger to bafflement to alarm. Chance rolled back in his chair—his face was hot with color—and addressed Carson.

"Carson, are you a man of God?"

"Yessir, I am."

"And do you read the Good Book?"

"Yessir, I do."

"And what does the Good Book say about retribution?"

"An eye for an eye, a tooth for a tooth."

Burl finished what he was doing and stepped back. Chance looked at the screen and grinned.

"An eye for an eye," he said. "And so we come to this."

He flipped the computer around, and every sister screamed.

# TWELVE

Both Brea and Flo lunged forward, bringing their chairs with them, but didn't get far before toppling. They landed hard and writhed on the floor, still shrieking. Jessie twisted, jerking her cuffs against the spindle, but it wouldn't break. Her chair shifted across the floor and also nearly went over.

"Let 'em be, they'll soon tire," Chance said to Burl, who'd stepped toward Flo. "That noise, though."

"Tay, go fetch the duct tape," Burl said.

Tay—the dumb-looking goon standing next to Carson—nodded and left the room. Burl stooped and righted Flo's chair, dragging Flo up with it, but she bucked and went over again.

"I said to leave 'em."

Burl nodded at his boss, then they all—even Errol—looked at the sisters writhing and cussing and screaming. Chance plugged fingers into his ears and said, "Lordy."

Tay returned a couple of minutes later with a roll of duct tape. Burl took it and tore off a seven-inch strip. He slapped this over Jessie's mouth. He righted Flo again, and Tay held her head steady while Burl ripped off another short piece and quieted her mouth. Brea was last. She snapped her teeth at Burl as he lifted her off the floor—almost caught him, by God—and he slapped her hard. He tore off a longer strip and covered her mouth, making sure he got some of her hair, too.

The sisters were quieter, but they still writhed and grunted. Their throats bulged. Their eyes were wide and red. To a woman, they looked at the computer screen and did not want to believe what they were seeing.

A ROOM WITH PLAIN BRICK walls and a meager source of light. Two women secured to chairs. Both were gagged and crying. The woman on the left was Aubree Vernier—Brea and Jessie's fifty-nine-year-old mother. She appeared unhurt but scared. The woman on the right was Imani Bella—Flo's little sister. All the beauty and radiance had been removed from her. She looked shocked and shattered.

There was one man in the shot but more in the room—three or four, perhaps, judging by the shadows on the wall. This man stood behind Aubree and Imani. He wore a black ski mask and a woodland camo field jacket. The pistol in his hand was the kind that didn't ask twice.

Burl took out his cell phone and thumbed the screen. Seconds later, the man in the black ski mask hooked his own phone from his jacket pocket and held it to his ear. The was no audio on the video feed, but the sisters heard his voice through Burl's device.

"We live, Burl?"

"We are live," Burl confirmed, and smiled. "Why don't you have those ladies give the camera a wave?"

"Shit, Burl, I got their hands all tied up."

"You can cut them loose for a second," Burl said. "Just the one hand."

The man in the black ski mask put his phone down, took a knife from his pocket, and made cutting motions behind Aubree and Imani. His voice came through faint: "Wave to the camera." Neither woman did, so he leveled his gun, first at the back of Aubree's head, then at the back of Imani's. "*I said wave to the fucking camera.*" Both women nodded and raised their one free hand, waving it feebly, whimpering through their gags.

"Ain't that sweet?" Chance said.

THE SISTERS STRUGGLED A WHILE longer but eventually exhausted themselves and sat slumped. Chance gave them another ten minutes. He left the room and came back eating a bowl of cobbler, spooning the dessert into his mouth with agreeable sounds. The video feed played throughout. The man in the black ski mask had grabbed a couple of zip ties and resecured Imani's and Aubree's hands to their chairs, then was replaced by a man in an olive-green ski mask. His gun was equally serious.

"I hafta say, Burl, your wife makes the *best* cobbler," Chance said.

"That she does," Burl agreed.

"Where'd she get these pears?"

"Rosalie's."

"Right off the farm?"

"Right off the farm."

"Mm-mmm." Chance nodded and shoveled the last spoonful into his mouth. He set the empty bowl down, then dropped one ass cheek onto the edge of his desk and looked at the sisters. "I said we wouldn't need restraints. I thought Errol and my men here would be enough to keep you from turning feral. Burl insisted, though, and I'm glad I listened. You gals have got some *fight* in you."

Their cuffs rattled. They looked at Chance through the clumps and straggles of their hair.

"Pull that tape off, Burl. They can barely breathe."

Burl did as Chance requested. He yanked Brea's tape off with a little extra zip, pulling out several long hairs for good measure. She winced and drew a rattling breath.

"Better?" Chance asked, wiping cobbler crumbs from the corner of his mouth.

"Kill . . . I swear . . . fucking *kill* you," Brea gasped.

"Not in this lifetime, missy." Chance gestured at the older woman on the laptop's screen. "But I might make you watch as my fellas kill *her*. Cover the walls with her brains. What do you think of that?"

"*Kill* you—"

"And this one." Chance looked at Flo, tapping one pudgy digit against Imani's half of the screen. "We'll put a bullet right between her eyes. Does that sound familiar?"

"She's *pregnant*," Flo hissed. She made a retching sound, then spat on the floor. "Jesus Christ, she's . . . she's—"

"I would never take a life in the womb, no matter the circumstances. An unborn child shouldn't be punished for the sins of others." Chance smeared more cobbler crumbs from his lips and pointed at the screen. "I can't say what fate will befall this young lady—that's up to you—but her baby will be fine. On that you have my word."

"Fuck your word," Brea snapped. "And fuck you."

"What do you want?" Jessie asked, applying a more diplomatic tact. She looked at Chance imploringly. "You want us to do a job for you? Take out one of your competitors? Burn down a rival meth lab?"

Chance slapped his thigh and laughed. "Sweet Lord. You think we're all meth and moonshine. You hear that, Burl?"

"I heard it."

"Burn down a rival meth lab, she said."

"Yessir, I heard it."

"I already told you," Chance said, looking at the sisters. "I'm an honest businessman . . . and I can handle my competitors just fine."

"What *is* it you want, then?" Jessie's throat cracked dryly. "We'll do it. Whatever it is. Just . . . please . . . *please* . . . let them go."

On screen, Imani wriggled in her seat. The man in the olive-green ski mask yelled at her, and she shrank away from him. It was impossible to tell where they were. A derelict foundry, perhaps, or warehouse, judging by the old brickwork. They might be underground, but not too deep under; they had a cell phone signal and, presumably, data or Wi-Fi to run the video feed. They likely hadn't been taken *too* far from their homes in Chatsworth and Panorama City. Somewhere in between? Any one of a thousand possible locations in the Valley. Maybe *ten* thousand.

"*Please*," Jessie said again.

"Let me tell you a little something about me," Chance said, drumming a fist against his chest. "I am, above all, a man of my word. If I say I'm gonna do something, I *will* do it. It's important you know and believe that."

"We believe it," Flo said. Her face was a mask of absolute pain. "Just . . . don't do this, don't—"

"Something else: I ain't much for drinking. A glass or two on special occasions, is all. I do not smoke, and I do not womanize. My only vice, if you can call it such, is that I like a wager every now and then. I also enjoy blood sports—hunting, bare-knuckle boxing, cockfighting, that kind of thing—and I've been known to combine the two." Chance drummed his chest again but rhythmically this time. *Ba-bump, ba-bump, ba-bump.* "It sets the heart racing. The higher the stakes, the faster this old ticker runs."

He smiled, slipped off the desk, and walked a circle around the sisters. He did so slowly—there were two full seconds between every click of his heels—and his eyes remained locked to them. Occasionally, he leaned closer, appraising them: their fatigue, their injuries, their fire. The smile never left his face.

"Who's your money on, Wilder?" he asked.

"The big blonde," Wilder replied. "She's got some balls on her."

"Carson?"

"Same."

"Yeah, I get it, but I keep thinking about the dogfights out at Cobb's place." Chance paused in front of Jessie and lifted a tress of dark hair out of her eyes. "It's the smaller dogs that pack a nastier bite."

"Get your fucking hands *off* me." Jessie pulled away from him.

"Vicious, some of 'em."

"Jesus Christ," Flo shouted. A long strand of saliva dangled from her lower lip. "Just *tell* us what you *want.*"

"They want us to kill each other," Brea said. Her voice was cold, steady, and hard. She looked from Flo to Jessie, then up at Chance. "A fight to the death. They're placing bets on who they think will win."

"You got it, sweet pie. Nail on the head." Chance clapped his hands and hooted. "Three badass, competitive gals, all trained up in kung fu and such. That's too good an opportunity to waste."

Wilder hooted, too, and offered Chance an adoring look, as if the big man had tipped a bucketful of good times into his lap. Carson and Tay high-fived clumsily and beamed. The sisters looked at one another. Jessie mouthed, *No way,* but then looked at the screen, where her mom and Imani sat with their heads lowered.

"You going to put us in a cage?" Brea asked. "Or in a pit, like dogs?"

"I thought about doing that, but it'd be over too soon," Chance replied. He stood with one heel cocked and his hands across his belly. "It don't take but a second to snap a neckbone."

"This'll be more . . . *drawn* out," Burl said. "More satisfying."

"Don't think of it as a fight. It's more like a game. An *event*." Chance studied the laptop screen for a moment, then stepped behind his desk and dropped into his seat. "Strength and technique will play a part, but it'll also come down to stealth, strategy, and instinct. True competition."

"The thrill of the hunt," Burl added.

Chance pointed at Burl and clicked his tongue.

"This is bullshit." Brea licked her wounded lip and regarded Chance with nothing but hate. "You say you're a fair man, but you're not. Johnny Rudd was drunk off his ass. He killed Flo's mother. And you, with help from your police chief sister, falsified the evidence and got him off the hook. There's nothing fair about that."

"It was an accident," Chance responded, trying to keep his manner cool and unaffected. "A terrible accident. I don't know if Johnny was drunk that night and neither do you. Not for certain. Maybe that breathalyzer really was faulty. But even if he *did* drink a little too much, you can put that down to stupidity—the exuberance of youth. There's not a judge in the world would sentence him to death for that."

"Exuberance?" Brea rolled her eyes. "I can't believe I'm hearing this shit."

"Your *unjust* retribution caused a lot of pain." Chance made no effort to appear cool now. He pointed at Brea with a trembling finger, and that hot color was back in his cheeks. "Like I said, you mess with my family, and we got a problem."

A strained silence fell on the room, disrupted only by the sound of the sisters' fearful breathing. Flo had lowered her head. She trembled so hard her handcuffs jangled. Some of that was rage. Jessie looked at the ceiling and swallowed with uncomfortable little clicks. Brea kept her eyes rooted on Chance.

"Here's how it's going down," the big man said. He leaned back in his seat and looked at his watch. "It is now just after eight P.M., Friday, September twenty-second, in the year of our Lord 2023."

The sisters did the math. They'd been ambushed Monday morning, which meant they'd spent four and a half days in their respective prisons. Long enough for Chance's goons to kidnap Aubree and Imani and drive them . . . wherever. Long enough for Chance to get all his crooked ducks in a row.

"At ten P.M.," he continued, "you'll each be dropped in a different part of the city. You'll have nothing but the clothes on your back and your knowledge of each other. No cell phones. No money. No weapons."

The sisters looked at one another again. It was hard to see such pain and uncertainty where before they'd seen only love.

"You will then have forty-eight hours to hunt each other down. Sister against sister. Kill or be killed." Chance had adopted the tone of an army captain imparting mission objectives to his platoon, but he couldn't keep the glee out of his eyes. "I do believe in second chances, however, and one of you *will* earn her freedom. The last woman standing gets to go home to California, be with her family."

Brea's breath hitched in her throat. "You better hope that woman isn't me, because I will be back here when you least expect it, and I will take your fucking head."

Chance flapped a hand. "You think I'm scared of a little thing like you? What you see here is just the tip of the iceberg. Tell her, Burl."

"Friends in high places. Friends in low places. And a small army in between." Burl spread his arms in a *sorry about your luck* kind of way. "From the gutters to the penthouses, we've got this town covered. You better trust we'll see you coming."

"And when we do, I'll be on you like dirt on a coffin. I'll bury you dead." Chance leaned forward. His belly nudged the edge of his desk and the items on it wobbled. "Then I'll drive out to California and bury everyone you love. Believe *that*, missy."

Any response would seem petulant, small. Brea knew this and opted for silence.

"Two dead, one survivor. That's what I want." Chance held up two fingers on his left hand, one on his right. "Forty-eight hours. That's more than enough time to seek and destroy. Reedsville is a small city—"

"Sixteen miles square, give or take," Burl put in. "You can walk from one end to the other in two hours."

"My fellas here"—Chance tapped the laptop's casing—"are under strict instruction to shoot your family members to death at *precisely* ten P.M. on Sunday. Only a call from Burl will stop that from happening."

Burl made a phone shape out of his right hand, thumb and pinkie extended, and held it to the side of his face.

"You do what we want," Chance said. "You play the game as we've laid it out, and Burl *will* make that call. These ladies'll be set free, and that sweet baby will be raised by his or her rightful mama."

Flo hissed through her teeth and pulled at the handcuffs yet again.

"Now . . ." Chance leaned back in his seat. "What do you think of that?"

Nothing for a long time, only pained grunts and movements, the hopeless clank of the handcuff chains striking solid wood. Then Jessie flicked the hair out of her eyes, drew an exhausted breath, and said:

"I think you'll get what you want, but not in the way that you want it. We're sisters, not opponents. We'd sooner kill ourselves than kill each other."

"That so?" Chance flashed a big smile and got to his feet. He walked around his desk, stood in front of Jessie, and lifted her chin so that their gazes locked. "Hmm. Yeah. You got that look in your eye. What's that look, Burl? The word escapes me."

"Devotion," Burl said.

"*Devotion.* That's it, by God. I think you'd do anything for your sisters, including lay your life down for 'em. But I can't say the same for thissun." Chance pointed at Flo. "And I *definitely* can't say the same for thissun." He pointed at Brea. "In case you haven't noticed, they been shooting daggers at each other from the moment they sat down. I'd say there's more than a little spice between 'em."

Brea and Flo glanced at each other for no more than a second—long enough to see that the daggers were still active.

Chance removed his finger from beneath Jessie's chin and took a backward step. "But let's say you *do* join hands and take a three-way header off the Wishbone Bridge. Well, that'd sure spoil our fun and upend all these weeks of careful preparation—the money spent, the good soldiers killed. Jesus, Howie's got a whole lotta nothing where his nut sack use to be, and Kyler don't have a single memory left in his skull."

"A crying shame," Wilder remarked, shaking his head. "Still, I'd sooner be Kyler than Howie."

"Ain't that the truth," Tay concurred.

"If all that ends up being for nothing more than three pitiful suicides, well . . . I might get redder than hell and kill these two women anyway." Chance gestured at the screen, then raised his hands defensively. "Now, I ain't saying I will, but I ain't saying I *won't*. I *do* have a miserable temper. Tell 'em, Burl."

"Like a kicked dog," Burl said.

"Let me be very clear: the only way to *guarantee* these women go free is to play my game, *my* way. That means up close and personal, hand-to-hand combat. *No* suicides." Chance folded his arms and nodded seriously. "Two dead. Forty-eight hours. Do you understand?"

Jessie murmured that she did. Brea and Flo said nothing.

"Do you *understand*?"

Flo whispered yes, but still nothing from Brea. Chance whipped out a hand—he was quick for a big guy—and struck her hard across the face. Brea's head snapped to the side, blood spouting from her lip. She groaned through gritted teeth, then looked at Chance and nodded.

"Good. That's good." Chance shook his right hand and returned to his seat. "Okay, as with any competition, there are certain rules you need to follow. Burl?"

Burl puffed out his chest and took up position next to Errol, stroking the dog with one hand as he spoke to the sisters. "You'll each be fitted with an ankle monitor—a GPS tracker similar to those given to offenders on house arrest. We'll know exactly where you are at all times. If you remove the tracker, or attempt to break it, an alarm will sound—"

"And we *won't* be waiting forty-eight hours," Chance interjected, motioning at the screen. "We will straight up execute these women."

Burl continued: "If any of you leave town, if you set so much as one foot outside the city limits, I will be forced to call my associates, and your family members will be killed."

"Immediately," Chance added.

"Do not even *think* about approaching this property. Not only will your GPS blips give you away, but we are equipped with a state-of-the-art security system: alarms, motion sensors, armed guards, twenty-four/seven video surveillance, the whole nine yards."

"If I catch even a *whiff* of a threat—from you or any outside help you might think of recruiting . . ." Once again, Chance tapped the laptop's casing. "We will cut that baby out of the womb, swaddle him or her up in a nice clean cloth, then shoot both these mamas in the head."

Flo let out a long, hopeless moan, which turned into a long, terrified scream.

"Couple more things," Burl said, as soon as there was enough quiet for him to be heard. "First: melee weapons are allowed. Knives, baseball bats, crowbars. Whatever you can procure in the field. No guns, though. We don't want you taking potshots at each other from fifty yards."

"Where's the fun in that?" Chance said, and grinned.

"Second: if we are forced to kill these women"—Burl nodded at Chance's laptop—"then we will round you up and kill you, too. Not because we fear reprisals, but because you didn't follow the rules."

Chance allowed a moment for this to sink in, no doubt enjoying the mood, the tension. This was the plan—the *game*—all laid out. It hadn't even started yet, and he was already wallowing in it. A pig in shit.

"Be smart, is all," he said, and tapped a finger against his temple. "This city belongs to me. I got eyes and ears everywhere. Friends on every corner. You won't be able to do a goddamn thing without me hearing about it."

Chance, Burl, and their little band of redneck thugs looked at one another in a self-congratulatory way. Tay rubbed his hands together, perhaps thinking of the money he'd win should his sister of choice be victorious. On screen, Aubree Vernier and Imani Bella squirmed in their seats and cried.

"Eight twenty," Chance said, looking at his watch. "Where's Goose? Shouldn't he be here by now?"

"I messaged him a few hours ago," Burl said. "But I haven't seen him since Tuesday."

"He disappears every now and then," Wilder added. "I think he's got a fancy woman out in Selma."

"Can't hardly blame a man for wanting to sow his wild oats," Chance said with an appreciative nod. "But get his ass out here. There's work to be done."

"On it," Burl said.

"I know you are. That's why I pay you the big bucks." Chance and Burl shared a winning smile. All was hunky-dory in their worlds. "Okay, fellas, let's get this show on the road. I want these gals patched up, ankle-tagged, and into their own clothes by nine thirty. Burl, make sure there are three men to a vehicle, not including the driver. We are throwing down at ten P.M. Not a second before. Not a second after."

Wilder and Errol loomed threateningly—Errol on all fours now, his teeth showing—as Burl unlocked each of the secondary sets of handcuffs, freeing the sisters from their seats. They were lifted to their feet by Burl, Tay, and Carson respectively.

"Give 'em a moment," Chance said, gesturing for his men to let go and back up a touch. They did but remained alert. Carson pulled his stun baton from where it was tucked inside his belt.

The sisters straightened to their full heights, rolling their shoulders, cricking their necks. They looked at Chance and his goons. The air sizzled. They looked at the computer screen, where their family members pleaded, unheard, through their gags. Finally, they turned toward one another.

"I don't know what to do," Jessie said.

"Do whatever you have to," Brea said.

The tension between her and Flo had not lessened. They stared at each other like hurting lovers. Jessie tried to bridge the divide. "Bring it in," she said. Reluctantly, Brea and Flo did. They got close but wouldn't touch foreheads. Their triangle—the special shape from which they drew such steadfastness and affection—was incomplete.

"We'll always be sisters," Jessie said, attempting to find their harmony in all the noise. "They can separate us, but that will never change."

"That's just so damn adorable," Chance said. He picked up his dessert bowl, ran his finger around the inside, and sucked it clean. "Share the love while you still can, gals. The next time you see each other, you'll have killing on your minds."

# THIRTEEN

His *nonna* was eighty-three and deteriorating rapidly. She used to know some English, but in recent years every word had faded from her crumbling brain, and he knew very little Italian. His visits were quiet but cordial. Usually, he'd fix her a snack and they'd watch TV together (he'd directed her router through a VPN and subscribed to the most popular Italian channels). Her favorite show was *Un medico in famiglia*. He couldn't follow what was happening, but Nonna would laugh and clap her hands and sometimes weep, and that was good. It occurred to him that many people's lives—including the most storied and complex—were bookended by impressionable, uncomplicated years, where even the slightest thing could bring joy. It was something to look forward to.

That afternoon, after eating her soup and watching some nonsensical game show, Nonna fell asleep in her armchair. The wren collected her dirty bowl, placed it in the sink, then grabbed his backpack and ventured out to her backyard. He'd modified the backpack a few years ago to accommodate his oxygen concentrator, first by cutting a hole in one side—this allowed airflow into the compressor—and then stitching around the edges to tidy it up. It worked perfectly. (Now he looked like a guy with a backpack instead of an invalid with a medical-grade machine strapped to his body.) The wren didn't think he'd need purified oxygen in Nonna's backyard, which was large and private, but he had it with him just in case. He'd also brought his air pistol.

Nonna's yard was full of bird feeders. They stood on pedestals and hung from the branches. Most were weighted for smaller species, but some tolerated crows and grackles. The neighborhood birds had learned that Nonna's backyard was the best hangout in town, although it didn't come without risk.

The wren removed the pistol from his backpack, its magazine already loaded with .177 BBs. He took aim at a crow perched on a feeder fourteen feet away. The crow fed contentedly, dipping its beak into the tray, gobbling down cracked corn and sunflower seeds. Such a happy bird. The wren squeezed the trigger and shot it through the wing. It cawed and flapped and tried to fly away but fell into the leaves below, where it struggled for some time. The pistol's pneumatic report wasn't loud—certainly not loud enough to wake Nonna—but it was sudden and different enough to scare many of the birds away. The wren waited. He took out his phone and checked his messages. Nothing important. He flipped over to Facebook (where he was logged in under a fake account) and perused photographs of his next victim.

Looking at her—at the span of her shoulders, her eyes, her slender throat—caused a sudden shortness of breath. The wren reached into his backpack, turned his concentrator on, and inserted the cannula prongs into his nostrils. Within moments, the pressure on his lungs eased.

The wren put his phone away. He kept the oxygen flowing for now. The birds settled again. He killed a second crow and a sparrow. Seven minutes passed before another bird came to feed. A northern cardinal. The wren shot it in the chest and it died instantly.

His concentrator was down to 37 percent battery life. He hit the off switch, removed the cannula, and went inside to check on his *nonna*. She was still asleep. He plucked a Kleenex from a box on the table and used it to wipe drool from her whiskery chin. The TV was still on, blaring in Italian. The wren considered turning it off but decided not to. It would present a distraction if Nonna woke any time soon, and he hadn't finished outside quite yet.

Over the next hour, he killed fourteen more birds, nine of them crows. He walked around the yard gathering the corpses, then arranged them on the ground in a pillow shape and lay down with his head on them. He looked at the sky. It was edging toward darkness, and there was a beautiful smoky purple color in the west. He thought about elevation and freedom and how that shade of purple would look on his wings. In time, the birds—such short memories—flew down again, alighting on the feeder perches and branches. They fed and squabbled and sang, but of course the wrens sang loudest of all. For such a diminutive species, their voices were extraordinarily pronounced. Nonna once told him that wrens made up in personality for what they lacked in size. They weighed little more than the air around them, but in their souls they were as large as eagles.

THE WREN STRIPPED THE DEAD birds, placing their feathers in an empty plastic bag he'd taken from his backpack. By the time he finished, the bag was mostly full. He got a small fire going in the firepit and threw the birds' naked corpses into the flames two at a time. They crackled and spat and smelled good. He went back inside to find his *nonna* awake and watching another of her favorite shows. It was close to eight P.M. The wren made her an herbal tea and rinsed a handful of black grapes and served them on a plate with a chocolate chip cookie.

"I should go," he said, giving the old lady a big smile. She was his only living relative. "*A presto, Nonna.*"

She reached and took his hand, and her rheumy eyes filled with affection. There were cookie crumbs on her chin. She looked lovely. "*Grazie di cuore. Buona seratata, piccolo santo.*"

She had called him this for as long as he could remember. *Piccolo santo*, meaning "little saint," and she would go to her grave believing this.

THE FIRST BUS THAT CAME along was nearly empty, so the wren got on but rode only two stops before a loud gang of youths boarded. They were threatening by their very presence and sat too close to the wren. He switched seats, but it didn't help, even with his oxygen cranked to 100 percent, so he got off at the next stop and waited twenty-seven minutes for another bus. It arrived in a cloud of exhaust fumes. The windows were slathered with grime, and something beneath his seat rattled uncomfortably. Despite the bus being only one-quarter full, the wren disembarked after a short distance and walked from there. Going the quickest route, it should take only twenty minutes, but he stuck to the quieter, more breathable roads and was home in just over an hour.

His hands still smelled of dead birds, with a hint of fire smoke. He washed them meticulously and scrubbed beneath his fingernails, then made himself a PB&J for dinner, with a handful of fresh raspberries, some dried apricots, and an ice-cold glass of water. The wren didn't need a surplus of fuel to keep running. It was one of the advantages of being slight in build.

Not that he was *tiny*. He was five-two, the same height as Charles Manson *and* Prince, who both, like wrens, had expansive (although vastly different) personalities. Manson once claimed that being incarcerated had caused him to shrink—that he'd measured five-seven at the time of his arrest. The wren didn't believe this to be true. He'd also heard that grief and trauma can stunt a child's growth. This didn't seem likely, either. Whoever had said this had probably meant it in regard to emotional and social development. A different kind of growth. Even so, the wren often wondered if he'd be taller and broader if not for the accident that had killed his parents and almost killed him.

HE REMEMBERED NOTHING ABOUT THE accident itself, but the immediate aftermath was seared into his soul. One moment the world was as bright as fresh paint, in the next their car had flipped onto its roof and was positioned halfway down an escarpment, with only a screen of thin trees keeping them from toppling into the gorge fifty feet below. His father was dead in the driver's seat, his skull crushed between the caved metal-work and the steering wheel. His mother's body was all wrong. She'd half slumped out of her seat belt, her chest twisted so that she stared at him in the backseat. Most of her lower body was buried beneath the mangled dashboard.

"Baby," she said faintly, blinking through the blood covering her face. "Baby, you're okay."

He looked at her. Nothing made sense. He remembered the movie they'd all been to see—*Con Air* with Nicolas Cage, so *exciting*—and they'd left the multiplex in high spirits. His dad had tuned in to the Braves game on the car radio, and Chipper Jones had just struck out with runners in scoring position. This was the last thing the wren—at that time just an unremarkable twelve-year-old boy—remembered before there was a loud, dark rip in the fabric of time, and now here he was.

"Baby, you're okay . . . you're—"

One of the trees supporting their battered Ford Taurus snapped beneath the weight, and the car edged farther down the escarpment. It was halted by another tree, but this bowed and creaked and would give way soon.

"Have . . . go . . . get help . . ."

It occurred to the boy that his mother was dying in front of his eyes. Her injuries were too catastrophic. There was so much blood, and every word out of her mouth took excruciating effort. He understood what she wanted, though: for him to clamber out of their car, make his way up the slope, then wave down help on the road. Not for her—it was too late for her—but for him. At the very least, she wanted him out of this car before it slipped another fifteen or twenty feet, to where the escarpment's gradient went from steep to sheer.

His seat belt held him in place, locked tight across his chest. He tried to reach the buckle but couldn't. His arms were over his head, the backs of his hands resting on the roof. He couldn't move them. He was either paralyzed or in complete shock.

"Now," she croaked. "Go . . . guh-guh-go . . ."

"I can't . . . *can't* . . ." His words surfaced on a bubble of confusion and fear. "Mom . . . I can't . . . *Mommy* . . ."

"Go."

The boy gasped. Tears brightened his eyes. He looked at the red button on the seat belt's buckle and it seemed a thousand miles away—a vast and epic journey for his hand to make. He glanced at his mom. She was spasming, showing her teeth in an awful grin.

He managed to drag his hand across the roof and lift it just a little. His heart thundered. His tears trickled upward, over his forehead, into his hair. He took a rasping breath, then something caught his eye. It was not an exceptional thing. On the contrary, it was quite ordinary, but it claimed his attention all the same.

A small brown bird had fluttered down and positioned itself on a rock three feet from the car. The boy looked at it through his broken window. It was a wren, of course. A house wren. He knew this because his maternal grandmother had taught him about common North American birds. Whenever he visited, they would sit in her backyard and watch them come down to feed. It amused him that the wren's voice was so big and interesting, especially for such a forgettable-looking bird.

This wren wasn't singing, though. It looked at him through the window, its head cocked inquisitively. The boy stared back, fascinated not by the bird per se, but by its spectacular freedom—its ability to lift so effortlessly from the ground and fly away. More tears ran from the boy's eyes. The tree groaned, and the car shifted several perilous inches.

He had no idea how long he stared at the wren. Thirty seconds? Five minutes? Ten? However long, his mother died during that time. There were no final words. Her eyes were open, and she still had that terrible grin on her face. The boy wanted to scream, but all he had in his lungs was a weak, bubbling hiss.

Time passed. The light between the trees grew rich and red. Before long, the boy started to hallucinate. The radio had been destroyed, but his father's voice came through the speakers: "Listen to me, son. When you die, you are asked to place all of your achievements into a box. If the box doesn't weigh enough, you are turned into a mealworm. If the box's weight is sufficient, then you get to eat the mealworm." He repeated this message five or six times, always with a squealy, staticky interference over the airwaves, as if being broadcast from very far away. Midway through the third repetition, his mother started to wink and blow kisses at him. The boy tried to scream again. It was another trembling, unworkable effort, so the wren screamed for him, spreading its wings and making the trees shake.

He faded away for a time and stirred awake to yet more hallucinations: strident voices and lights between the trees. Except they weren't hallucinations. A firefighter looked at him through the broken side window. "Hey, kid. We're going to get you out of there." More firefighters secured the car and removed the rear passenger door so that they had more room to pull the boy free. He looked around, believing the wren must have flown away, but he saw it inside the car, perched on the inverted roof.

The little bird paid him no attention. It was too busy pecking hairs from his mother's head—to line its nest with, perhaps. This reminded the boy of something else he knew about wrens: that they were bold opportunists and often callous.

**TWENTY-SIX YEARS HAD PASSED, AND** he was still in the car. That's how it felt. His agoraphobia made him a prisoner, trapped inside by fear and anxiety. The little brown wren symbolized freedom, strength, and flight, everything he strived to attain.

His apartment was a safe space. He had it built to his specifications and had furnished it with comforts: TVs, video game systems, paintings (mostly cloudscapes), a king-sized bed fitted with sky-colored sheets, a chenille barrel chair as soft and round as a nest. He had a shrine to his victims: a locked room with their photos on the walls and corresponding haikus, written in his elegant cursive. There was also a laptop computer on a small desk, and this was where he researched potential victims, using the social media windows they'd built into their lives. *Look at me*, those windows said, and he obliged. He also went there to stare into his victims' eyes and recall the breathtaking heights he'd reached with them, the freedoms he couldn't experience anywhere else.

The wren left his apartment only when necessary and never without his oxygen. It made the outside world vaguely manageable. When everything became too much, he increased the flow rate. It wasn't escape or elevation, but he felt lighter. A balloon in a box.

The oxygen wasn't prescribed. He discovered this remedy by himself, during his torrid years in the foster care system. The matriarch at his third home used to make the children spend time with her sick father, whose many ailments included emphysema and chronic bronchitis. The old man was sweet enough, and the wren—again, just a boy at that time, albeit one with severe PTSD and undiagnosed agoraphobia—didn't mind whiling away the hours with him. It removed him from the clash and bang of the other children and the house in general (the boy suffered more than two hundred panic attacks during the five years he spent in foster homes). One summer evening, the boy asked the old man if he could breathe without the tubes running up his nose. "Not very well," the old man had replied.

"When I take them out, it feels like a rhinoceros is sitting on my chest." The boy had smiled politely at this, but he knew that crushed, constricted feeling all too well. Later that evening, while the old man was sleeping, the boy removed the cannula prongs from his hairy nostrils and inserted them into his own. He fully opened the valve on the oxygen bottle. The rush of cold air into his lungs was immediately blissful. His rib cage expanded, his pelvic floor relaxed, and a lightheaded smile touched his face. More important, the clamor of his surroundings eased notably. The boy worked his thin arms and fluttered on the spot.

He kept the oxygen flowing until the old man started to crackle and gasp, then returned the prongs to their rightful owner. But from that point forward, whenever the old man slept, the boy would sneak into his room and—with a wren's opportunism—appropriate his oxygen.

That was when the sky first called to him, promising openness and light.

THE WREN FINISHED HIS PB&J, drank his water, then removed the concentrator from his backpack and plugged it into the wall. The display showed 0 percent battery life. The last few blocks of his walk home had been touch and go.

He also removed the bag of feathers from his backpack. It was a decent haul, but he would need more than this for his next victim, for whom he had something different—*special*—planned. Not just knife wounds.

She flashed through his mind and his chest tightened again, like it had in Nonna's backyard. He tore the bag open, inhaled the smell of the feathers, then stepped toward the window and looked at the night sky.

The wren's chest expanded, but his eyes blurred with tears and his shoulders ached where wings would grow.

# FOURTEEN

It was a clear night and warm, and there were doubtless areas of the city—on the banks of the Mary, perhaps, or on the patios of any of the upmarket eateries in Waterloo Square—where it might be considered beautiful. The Fort was *not* one such area. Located west of Main, it comprised three neighborhoods, each steeped in degradation. Shovel Town and Upper West were primarily residential, with rows of smoke-colored tenements and shotgun shacks housing 70 percent of the city's population. Gangs cruised their own section of the grid, ostentatiously armed. The crack houses were many and overcrowded. Lower West was largely commercial, catering to the demographic: liquor stores, pawnbrokers, fast-food joints, dive bars, laundromats, convenience stores. There were six churches, two strip joints, a barely operational movie theater called the Utopia, and three nightclubs—one of which, Heat of the Moment, entertained sins of every flavor.

Reedsville's Lower West Precinct patrolled the Fort, a 115-strong team of street-savvy policepersons. They flashed their badges and flexed their muscle, but it would always be an uphill battle. "There's too much trash to clean up," Police Chief Bethany Kotter was fond of saying, usually after she'd sunk a few at Fat Fanny's Ale House. "The best we can do is keep it in the gutter."

THE ESCALADE ROLLED NORTH ON Independence Boulevard, the main thoroughfare running through Lower West. It caught the city lights like a polished black stone—gaudy frontages, neon signs, digital billboards. A red eye settled on the front windshield as it paused beneath the light at the Brooks Street intersection. Goose was behind the wheel. Burl occupied the passenger seat, muttering under his breath as he regarded the overflowing garbage cans and boarded-up windows. Brea, still cuffed, sat in the back between Wilder and a bruiser named Stratton—Strat for short— whom she might have nicknamed Black Teeth if she hadn't learned his name early. It was 9:53 P.M.

A bony homeless man holding a sign reading PLZ NEED $$$ FOR FOOD NEW SHOES stepped barefoot off the sidewalk and approached the passenger-side window. He extended one hand palm up and mouthed through the glass. Burl lifted a Walther PDP from inside his jacket, buzzed the window down, and pressed the tip of the barrel to the side of the homeless man's nose.

"Back the fuck off."

The homeless man made a startled sound in his throat, stumbled backward over the curb, and fell hard. His head struck the sidewalk with an audible thud. Brea saw blood run down one side of his face as the light turned green and Goose pulled away.

"I hate this goddamn neighborhood," Burl said, tucking the pistol back inside his jacket.

Across the street, beneath the glare of the Utopia's marquee, two bulky cops threw a Black teenager over the hood of their cruiser, and one of them cracked him between the shoulder blades with his nightstick.

THEY PASSED A JAZZ CLUB called Sax to the Max where the music leaked onto the street and a Charlie Parker mural adorned the brickwork. Youths gathered beneath the awning, some very young, maybe only eight or nine, eyeballing the Escalade as it purred by.

Strat raised a middle finger that couldn't be seen through the tint. He said, "Someone needs to burn this side of town to the ground." There were mumbles of agreement from Wilder and Burl. Brea rolled her eyes— the ugliness was off the chart—then noticed Goose studying her in the rearview. He held her gaze for an uncomfortable second before turning his attention back to the road.

Nine fifty-six. They continued on Independence for three blocks, made a left on a street that Brea didn't catch the name of, then a right onto a scrub lot with weeds growing through the asphalt. Goose directed the SUV to the back, its headlights cascading over a graffitied wall and a wrecked Chevy Impala that needed a date with a crusher. Anything of potential value—the radio, mirrors, steering wheel—had been stripped. It sat on its rims in a scatter of broken glass. Goose pulled to a stop close by. He shifted into park but kept the engine running.

Three doors opened. Burl, Wilder, and Strat got out—Wilder dragging Brea by the elbow. "Get over there, by the car," he said, and gave her a firm kick in the ass to hurry her along. Brea walked at her own pace, turning her head to keep the three men in her sights.

"Stop," Burl said. "Get on your knees."

Brea stopped. She took a deep breath and dropped to her knees. Glass crunched beneath her. She heard sirens and distant music. The Escalade's engine ticked over.

"Who have you got your money on, Burl?" she asked.

"Not you," Burl replied. He removed the pistol from inside his jacket again. "I wouldn't mind popping a bullet in your leg right now, only Wilder's got five large riding on you, and I think he'd get mad as hell."

Wilder cracked a smile. "Yessir, I would."

Burl dug into his pants pocket, pulled out a handcuff key on a ring, and tossed it to Wilder.

"Wilder is going to unlock your cuffs. You will remain on your knees until we are back in our vehicle and driving away." Burl and Strat stood in front of Brea and aimed their pistols at her. "One sudden move and Wilder is out five grand. Do you understand?"

Brea nodded.

Burl nodded, too, but at Wilder, who crouched behind Brea and started on her restraints. He was nervous, Brea realized. She heard his jerky breaths and felt the tip of the key dancing around the little hole, then he slotted it home and twisted. *Snick.* The cuffs loosened and Wilder pulled them off her wrists.

"Five large," he whispered in her ear. "Don't let me down, bitch."

Brea flexed her fingers. Her hands were free, and she was twelve inches away from the pistol that Wilder undoubtedly carried in a side holster. Three seconds. That's how long it would take to grab Wilder, pull him in front of her—a human shield—then snatch the handgun from its holster and use it on Burl and Strat. Such a desperate maneuver required absolute precision, with no margin for error. Fully focused and fit, *maybe* Brea would have chanced it. But not now. Burl had his finger on the trigger and was looking for a reason to shoot her. One in the leg would give her sisters—her *opponents*—an insurmountable advantage.

Wilder stood and backed away with the cuffs in his hand. Brea remained on her knees, rolling her wrists, returning the feeling to her hands and forearms. Burl nodded at Wilder and Strat. They retreated to the Escalade, and Burl followed slowly, walking backward, still with his pistol leveled. Did these men really fear her that much? Brea didn't think so. They were emphasizing how diligent they were—reinforcing, for Brea's benefit, the thoroughness of their plan.

She watched them climb into the vehicle. Burl sat on the edge of the passenger seat with the door open. He took his cell phone out with his left hand and aimed this at her, too. A photo: Brea on her knees with the junked Impala and graffitied wall in the background. Ready player one.

"Wave howdy to Mr. Kotter," Burl said.

Brea didn't wave howdy. Burl snapped the shot anyway. The flash illuminated the scene. He swung his long legs into the footwell, closed the door, and looked at Brea through the open window.

"Ten o'clock," he said. "It's showtime."

The Escalade pulled away, bathing Brea in the blood red of its taillights.

BREA GOT TO HER FEET and brushed the broken glass off her knees. She was wearing her own clothes—her superhero outfit, sans ski mask—freshly laundered. Their familiar fit and feel gave her some comfort. Conversely, the GPS tracker attached to her right ankle made her feel sick and defeated, like an animal in a cage, existing only for the entertainment of others.

She inspected the device: a solid black band with an LED that blinked green once a second. It was as diminutive as a mouse's eye but felt as tall and communicative as a smoke signal. A picture formed in Brea's mind: Chance Kotter opening a GPS app on his computer and, with one click of a button, zooming in on a green blip flashing in the slums of downtown Reedsville. It was ten o'clock, though—showtime, as Burl had announced—which meant there'd be two other blips, probably different colors, blinking brightly on that same map of the city.

Brea looked at the night sky, at the few stars winking through the murk of light pollution. *I don't know what to do,* Jessie had said. Brea's response had been hard-hearted, as if the matter required no deliberation. The truth was she didn't know what to do, either. Her emotions had set inside her like concrete. She needed to chip away at the mass, separate the pieces, and feel again. Then, maybe, she would have a clearer idea how to proceed.

She stepped closer to the junked Impala and kicked the driver's door as hard as she could. The sound of her boot striking metal was undeniably satisfying. She kicked the door again and heard the paneling pop loose on the other side.

There had to be a flaw in Chance's plan, but Brea couldn't see it. He'd put money, effort, and influence into this and appeared to have his bases covered. Brea could bypass Reedsville's corrupt—and complicit—law enforcement and bring in the state cops, but could she trust *them* not to involve the local authorities? Brea didn't think so. And even if she could, it was still too high a risk with her mom's and Imani's lives on the line. At any given moment, they were one phone call away from being shot to death. Even if Brea had access to a team of covert operatives (she didn't), one wrong move, one triggered alarm, one tip-off, was all it would take.

Brea kicked the car again, putting a boot-sized dent in the front fender. Chance Kotter had tricked them, bested them, and at every turn he had them beat. The only way out was to play his game.

Which led to two questions: Could she kill her sisters? And would her sisters kill her?

Three more kicks to the front fender, deepening the dent. The hood clapped up and down. Brea felt a faint pulse of emotion. There one second, gone the next. She crossed the weedy lot and turned left toward Independence Boulevard. Her body still ached from the abuse she'd suffered in the shed, but this didn't concern her as much as her blunted instincts.

Jessie was quick, skillful, and strong, but she lacked the cold-bloodedness it would take to kill one of her sisters. Brea had no such reserve, and neither did Flo. Brea knew that Flo would do whatever it took to save Imani, and rightly so. Wherever she was in this city, Brea suspected she was already in hunting mode.

A bus roared past, rattling as it hit the potholes in the road. Several passengers stared at Brea through the murky glass. She stared back, feeling an acute desire to be one of them, just another everyday person rumbling toward an everyday destination. A crack appeared in her emotional concrete—regret or grief or something between the two. Brea walked on, passing shuttered businesses, an adult store, a twenty-four-hour grocery. An oncoming car slowed as it approached and the driver leered at her through the windshield. If he stopped and invited her to get in, she would do it . . . and when they pulled over, probably on some darkened back street, Brea would smash his face against the steering wheel, over and over, until it was a mess of broken pieces.

The car passed her and kept going. It accelerated away. Taillights. The violent imagery had quickened Brea's heartbeat, though, and that was good. She was beginning to feel again.

There was a blind guitarist on the corner of Independence Boulevard, not really playing, just tapping the strings in a vague twelve-bar progression. A tip jar swung from the headstock on a piece of string. Brea stopped to listen, letting the rhythm do its thing. A little more feeling, a little more soul.

"Hey, girl."

Brea blinked and drew in a quick breath. She turned away from the guitarist to see a man approaching her. He had a beautiful Afro and a musical walk. Vape smoke surrounded him.

"Yeah. You."

"What?" Brea said.

"Shouldn't you be home? House arrest, right?" He nodded at the band around her ankle, its green light still flashing. "Whatchoo do wrong, girl?"

Brea considered the question for several seconds, then sighed and walked away.

"Everything," she said.

HER POCKETS WERE EMPTY. NO money. No phone. No weapons. "Stripped" was the word that came to mind. Her sense of vulnerability was amplified, and it didn't help that she was being watched. *I got eyes and ears everywhere*, Chance had said. *Friends on every corner.* Brea had assumed he was talking figuratively—emphasizing his place in the city and how the sisters had no safe harbor—but now she wasn't so sure. Blond, female, and alone, she turned plenty of heads, but there were also cooler, more evaluative stares. Two heavyset guys in ball caps surveyed her from a parked Silverado. Another man followed her for four blocks and winked every time she turned around. Brea entered a laundromat and sat on one of the dryers, facing the door. The man lingered outside for ten minutes or so, then called someone—Burl, probably—on his phone and walked away.

*I don't know what to do.*

Brea closed her eyes and Jessie's face floated into her mind. Where was she now? Was her GPS blip closer to Brea's or Flo's? And what would happen when those blips came together? Brea imagined a montage of upsetting scenarios and pushed them all away. One irrefutable notion persisted, however: of the three of them, Jessie was the most likely to lie down and die.

A tear trickled down Brea's cheek. She wiped it away, but it was soon followed by another, then another. Before Brea knew it, she was crying profusely into her hands. Deep, wrenching sobs bubbled from her chest. It was both totally unlike her and yet the most like herself she had felt for many days.

Emotion, finally. *Feeling*, at last. But Brea knew that the real reason for her tears was because she had seen the way ahead, as clear as rainfall.

She knew what she had to do.

# FIFTEEN

Flo had met Jessie and Brea in 2004, at the All-Valley Under-Sixteen Battle of the Bands. This was, until now, the only time they had competed against each other. Flo's band, Sweet Collusion, went on to win the whole thing, but there was no animosity between the girls. Quite the opposite. They clicked immediately and maintained a close friendship from different parts of the Valley (Flo was in Panorama City; Jessie and Brea, in Chatsworth). Their early collaborations included a YouTube channel reviewing reality TV shows and a short high school–themed film called *Played*. At the age of sixteen, Flo was inspired to take up kung fu after seeing Jessie and Brea win their respective age groups at the SoCal MMA Throwdown, and it was Jessie who, four years later, persuaded Flo to travel to China, where she studied under the tutelage of Shaolin grandmaster Yao-Chang Kwan.

On her return Stateside, Flo moved in with Jessie and Brea, who'd rented a house in North Hollywood. They spent their days training, getting stronger, and their nights rocking out. This was when their togetherness deepened and their shape was defined. They wouldn't become a sisterhood until they'd locked arms and walked through darkness (rest in hell, Johnny Rudd), but even before that first kill, Flo believed they were eternal.

Recent events had sent shock waves through their geometry. The sisters were no longer a powerful triangle but three ragged, disjointed lines. And yes, Flo's love remained. Something that deep and honest couldn't so quickly be eradicated. Brea and Jessie were a *part* of Flo. They were her support and her light.

Now, though . . . now she planned on killing them both.

REEDSVILLE'S BUSINESS DISTRICT WAS ON the east side of town, across the Mary River. It was small—several blocks of financial institutions, hotels, and office buildings, dominated by the Kotter-Bryce Tower. Several bars and restaurants offered a post-six P.M. pulse, although the livelier establishments were in Waterloo Square, on the other side of the river. The traffic—foot and road—was minimal this late on a Friday night. Flo walked alone.

*Mostly.* Shortly after being dropped off—Carson had done the honors, along with three heavies she didn't recognize—Flo noticed she was being watched. She thought it was paranoia at first, but the pickup truck idling outside the Bank of America was the same one she saw thirty minutes later, cruising slowly past as she walked west toward the Wishbone Bridge. And not five minutes after that, she saw a shadowy figure standing in the doorway of an office building, filming her on his cell phone. Flo imagined the footage gracing Chance Kotter's computer screen, with the big man and his cronies sitting around it, smoking cigars and discussing her chances. Her impulse was to run and hide, but what would that achieve? Flo had a task ahead of her—a tortuous, heart-wrenching challenge—and hiding wouldn't make it go away.

She crossed Atlantic Avenue and the Wishbone Bridge came into view, with the rest of Reedsville on the other side. Brea and Jessie were out there somewhere, alone and scared. How long before they found each other?

The clock on the Kotter-Bryce Tower read 11:17.

LIKE BREA, FLO HAD TAXED her mind, believing there must be some other way, a means of escape that Chance hadn't considered, but every avenue she explored finished in a dead end. The tracker around Flo's ankle—her LED was blue—may as well have been a leash, secured to a post, designed to tighten and choke if she tested its durability.

An idea occurred to her, though, as she approached the bridge. It was fanciful, almost certainly impractical, but it was *something*. Flo paused, pressing the heel of one hand to her head. Should she let the idea gestate at the risk of it becoming a distraction? Or was it better to focus on the task at hand—her one guaranteed way of escaping this nightmare?

"Focus," she said, but the idea tapped and scratched, demanding her attention. Flo shook her head. She slumped against a nearby wall, first leaning, then sliding into a sitting position. She visualized breaking Jessie down—sweet, beautiful Jessie—punch after punch, kick after kick, then snapping her neck with one brutal twist. Brea would be more challenging. Flo would want a weapon. Guns were against the rules, but knives were not.

She pushed herself into a standing position, ran both hands down the length of her face, and continued walking. The Wishbone Bridge was 1,300 feet end to end, four lanes of road and a walkway along one side. Flo started across it, keeping low. Its structure was ablaze with lights, and she felt horribly exposed. The pickup truck she'd seen earlier passed her again, its driver slowing to snap her photo on his phone. Flo concentrated on the tops of her boots and walked faster. She reached the end of the bridge and tucked herself into the shadows of the nearest building. Short breaths rasped from her lungs. She waited ten minutes. Her heartbeat slowed but her adrenaline remained up.

"Hey, are you okay?"

The voice made her jump. A man stood on the sidewalk twenty feet away. He'd approached so silently that Flo hadn't noticed him. One of Chance's crew, perhaps, watching her? She didn't think so. He didn't have quite the right deportment—that redneck machismo, that country snarl. Nor did he look entirely benevolent. His eyes were misaligned. A cigarette burned between his fingers.

"I'm fine," Flo said. She stepped out of the shadows so that he could fully see her, shaken and alone, maybe, but with a fire in her eyes.

"You need some help?" The man took a step toward her.

"Stay the fuck away from me." Flo also stepped forward, spreading her shoulders, making herself bigger. The man faltered. He parked the cigarette between his lips, raised both hands defensively, then backed away. Within moments he had ghosted across the road and disappeared.

Flo exhaled, relaxing her posture. The tightness across her shoulders eased. Her emotions surfaced then, and suddenly: a wave of sadness, anger, and self-pity. She lowered her head and covered her eyes. Imani called to her from some unknown location. She told Flo to be strong, even though Imani was the one being held at gunpoint.

A breeze roused her. It smelled of the river. Flo stepped onto the sidewalk and looked west along Harper Avenue, a mile and a half of stores, bars, and restaurants leading uphill toward Main. It was after midnight now. A handful of late-night revelers dotted both sides of the street. Upbeat music spilled from a bar called Noah's Tap.

Flo looked for her sisters, scanning the sidewalks on both sides, studying the shadows, the doorways, the rooftops. She wondered what would happen when, finally, they came face-to-face. Would they talk first—console one another as they had so many times before? Or would they forgo the sentimentalities and collide?

No sign of Brea or Jessie. Of course not. It was too soon. They were likely miles apart. Flo placed one hand on her chest. Her emotions simmered, under control but still present.

She needed a weapon.

HER FANCIFUL IDEA HINGED NOT on taking Chance Kotter down or finding a loophole in his game, but rather on removing his bargaining power. Imani and Aubree were his trump cards. Freeing them would give the sisters more options and level the playing field.

The concept was solid but collapsed when Flo thought about how to implement it. She could probably find a discreet way to alert the authorities in California, but she couldn't give them any substantial information. All she had to go on was what she'd seen in the live feed: a windowless brick room that could be anywhere, and a couple of masked assailants. There was a possibility the police were already on the case. They wouldn't be overly concerned about a missing Black woman from Panorama City, but the wife of a prominent record company executive would've kicked their asses into gear.

Given how carefully Chance had laid all this out, it was safe to assume that the men who'd abducted Imani and Aubree had covered their tracks. They would have gone in at night, used a nondescript vehicle with bogus plates (much like the sisters' tour van), and left not a single speck of evidence at either scene. All Flo could add was that both women had been snatched by the same people and taken to the same place. This might be useful information, but it wasn't enough. The police would spend too long spinning their wheels, foraging for leads. Meanwhile, the clock in Reedsville was ticking.

There was another consideration: if Flo communicated with L.A. law enforcement and Chance found out, he would see this as a violation of the rules. His warning recurred, verbatim: *If I catch even a* whiff *of a threat—from you or any outside help you might think of recruiting . . . We will cut that baby out of the womb, swaddle him or her up in a nice clean cloth, then shoot both these mamas in the head.* Chance would have someone monitoring the police involvement in Los Angeles. He might even have a person on the inside. A man who'd apparently thought of everything would have a contingency plan if the heat closed in.

**FLO VISUALIZED CUTTING BREA'S THROAT** with a knife and holding her as she died. The image was so stark that she apologized out loud. "I'm sorry, Brea. We've had our differences, but I love you. I want you to know that."

Twelve forty. She walked half the length of Harper Avenue and took a right turn—a pedestrianized thruway into Waterloo Square. The lights here were still burning, the bars were bright and loud, and there were people—normal people, living normal lives—all around. They laughed and chatted and smoked and perused their cell phones and sat on benches eating. A busker with a beautiful voice and a beaten-up acoustic guitar performed her rendition of Wilco's "Jesus, Etc." Nobody looked twice at Flo. She walked among the late-night disciples, trying to absorb some of their ordinariness.

She saw someone who looked like Jessie—the same dark hair and athletic build—and her heart jumped. It wasn't Jessie, though. This young woman was radiant, not broken, and she wore warm colors. Flo stared at her, remembering Jessie's sunshiny, infectious laugh and the way she clicked her tongue when she was lost for words. Flo's breath caught in her throat. Once again, she imagined twisting Jessie's neck until the bone cracked.

Moments later, she stopped outside a restaurant called Flavor Moon. It wasn't particularly busy, not this late. Flo looked through the front window and saw that a third of the tables were occupied. She went inside. Nobody looked at her. There were two servers, one pouring coffee, the other clearing a table. Flo walked through the restaurant toward the kitchen.

It helped to visualize the grim work, the killing. She would be better equipped to act when the time came, if only mentally. It also helped to focus on the prize. There was a wide, bright future where she and Imani took the baby to the park and picnicked and fed the ducks and laughed until their bellies ached. There'd be sleepovers at Aunt Flo's and family Christmases and Lakers games and weekend getaways. They would grow together, a new triangle, perfect on every side.

The kitchen was a small, rectangular space with an island in the middle and burners along one wall. There were three staff: an older Black man in chef whites and his assistants. They looked at Flo as she passed through. An objection formed on the senior man's face, but Flo gave him a cautioning look and he remained silent. She found what she was looking for on the island: a half-loaded knife block. She grasped one of the handles and pulled out a five-inch utility blade, sharp but too narrow. The next one she selected was better: a seven-inch santoku knife. Flo gave the kitchen staff another hard look, then slipped the knife inside her jacket.

She exited via the back door, which was propped open. Moths had gathered on the screen in their dozens, a crawling brown mass that lifted in a cloud as she pushed through. She stepped into an alleyway illuminated by the rear windows of the flanking buildings. Soon, she would need to decide whether to hunt or lie in wait. For now, she walked aimlessly. Rats crisscrossed her path. A homeless man slept between garbage cans with a dog curled into him. Flo passed without waking them.

# SIXTEEN

At around the time that Flo walked into Flavor Moon to procure a knife from the kitchen, Jessie entered a drinking joint called Cheap Spills, situated in a strip mall on the northern edge of the industrial district. She grabbed a stool at the bar and glanced around listlessly. A dive bar, like hundreds she had played in across the country. There was a pool table, a pinball machine, license plates nailed to the walls, and neon in the windows. Three middle-aged men sat at the bar sipping bottled beers. There were louder voices at the back, maybe half a dozen more guys occupying the booths there. "Paint It Black," by the Rolling Stones, played on the sound system.

"Hey." The bartender wore a faded Ramones T-shirt, sleeve tattoos, and a questioning frown. Clearly, he wasn't accustomed to seeing attractive young females in here by themselves. "Everything okay?"

Jessie's mouth trembled. Bartenders were renowned for being good listeners, and maybe some were adept at giving advice, but this guy wasn't ready to hear just how goddamn terrible everything was for Jessie. Well-meaning conversation couldn't ease her woes. Only a couple of high-caliber bullets would do the trick—one in Burl's skull, the other in Chance's.

"I just need a glass of water," Jessie replied.

The bartender nodded. He fetched a tall glass from beneath the counter, filled it from the faucet, and pushed it in front of Jessie. She thanked him with a tip of the head, lifted the glass to her lips, and guzzled.

The music changed. Same band, different song. "Brown Sugar." The sisters used to cover this one back in the day. Open G tuning and a truckload of sass. Listening to it now brought a wave of memories, to which

Jessie gave herself entirely. Better to relive the past than face the present. Such was her mindset since being separated from Brea and Flo. She'd shuffled through the industrial district, passing factories and warehouses, aware of her surroundings but completely lost to yesteryear: countless gigs, parties, road trips, music festivals, and girls' nights out. Jessie had sat beside a railroad crossing as the bell clanged and a freight train chugged south out of town, with enough good memories to place a different one in every boxcar. She watched the train until it was out of sight and wished that she and her sisters were on it, barreling toward the Gulf of Mexico.

"Water? You look like you need something stronger."

Jessie heard these words, slowly registering that they were directed at her. She turned toward the speaker. It was the guy to her immediate right, three stools away. He had cracked, sunken cheeks, a receding hairline, and gray in his goatee. His work shirt had the name "Todd" embroidered onto the breast pocket.

"Water's fine." Jessie took a long drink from the glass, just to show how fine it was.

Todd raised his bottle of Yuengling like a man in a commercial. "Let me know if you change your mind."

Jessie nodded. She leaned on the bar with her left palm cupping her jaw. In truth, beer sounded great, and not just one. Being blind drunk would obscure everything for a few hours—perhaps not what she needed, but exactly what she *wanted*. It was as close as she'd get to hopping on that freight train and riding it south.

"Okay," she said to Todd. "One beer." A single bottle wouldn't carry her away, but it might erode some of her anguish, which in turn would allow her to think. "But I have to warn you, I'm not in the mood for conversation."

"Understood," Todd said. He gestured at the bartender, and five seconds later a bottle of Yuengling lager appeared in front of Jessie. She picked it up and angled the neck toward Todd in acknowledgment of his generosity. Todd mirrored the gesture with his own bottle.

"To a happier tomorrow," he said.

"I'll drink to that."

**WITHIN A FEW COLD SIPS,** Jessie had relinquished the past and embodied the here and now. Certain determinations were made immediately.

Foremost: she wouldn't kill her sisters, regardless of the consequences. She *couldn't*, because what would her life be worth afterward?

They'd been given forty-eight hours to hunt down and kill one another. It was enough time, but Jessie planned on spending every minute of it in her own way, with a single goal in mind.

She was going after Chance Kotter.

It was risky, but it didn't have to be reckless. She would be smart about it. All her life, Jessie had gone up against larger opponents, which often necessitated a different approach. As always, it would come down to careful movements and doing the small things right.

Jessie sipped her beer, breathing slowly through her nose, sorting through the pieces in her mind. Many of them were obscure or broken and would cut if she handled them carelessly. Some were smoother, shapely, weighted like coins. She started to stack them, looking for symmetry and balance.

The Trace was one such piece. It had been compromised, but it wasn't complicit in setting the sisters up. *My computer fellas hacked the hackers*, Chance had said—a statement that, while troubling, came as no small relief to Jessie. It meant that the Trace was not on Chance's payroll. Did it know that it'd been hacked and that the evidence it'd been fed about the wren was mostly bogus? If so, would it want to even the score?

Jessie didn't have the answers, and she wouldn't until she'd logged in to the Trace and reestablished contact with 9-$tar. But to do that, she needed to find a way to get online.

The door to Cheap Spills swung open and three people staggered in: two jacked dudes and an older woman with pink-and-blond hair, her upper half squeezed into a tube top. They'd all had too much to drink, but the bartender served them anyway. It was that kind of joint. The exuberant trio took their bottles and bumbled toward the pool table, where the dudes racked 'em up and the woman danced alone.

"Someone's having a good night," Todd remarked.

Jessie didn't respond. She watched the woman dance and sing along to the music. "Stay with Me," by Faces, another classic the sisters used to cover. A guy at the far end of the bar howled and raised his drink. "Shake yer ass, Betty," he said, and Betty obliged, displaying a gap-toothed grin.

Todd chuckled. He shook his empty at the bartender, then looked at Jessie. "How's the beer?"

"Good enough."

"You need another?"

"Nope."

Todd shrugged and sipped from his fresh bottle. After a beat, he hopped one barstool closer to Jessie. "So, what's your story?"

Jessie shot him a cold look, her bottle lifted halfway to her lips. "I told you, I'm not in the mood for conversation."

Todd made a *hmph* sound in his chest, swiveled his body, and watched Betty dance. Jessie went back to sorting and stacking pieces, focusing on the Trace. She visualized a small group of hackers from around the country, working together to break into Chance's computer. Maybe they could tap into the video feed and uncover where her mom and Imani were being held hostage. They might also be able to scramble the GPS signals on the trackers the sisters wore on their ankles (Jessie's winking LED was red), effectively disguising their whereabouts.

The Trace was capable of wizardry, that much was certain, but the irregularities in its shape could not be ignored. It was clandestine, yes, but not impenetrable. Chance Kotter likely had no further use for it, but were his hackers still monitoring its hardware? Would they register a correspondence between Jessie and 9-$tar and inform Chance that she had enlisted outside help?

Jessie closed her eyes, trying to extinguish the image that had jumped into her mind: Burl making a call to the masked assailants in the dingy brick room. The visual faded, but Burl's voice persisted, black and echoey, as if coming through a drain: *One of these dumb bitches just broke the rules. You know what to do . . .*

Was there a medical professional on hand to remove the baby from Imani's womb, or would Chance's goons do it themselves?

A CLOCK ON THE BACK wall, emblazoned with the Budweiser logo, ticked over to 1:45. Jessie finished her beer and banged the empty down on the bar. She was emotionally exhausted and wondered if she might find a place to rest for a couple of hours—a doorway, perhaps, shielded from the wind, or the backseat of an unlocked vehicle.

"Thanks for the drink." Jessie didn't look at Todd. She slipped off the stool and started toward the restroom, which was in back, past the pool table and the booths.

Betty had stopped dancing and had slumped into a seat, her tube top rucked up, exposing her belly. The greenish lines of an old tattoo crept out from one of the folds. "They think they're too good for me," she slurred at Jessie, and gestured at the two guys playing pool. One of them took an aggressive shot and lifted the cue ball off the table. It bounced across the floor, and Betty went after it, her heels clattering.

Jessie found the restroom at the back of a narrow, L-shaped corridor. It was exactly what she'd expected, with its dripping faucets and cracked tile floor. One of the lights was out and the other flickered. The chemical smell was eye-watering. Jessie entered the only stall with a lock on the door and managed to pee without any part of her body touching the toilet. She used the tip of her boot to flush. She then stripped off her jacket and shirt and examined her ribs. They'd been taped on the left side, but the bruising reached all the way down to her hip. Jessie arched her back gingerly and twisted at the waist. The pain was dull and grinding, but she was moving more freely than she had been earlier in the week.

Maybe not broken, she thought. She reached into the back pocket of her jeans and took out a strip of twelve Advil, given to her by one of Chance's men. "Don't take 'em all at once," he'd whispered, and winked as if they shared some secret. Jessie punched two of the capsules out of their plastic beds and tossed them into her mouth.

Beer and painkillers. Some way to begin this shitshow.

SHE WONDERED WHAT HER SISTERS were doing. The man who'd given her the ibuprofen had hinted that their starting points were geographically closer to each other than to hers. Jessie didn't think Brea and Flo would charge wildly toward confrontation. They'd hang back—see if anything changed over the next twenty-four hours or so. On the heels of this thought came another. A memory, specifically, of her telling Chance that they'd sooner take their own lives than kill each other, and the big boss man flashing a confident smile in reply and pointing out that her two sisters didn't appear to share the same level of devotion.

Jessie put her shirt and jacket on and exited the stall. Chance's assessment wasn't wrong: the friction between Brea and Flo had been uncomfortable, to say the least. This didn't mean that they'd go at each other like stray dogs, but those tensions would only increase as the hours ticked by. Whatever retaliation Jessie mounted against Chance Kotter, she knew she didn't have much time.

"But rest first," she whispered, because everything hurt, not just her ribs. The kind of pain that ibuprofen couldn't touch. She crossed to the sinks, turned on the faucet, lifted her gaze to the mirror. Damn, she looked wretched. Tired. Weak. Empty. The .40-caliber goth was dead, and here was her ghost.

SHE OPENED THE RESTROOM DOOR and Todd was there, blocking the way out with his arm.

"You ain't in the mood for conversation," he said. One of his eyelids drooped and his lips were wet. "I hear that, but maybe you're in the mood for something else."

Jessie was so surprised that she took a step back. Her mind reeled for two seconds, and she clicked her tongue. Todd apparently viewed this as acquiescence. He stepped into the restroom, placed his palm on Jessie's upper chest, and eased her up against the wall.

"I'm just reading the signals," he said.

Any part of Jessie that might opt for a nonviolent resolution was out of commission. She was dynamite without a fuse. Todd—clearly bereft of any skill when it came to reading signals—edged closer, rolling his shoulders in a salacious way while exerting more pressure with his hand. This was as far as he got. With snakelike precision, Jessie jabbed her fingers into his eyes. This was one of the first self-defense techniques that Uncle Dog had taught her. It wasn't as damaging as a thumb poke, but it was quick and effective and could be used against opponents of all sizes. Todd reeled away from her, temporarily blinded, raising the hand that he'd placed on her chest up to his face. Jessie followed with a front kick to the sternum that sent Todd skating across the slick tile floor. He hit the wall and slumped to one knee.

With her opponent subdued (and taught a lesson), Jessie would ordinarily walk away. But she was in a dark place, susceptible to her emotions. She lunged forward and threw a right hook that connected with Todd's jaw. He went down with a thud. Blood leaked from his mouth. Jessie stomped on his hip bone and heard it crack.

"Motherfucker." She stomped on him again.

The music flooding from the bar was equally energetic. Nirvana's "Scentless Apprentice." Todd shrieked, but nobody heard him. Jessie grabbed the collar of his work shirt and dragged him across the tiles toward one of the stalls. He resisted as much as he could, swinging his arms and kicking one leg limply. It was all ineffectual. He looped his left hand around the bottom of the stall's pilaster as Jessie pulled him in. She kicked his fingers—more cracking sounds—then lifted the toilet seat, yanked him up by the hair, and slammed his face against the lip of the bowl. His blood splashed the porcelain, appearing dark in the flickering light. Jessie's anger bubbled over. She stepped back quickly, afraid that she might kill this man. The grief she felt for her sisters, for her mom and Imani, emerged in a tight, hissing scream. She turned and punched the mirror twice, cracking it in three places.

Todd groaned, his face in the toilet bowl, his body slumped across the stall floor.

"You picked the wrong night to fuck with me," Jessie said. She inhaled the pungent chemical smell, breathing deeply into her lungs. Several seconds passed, perhaps as long as a minute. The music switched up again. Something equally loud.

Jessie recognized the shape of a cell phone in the back pocket of Todd's jeans. She stepped into the stall, hooked it out, and brushed a trembling finger across the screen: 2:03. The night—the game—was four hours old, and she already had blood on her hands. There'd be more, of course. There *had* to be. Jessie vowed that next time it would belong to Chance Kotter.

She swiped up on the phone and got the lock screen.

"Passcode?" she said to Todd, and gave him a little kick in the ass.

"Hnggh . . ."

"The passcode? For your phone."

Todd mumbled something. He lifted his head, then lowered it again. Jessie heard his blood dribbling into the bowl.

"Use your fingers if you're having trouble speaking," Jessie said.

Nothing from Todd. Jessie kicked him in the ass again, harder this time. He whined, lifted his left hand off the tiles, and slowly erected his fingers. Three, then one, then one, then three.

"Thirty-one thirteen?"

A grunt, then a reluctant thumbs-up.

Jessie tapped in the code. It worked. Todd's phone had 83 percent battery life and 5G. She turned it off and slipped it into her pocket. Maybe a connection to the outside world was dangerous, given Chance's strict rules, but having the option made her feel less helpless.

SHE VACATED THE RESTROOM AND walked back through the bar, making eye contact with no one. There was a half-empty bottle of beer in front of Todd's barstool. Maybe, when he failed to return in five, ten minutes, someone would go looking for him. Or maybe not. Either way, Jessie didn't care.

She pushed open the door and stepped outside. Three custom-painted muscle cars rumbled in the parking lot. Chicano rap thumped from a bass-heavy sound system. Youngish men stood around the cars, vaping, drinking, smoking. One of them called out to Jessie—something in Spanish—and his amigos laughed. Jessie put her head down and kept walking.

She had no idea where she was going. Tiredness, grief, and anger swamped her. Within twenty minutes, she found herself back at the railroad crossing she'd sat beside earlier, listening to the bell clang, watching the boxcars rattle their way out of town. Eventually, she moved on. Instead of crossing the tracks she followed them, heading north into the city, the soles of her boots coming down on every other crosstie.

The clock on Todd's phone read 2:52. Jessie passed a junkyard and a substation and a run-down motel. The thought of a bed—even a lousy motel bed—filled her with longing. She considered breaking into one of the rooms, then spotted a small maintenance shed up ahead, beside the tracks. Jessie walked to it. She took Todd's cell phone from her pocket and shone the flashlight through the only window. There were tools on racks—sledgehammers, pickaxes, ballast forks—and light kits lined up along the floor. Jessie also spied a caddy filled with high-visibility vests.

"That'll work," she said. There was a padlock on the door, but she dealt with this with a hefty rock and a well-placed blow. Once inside, she upended the caddy and laid the vests on the floor. Jessie crawled on top of them and put her head down.

**DESPITE HER EXHAUSTION, IT TOOK** Jessie some time to fall asleep, and even when she did, it was light and troubled. She was woken twice—first by a train (she thought the entire shed was going to leave its foundations), and again when Todd's phone rang. Jessie rejected the call and put the device into Do Not Disturb mode. She wondered if Todd was still lying on the restroom floor with his face in the toilet bowl. Eventually, he would be alert enough to contact his provider and have it block the SIM, but for now his phone was working.

Motivated by this, Jessie propped herself on one elbow, accessed the internet, and downloaded Tor—the only browser that worked with the Trace. She typed in the URL and cleared the various security protocols. There was nothing new and the landing page looked the same. Maybe the Trace *didn't* know it'd been hacked. Jessie had two new DMs, both from 9-$tar. The first, sent last Monday at 10:01 P.M. CT, read, **72-HR EXCLUSIVE WINDOW CLOSED**. The second, sent a few hours later, on Tuesday morning, read, **Status?**

Jessie stared at this second DM for a long time, thinking of various responses. "Broken" summed up her status pretty well, she thought. As did "Finished," "Helpless," and "Dead woman walking." After a long moment—long enough for morning light to paint the murky window—she typed the word **FAIL** into the message window but hesitated before hitting the send button. That terrible image had dropped into her mind again, of Burl making the call to the masked assailants holding her mom and Imani hostage . . .

Jessie closed her eyes, clenched her jaw, then clicked the send button anyway, because doing nothing, being Chance Kotter's plaything, was destroying her. Besides, it was a single word, a response, and couldn't be construed as breaking the rules. In short, she had not enlisted outside help.

Not yet.

**JESSIE LOGGED OUT OF THE** Trace, then checked various Los Angeles news sites for any mention of Aubree Vernier or Imani Bella. She found nothing. Clearly, the two women hadn't been missing long enough to be newsworthy. From this, Jessie surmised that they were probably being held close to home.

Daylight gradually filled the shed. Jessie stood up and stretched. Her stomach panged and her mouth was dry. She stepped outside just as another train thundered along the Waynesboro-Conecuh Southern Line, lifting grit and trash and dust. Jessie shielded her eyes and walked on.

# SEVENTEEN

Saturday morning broke with birdsong in some areas and traffic noise in others. The rising sun edged across the city, creating as many shadows as bright spaces. It set a gentle orange light on the Mary, and for ten minutes, give or take, the river looked pretty enough to put on a postcard. A westerly breeze accentuated a variety of aromas, depending on the neighborhood. Honeysuckle, baking bread, chicken manure, and sewage were most redolent. For every sweet thing in Reedsville, there was a flip side.

Seven A.M. signaled a shift change at the Lower West Precinct. Outgoing officers filed their paperwork and returned gratefully to their homes and families. It had been a busy night, with, among other incidents, two drug-related homicides, eleven domestic disputes, four armed robberies, and thirteen assaults. On the other side of the tracks, the police headquarters on Franklin had responded to a break-in, a car theft, three DUIs, and a drunk and disorderly at Fourth and Inches. Officers coming off *that* shift did so in a notably less traumatized state of mind.

THE WREN GOT OUT OF bed at 7:11 and ate half an apple for breakfast, then spent an hour working on his haiku. Descriptions of birds and elevation were not enough. His next victim demanded more majestic adjectives. He wrote down words like "ethereal" and "exospheric" but immediately scribbled them out. The line between majestic and pretentious was thin, but he would find it. The wren worked until his brain creaked in a way that made him feel low, then curled up on his barrel chair—his nest—and wept for a while.

BURL ROWAN BEGAN HIS DAY like he always did, by rolling over and kissing his sleeping wife's shoulder. Caroline worked from home, a ghostwriter and night owl who did most of her work between midnight and four A.M. and often slept until late morning. As such, it was Burl who woke first and kick-started the household, which on weekdays entailed waking his daughters, making them breakfast, and getting them out the door and on the school bus, and on weekends meant frying up some bacon and building a whole stack of pancakes. The smells would invariably wake Megan, thirteen, and Joanne, eight, and the three of them would sit at the kitchen table and devour. But no matter the day or the duties involved, nothing started until Burl had rolled over in bed and kissed his sleeping wife's shoulder.

He did so now. Caroline didn't stir or whimper. She slept like a stone, which was just as well, because Burl's phone chirped on the nightstand, sounding especially loud in the Saturday morning stillness.

A message from Chance: Need help.

Burl read it sleepily, half yawning. Still holding the phone, he got out of bed and shuffled to the en suite. He emptied his bladder, washed his hands, pulled on a pair of track pants, and replied to Chance's message as he walked to the kitchen.

What's the problem boss?

Burl started a pot of coffee and put a skillet on the stove. Joanne—awake before the breakfast smells reached her nostrils—came into the kitchen with her bare feet slapping and her hair adorably mussed.

"Good morning, sweet thing."

"Good morning, Daddy."

"You're up early."

"Thirsty."

She grabbed a carton of chocolate milk from the refrigerator and poured herself a tall glass, then drank directly from the spout.

"Hey," Burl said, one eyebrow raised, pointing at her with a spatula. "Not from the carton, sugar. You know that."

Joanne lowered the carton, displaying a cheeky smile and chocolate mustache. "There ain't but a dribble left. I was just finishing it."

"Well, I guess that's all right," Burl said, thinking he would have done the same. "You ready for pancakes?"

"Yummy!"

Burl's phone chirped again.

**This dang computer. I can't get shit running on it.**

"And by the way," Burl said, looking from his phone to his daughter. "Where's my hug?"

Joanne smiled, set her glass down, and stepped into Burl's open arms. She gave him a good squeeze, too, but pulled back in a hurry.

"Oh, Daddy. Your chest. I forgot."

"Don't you worry about that." The bruise on Burl's chest was as wide and round as the skillet on the stove. It had yellowed at the edges in the five days since Brea—that fierce bitch—had shot him, but he could live with an ugly contusion for a week or two. Besides, his injuries would have been considerably more serious if he hadn't been wearing a ballistic vest. "Ain't nothing better than a hug from my little girl, so you squeeze away."

Joanne did, and yes, Burl winced with the discomfort of it, but his heart flooded with joy nevertheless. He kissed the top of her head and set her loose.

Burl told his family that he'd been kicked by General Custer, Chance's horse (and a properly vindictive bastard)—one of thousands of lies he'd told over the passage of time. They knew that he was Chance Kotter's head of security but not exactly what the job necessitated.

"I take care of Mr. Kotter's assets," Burl had explained vaguely. "He's a successful businessman. A lot of people want a piece of him, and they'll take it by any means. It's my job to make sure they don't succeed."

He'd said nothing about the blood he'd spilled, the bones he'd broken, and the bodies he'd disposed of (Burl had his own key to Ernie Pink's crematorium). Caroline and the kids were fully in the dark, and Burl intended to keep it that way.

They had enough to think about, after all. Joanne had recently been diagnosed with generalized anxiety disorder, which came with an abundance of demands, including financial. Burl's medical insurance was good, but it covered only one psychotherapy session per month (currently used by Burl), and this didn't come close to the extra support Joanne needed. Also, his copay on the brand-name SSRIs, to which Joanne had fewer troubling side effects, was 80 percent. This alone meant their monthly expenses had increased by hundreds of dollars.

Compounding their fiscal concerns, Caroline's income had taken a hit in recent months, as many potential clients had turned to ChatGPT for their creative writing needs. Combined with the higher cost of living, it was all looking increasingly bleak. Perhaps the bleakest they'd known. Caroline had suggested remortgaging or maybe off-loading one of the cars. Burl assured her he'd think of something.

He got the griddle hot, added a tablespoon of oil, then messaged Chance: Give me 5. I'll call.

I am so fucking close to throwing this fucking computer out the fucking window.

Roger that. Hang tight boss.

AT HIS IMMODEST ABODE ON the outskirts of Reedsville, Chance Kotter slammed his phone down and swept a meaty hand across the top of his desk, knocking the laptop and the framed photograph of his dear sister to the floor.

"Sweet Christ," he said, standing up quickly. He retrieved the photograph first, relieved to see the glass wasn't cracked. "I'm so sorry, Bethany."

He kissed his sister on the lips and set her back on the desk, angling the frame so that the morning light caught her lovely face. He then picked up the computer, gave it a quick once-over, and returned it to its original position. The screen was black. He jabbed a couple of random keys. Nothing.

"Fuck you, Mr. Computer."

Chance's morning had started delightfully, with an hour-long horse ride through Aldrich Woods. Afterward, he enjoyed a generous serving of eggs Benedict, southern style, and a glass of Chandon Brut just because. He'd barely wet his lips when Tucker Presley called. Tucker was Chance's longtime friend and an unbridled spender. He and a few of the boys were coming over later to drink high-rye bourbon, shoot some pool, and watch the "game" unfold. Tucker, like Chance, had placed fifty big ones on the blonde.

"How's my gal doing, Kott?" Tucker had drawled over the line.

"I'm about to check in," Chance had replied truthfully. "But she's still in the game. They all are. I'd have heard otherwise."

He would have. He'd had a team out all night, keeping an eye on the sisters, with instructions to notify him if anything significant happened, even if that meant waking him up. The fact that he'd risen from his bed at 6:30 A.M., the same as always, told him that the night had been uneventful.

Chance chatted with Tucker a while longer, then finished his breakfast and crossed the house to his study. A message came in as he walked. It was from Carson, informing him that the little one, Jessie, had slept a few hours in a maintenance shed near the Happy Cat Motel but was on the move again now.

Good to know, Chance texted back, and added a thumbs-up emoji for emphasis. He was feeling particularly chipper and smart.

The feeling didn't last. In his study, he powered up his computer, intending to access the GPS app that Burl had installed and see for himself where the sisters' colorful little blips were on the map. There followed five infuriating minutes where he and his computer developed a hateful attitude toward each other, and that was when he sent that first text message to Burl.

Now, he stood looking out his study window, pulling snarly breaths into his chest, waiting for Burl to call. Five minutes, he'd said. It had been closer to fifteen. Chance was about to send another message when his phone lit up and the ringtone sounded: the theme tune from *The Dukes of Hazzard*.

Burl said, "Sorry, boss. A hundred things going on here. What do you need?"

"What I *need* is for this goddamn hunk-of-shit computer to do what I want it to do."

"Which is what, exactly?"

"I'm trying to get into that fancy GPS program you installed."

"Okay, I can talk you through that." And Burl no doubt would have, but he soon realized that the Track-U-Gen app wasn't working because Chance had inadvertently locked himself out of it.

"I guess that's what happens when you thump the shit out of the keyboard," Chance said. He felt a little foolish, truth be told.

"Listen," Burl said. "I need to shower, get dressed, but I'll be there in an hour. I'll get everything up and running. Get some live video up, too."

"Good," Chance said. "Because I got the boys coming over."

"Yessir, I know. In the meantime . . ." Burl took a minute to access Track-U-Gen on his phone and give Chance a real-time update: "The red blip—that's Jessie—is in Lower West, heading north on Refinery Road. She's covered some miles already. The green blip—Brea—has crossed Main. She's in Colonel Park, not far from the mall. Flo spent the night in Waterloo Square but has moved north. She's on Franklin now, just outside Bunny Digg's Auto."

Chance declared Burl a godsend and ended the call. He sagged in his seat, suddenly aware of just how rapidly his ticker was ticking. This was his most ambitious scheme to date, with so many moving parts and considerable amounts of trust placed in other people. But for everything that could go wrong, Chance was impressed by how much had gone *right*. He'd lost a couple of good soldiers, sure, and Howie Chisolm's man grapes had been blown to kingdom come, but all things considered . . .

"Everything's going to plan."

Chance linked his hands across his belly and grinned. The good Lord was rooting for Team Kotter. This he believed. Chance further believed that, by the end of the day, one of these sisters would have her blood spilled.

In this, at least, he was correct.

BURL HAD REVEALED THAT THE green blip was in Colonel Park, a neighborhood in the southeast of the city, home to the Reedsville Roosters baseball team, a sixteen-screen cineplex, and the Colonel Park Mall. If Burl had zoomed in any closer, he'd have seen that the blip was signaling from Chip & Chick's Homestyle, where Brea was enjoying a hearty breakfast.

"What's that on your ankle, Blondie?" an old fella sitting at the bar asked, swiveling on his stool to get a good look-see under her table. "You some kinda prisoner?"

"Yup, I killed a man who asked too many questions," Brea replied, affecting a southern twang. She tipped the man a wink. His hazy blue eyes flared, and he went back to his grits.

She was awake, alert, and feeling strong—no small wonder, all things considered. It helped that she'd had a reasonable night's sleep. Brea had walked through several parking lots in Lower West and had tried more than a hundred vehicles until she finally found one that was unlocked: a Sable from the aughts with rusted rocker panels and a backseat covered in dog hair. Brea crawled in, closed the door, and succumbed to her exhaustion. She was woken six hours later by the owner and her dog, both fearless. "Get *out*, motherfucker. Get the fuck out *now*!" Brea had edged from the Sable, blinking sleep from her eyes, raising her hands to show that she meant no harm. "That's right, motherfucker. Walk the fuck away. And don't you come round here no more." The woman's chest was puffed starling-like, and her dog ran back and forth at the end of its leash. Brea nodded and backed away. The woman's voice followed her across the parking lot.

And so began Saturday morning—8:07, as indicated by the glaring blue digits at the top of the Kotter-Bryce Tower, which Brea saw as she hopped seven feet of chain-link and crossed the railroad tracks. She kept her eye out for her sisters, Flo in particular, who she suspected would come at her like a bullet.

Brea was in Colonel Park thirty minutes later. She was rested, but her belly grumbled. An A-board outside Chip & Chick's Homestyle announced breakfast specials. Without a penny in her pocket, Brea went inside and ordered coffee, toast, biscuits and gravy, a three-egg omelet, and a fat wedge of apple pie. Everything was delicious, and she left not a scrap.

"Good Lord above," her server said, all lipstick and eyelashes, collecting Brea's empty plates. "Where'd you put all that food, hon?"

"I was hungry."

"I'd say! Can I get you anything else?"

"You can refresh my coffee and bring me the check."

"That I will."

The server stacked the last empty plate and wobbled away. Brea watched her go, sitting back in her seat with one hand on her satisfied belly. The old fella at the bar glanced sidelong at her, then faced forward when she curled her busted lip at him. She drank the cool dregs of her coffee and thought about Jessie and Flo. Had they found each other yet? Was Jessie lying dead in some garbage-strewn back alley? Unlikely, Brea thought. Both sisters would have laid low for the night, recouping their energy for the punishing day ahead. Brea looked at her feet beneath the table, at the green light winking on the device around her ankle, and knew one thing for certain: that her plan—the thing she didn't want to do but *had* to do—was the only way forward. The first step was to find Flo before she found Jessie.

The server returned with a carafe of steaming coffee and Brea's check. She poured the coffee, scooped more creamers from a pocket in her apron, and placed them and the check holder in front of Brea. "Take your time, hon," she said with a grandmotherly smile. Brea splashed cream into her coffee and assessed the bill: $48.60. There was a pen in the holder and a clear pocket in which to place her credit card. Brea picked up the pen, added a fifty-dollar tip, and wrote across the bottom of the check:

CHARGE TO CHANCE KOTTER
THE BIGGEST SWINGIN' DICK IN REEDSVILLE

Pleasures were in short supply, but a tiny smile touched Brea's lips. She closed the holder, finished her coffee, and left the restaurant. The old fella forked his grits silently and didn't dare look at her.

JESSIE PULLED A SIMILAR, IF less audacious, trick. She ordered a breakfast bagel and a large coffee from Pick-Me-Up Deli and walked out without paying. The boy-sized deli clerk followed her out to the street. "You gotta pay for those items," he called after her, not wanting to drift too far from his post.

"Take it up with Chance Kotter," Jessie called back, and tore a delicious, greasy chunk out of her bagel.

She had followed the railroad tracks into Lower West, where stores and businesses rolled open their shutters for another day of commerce, and the streets began to populate. She kept her eyes peeled for either of her sisters, now actively seeking them out—not to fight them, but to stop them from fighting each other. *Give me until seven P.M. Sunday*, Jessie wanted to pitch to them. *That's three hours before the deadline. If I haven't put a plan into action by then, we'll meet in the middle of the high school football field and see what happens.* If it came to that—an unavoidable kill-or-be-killed situation—Jessie would throw the fight. Chance had warned them against suicide, but there was more than one way to sacrifice herself.

Hot coffee slopped out the lid of the paper mug, scalding Jessie's hand. She swore, then crossed the street and climbed the steps of the Lower West Hispanic Church of the Nazarene. They were steep and many, clearly designed for a more determined class of worshipper. Jessie sat near the top, a good spot to eat her sinfully appropriated breakfast and survey the gathering traffic for Brea and Flo. Plenty of people looked at *her*—the goth chick who could at any moment be blasted by lightning—and some were Chance's men. She recognized Carson and Tay, who cruised past in a black pickup truck with old country blaring from the speakers. Carson snapped a photo of her on his cell phone, and Jessie struck a pose with her middle finger raised.

She finished her bagel and coffee, disposed of the trash, then descended the church steps and found a quiet side street where she could avoid being spied on. Todd's phone was still working. Jessie ducked into a doorway and logged in to the Trace. There was another DM from 9-$tar, replying to the one-word message—FAIL—that she'd sent from the maintenance shed.

**What happened?**

Jessie's heartbeat quickened. A response. Two words to her one. But it meant that she was now, inarguably, in active communication with someone on the outside. This could be a promising development or extremely bad, depending on whether Chance Kotter's hackers were watching the Trace. Either way, she was going to reply. It was a thin, dangerous hope, but it was all she had.

She typed, **IT WAS A SETUP**, in emphatic caps, deliberated for at least thirty seconds, then tapped the send button. A ripple of nervous energy shortened her breath. Perhaps 9-$tar was online and would respond immediately. Or maybe someone else was monitoring the DMs and was already making the call to the big bad boss.

Jessie focused on her breathing, unable to tear her gaze from the screen. Five minutes passed. No response. Ten minutes. Nothing. She turned off the phone, slipped it into her back pocket, and edged out of the doorway. For one terrible second, she expected a black SUV to come speeding down the side street and screech to a halt in front of her—for the doors to open and Chance's army to roll out. *You just put a bullet in your mama's head*, Burl would say. *Your turn next.*

This image was so vivid that Jessie retreated into the doorway and pressed herself against the wall. She counted to sixty, breathed deeply, then emerged. There was nothing in the street except for a few parked cars and some blowing trash. Jessie walked east and came out on Independence Boulevard. It was lively and loud.

Carson and Tay drove past moments later. They didn't slow down, only sneered at her through the open window. Farther north, a narrow-faced dude with a scar across his throat approached her. He pointed at his watch and grinned.

"Ticktock, little bunny," he said. "It's ten A.M. Thirty-six hours remaining."

When Jessie checked Todd's phone twenty minutes later—ducking down another side street to do so—she was greeted with a "SIM blocked" message. Todd had picked himself up off the restroom floor and notified his provider.

Jessie gritted her teeth. She'd need to steal another phone to continue her communication with the Trace. For now, she threw Todd's into a garbage can and continued looking for her sisters.

FLO HAD SLEPT FOR SIX hours in the back doorway of an art gallery north of Waterloo Square, on a cold concrete step too small for her to stretch out on. She was fine with this. Minimalism was the cornerstone of her kung fu training. Grandmaster Yao-Chang Kwan had taught her that simplicity purified the body and mind, and in purity there was strength. For five years, Flo's bed had been nothing but a thin bamboo mat. She had eaten basic, tasteless nutrition—often went days without eating anything at all—and drank only water. Six hours in a doorway, mostly sheltered from the wind, was not such a hardship.

She woke with a headache, as she had for the past five mornings—a little post-concussive bonus, courtesy of the golf club she'd been cold-cocked with. Flo used her fingers to inspect the bump on the back of her skull. It was knuckle-sized, as opposed to egg-sized, and the laceration was dry and tight. Healing, no doubt, but still tender. She popped a couple of the Advil Chance's guys had given her, then removed the santoku knife from inside her jacket, placed it on the step, and stretched out the cricks in her body.

A few hours' sleep hadn't altered Flo's mindset nor presented a preferred course of action. As she stretched and breathed, a rudimentary plan formed: first, a disguise. Different clothes, headwear, and sunglasses. She needed to blend in with the environment. Next, locate a public hub—Waterloo Square, perhaps, or the intersection of Harper and Main. It might take all day, but eventually Brea or Jessie would pass through. Flo would sneak up behind them, knife in hand. Several quick thrusts between the ribs would do it.

Then repeat.

It sounded simple, and in practice it *was*, but Flo was working against a soulful and emotional headwind. She tried telling herself this was just another Bang-Bang Sisters job—a solo gig—and the reward was the biggest she had ever known. But her heart wouldn't be fooled.

She stretched. She breathed. She imagined Imani's baby nestled securely in her arms, looking up at her with huge brown eyes. "Leon," she said. If Imani had a boy, she would call him Leon. A girl: Esther Grace, after their mother.

Flo picked up the knife, secured it inside her jacket, and moved on. She headed north out of Waterloo Square into a neighborhood of prettily painted houses and double-wide driveways. This was Pine Vista, positively bougie compared with the ash-colored slums west of Main. One of the houses was not so appealing, though. It was dark and cold, with a FOR SALE sign posted on the lawn and bundles of dead flowers on the front steps. Susan Orringer had lived there once. It was her haven, her supposed safe place. Flo walked past with heavy steps. Via the Trace, she had seen crime-scene photos of Susan's bloodstained corpse on her bedroom floor, surrounded by feathers—a reminder, amid the rest of this awfulness, that the wren was still out there.

She got lucky on the next street (if anything could be construed as luck). There was an electrician's van reverse-parked in the driveway of a tidy brick bungalow. No sign of the driver. As Flo walked past it, she spied a Crimson Tide ball cap on the dash. She edged toward the passenger-side door, peered in, and saw a matching red hoodie on the passenger seat. Flo didn't think twice. Working swiftly, she removed her jacket—the knife now tucked inside her belt—and switched it for the hoodie, then whipped the ball cap off the dash and slapped it on her head.

Better. Less conspicuous. Brea and Jessie would have to get close to make sure it was her. Of course, they might be armed—they probably *were*—but Flo would deal with that if she had to.

She continued north through Pine Vista and emerged on Franklin Boulevard. Here, she headed west, looking along both sides of the street, occasionally turning to glance behind her.

A partial disguise was one thing, but she couldn't stop the tracker from revealing her location. Flo drank from a water fountain in a children's playground, then sat on a swing collecting her thoughts. She'd just knuckled the first tear from her eye when a silver GMC Yukon pulled up beyond the chain-link fence. Burl, alone, was behind the wheel. He buzzed down the passenger-side window and called out to her. She ignored him. He called again with more urgency. This time Flo sighed, slipped off the swing, and exited the playground. She approached the SUV's open window cautiously.

"Here," Burl said, and handed her something warm and foil-wrapped from a paper bag on the passenger seat. He pressed a finger to his lips. "Shh."

Flo flashed back to the room she'd been confined in, when Burl had brought her steak and eggs with a glass of milk. He'd made the same *shh* gesture then.

"It's from Bo Peep's," Burl added, stealing a glance in the rearview, as if to make sure *he* wasn't being watched. "Best breakfast joint in town."

Flo wanted to throw the offering back at him—fuck this guy and fuck Bo Peep, too—but she smelled bacon and her stomach boomed. She cracked open the foil and saw a sandwich loaded with everything.

"I didn't know food was included with your murderous game." Flo gave Burl a bitter look but kept hold of the sandwich.

"It's not," Burl said. "But your friends have proved quite resourceful. Shit, Brea just ate a fifty-dollar breakfast at Chip & Chick's. She's fully recharged and ready to rumble. I'm just trying to keep everything fair."

Flo pressed her lips together. She noticed Burl had referred to Brea and Jessie as friends, not sisters—a subtle but deliberate attempt to draw a line between her and them. In fairness, Flo had drawn that same line herself. She *had* to. How else could she do what needed to be done?

"Speaking of Brea . . ." Burl removed his cell phone from a clamp attached to the dash, tapped the screen a couple of times, then turned it toward Flo. It showed a zoomed-in view of a city map with a green dot flashing in the middle. "She is currently on Water Street, moving north toward Harper."

Flo shook her head, looking from the screen to Burl, then back again. A weight settled on her chest and the next few breaths were hard. The green dot moved incrementally as she watched.

"If you continue on Franklin," Burl said, motioning west with a manly thrust of the chin, "then take a left on Main, you'll be at Harper in twenty-five minutes. Fifteen if you pick up your heels."

"Why—"

"*Why?* You want to find her, don't you? You want to increase your chances of winning this and going home to your sister. Your *real* sister."

"That's not what I mean." Flo shook her head again. She searched Burl's eyes carefully. "Why are you telling me this?"

Burl flicked his phone off and placed it back in the clamp. "I'm not *helping* you, if that's what you think. A few of Mr. Kotter's big-spender friends arrived this morning, and they're keen to see some action."

"Right," Flo said. "Blood for the emperors."

"Something like that." Burl glanced in the rearview again, then nudged the shifter into drive and pulled away. Flo swayed on the sidewalk. It was still hard to breathe.

Moving slowly, almost *dreamily*, Flo reentered the playground, went back to the swing, and sat down. She had no appetite for the sandwich but ate it anyway. She needed the protein. The fuel. Brea had eaten a fifty-dollar breakfast, after all, and was ready to rumble.

*She is currently on Water Street, moving north toward Harper.*

"Okay," Flo said. Her wet eyes flashed beneath the brim of her newly acquired ball cap. She dabbed them with her palms and got to her feet. Her heart galloped.

She ran all the way to Main Street, then forced herself to walk. Brea was strong. *Savagely* strong. Flo wanted this to be over in a blink, a quick and decisive attack from behind, but she'd need all her energy if it turned into a war.

# EIGHTEEN

There'd been an unspoken alpha-female rivalry between Brea and Flo for as long as they'd known each other. It wasn't caustic or obvious. It existed beneath the surface and very occasionally announced itself, usually when sparring. There was extra spite in their blows when they went head-to-head in the ring, as opposed to when they faced Jessie. Each had hurt the other numerous times, even though they wore headgear and seven-ounce gloves, but they always hugged it out afterward.

"I'm glad we're on the same side," Flo had said once, after a particularly attrite ten-round session. She had a cold pack pressed to a swelling beneath her eye, while Brea nursed a bleeding nose.

"I hear that," Brea had agreed, and smiled. She had blood on her teeth, too. "If the gloves ever come off, neither one of us is getting out alive."

FLO FOUND BREA LATER THAT morning, almost an hour after Burl had shown her the flashing green blip on his phone. She had walked up and down Harper Avenue, scouting both sides of the street, aware that Brea might have acquired a disguise of her own—if only a beanie to conceal that distinctive mop of blond hair. Flo looked twice at everyone. Eventually, she veered off Harper and spotted Brea moments later, walking through a small park west of Waterloo Square.

Flo's breath caught in her throat. She froze in her tracks, listening to the thrash-rock soundtrack of her heartbeat. Again, she tried convincing herself that this was just another hit, another contract. She watched Brea exit the park and head east. Flo checked the knife in her belt and started to follow.

She maintained a prudent distance, staying on the other side of the street. Brea turned around every now and then—walking backward, surveying her six—but didn't pay particular attention to the person in the red hoodie and baseball cap. Conversely, Brea had made no attempt to camouflage her appearance. Black jacket, black jeans. She'd tied her hair into a ponytail, but that was all. In true Brea style, she wasn't hiding from anyone.

Even so, Flo lost sight of her more than once—at busy intersections, mainly—but it never took long to find her again. She closed the distance incrementally as Brea headed east toward the Mary River, waiting for the right time to strike.

BREA FELT AN ODD GRAVITY in her chest and knew she was being followed. Nothing new about that; Chance's dipshit goons had been keeping tabs on her since the game began. This felt *different*, though.

She looked left and right, then turned around and took everything in. Nobody stood out, but there were a lot of people. Brea resumed her random course, breathing meditatively through her nose. She turned a corner and considered scrambling beneath a parked car, studying the feet of everybody who passed by, knowing she'd soon see an ankle cuffed with a GPS tracker. She could then crawl out from behind and turn the tables. For now, she kept walking. Adrenaline amped her senses and painted a wild expression on her face.

A CITY BUS CAME TO a puffing, rumbling halt directly in front of Flo, breaking her sight line. She hastened around its front end and almost got hit by a Durango with six-foot steer horns mounted to its hood. The driver jumped on the brake and swore. Flo raised one hand apologetically, then lowered her head and dashed to the opposite sidewalk. She kept her head down as she walked, knowing that she'd drawn some attention, glancing up in time to see Brea turn left at the next block. Flo followed. This was not a busy part of town. There was an indoor market, a Starbucks, a

Walgreens, but most of the stores were of the boutique variety. This meant fewer pedestrians, which made it harder for Flo to blend in. She would have to make her move soon.

The left turn—the dubiously named Robert E. Lee Avenue—led downhill to the waterfront. The landscape was notably different here. A promenade paralleled the river, with a parking lot on one side and a strip of woodland on the other. Flo watched as Brea walked across the parking lot and started south along the promenade. The Wishbone Bridge spanned the river two hundred yards away, its distinctive steelwork glinting in the sunlight.

Flo quickened her pace. With so few pedestrians, she couldn't risk attacking Brea from behind. Brea would hear her footfalls, her breaths, giving her time to react. Flo's best move was to get into tree cover, run ahead of Brea, then position herself behind the broad trunk of a maple and strike from the side.

"Just another job," Flo whispered, beginning to hate these three words almost as much as she hated the situation. Maybe one day she could make peace with herself for what she was about to do, but that was a distant future. There'd be a lot of regret, self-reproach, and therapy before then. Flo focused her mind and pushed forward. She zigzagged through the parking lot, crossed the promenade, and ducked between the trees.

Her camouflage wouldn't work here. Black was better. Flo stripped off the bright red hoodie and ball cap, pulled the santoku knife from her belt, and started to run. The river rolled to her left, the promenade to her right. She flitted silently from one shadow to the next, catching up to Brea.

She imagined Chance Kotter and company huddled around a computer screen, slapping one another's backs and guffawing as the distance between the blue and green blips decreased.

BREA HAD SEEN THE SAME person in a red hoodie and ball cap four out of the ten times she'd turned around, over a thirty-minute period, through multiple streets, most notably when that person nearly got smoked by a truck crossing Crawford Avenue and again when running across the riverside parking lot. The person was too far away to make out any detail.

She had her hood up, the ball cap's visor covered most of her face, and her hands were in her pockets, but Brea recognized her broad shoulders, the set of her hips, and the athletic way she moved.

Flo.

Brea eyed the trees and brush to her left, seeing an opportunity. She knew how Flo thought, and how she *fought*. Flo was quick but not necessarily soft-footed. She would want to deaden her approach, attack from the tree line. Smart, stealthy, but Brea would be one step ahead.

She glanced over her shoulder. There were several people on the promenade, but Flo, in her red hoodie and baseball cap, was not one of them. Either she'd had a change of heart and turned back, or she was already in the narrow stretch of woodland, running to catch up.

Brea stepped off the promenade and darted into the woods, weaving through the foliage until she found a tree broad enough to hide behind—an elm with high swaying branches and thick roots she could springboard off. She breathed through her nose and waited, attentive to every sound. The floor was all mulched leaves and needles. Very soft, very quiet. Brea wouldn't hear Flo until she was within striking distance.

Crows called back and forth. Brea wondered if Chance's men were communicating similarly, watching the colored blips on their cell phones, moving in to catch some of the action. Brea forced the thought away. It was a distraction. Her adrenaline climbed. She blended with the trees and listened for Flo's approach.

Seconds later . . . short, gasping breaths, the rustle of foliage, the softened thud of footfalls. This was it. Brea stared straight ahead, expanding her peripheral vision. Her body and mind came together and thrummed. Flo passed on the left, moving deftly. She had removed the bright hoodie and cap—an anti-camouflage in the woods—but this didn't throw Brea off. She was wired for action.

She exploded from behind the elm tree, digging the soles of her boots between its roots and pushing off hard. A distance of twenty feet separated her from Flo, and she closed that in seconds. She wanted to strike before Flo realized what was happening and had a chance to defend herself, but Flo had preternatural awareness and reactionary skill. She also had a knife in her right hand.

Flo came to a sliding stop, dragging up a cloud of dirt. She turned simultaneously, raising the knife, but Brea was already on top of her. She landed a kick to Flo's right forearm. The knife remained in her hand, but her grip weakened. She blocked Brea's next strike—a straight right—and countered, bringing the knife down in a loose arc. Brea anticipated the attack. She sidestepped, threw an elbow to Flo's chest that sent her staggering back, and followed with a side kick. Flo swiveled just in time, absorbing the blow with her upper left arm and stumbling backward. She tripped over a lacework of roots and fell. Her head thumped off the base of a pine. Her eyes fluttered, and the knife spilled out of her hand.

Brea pounced. Flo made a grab for the knife, but that knock to the head had momentarily scrambled her circuits. Brea kicked her hand away, then stooped and retrieved the knife. She twirled it between her fingers—the seven-inch blade flashing in the light—as Flo used the support of the pine to regain her feet.

"A knife?" Brea looked at her sister—her *former* sister—and shook her head. "Really, Flo, I'm disappointed in you."

Flo touched the back of her head and her fingers came away bloody. Brea smiled. She flipped the knife, caught it by the blade, and threw it between the trees to her left. It went end over end and stuck dead center in the trunk of the elm she'd hidden behind.

Brea unzipped her jacket and let it fall to the ground, exposing her tight black tank top and the angry ink across her upper body. Flo circled to her left, wiping her bloody fingers across the front of her black T-shirt. Her eyes were clearer now. Brea's smile lengthened. She rolled her shoulders and curled her hands into fists.

"Let's settle this like women," she said.

THEY CAME TOGETHER HARD, PUNCHING, parrying, kicking, blocking—two sparks on an updraft of misery and anger. Neither wanted to kill the other, but neither was prepared to lie down and die.

Brea slipped a high kick and saw an opening: the inside of Flo's supporting leg. She lowered her stance and drove her right fist forward. Flo's knee buckled, and Brea followed with a front kick that found the middle of her chest and dropped her. Flo rolled as she hit the ground, using the momentum to pop up to her haunches. Brea pressed her advantage—a middle roundhouse kick, pivoting on her support foot, generating incredible power. Flo threw up a turtle block. Her left arm absorbed most of the damage, but the kick was still vicious enough to drop her again.

Brea swept forward. Her face was empty—beaten and bruised from recent abuses, but otherwise stony. Flo had never seen her from this perspective. This was the face their adversaries saw in the moments before they were put down. It was terrifying.

She rolled to her left as Brea aimed a knee drop at her midsection, which would have hit like a 130-pound hammer and drained most—if not all—of the fight out of her. Gasping, scrambling to her feet, she grabbed a handful of needles, twigs, and dirt and threw it in Brea's direction. Brea instinctively flinched. Flo took her chance.

Two strikes, both hard, both on target: a spinning elbow to the face, followed by a front thrust kick—a move Yao-Chang Kwan had called "White Horse Presents Hoof." Brea retreated, ducking behind her guard. She used her footwork to create distance as Flo edged forward. The two women circled each other, moving between the trees. Flo limped slightly from the punch she'd taken to her left leg. Brea's mouth and nose were bleeding.

It was only then, circling warily, attuned to every movement, that they noticed they were being watched. Not just watched—*filmed*. Two of Chance's lackeys stood nearby, catching the action on their cell phones from different angles.

Flo wiped sweat from her throat. Her eyes flicked to the men, then back to Brea. Adrenaline had tightened her vocal cords. With some effort, she said, "It doesn't matter who walks away from this. Chance Kotter is the only winner here."

Brea spat blood. "You think I don't know that?"

Flo shook her head. She was too amped to cry, but she wanted to. "I hoped it wouldn't come to this. I racked my brain trying to think of another way."

"Me, too."

"Just know that I'm doing this for my sister."

Only loud enough for Flo to hear, Brea spoke the same two words: "Me, too."

They took a step toward each other, feinted, then backed off. One of Chance's goons chuckled and shot a snot rocket from his nose.

"It's *your* fault we're here," Flo moaned. It was a spiteful thing to say, but she couldn't help herself. "We were nearly home. We were three hundred fucking miles away, but you wanted to turn back and go after the wren. This is on *you*, Brea. This whole fucking mess."

"Keep believing that, Flo, if it makes you feel better," Brea said. "Truth is, we're only in this shitstorm because of Johnny Rudd."

The mention of his name filled Flo with fire. She surged forward, throwing a succession of quick jabs, then a flying knee. Brea blocked the punches, but the knee got through and drove her backward. She bounced off the trunk of a pine, then spun to her right. More nimble footwork reestablished the distance between her and Flo.

"Yeah, that's right. We had your back, but that was *your* vendetta." Brea showed her red-stained teeth. "You couldn't just shatter his kneecaps or cut off a limb. You had to put a bullet in his skull."

"That piece of shit killed my mom."

"Chance Kotter believes it was manslaughter," Brea said. "He thinks killing Johnny was . . . what did he call it? An '*unjust* retribution.'"

"Is that what you think, too?"

"I stand by what we did, for better or worse. Was it an overreaction?" Brea spread her hands but kept her guard high. "I don't know. Probably. One thing I know for certain is that you need to own your part in this, instead of throwing all the blame at me."

Flo considered this, then nodded.

"Attagirl." Blood trickled down Brea's face, onto her throat. "You ready for round two?"

FLO'S RESPONSE WAS A BARRAGE of punches, kicks, and elbows. She'd win no finesse points, and her accuracy was sacrificed for volume, but some of those shots found a home. Brea backed up, weaving and blocking. She looked for gaps, but they were hard to find. Eventually, Flo's attacks had less pop to them. She and Brea traded lefts and rights, then Brea parried a jab, threw her shoulder into Flo's middle, and drove her backward. They crashed through the understory and emerged from the tree line on the east side of the woods. Chance's guys followed, laughing and hooting. A third had joined the pack.

The ground here was dry dirt and stone punctuated with scrub. It was flat where it met the trees but sloped quickly and steeply to the river. The sisters fought on the edge of this embankment, Flo on the ground and Brea on top, both breathing hard and bleeding.

"Side bet!" one of Chance's men exclaimed excitedly. "I got fifty bones says one of these bitches goes down that hill and into the water."

The meathead who'd just arrived—the name REID was tattooed across his knuckles—said, "I got a hundred bones says they *both* go in."

Reid was right. The sisters took a recuperative pause, then resumed grappling. Brea dropped elbows but couldn't break Flo's shell-like guard. Flo arched her back and worked Brea with her knees. After ten enervating minutes of this, they separated and got wearily to their feet. Dust rose around them.

"I got the knife," Flo said, "because I wanted to make it quick. For me and for you."

Brea nodded, acknowledging the sentiment, twisted though it was. "Sorry to mess up your plans."

They came together again. Brea got the upper hand. She took a shot to the neck but managed to ram the top of her head into Flo's chest and knock her off-balance. Flo pinwheeled toward the drop, twisting her body. With a last-gasp effort, she grabbed the back pocket of Brea's jeans and pulled. Some of the stitches popped loose, but not enough to save Brea. Both women teetered on the edge, appearing to defy gravity for agonizing seconds, then over they went. They slewed, bounced, and tumbled their way down the thirty-foot embankment and splashed into the water below.

THE MARY WAS MUD BROWN and slow moving, but the current had something to it. Brea and Flo were carried downriver toward the bridge. They gasped and kicked, looking for each other in the water. Both were strong swimmers, but both were hurt and exhausted. The current pulled them under and turned them around. Brea came up reaching for air. Flo, by pure chance, was carried into her. She wrapped her arms around Brea's legs and dragged her down. Brea gulped water. Her eyes bulged.

Flo dragged her deeper still, curling one hand around her throat to keep her under.

They were carried through riverweed and over rocks. Brea managed to squirm loose. She kicked her legs, and both women broke the surface. Brea coughed up a gritty throatful of water. She flailed and splashed, then swam toward the bank. The current made fierce work of it, but she was soon within reach. Flo went after her. She lunged gator-like in the shallower water and took Brea down. They rolled in the silt and bulrushes and trash where the water lapped the bank, exchanging sloppy blows. Flo rattled a swinging right off Brea's jaw, stunning her briefly. Her eyelids fluttered and her body turned slack. Flo clambered higher onto Brea's chest, covered her face with one hand, and held her beneath the surface. The muscles in her arms and shoulders trembled with the effort. She screamed and cried. Brea didn't resist to begin with, then her head cleared and her fight returned. She bucked and twisted. She tried to bite. Flo held strong. She closed her eyes so she didn't have to see Brea's drowning face or the long hair—worked loose from the ponytail—swishing around her head. Brea shoveled her right hand through the silt and uncovered a good-sized rock. She swung it twice. The first strike hit Flo's left shoulder. The second cracked against her cheekbone and shook her. Brea rolled out from beneath Flo and dragged herself out of the water. She hacked and retched, then clambered up the embankment. Flo had staggered backward. She folded at the knees and the river took her.

**THE EMBANKMENT WAS MODERATE HERE** but longer. Brea crawled through sedge and thick weed, startling small wildlife, eventually regaining her feet and clomping the rest of the way in her soggy boots. She rejoined the promenade where it fronted a strip of waterside bars and restaurants and was greeted by Reid and his buddies, still filming on their phones. "You're puttin' on one helluva show, Blondie," Reid said. Brea wanted to rip the phone out of his hand and crunch it beneath her bootheel but needed all her energy just to walk. She passed the restaurants, earning curious stares from those dining outside. A steep cement walkway wound up to Harper Avenue and the west side of the Wishbone Bridge. Brea took several deep breaths before starting along it. She tasted blood at the back of her throat. Her knuckles were bruised, and her arms ached from the assault they'd absorbed.

She stopped halfway and vomited into a cluster of bright flowers. It was mostly river water, but some of the fabulous breakfast she'd enjoyed at Chip & Chick's came up, too. Chance's boys caught this on their cell phones. They laughed and hooted. "She's hurtin', boss," one of them reported. "She's hurtin' bad." Brea wiped her mouth and continued up the walkway. She reached the top, lightheaded. The bridge extended to her left with the business district beyond. Brea went this way, simply because there were fewer people. She needed breathing room—space to recover and realign her mind. Then she could track Flo down and finish the job.

Maybe a knife wasn't such a bad idea.

Brea started along the bridge but didn't get far before she heard brakes screeching behind her. She turned and saw two vehicles—a city bus and a minivan—come to a sliding halt, smoke rippling from their locked tires. They had braked to avoid the very wet Black woman recklessly crossing all four lanes.

Flo had ascended the walkway on the other side of the bridge. She clearly wasn't taking a timeout.

Brea clawed wet hair out of her eyes. She assumed a jaded fighting stance, and the two women went at each other again.

THEIR ATTACKS WERE LABORED AND telegraphed, but their defense was mostly ineffective. Flo started out stronger, slightly faster. She threw low kicks and uppercuts that landed. Brea stumbled away, shielded behind her arms. After another blow, she fell and her head thumped the guardrail on the way down. She saw her blood hit the sidewalk. The edges of everything turned gray.

Flo had lost all sense of herself. Her body was cumbersome, her hands too large. As she watched Brea push herself to her feet, she was aware, on some primal level, that she was edging the fight. It brought no satisfaction, only a numb acceptance of doing what needed to be done.

It didn't last. Flo threw her shoulder into Brea's chest, knocking her backward, giving her room to execute a high roundhouse—the attack that might have ended it. Brea stumbled more than dodged, but the result was the same: Flo's strike fell short. She overbalanced, turned clumsily, and Brea pounced. She threw wild hooks, and they all missed but one—a whistling right that struck Flo's temple and knocked her out on her feet. Her eyes rolled, and she slumped against the guardrail. Brea saw her opportunity. She reached with both hands, grabbed the backs of Flo's knees, and lifted.

One moment Flo was there, in front of Brea. In the next she was gone, toppling backward over the guardrail, falling eighty feet to the glassy brown surface of the Mary River.

BREA LOOKED OVER THE RAIL in time to see Flo hit the water. She landed flat on her back and sank and didn't come up. Brea covered her eyes. A conflicting ball of grief and relief climbed into her chest. She lowered her hands and stood aching. The traffic on the bridge was light—most of it had backed up behind the sideways bus. There were a few slow-moving cars . . . and Chance's goons, of course, catching all the action. Reid had his phone pointing down at the water. "Jesus Christ," he cried. "That's one down, boss. Holy shit, she went right off the fuckin' bridge!" Reid straightened and pointed the phone at Brea. She looked at it incredulously, then screamed until her throat burned. It freed something inside her, and she started to run—a slow, wounded animal's effort, but it was all she had.

# NINETEEN

**B**url had zapped the action from his cell phone to Chance's eighty-four-inch TV via high-tech hoodoo—screen mirroring or some such. Burl had started to explain how it worked. "Riding the same Wi-Fi connection, I can make my phone the sender and your TV—" Chance had flapped a hand. He didn't give one goddamn hoot how it worked, only that it *did* work. "Horseshit, horseshit," he'd said, and he and the boys sat in front of the big screen and watched the fight unfold.

Some of the camerawork was questionable—Burl switched between feeds to get the best angle—but it was better than nothing, and when Blondie straight up tossed the Black one off the bridge, most everyone leapt out of their seats (Brea was a heavy favorite). There was much cheering, howling, and high-fiving. Chance popped open a bottle of American bubbles and filled a dozen glasses. From the sound and celebrations, anybody'd think 'Bama had kicked the game-winning field goal in the CFP National Championship.

Burl put on a brave face but couldn't hide his disappointment. He killed the video feed and scrolled through his phone, nervously scratching the underside of his jaw. Chance grabbed a flute of Chandon Brut and took it over to his head of security.

"Tough break," Chance said, handing Burl the bubbles. "That cat-fight was vicious. Could've gone either way."

"Yessir," Burl acknowledged. He gulped from the flute, and tiny suds fizzed in his Burt Reynolds mustache.

"On the bright side, you'll get the chance to recoup some of your losses. I got a Caddy full of gals coming over this evening. We're gonna oil 'em up and have 'em ride El Toro Loco." Chance grinned and gestured toward the mechanical bull in the middle of the basement floor. "There'll be a wager or two made, no doubt."

Burl managed a smile. "It wouldn't be a Chance Kotter party without a few thousand dollars being thrown around."

Chance glugged his bubbles and hiccupped. Friends, booze, and retribution. He was having a fine old time. Yessir.

"And I may not have lost anything *yet*," Burl said. He glanced at his phone, one eyebrow higher than the other. "Strictly speaking, Flo isn't out of it until we ID a corpse."

"You'll be dragging it out of the Mary," Chance said.

"I don't think so." Burl flipped his phone around, giving Chance a good look-see. The Track-U-Gen app was open and fully zoomed in on Flo's winking blue blip. As the two men watched, it moved gradually across the lighter blue of the Mary River toward its eastern bank.

"What am I looking at here?" Chance asked.

"Flo," Burl replied, tapping the blue blip. "It might be the current, but in that direction, at that angle, I don't think so."

"She swimming?"

"I reckon."

"Well, I'll be double-dipped in dogshit." Chance finished his bubbles in a single swallow and hiccupped again. "That stone-cold piece of snatch is still alive."

BURL LEFT THE PARTY TO check Flo's status. Her blip was no longer moving, not even slowly, but she'd at least dragged herself out of the river. Chance announced that there were still three fighters in the game, which was met with a mixed reaction. "You know me, folks. I play by the rules. If that Black gal's still got a pulse, then she's still got a chance . . . and so does anyone who laid their money on her." Chance kept the good times rolling by opening a case of Kotter's Gold (his priciest bourbon) and kicking the jukebox into life. Hoyt Axton soon got boots tapping.

Bethany arrived twenty minutes later, dressed in full chief of police uniform (which, if Chance was being honest, made him feel a certain kind of way). She was on the clock but had three fingers of Kotter's Gold just the same, and didn't resist when Chance spun her around the room as Tammy sang "Stand by Your Man."

Tucker Presley took a turn with Bethany, which gave Chance the opportunity to catch his breath. He took a seat by the jukebox and checked his phone. Five messages—standard updates from Carson, Goose, and Strat. Nothing from Burl. Chance opened Track-U-Gen, expecting to be locked out again, but it opened just fine. The blue blip had moved but not far. Maybe fifty yards from the river's edge. Flo was hurting bad.

He put his phone away and greeted Mason Nurll, who'd sidled over to explain how a particularly dry September could decrease this year's peanut yield by 30 percent . . . and that was eight minutes of Chance's life that he'd never get back. Bethany rescued him. "A quick word, brother?" Chance said absolutely yes and left Mason standing alone.

"Thanks for that, sister."

"You're welcome, but I really do need to talk."

At fifty-eight, Bethany was four years Chance's senior, but she looked four years his junior with her full fiery hair and shimmery skin. She'd worked her way through the ranks of Reedsville's police department and was named chief in January 2017 (the same day that DJT was inaugurated, occasioning one *heck* of a double celebration). Chance admired her sass, stick-to-itiveness, and sense of honor. More than anything, he thought she looked mighty fine with a Glock on her hip.

"Just got word that two federal agents are inbound next week. Maybe Tuesday, but probably Monday." Bethany fixed her hair; some of it had come loose dancing with Tucker. "They're dotting i's and crossing t's in regard to our resident serial killer, but I need to know that this whole circus will be packed up by then."

"You've no need to worry. It'll be done and dusted by ten P.M. tomorrow. At the latest." Chance placed a hand on his chest and spoke his favorite phrase. "On that you have my word."

"Your word is fine and all, and I believe you mean to keep it. But you got three trained killers on the loose—"

"Two and a half killers," Chance interjected, and winked. "The Black gal just took a spill off the Wishbone Bridge. Only thing she's killing is time."

"The Black gal?" Bethany folded her arms. "She the one killed Johnny?"

"They're all to blame, but yeah, she fired the killing shot."

"Well, there's some justice served."

"Amen."

"My point is anything can go wrong, and I can only turn a blind eye—and redirect my officers—for so long." Bethany took a step closer, giving Chance a whiff of the Old Spice aftershave she splashed daily into her pits. "Listen, I support your desire for revenge, God knows I do, but there are simpler ways to go about it. And if this all backfires . . . if I hafta choose between my career and your elaborate game . . ."

"I get it. The buck stops here." Chance pointed at his boot tops. "I won't ask any more of you than I already have."

"I can't put my neck on the line, brother. Not again."

She was alluding to the "faulty" breathalyzer that had gotten their nephew out of extremely hot water, and to the understanding that she and Chance never discuss whether that evidence had been tampered with, or who'd suggested such a thing in the first place.

"I ain't sure what you're talking about," Chance said coyly. "But I will say this: Johnny was blood. You didn't want him getting his asshole popped in Staton, did you?"

"No, I did not, but it pains me even more to bring flowers to his grave." Bethany placed her hands on her hips and swallowed hard. "His mama's grave, too."

"You know I feel the same. Fiercely so." Chance twirled his forefinger, gesturing at everything—his powerful friends and abettors, his city, his scheme. "Hence the circus."

Bethany pressed her tongue into the side of her mouth and angled her head. "My brother the ringmaster."

"Hehe. That I am."

"Can't help but love you." A dainty smile. "You big ol' lug."

"Love you, too, sugar bunches."

Bethany nodded and swiveled on her bootheel. Her little tushy shook as she made for the door. "Just clean up your shit before the Feds get here."

CHANCE HAD BEEN MARRIED ONCE, in his early twenties, to a doll-faced southern gal named Josie-Ann, but Chance had not given his young wife the time, care, and attention he should have (he worked ungodly hours, in his defense). He came home one night to find a Dear John letter on the kitchen table, as clichéd an end to his marriage as it was sad.

*Do not go looking for me*, Josie-Ann had written in her gently flowing cursive. *I have fallen for another man. He has hips like an ox and a never-ending heart. Jesus brought him to me.*

Chance spent the remainder of that night with a bottle of sour mash whiskey, reflecting on his marriage, and had concluded that Josie-Ann was right to leave him. He had not fulfilled his marital duties, and her decision, though heartbreaking, was a *fair* one. After nineteen months as man and wife, he finally gave Josie-Ann what she deserved: an uncomplicated dissolution.

There'd been other romances, but none of them culminated in a walk down the aisle. Chance knew that work would always come first, and he made this clear to every woman he'd shared more than one evening with.

This tireless work ethic was hammered into Chance by his daddy, a battleship of a man without a scrap of patience in his soul, but whose commitment to his family could never be questioned. Chance was barely out of kindergarten when his daddy had him feeding the chickens, chopping wood, and raking leaves. At age nine, Chance earned his first wage: $42 for a whole weekend—twenty hours—picking cotton on Boz McCreary's farm. This, in 1978, was a kingly sum of money for the boy, and with it came a schooling that he never forgot. His daddy had him lay the bills out on the kitchen table—two tens, three fives, and seven singles—and for a long minute they stared at all that beautiful green. Finally, his daddy lifted his magnificent chin and spoke.

"Chance, son of mine, there ain't no secret to success, but there *is* a recipe. First, you pay what you owe." With this, his daddy removed the two tens and tucked them into the pocket of his grubby work pants. "This'll go toward the roof over your head and the food in that refrigerator."

"Yessir." Chance nodded. He was happy—proud, even—to contribute.

"Then you take whatever's left and split it three ways, as evenly as you can." His daddy gestured at the remaining bills. "Go on, do it."

Chance made three little stacks: an eight and two sevens.

"Okay then. That first third you spend on yourself, however you want. You've earned it."

"Yessir."

"That second third goes into the bank. Money for a rainy day."

"Yessir."

"Last third may well be the most important of all." His daddy drummed one callused finger on the five and three ones. "You put *that* toward something that'll make your work easier. Maybe a new pair of gloves or a better shovel. In time, as the money grows, that might be a bigger shed or a down payment on a truck. Eventually, it'll be an employee. Then two employees. Then three. You see where I'm going with this?"

"Yessir."

"Easier work is happier work. It's worth investing in." His daddy was not one for affection, but he ruffled Chance's hair and it felt uplifting. "You follow this recipe with every paycheck, son of mine, and you'll be cooking up success by the plate load."

Chance followed it to the dollar until he was eighteen years old, then added a couple of ingredients that his old-school daddy would never have considered: mutual funds and a retirement plan. And there was another critical ingredient that had been overlooked—one that Chance soon discovered added all the flavor: ruthlessness.

Chance's daddy was the ground he walked on. Jesus Christ was the sky overhead. In between, there stood a monolith—a formidable, upright slab carved from something ungiving, and that cut a mighty shadow. That monolith's name was Amos "Tusk" Sauerland.

Tusk taught Chance the importance of flavor.

"The trouble with success is the moment you have it, everybody wants a piece of you." Tusk wore a bolo tie and a black satin shirt and a ring on every finger. He was so named because of an enlarged, elongated canine that protruded from beneath his upper lip at an angle, a condition known as isolated macrodontia. Every dentist he'd seen wanted to yank that ugly tooth from his jaw, but Tusk insisted they leave it well enough alone. He said it made him look awful fearsome, and he was right. "What you decide to give should always be on your terms, but not everybody sees it that way."

Chance had nodded respectfully. He was twenty years old at the time and had been working for Tusk—a lot boy at his RV dealership in Sable Point, among other odd jobs—for about eighteen months. Tusk also owned businesses in Montgomery, Selma, and Colton. He was magnetic and imposing, yet as country as a longleaf pine. Chance all but worshipped him.

"And how do we best go about that?" Tusk asked. He pronounced it *betht*. His irregular tooth gave him an aggressive smile but also an interdental lisp that no one dared mention. "Keep folk from assuming they can have a piece of what you worked so hard to achieve?"

Chance pondered the question with one eye to the blue sky, but the answer wasn't there, nor in his young head. He shrugged. They were at Tusk's ranch in Colton, sitting on a clean white fence, watching five Thoroughbreds get their exercise beneath the striking Alabama sun.

"Hint," Tusk said, and patted the revolver on his right hip—a Smith & Wesson Model 29 in .44 Magnum, a goddamn Dirty Harry gun.

"Shoot 'em?" Chance ventured, and smiled.

"Hehe. Nope. Although there'd be a lot more winners in the world if you did."

Chance was not at that time worldly or experienced, but he nodded at that just the same. "Strike fear into 'em?"

"There you go." Tusk winked and clapped the younger man on the shoulder, good and hard. "You set your stall out early, letting folk know you ain't a man to be fucked with. You intimidate. You threaten. After that, should folk *still* decide that fucking with you is in their better interest, you back your threats up with action."

"*Then* you shoot 'em."

"Ain't you a bad dawg? Christ, I'll bet your blood runs redder than the background on a rebel flag."

"Yessir."

"Can't say as there's anything wrong with that, but you got a lot to learn."

Some weeks later, Tusk had Chance bring a livestock truck to his hog farm, also in Colton. "Need you to transport a dozen bacon-weights to Olsen's bloodhouse over in Marion." When Chance arrived, he found Tusk standing in the middle of a holding pen, surrounded by disturbed, squealing pigs. Tusk had the .44 on his hip and a four-pound engineer's hammer in his left hand. Chance backed up the truck and lowered the ramp.

"Look at these sweethearts," Tusk remarked, and mimicked their noises. "Some smart, too. They started squealing the moment they heard the truck heading along sixty-three."

"Guess they don't wanna make the trip to Marion," Chance said.

"You guess right, and loading 'em up is gonna be a problem." Tusk made a show of scratching his head. He flipped the hammer three times, catching it by the handle. "Any suggestions?" Then his eyes grew large and he drew his revolver. "Think we should shoot 'em?"

Chance looked at the pigs trundling on their dirty pink legs, each bouncing its body into the next. The force of them made the hard-packed dirt tremble. Their eyes were scared and bright.

"Not sure that fixes the problem so much as creates a new one." Chance pulled a stick of Juicy Fruit from his pocket, folded it into his mouth, and started chewing. "Those animals weigh two hundred pounds apiece, I'll say, and now you hafta *drag* them onto the truck."

"Also," Tusk said, holstering the .44, "nobody wants to find a bullet hole in their breakfast."

Chance chomped his gum and smiled.

"How about if we disorient them? Exploit a weakness?" Tusk shrugged and ran the tip of his tongue over the tip of his tooth. "Does that seem like a suitable way to overcome this show of adversity?"

Chance's eyes flooded with awe. He couldn't remember ever feeling so replete with admiration, not even when he met Merle Haggard after a show at Billy Bob's in Fort Worth.

"I'd say."

Tusk nodded. "A pig uses its snout like we use our hands. It helps them navigate, root, and identify. Most folk think it's just a big ol' nose, but it's more important to a pig than its eyes and easily the most sensitive part of its body." Tusk flipped the engineer's hammer again, then raised it above his head and brought it down on the snout of the nearest animal. It screamed and crumpled to its knees. "Get that gate, Chance."

Chance ran around and got the gate. Tusk booted the injured pig's rump, and it rose to its feet and walked a bewildered circle. "C'mon now," Tusk said, bumping its flanks with his knees, guiding it out of the pen. Chance closed the gate after them and watched as Tusk nudged the pig up the ramp and into the back of the truck.

"Christ," Chance muttered. His admiration only swelled.

Tusk stepped back down the ramp flipping the hammer. His grin was unruly. He walked toward Chance with the ornamental clasp of his bolo tie winking in the sunlight. His buckle, too.

"A snout-broke pig will go wherever you lead it," he said. His voice was cool and serious. His gaze didn't waver. "Bullets ain't always the answer. You hear what I'm saying?"

Chance nodded. He knew exactly what Tusk was saying.

"Good. Now get these bastards loaded up." Tusk handed Chance the hammer. "Olsen's expecting you by four."

Chance nodded and hopped the gate into the pen. His heart fluttered in a new way. Then he got an idea—a way of spicing up the work and perhaps earning Tusk's admiration. "Hey, Tusk." Chance bounced his gum between his teeth and pulled his wallet from the back pocket of his Wrangler jeans. He took out every bill inside—seven tens, two fives, and eight ones—and slammed them down on top of the fencepost. "I got eighty-eight dollars says I can load these bacon-weights in twenty minutes."

Tusk sucked his big tooth. "Shoot, son, you *are* a dawg."

"Yessir."

"But let me ask you this: Can you afford to lose that money?"

"Yessir." It was the slice of his paycheck that he'd set aside to buy something for himself.

"Only a fool gambles what he can't afford to lose."

"A *damn* fool," Chance agreed.

Tusk clattered with laughter. The sound came from his chest, not his mouth, like banging inside a mine. "Then I'll tell you what . . ." He

hooked a money clip from his pocket and counted off a chunk of twenties. "I'll give you better than four-to-one odds. Three hundred and sixty
dollars"—he slapped his wager down on top of Chance's—"says you'll still
be swinging that hammer twenty minutes from now."

Chance grinned and went to work. He lost the bet—it took him closer
to forty minutes to load the animals, and that hammer was wet with blood
by the time he'd finished—but he made the thirty-mile trip to Marion
feeling like he was driving on sunflowers.

EARL KOTTER—CHANCE'S DADDY—AND Amos "Tusk" Sauerland died
on the very same day, an hour apart and two towns from each other.
Some declared this a woeful coincidence. Others preferred to think of it
as God's work. Whatever it was, Chance's heart was kicked from one side
of his body to the other, leaving a vast emptiness behind his ribs. At least
they died in different ways—a wood-chipper incident for Daddy, a good
old-fashioned American heart attack for Tusk.

Chance was thirty-three at the time and had more than enough rainy-
day money to buy a family plot at the Garden of Everlasting Light, a private
cemetery overlooking the Mary River. He had the men in his life planted
there and erected angels around them. There was space for other graves, but
he'd marked the plot between his daddy and Tusk as his own. Sometimes
Chance visited and sat talking to both for hours. Occasionally, he'd lie
in the lush grass with Tusk on one side and Daddy on the other—as if
getting some practice in—and fall asleep. He earnestly believed that one
day, centuries into the future, a tree would grow in that generous soil, the
tallest, most colorful tree in the entire state, and it would bear an abundance of fruit.

EMMETT POUND WAS CHANCE'S LIFELONG friend and a ruthless businessman in his own right—a thorny sumbitch, truth be told. "He came
outta my belly snappin'," his mama said of him. "I knew right away he'd
be hard to love." Chance never had a brother, but Emmett was close.
They'd met in third grade and ran headlong into the days ahead, at least
until Emmett pursued a business opportunity in Nashville. That was
thirty years ago. Presently, Emmett resided in Chattanooga with a soulless

wife and an ugly kid. He'd flown to Reedsville in his Bell 206 helicopter and landed it in Chance's backyard.

"I hafta say, Chance . . ." Emmett had a bobblehead, in that it trembled delicately whenever he spoke. "This beats the time you had those two crack whores go at each other with straight razors."

Chance grinned at the memory. "I won six thousand dollars that day and only had to spend six hundred on coke."

The party was moving along nicely. The booze was flowing (a keg of Busch had been added to the mix), the big TV ran an old Dale Earnhardt race, and Kristofferson graced the jukebox. A few fellas sat around talking. Others played pinochle. Others played pool. Even Mason Nurll seemed more relaxed, having drowned his peanut woes in a steady stream of bourbon.

Chance's phone was still in his hand. It lit up and buzzed, startling him. He dropped it. "Goddamn thing." Stooping to retrieve it wasn't easy. Emmett—leaner but creakier in the knees—didn't help. Chance managed to tweezer the edge of the case with his fat fingers. He woke the screen and read a message from Burl.

"It's from Burl," he said, flicking his gaze to Emmett. "He says Flo—the Black one—is still in the game. She's hiding out, licking her wounds. Alert, though."

"Tough gal," Emmett said.

Chance nodded and opened the Track-U-Gen app. He zoomed in and saw that Flo's blue blip was "hiding out" on Choctaw Street, maybe in one of the empty office units there. Chance scrolled the map northwest and found the green and red blips. They were both in Lower West, only a few blocks from each other.

"How'd you do it, Chance?" Emmett asked. He clamped a Padrón between his teeth and got it burning with something that looked like a mini welding gun. Smoke momentarily veiled his snaky green eyes. "How'd you get them gals to go to war with one another?"

Chance inhaled proudly. He remembered Tusk's words from thirty-four years ago: *A snout-broke pig will go wherever you lead it.* He considered saying exactly this, then smiled and opted for a less recondite response.

"Let's just say I exploited a weakness."

Emmett puffed his cigar and quacked laughter. His head wobbled every which way, as if it might, at any moment, overspill and topple off. "You're as mean as a wet panther, Chance Kotter."

"Mean but *fair*." Chance angled his phone so Emmett could see the screen and indicated the proximity of the green and red blips. "Lookee—we might get some fireworks soon. And Burl's on his way back. I'll get him to hook up a live stream."

"Prime time!"

"You know it. In the meantime . . ." Chance gave his old friend a playful punch on the arm. "Let's shoot some eight-ball."

# TWENTY

Flo opened her eyes. She saw bare white walls and a white drop ceiling. White blinds covered the only window. She suffered a moment's disorientation, then a school of quick, bright memories swam through her mind. She sat up with a start and her head whirled. The blue light on her tracker winked, and she stared at it until her equilibrium returned.

Pain came with it, deep in places, superficial in others, stabbing in others still. Flo looked down and saw a rudimentary splint on her left forearm: two pieces of folded cardboard cinched with several strips of cloth. Her hips moaned. Her legs cried. She tried getting to her feet, but there was no way, not yet, and perhaps not for a long time to come. Another wave of dizziness crashed through her and she flopped onto her back.

Time ticked along.

SHE HAD BEEN STRIPPED TO her underwear. Her T-shirt and jeans were drooped over a chair, drying out. Her boots were by the window with her socks laid out beside them.

Burl had done this. He'd brought her here. Snapshots recurred, all from the rim of consciousness: the blackness of his mustache, the view from his arms, the St. Christopher pendant swinging from the rearview mirror of his SUV. He'd *helped* her, just like he'd brought her the breakfast sandwich from Bo Peep's and the steak and eggs when she'd been imprisoned in the room.

*Shh.*

Flo stared up at the drop ceiling, trying to make sense of this. There was still too much pain. She'd catch the tail end of a thought and try to hold on, but her body would bang, burn, and rebel, demanding all her attention. At length, she gave up. She closed her eyes and muttered nursery rhymes through gritted teeth, imagining every word traveling through a metaphysical gateway and reaching Imani's perfect melon of a belly.

SHE LAY ON A DAMP, coffin-sized piece of cardboard. Burl had rolled up a small blanket for a pillow. The room was empty except for the single chair that her clothes were draped over. A profusion of power outlets led Flo to believe this was vacant office space, which made sense considering she'd pulled herself out of the river at the southern edge of the business district.

The single door was featureless and brown and probably led to a narrow hallway with the same white walls and drop ceiling, with more vacant office space leading off it. Cars ripped past the window semiregularly, flashing through the gaps in the blinds. She was on the ground floor.

Flo sat up again, moving oh-so-slowly. She examined the splint, turning her left arm gingerly. It was broken. No doubt about it. Her skin had a bruised hue, and her left hand was swollen. Her right arm hurt, too, but she could move it and make a fist. Once again, she tried getting to her feet but wasn't quite ready for it. She overbalanced and crumpled to the floor, twisting her body so that she didn't land on her broken arm. She counted to one hundred and tried again. This time, she made it to her feet. She took a couple of shaky steps, then had to lean her back against the wall and gradually lower herself into a sitting position.

Progress.

It was still light outside. Flo couldn't have been here long, unless she'd been unconscious all day and right through the night. Her underwear was still damp, though, so she didn't think this was the case. Either way, she needed to get moving, get back in the game. She could neither kill nor be killed from this room, and she had to do one or the other to save Imani.

THE PAIN MOVED AROUND, FROM her hips to her head to her shoulder to her left arm to her legs. Sometimes it was everywhere at once. Flo gritted her teeth and waited it out, sweating into the cardboard beneath her.

The next time she got to her feet, she was able to take several steps. Her legs were weak but didn't buckle. She crossed to the chair and retrieved her T-shirt. It was damp and smelled of the river. There were striations in the fabric where Burl had wrung it out. Flo put it on carefully. She was still half naked and half broken, but the simple act of dressing helped her feel closer to normal. She wasn't ready to get into her jeans yet, and the thought of tying her bootlaces one-handed made her head spin.

"One step at a time." Flo grabbed her jeans, reached into the back pocket, and, to her immense relief, found the strip of Advil that Chance's thugs had given her. There were six remaining, still sealed and dry. She swallowed three of them, then shuffled to the window and cracked the blinds. The view was post-COVID regressive: empty sidewalks, a two-lane road, and a row of three-story office buildings, each displaying an identical COMMERCIAL SPACE FOR LEASE notice. She couldn't see the Kotter-Bryce Eyesore from this window, or even the sun, so she had no idea of the time.

Maybe it was the skin of dust on the outside of the glass, but she was sure the light was fading.

FLO STARTED TOWARD THE DOOR, taking a deep breath every third step. Maybe there was a clock in the hallway or—bliss—a watercooler. Also, a different office would offer a different view. Not necessarily a *better* view—this was Reedsville, after all—but one that would help Flo get her bearings.

Three feet from the door, she heard a vehicle pull up outside. The engine shut off, then a single door opened and closed. One person. Flo took a shuffling step backward. She was exposed, defenseless, and there was nothing she could do about it. The feeling sickened her. She looked at the blue light flashing on her ankle. If this was one of Chance's guys, here to take advantage of her in her weakened state . . .

Another possibility occurred, infinitely darker.

The wren.

She heard the pneumatic hiss of another door opening and closing, then the echoey tap of bootheels on a tile floor. They got steadily louder.

Flo took another uncertain step backward. She raised the only fist she could make.

The door opened. Flo's legs trembled. Her left knee buckled, but she stayed on her feet.

Burl stepped inside, a brown paper bag bundled in one arm. He'd loosened his necktie to a sloppy height, but his expression, as ever, was all business.

Flo exhaled. She hated this man absolutely but couldn't deny being relieved to see him. He didn't appear to share this sentiment. He looked at Flo and said in a drab, compassionless tone, "You should be resting."

SHE SAT IN THE CHAIR with her jeans still draped over the back of it. Sitting was as uncomfortable as standing, but lying down, half dressed as she was, made her feel especially vulnerable. Burl assessed her, stroking his mustache, then placed the brown paper bag on the floor.

"What time is it?" Flo asked. She'd lowered her hands into her lap for a little more cover. "Let me rephrase that: How long do I have left to kill my sisters?"

"Don't sound so outraged. Killing is what you *do*." Burl curled his lip. "I'm sure your body count is much higher than Chance's."

"There's a difference. I only kill scumbags." Flo winced as pain rattled her hips. "Men like you."

Burl let that one go. He shook his head and looked at his phone. "Six twenty-three. You've been here five hours, give or take."

"Brea and Jessie?"

"Still alive. Still in the game." Burl checked his app. "Brea's on Oriole Avenue, Upper West. Jessie's about half a mile away, heading south on Main. They haven't connected yet, but they came close—got to within a block of each other at one point."

Flo closed her eyes. She recalled the woodland retreat in Vermont, where she'd said to her sisters how the three of them were the same entity. A force of nature divided into three parts. Jessie had likened them to a typhoon: the eye, the eye wall, and the rainbands. *We roll in, cause chaos, then leave.* Now they were *in* chaos, and only one of them was leaving.

"Here."

Flo opened her eyes. Burl had unscrewed the cap on a one-liter bottle of Pedialyte and held it out to her. Her dry throat rejoiced. She came close to snatching the drink out of his hand but didn't want to appear too needy.

"Pedialyte? Was the store out of Gatorade?"

"This has more electrolytes than Gatorade," Burl responded blankly. "You need to rehydrate, balance your levels."

Flo took the bottle. Her right shoulder pulsed angrily as she lifted it to her lips and drank, but she didn't care. The Pedialyte was cold, delicious, and revitalizing.

"There's another bottle in the bag," Burl said, nudging the bag with the side of his boot. "Some other things, too."

Flo nodded and lowered the bottle. She belched, then took another big drink. It was two-thirds finished already. Burl examined the cardboard splint, turning her left arm gently.

"I didn't need an X-ray to see that your forearm is busted. What I *can't* tell is how serious it is." He retied one of the fabric strips, pulling it tighter. "Plenty bruised and swollen, though."

"No deformity?" Flo licked her lips. There was a mouthful left in the bottle, but she held off.

"No. So maybe a greenstick fracture in one of the bones." Burl tapped his knuckles on the cardboard and winked. "Painful, huh?"

Flo hissed through her teeth and pulled away from him. The sudden movement brought more pain.

"Your right shoulder was dislocated. I clunked it back in." Burl made a pulling motion. His teeth flashed. "I don't know how you swam to shore with a broken left arm *and* a dislocated right shoulder. Determined, I guess."

"I don't remember," Flo said, shaking her head. This was true. She recalled dragging herself out of the river the *first* time, then staggering up the walkway and fighting Brea on the bridge. Suddenly, the lights went out, putting truth to the old boxing adage: that it's the punch you don't see coming that knocks you out. Flo had a disjointed memory of being dragged through the river, scuffed along the stony bottom. The next thing she remembered was the blueness of the sky. Those hazy snapshots followed: Burl's dark mustache, the St. Christopher's pendant hanging from his rearview.

She finished the drink with a single, satisfied swallow and tossed the empty bottle across the room.

"Yeah. You got your bell well and truly rung. Ninety-nine percent chance of a concussion, I'd say. I'm surprised you remember anything." Burl removed a bottle of iodine solution and a cotton ball from the paper bag. "There's bruising up and down your body. Scratches and scrapes. You're breathing okay, though, and moving around, so likely no serious internal injuries."

He wet the cotton ball with the iodine solution and applied it to Flo's left cheekbone, disinfecting an open wound she didn't know she had (although the memory of Brea hitting her in the face with a rock came howling back). For a big, macho guy, Burl worked with surprising tenderness. Flo knew he had a wife at home—maker of the *best* pear cobbler, according to Chance—and wondered if there were a couple of little Burls in the household, too. She imagined a five-year-old with a mop of black curls sitting on the kitchen countertop, whimpering as Burl tenderly dressed a scrape on their knee.

"You get your first aid merit badge at Boy Scouts?" Flo asked, wincing at the sting of the antiseptic.

"I patched up my fair share of brothers in Afghanistan," Burl replied, then elaborated: "US Army, 173rd Airborne Brigade. Eight years of service. A lifetime of memories."

Flo caught his eye and saw some of the memories there, few of them good.

"Why are you patching *me* up?" Flo asked. "Bringing me food, giving me Brea's location. Why are you helping me?"

Burl lowered the cotton ball. He examined it briefly, then dropped it and the iodine solution back into the paper bag. "I'm helping *myself*. Don't think for one second that I like you, because I don't. Not at all."

It clicked then, with an exact and satisfying sound, and in a way that made Flo wonder why it had taken her so long to realize. "Okay, I get it now. You have money riding on me. You're *cheating*."

"I'm keeping it interesting," Burl said.

"Right, and how does your boss—a man of his word, a *fair* man— feel about that? Or wait, maybe he's not so fair. Maybe he's in on it, too."

"Chance doesn't *need* the money," Burl said, and made a sound in his throat, somewhere between a cough and a grunt. "He's got fifty thousand on Brea. A big chunk of change. She's the favorite, but her odds aren't juicy enough for me."

"Yeah?" Flo cocked an eyebrow. "What are they?"

"Minus one hundred," Burl replied, and gave his mustache a slow, indulgent stroke. "You, on the other hand, are plus three hundred. That kind of return makes it worth the risk, especially if I can use my position in the field to give you a leg up."

"Hmm, better hope the big boss man doesn't find out."

"He won't. Only person who knows is you. And seeing as I'm your only hope of winning this thing, I figure you'll keep your mouth shut." Burl took out his cell phone and accessed an app called StreamSphere. He logged in and brought up the live video feed of Imani and Aubree, tied to chairs in that dank brick room. Aubree had her head down, maybe sleeping. Imani wept and pleaded with someone off camera. Burl held the screen close to Flo's face, giving her a good look. "Still alive, see? I assume you want to keep it that way."

Flo had stopped breathing. She heard her heartbeat in her skull.

"It's worth remembering that I have a direct line to the men holding these women hostage." Burl tapped the screen, then shut off the app. "They'll do exactly what I say. You better not fuck with me."

Flo's gaze flicked to Burl's left side, where, when his jacket flapped open, she saw the grip of a semiauto extending from its holster. If she wasn't so busted up, she might have made a move for it.

Burl put his phone away. "You got anything to say?"

Flo swallowed hard, then shook her head no. A shuddering breath caught up to her.

"Okay. We have an understanding." Burl displayed something like a smile and pulled a leatherette case from his jacket pocket. The last time Flo saw that case—hog-tied with duct tape on Chance Kotter's driveway— Burl had injected her and her sisters with a strong anesthetic, and she'd woken up several hours later, handcuffed to a pipe in a small room.

She watched as Burl unzipped the case and screwed a clean needle onto a syringe. Her stomach tightened. "Shoot me up with that, and my chances of winning go from slim to zero."

Burl gave her a sideways look, realizing what she was referring to. "This is different. Think of it as a firm kick in the pants." He inserted the needle into a vial with a red-and-white label and half filled the syringe. "It's mostly vitamin B$_{12}$ with some Ritalin and *myo*-inositol. I sourced it from a vet friend of mine. They give this to horses to make them run faster."

"Are you shitting me?"

Burl winked. This was as close as Flo got to an answer. Before she could protest, he jabbed the needle into her right quad and pressed the plunger.

"You son of a bitch." Flo jerked in the seat.

"That'll take a moment to kick in. Once it does, the effects will last up to thirty-six hours." Burl packed the used syringe away and dropped the leatherette case back into his pocket. "You'll either be on your way to California by then, or a forgotten pile of ashes at the bottom of Ernie Pink's cremation chamber."

Flo looked at the needle's point of entry, indicated by a swelling droplet of blood. She smeared it with her thumb, blinking disbelievingly, then stood up suddenly. Burl sat her back down without any effort.

"I'm not done with you yet."

Her mouth opened and a crack of air escaped, which turned into a word, then a question: "*Whaaaaaat* the fuck was that?"

"A pick-me-up. Like I said, *mostly* B$_{12}$."

"I don't believe you."

Burl shrugged: *I don't care.* He stooped and picked up the brown paper bag. "There are more provisions in here. Nuts and such. Painkillers, extra strength. Use what you need. And get some rest. If I can check on you, I will."

"Rest won't help." Flo held up her left arm. It felt heavy and raw, but the pain had diminished considerably, no doubt due to the three Advil she'd recently swallowed—unless there was some fast-acting morphine in that fucking horse stimulant he'd shot her up with. "How do you expect me to beat Brea and Jessie with a broken arm?"

"By using your advantage," Burl replied.

Flo frowned, wondering if she was missing something. The question formed on her lips, then Burl preempted it by lifting a cell phone from the paper bag and handing it to her.

**SHE TURNED THE PHONE ON.** No security measures. The home screen appeared immediately with a bland gray wallpaper and just one app icon—a magnifying glass on top of a map: Track-U-Gen. Everything else had been either hidden or deleted.

"Incoming calls only," Burl said. "You have data, but only access to one app. Go on . . . open it. You're already logged in."

Flo tapped the Track-U-Gen icon with the tip of her thumb. The logo bloomed in bright colors, followed by a loading screen. Flo watched the percentage number quickly count from zero to one hundred, then planet Earth appeared.

"Swipe up," Burl said.

Flo did. She got an options screen.

"Live tracking."

Flo tapped it and saw three monitored devices, denoted by a colored blip and a seven-character code. Hers was blue, XC70-FB. She selected it. The bird's-eye view of Earth appeared again, but rapidly zoomed in on North America, breaking through feathery clouds, closing in on the Lower 48, on the Deep South, on Alabama, on Dallas County, on Reedsville. She saw streets and places that had become all too familiar: Franklin Boulevard, Harper Avenue, Waterloo Square, the Wishbone fucking Bridge. The view continued to zoom in until she saw her blue blip three blocks east of the Mary River, on Choctaw Street.

"It's an older phone," Burl said. "The battery's not great, so use it sparingly."

Flo nodded distantly. She moved her thumb and forefinger together on the screen, zooming out, and scrolled to Jessie's red blip, now in Colonel Park. Brea was still in Upper West, on Blount Road, four blocks from Main.

"You can't go toe-to-toe with them." Burl scratched his throat, squinting one eye. "You're not fast enough or strong enough. They'll cut you down. And quickly."

"I know that."

"You need to anticipate their movements. Use stealth. Better yet, attack them while they're sleeping."

"No," Flo said, and glanced at Burl. "They'll be hypervigilant, even in their sleep. It's how they've been trained."

"Jesus Christ," Burl snapped. "They're not special ops. They're a couple of California gals with some krav maga lessons under their belts."

"*Hujan badai*," Flo corrected him. "And if you truly believe that"—she held up the phone—"you wouldn't have gone to all this trouble."

Burl expanded his chest. A vein in his temple swelled. "Just find a way to get it done. And be discreet with that phone. If you're seen following the map like a goddamn tourist, questions will be asked."

Flo checked the red and green blips again, then turned the phone off. "Have you thought about what's going to happen if I'm killed—probably *when* I'm killed—and the phone is found on me?"

Burl waved that concern off. "It's me who'll confirm the kills, ID the bodies. I'll just dig the phone out of your pocket and throw it in the river."

"Hmm." Flo nodded. "Chance really trusts you."

"Like a brother," Burl said. "That's why this is the perfect crime."

Flo got to her feet, stretching her back and shoulders. Her joints and tendons creaked. She walked to the window and back. It was easier than the last time she'd hobbled around the room, but not *much* easier. This was going to take some time.

"One more thing." Burl reached into his front pants pocket and took out a folding knife—a balisong. He flipped it open with a neat flick of the wrist, looking pleased with himself, then closed it again with another flick. "A butterfly knife. Easy to conceal, and you won't stab yourself in the leg if you fall over."

"It's called a balisong," Flo said dryly.

"That so? And am I supposed to be impressed by your knowledge of Chinese weaponry?"

"Filipino."

Burl's lips turned down in a long, ugly sneer. He held the balisong out to her, then thought better of it; he dropped it into the paper bag, giving him time to introduce his boot to her ass if she made a sudden move for it. "I took the liberty of sharpening both sides."

Flo pressed her lips together. She hated this man with every wounded scrap of her soul.

He walked toward the door. "I've been here too long. The boss'll want a debrief." He gave her a deep look before leaving, as if wanting to impart a final motivating salvo. Anything he said would be redundant, though; Flo had more motivation than she could reasonably bear. Burl rocked on his heels and stroked his mustache, then he was gone. Flo heard his big silver SUV start up and pull away.

She stood for a moment, making small movements to test her body: rolling her right wrist, extending her ankles, twisting her hips—the kind of light warm-ups seniors did before walking the mall. The Advil had partially numbed the pain, but her range of motion was limited. She returned to the coffin-sized sheet of cardboard, lay down, and stared at the white drop ceiling.

THERE WAS NO POWER IN the empty building. The sun went down and the room got dark. Flo cracked the blinds, and a nearby streetlight painted stripes across the wall.

She walked three slow laps of the room, moving a touch more freely, then tore open the paper bag. The contents spilled: two bottles of water, another bottle of Pedialyte, three bananas, two Clif Bars, the bottle of iodine solution, one Kit Kat, a box of Advil extra strength caplets, the balisong, and a bag of mixed nuts. Flo ate a Clif Bar and half the nuts and washed them down with a bottle of water. She walked another two laps, then checked the phone Burl had given her. Brea and Jessie had drawn closer to each other. The same neighborhood, different streets. Heartbreakingly, Flo thought that if one were to kill the other, her task would be 50 percent less challenging.

There was no hope of sleep or even rest. Whatever Burl had injected her with was working. Her heart raced. Her muscles twitched. She drained the second bottle of Pedialyte and took more painkillers, then walked laps. Five . . . ten . . . fifteen. Either the room grew smaller or her legs got faster. She lost count somewhere between twenty and thirty.

In time, she stopped. She sat on the cardboard and played with the balisong, twisting her wrist, flipping it open and closed. She liked the quick sound it made. *Snick-snick-snick . . . snick . . . snick-snick.* A metronome for her heartbeat.

# TWENTY-ONE

The red and green blips had failed to make contact. They'd gotten awful close more than once, only to miss each other by a matter of minutes—perhaps seconds. Despite the NASCAR reruns and the oiled-up gals riding El Toro Loco, Chance's hombres were growing impatient.

"This good time has fallen flat on its ass," Emmett Pound slurred, head trembling. "You need to go grab those bitches and throw 'em in a cage."

"Cool your jets, Em," Chance countered. "This is all about the thrill of the hunt."

"Ain't much thrilling about watching a few colored dots on a screen."

Chance placed both hands across his belly and pondered this. He didn't care to mess with the system, but maybe dropping a couple of hints, subtly guiding the red blip and the green blip closer to each other, wasn't a terrible idea. Besides, nobody had a stake on there *not* being a fight, so he didn't view it as unfair in any way.

"I'm telling you, Chance, if I don't see a catfight soon"—pronounced *shoon*—"I'm getting in my 'copter and flying back to *Ch-Ch*-Chattanooga."

"Christ alive, Em, you've had a skinful of Gold." Chance mimicked Emmett's piss-drunk expression and flapped a hand. "You ain't flying nowhere."

**AS THE HOURS MOVED ON** and darkness fell, Jessie became more and more certain that the Trace was their only hope. Making contact, though, was a considerable obstacle. She had, while looking for Brea and Flo, stolen two cell phones. The first was in Waterloo Square, when some guy had placed it on the bench beside him while he ate a sandwich and read his comic book. The second was in the Glass Garden on Harper Avenue, where several patrons sat at a table crowded with cocktails and cell phones, engaged in such animated conversation that they hadn't noticed when Jessie strolled past and made one of those phones disappear. Unfortunately, getting *into* the devices wasn't as easy as appropriating them. One needed a passcode, and the other, facial recognition. Without the technical know-how to get around these barriers, the phones served no purpose.

She'd walked past the city library three times, imagining all the public computers inside. Chance probably had someone monitoring them, but even if he didn't, Jessie still needed to download the Tor browser to access the Trace, and library computers invariably employed internet filters and user permissions. Like the cell phones she'd stolen, they were effectively useless.

Jessie trusted that a solution would reveal itself. It *had* to. Maybe Brea or Flo had access to a working phone—another reason for wanting to find them, along with trying to convince them that there was another way through this ordeal, that they didn't have to kill one another.

Yet.

She traipsed the darkened streets, hungry, scared, with time slipping away. On the corner of Main and Jackdaw, she was approached by the same man she'd seen twelve hours earlier—the narrow-faced dude with a scar across his throat. He grinned and tapped his watch again, delivering a similar message.

"Ticktock, little bunny. It's ten P.M. Twenty-four hours remaining."

"Fuck you, man." Jessie spat at his feet as she passed, then stopped, turned on her heel, and got all up in his personal space. "Are my sisters still alive? Tell me. I don't think there's any rule against me punching you in the fucking mouth."

"Fuck you. Bitch skeeze."

Jessie punched him in the mouth. A quick, hard strike. He folded at the knees, but Jessie grabbed his shirtsleeve before he could fall and dragged him back up.

"Are my sisters still alive?"

The man wiped his bleeding lip. The scar across his throat was too big to have been made by anything but a blade. Jessie knew she could do a better job of killing him.

"Tell me, man. Next time, I break your nose."

"Alls I know . . ." He wiped his mouth again and played with the blood on his fingers. "Yeah, alls I know is that they came together, and it didn't end well for one of them."

Jessie let go of his shirtsleeve and stepped back. A hole opened in the sidewalk beneath her and she fell but didn't go anywhere. All the breath rushed from her lungs.

"Frederick Plaza . . . a strip mall in Upper West." The man started away from her, spitting blood. "Maybe you'll find more answers there."

JESSIE WALKED THE MILE TO Frederick Plaza in a daze. She found drug dealers and prostitutes. Crunk blared from the open windows of a smoking, tricked-out Eldorado. She crisscrossed the lot, ignoring the comments. "This ain't yo' track, bitch, keep movin' . . . I got what you *need*, baby . . . She ain't hood but she fine . . ." The temperature had climbed ten degrees, or so it felt. Her hair was limp with sweat. She checked the businesses that were still open: a laundromat, a fast-food joint, a Circle K. No sign of Brea or Flo. No *answers*. Jessie checked the lot again. A red pickup truck pumping country pulled up beside her, driven by a good ol' boy with a missing front tooth and a ROLL TIDE tattoo.

"Independence Boulevard. She cut all her hair off," he said, and drove away.

BREA STEEN WAS DEAD. DECEASED. No more. Rest in fucking peace.

It was easier for her to think of it this way, because she no longer felt connected to the woman she used to be—the sister, the friend, the band-mate. Her body was still intact, but her defining qualities were gone. It happened the moment she threw Flo off the Wishbone Bridge and watched her fall eighty feet to the water below. *Flo*, with whom Brea had shared so many miles and moments. *Flo*, who'd had her back a thousand times.

Brea had wandered for hours, wet from the river, beaten up from the fight. Eventually, she'd dried out, but people still stared and gave her a sizable berth when passing her on the sidewalk. Chance's goons kept track of her. They took photographs and recorded video on their cell phones. They coaxed. They hollered. Only Chance's driver—Goose, that was his name, like the character from *Top Gun*—was any different. He only watched her, with no interaction. Brea would look up and he'd be there, positioned behind the wheel of Chance's Escalade, just staring.

Darkness edged across the city. The hustlers, freaks, pimps, pushers, hoods, and hookers emerged, like coyotes on the hunt. At a strip mall where Upper and Lower West came together (Brea was getting to know this damn city too well), she paused at a storefront window, looking at her reflection in the glass. She couldn't collate the woman staring back at her with the emptiness she felt inside. Her vision blurred. Tears, maybe, but nothing spilled over her eyelids onto her cheeks. That's how empty she was. She blinked, tried to focus, and realized then that she was standing in front of a barbershop, not a store. An elderly Black gentleman was inside, trimming another Black gentleman's beard.

Brea didn't think twice. She entered the establishment.

"We're just closing up," the proprietor said, beard-trimming scissors in one hand, comb in the other. He had a journeyed face, every groove a story. The skin around his eyes was identically mottled, like a butterfly's wings.

Brea ignored him. She walked past his station to a chair at the back of the shop.

"Hey, excuse me . . . excuse me, ma'am, I said we'll be closing up soon."

Brea grabbed a set of hair clippers from a rubber mat on top of the station, then opened a drawer, selected a number one guard, and fitted it over the blades. She hit the power button, placed the flat of the guard to her forehead, and ran a trench through her long blond hair.

"Oh shit." The barber jumped up, tucking the scissors and comb into a pocket in his apron. He hastened over to Brea as she made a second cut. "Oh my goodness, stop. *Stop.*" The barber—his name tag read MO— gently closed his hand around Brea's as she lifted the clippers for another go. Hair tumbled onto her shoulders and swayed to the white tile floor.

They looked at each other. Brea saw only concern and kindness in Mo's eyes. He must have seen the brokenness in hers, because he lowered her into the seat and said, "Let me help you." Brea frowned at that. Help? The concept of *help*, here in Reedsville, was entirely foreign, especially to the fractured person she had become.

"Help?"

Mo nodded reassuringly, eased the clippers from Brea's hand, then gestured at the other customer. "I need to finish up with Jarien here. He's my sister's husband, and I won't hear the last of it if he goes home to her looking like *that*."

Jarien regarded himself in the mirror from beneath knitted eyebrows.

"Three minutes," Mo continued. "Maybe five, then I'll be back, and we'll do this properly."

Brea nodded and waited, looking down at her hands—she couldn't stare at the stranger in the mirror—while Mo tidied up his brother-in-law's beard. He then shuffled over to her, with all that kindness still in place.

"I'd suggest something a little longer than one-eighth of an inch," he said, lifting a pair of scissors from a bright blue jar of Barbicide. "But I guess I need to finish what you started."

"Finish it," Brea said.

Mo used the scissors first, lopping off all that golden hair close to the scalp. Then he fitted a number eight guard to the clippers and ran this over her head. Finally, he went with the number one. "I think all women look beautiful with short hair," he said. "It brings out their eyes. Their truth."

He finished up and used a duster to brush the small hairs from her forehead, neck, and inside her ears.

"All done."

Brea looked at herself, divested, shallowed, the curves of her jawline accentuated, the hollows of her temples pronounced. Her truth had indeed been brought out. She looked closer now to the creature she felt like inside. No more Brea. No more sister. No more friend.

"I have nothing to pay you with," she said to Mo, meeting his gaze via the mirror.

He shook his head and smiled, then asked her if she needed anything else.

"Water," Brea replied.

"You need anything to eat?"

"Not hungry."

Mo fetched her a tall glass of water with ice cubes tinkling against the sides. There was a small white hair floating on top, but Brea didn't care. She emptied the glass without coming up for breath, and Mo brought her another. Brea drank this slower, blinking invisible tears, then she thanked the kind old barber and left his shop. It was full dark now, and the strip mall teemed with degeneracy. A skinny white kid with oversized jeans hanging around his ass postured in front of her. Brea stepped around him and kept walking.

She headed south, into Lower West, more stores and businesses, but just as much plight. Every street was familiar. It felt like she'd walked them a thousand times. She turned onto Independence Boulevard and passed Sax to the Max, the jazz club she'd first seen from the backseat of Chance's Escalade, with Wilder on one side and Strat on the other. The same youths loitered outside, their faces colored by flickering neon. Brea remembered Strat saying that someone needed to burn this side of town to the ground. A spark of anger flashed inside her. To have been played by these morons— these redneck jackholes—was an indignity she still felt, in spite of her emptiness. She had not forgotten her plan, though. In fact, she was better suited for it, and with Flo removed from the picture, everything was lining up. All she needed was to find Jessie, and this nightmare would be over.

Brea ran a hand over her newly smoothed head and crossed the four-lane street. She walked another block, looked around, and saw Goose again. The Escalade was parked outside the Utopia, its marquee lights re-flected across the pristine paintwork. He sat behind the wheel and stared at her. She was about to cross the street again and find out what his fuck-ing deal was—maybe she wasn't *completely* dead—when Carson and Tay pulled up in their truck, its front tire scuffing along the curb.

"Your sister's six blocks behind you," Tay said, glancing up from the app on his cell phone. "She's coming this way."

Brea looked north on Independence, as if expecting to see Jessie ma-terialize through the glare and traffic. She waited a moment, then turned back to Tay, but the truck was already pulling away. Goose moved out, too. He shot her a final brooding stare, then he was taillights.

"Jessie," she whispered.

Brea headed back the way she'd come, slowly at first, then picking up the pace. She swiveled her neck left and right, checking both sides of the street. To begin with, she couldn't comprehend why Tay had given her Jessie's location, then it dawned on her. The lions were getting hungry. They wanted blood.

She would give it to them.

BREA AND JESSIE SAW EACH other at the same moment, at the intersection of Calhoun and Independence, from opposite sides of the street. They were a stone's throw from the scrub lot where Brea had been dropped off, with its graffitied wall and trashed Chevrolet. Brea recognized the area not from any particular landmark but from the blind guitarist on the corner. He tapped the strings in his cool, bluesy way, his tip jar swinging rhythmically from the headstock.

The sisters locked eyes. In that first instant, it was surreal, as if they had been apart for years, the memories and experiences they'd shared separated by a thousand complicated obstacles. A strange, bruised love flowed between them. Saturday night traffic accumulated at the lights, and Brea crossed, weaving between grilles and rear bumpers. She took her eyes off Jessie only once, looking for Chance's guys. A silver pickup truck idled in traffic a block south. She thought it was probably them, but they were too far away for her to be certain.

*Brea*, Jessie mouthed as Brea closed the distance between them. The guitarist sang about how he got no job, got no woman, and was ridin' a slow train outta town. His voice cut through the ambient noise: the sirens and horns and rumbling engines. Brea waited for a beaten-up minivan to pass, then stepped onto the sidewalk in front of her sister.

Jessie looked her up and down. Tears gathered in her eyes and made them huge. "Brea . . . oh, Brea." She touched her head, as if to make sure her own hair was still there. "What did you do?"

"Follow me," Brea said, and ran.

BREA SPRINTED HALF A BLOCK west on Calhoun and turned right into the scrub lot, dimly lit by a streetlight bolted to a neighboring building. She whipped through the high weeds and trash and came to a sliding, breathless stop not far from the junked car. Jessie wasn't far behind.

At some point after her confrontation with Flo, Brea had returned to the narrow strip of woodland beside the river and yanked the santoku knife from where she'd thrown it into the tree. She'd tucked the blade inside her left boot and pulled the hem of her jeans over the handle, and there it stayed as she traipsed across the city. Now, she quickly dropped to one knee, yanked up her pants leg, and pulled the knife free. As Jessie skidded to a halt in front of her, Brea raised the knife and pressed the tip to her own throat.

Jessie's mouth fell open. She held out her trembling hands. "Brea. *Stop*. My god, what are you *doing*?"

"This is the only way," Brea said. She glanced over Jessie's shoulder, knowing that Chance's thugs would soon appear, cell phones in hand. She needed to do this *now*. "You could never kill me, Jessie. I *know* that. It has to be this way."

"No, Brea. *Please—*"

"I already killed Flo. I didn't want to, but I did it because I knew she'd take you out to save Imani." Brea shook her head, and all the feelings were still inside her. No, she wasn't dead at all. "I couldn't let that happen."

Jessie took a step backward. Her expression crashed. In all their years together, the experiences and heartaches they'd shared, Brea had never seen her like this. It was eviscerating. A terrible pain to feel. Brea watched more tears gather in Jessie's eyes and spill down her cheeks. She doubly hated herself.

"I *had* to." She flexed her fingers around the knife handle.

"Brea . . ."

"Remember back in Jersey, when you told me you didn't know how long you could keep going with the Bang-Bang Sisters? You saw a future for yourself. A normal job. A family. I saw all those things in your eyes, Jessie, and now you get to go live them."

"No, Brea. There's another way." Jessie held her hands out again. "I *know* there is."

A car thrummed west on Calhoun Street, passing the entrance to the scrub lot without slowing. It wasn't one of Chance's guys, but they were coming. No doubt about that.

"This is who *I* am," Brea continued. She thrust out her chest and angled her left arm, showing the abrasions, bruises, and tattoos. "I'm a soldier. A Viking. I was always meant to die on the battlefield."

"No."

"*Yes.*"

"The Trace," Jessie said imploringly. She brought her hands together, as if she might fall to her knees and pray. "They can *help* us. We've got a contact there, remember? We can get them to hack into Chance Kotter's computer, find out where Mom and Imani are being held."

Brea faltered for a moment, her weary mind assessing the pros and cons of Jessie's ballsy idea. She felt a warm rill of blood trickle down her throat where the point of the blade broke her skin.

"No," she said, snapping back to her own grim plan. "It's too risky. Chance has every angle covered. There's only one way you survive this."

"Please, Brea. Give me a few hours." Jessie reached for the knife, then drew her hands back. Her breath hitched in her chest. She used to cry like this when she was a kid. "Until morning, yeah? I just need . . . need a little time to work this out."

"Chance is too smart," Brea said. "He's too dangerous."

She heard the growing roar of trucks' engines and glanced over Jessie's shoulder again. Two pickups rumbled toward the lot, accompanied by the customary backing track of country music. Brea wrinkled her nose. She'd always envisioned dying in an explosion of dirty rock and roll.

"They're coming. Don't let on that this was suicide." Brea clamped her left hand over her right to keep the knife steady. A single, very visible tear curved around her cheekbone. "Chance won't want to feel cheated, so take credit for the kill."

"*No.* Please, Brea. Don't . . . *don't*—"

"I love you, Jess."

BREA WAS GOING TO DO it. It was in her eyes, in her body language. She was going to plunge that seven-inch blade deep into her trachea, and when the trucks pulled to a stop and Chance's goons jumped out, they would find Jessie staring down at her sister's wheezing, dying body.

The last one standing.

It was a beautiful, selfless act, and so typical of Brea, who'd always been there for Jessie and looked out for her like any big sister would. That unconditional love was a two-way street, though, and Jessie wasn't about to stand there, crying like a six-year-old, while Brea sacrificed herself.

It happened in a single frantic blur. Brea lowered the knife three inches, to better put some momentum behind the thrust, and Jessie saw her chance. She struck with her right hand, fingers extended, poking them into Brea's eyes, the same move she'd used on Todd the Pervert. Brea jerked backward, scrunching her eyes shut, giving Jessie another free shot and more time to execute it.

She didn't need to disarm Brea. That would be ideal, but Brea's plan to kill herself and make it appear that Jessie had beaten her in a fight could only work if they were within striking distance of each other. All Jessie needed was to get *away*.

Two attacks: The first, a leg kick, catching Brea below the right knee and unbalancing her. The second, a thumping roundhouse that connected with Brea's upper left arm. She staggered to one side and would have gone crashing to the ground if the wrecked Chevy Impala wasn't there to keep her up. Brea banged into the dented fender and splayed across the hood. The impact echoed between the darkened buildings like a gunshot.

It faded quickly, replaced by the chomp of heavy-duty tires and swelling engine noise. The trucks swept into the lot, bouncing on their suspensions over the uneven asphalt. Their headlights dipped and swayed. Jessie glanced at them—captured in their glare for a moment, like urban wildlife—then ran at the graffitied wall. She intended to scale it, drop down the other side, and run like hell. It was eight feet high, though, requiring strength and technique to get over. In her current condition, both were in short supply. Jessie clasped the top of the wall and pulled herself up, scrabbling with the toes of her boots. She managed to hook an elbow over and was about to lift her battered rib cage onto the wall when Brea grabbed her right ankle from below. She pulled hard. Jessie struggled to hold on but didn't have the purchase. She toppled backward, landed awkwardly on one foot, and spilled to the ground. Her right shoulder took the brunt of the fall, but she felt it in her ribs, too. Stars zipped across her vision, leaving jagged trails.

The trucks stopped close by. Doors flew open. Three of Chance's boys jumped out. Two had cell phones. "We got ourselves a rumble, Mr. Kotter," one of them commentated. It was the good ol' boy with the Roll Tide tattoo who'd directed Jessie toward Independence Boulevard.

Brea stood over Jessie. She still had the knife in her hand but had it concealed behind her forearm. Jessie guessed her strategy: to fall on top of her and wrestle and, during the obscure, close-up work, maneuver the blade up to her chest and lower herself onto it. Chance's guys would be none the wiser.

Knowing this, Jessie was able to anticipate the move. She rolled to her right as Brea dropped, then scrambled to her feet. Now *she* was standing over her sister. Brea looked up, her eyes etched with frustration. She pushed herself to one knee and swiped at Jessie's calf with the knife, wanting only to disable her—slow her down. Jessie anticipated this, too, and sidestepped the attack. She countered with another kick, striking the delicate nub of bone behind Brea's left ear. It was savage but necessary. Brea flopped onto her back with a loud grunt.

"Christ shit," the good ol' boy cackled. "This littlun's got a strip of *dawg* in her."

Jessie wanted to show these redneck fucksticks just how ferocious that strip was—an up close and personal education—but she had to use this window to put some distance between her and Brea. She took another shot at the wall, this time using the trashed Impala, leaping first on the hood, then the roof, then propelling herself toward the graffitied brickwork. Jessie caught the top of the wall with her elbows, dragged one knee up, and flipped herself over. It was an equivalent drop on the other side. She landed on her feet but staggered, bounced off a dumpster, and fell on her ass.

Brea cried out—a wordless, exasperated howl rising above the country music and the hooting of Chance's men.

"Get after her, ya big blond bastard," one of them cawed. "Get over that fuckin' wall."

Jessie didn't stick around to see if Brea would heed this instruction. She got to her feet and ran with no destination in mind, only *away*. She made haphazard lefts and rights, cutting through side streets and alleyways and seedy all-night establishments, not stopping to catch her breath until she was in the hurting ghettos of Shovel Town.

# TWENTY-TWO

Jessie had traversed Upper and Lower West multiple times. She'd seen the desperation, bullet holes, and boarded-over windows prevalent in these neighborhoods, but Shovel Town was different again. It was neglected at best, but more likely forgotten.

She walked potholed roads lined with lowly shotgun shacks with bars across the windows and patched-together walls. Stray dogs eyed her indifferently. Some fought in the trash. A kid, maybe eight years old, swore at her from the steps of a burned-out tenement building. He had a scarred eyelid, and his dirty white tank top poked out on one side, barely concealing the handgun tucked into his jeans. The next two blocks were nothing but rubble. Farther along, she passed an overturned car, a derelict gas station with indigents camping on the roof, and a high school with razor-wire fencing. Gangs occupied street corners and cruised in beaten-up sedans. A shirtless body lay facedown on the sidewalk outside a 24/7 bodega, maybe drunk, maybe dead.

One good thing: no fucking rednecks.

THIS WAS THE MOST DANGEROUS part of the city, and the most comfortable Jessie had felt since arriving. Chance Kotter claimed to have eyes and ears everywhere, friends on every corner. This might be true in Waterloo Square, Colonel Park, the business district, even Upper and Lower West, but it wasn't the case in Shovel Town. It'd be foolish to assume that Chance's influence was nonexistent here, but it was certainly *thinner*. Jessie saw no MAGA ball caps, steel-tipped cowboy boots, or flannel shirts. She heard no Toby Keith or Jason Aldean songs pumping from passing speakers. The pickup trucks with country music on their radio presets and rebel flags on their bumpers did not venture readily this far west of Main.

Jessie was left to her thoughts and to her grief. Both were too burdensome to carry, gathered like boulders in her mind and heart. She did her best to smooth their surfaces, to rearrange and stack them in a way that wouldn't crush her.

There was some light, though. Above the dark houses and broken streetlights, the stars appeared more plentiful in Shovel Town. Her route was arbitrary but consistently took her past a neat little church house with unblemished siding, intact stained glass, and a sublime white cross rising above the door. A sign outside provided a quote from Proverbs: BETTER IS A POOR MAN WHO WALKS IN HIS INTEGRITY THAN A RICH MAN WHO IS CROOKED IN HIS WAYS.

SHE HEARD GUNSHOTS BENEATH A shadowy overpass and didn't go that way. An hour or so later, she was held up by four teenagers. Two of them pointed semiautomatic pistols at her. They wanted her wallet and her phone.

"My pockets are empty. You're welcome to check."

They checked.

"Your jacket then. And your boots."

"These boots won't fit you."

"They'll fit someone."

Jessie sighed and lowered herself to one knee and started to unlace her right boot.

"What's that shit on your ankle?"

"It's a GPS tracker."

"House arrest?"

"No. There are some very bad men tracking me. It's part of a game they're playing."

The teenagers glanced at one another and shrugged. The one who'd done all the talking said, "Keep the boots."

They took her jacket and ran.

SHE RESTED PERIODICALLY, NEVER FOR long. It was better to keep moving. Chance's dipshit army might be reluctant to venture too deep into

Shovel Town, but Brea was not. If she found Jessie—if their two blips came together on the tracking app—she'd likely try that suicide shit again. And with nobody around to prove that Jessie *didn't* kill her, Brea's dark plan might actually work.

*Give me a few hours*, Jessie had pleaded with her. *Until morning, yeah?*

Those hours had passed, though, and morning came. It brought mist and warm rain. The gangs slunk from their corners. More cars appeared on the streets. Residents sat on their front stoops, surveying the new gray day with Sunday morning coffees in hand. The body outside the 24/7 bodega had disappeared.

Jessie walked, splashing through puddles, her arms wet with rain. She passed the little church again and noticed the front door partway open.

RELIGION HAD NEVER BEEN A part of Jessie and Brea's upbringing. Their mom was agnostic. Their stepfather was a Scientologist, a faith he maintained quietly and in his own way. Flo had been religious, though, at least until Johnny Rudd killed her mother. While not *devout*, she had spent weeks in her youth at Bible camps and had told Jessie anecdotes about her family, friends, and neighbors all bundling into a midsized Pontiac to go to church on Sundays. "God's clown car," she'd called it.

Jessie recalled the mirth in Flo's eyes as she regaled her with these stories . . . and it was for Flo that she walked up the short cement path and entered the church that morning.

One prayer, not for salvation, not for mercy, but for her friend.

Her sister.

THE WOODEN PEWS WERE EMPTY. Light came through the stained glass in faintly colored shafts. Jessie marveled at the stillness and silence—a tranquility she'd been bereft of for so long. She started down the aisle, her steps weary but soft. The floor was solid.

She knelt at the altar, looked up at Christ on the cross, then closed her eyes and prayed. It took less than a minute, but she remained on her knees a moment longer, absorbing the incredible peace. Standing afterward, opening her eyes and taking a deep breath, she noticed a door on the other side of a fine grand piano. It, too, was partway open.

Jessie stepped backward to look through the narrow opening. She glimpsed part of a room—an office, obviously, with a computer on the desk. Her eyes grew wide.

A *computer*. Internet access. Somewhere she wouldn't be seen. If Chance or Burl looked at her location on his phone, he'd assume she was praying for guidance.

Jessie crossed the front of the nave, stepped around the piano, and approached the door. She took a calming breath and poked her head through the opening. There was a short hallway beyond with the small office leading off it and two other doors, both closed. A bathroom and storeroom, presumably.

Not a soul in sight.

She stepped into the hallway and then into the office. It was modest, just enough room for the desk, a chair, and an old metal filing cabinet. The window looked out on a stretch of yellow grass with a row of condemned houses beyond, marked for demolition. Scenes from the Old Testament graced the walls: Daniel in the lion's den, Hagar and Ishmael saved, Moses dividing the Red Sea. Jessie sat and looked at the computer. The screensaver was a slideshow of jubilant worshippers. She jiggled the mouse, hoping to be taken to the desktop, but got a lock screen instead. A blinking cursor challenged her to enter a password.

"No," Jessie hissed. She curled over the keyboard and drummed her fists against the sides of her skull. The fates had no love for her.

"You shouldn't be back here."

Jessie snapped backward in the seat and looked up. A thirtysomething female pastor stood in the doorway with her arms folded and one eyebrow raised. She appeared both benevolent and strong—a mother, nurse, and teacher all in one. Her posture was slightly off-center, her face round and gently worn. Jessie wondered at the fortitude required to serve as a conduit to hope in such a downtrodden and abandoned place.

The two women looked at each other. Jessie wanted to say something but could only click her tongue.

"What do you need?" the pastor asked.

"What *don't* I need?" Jessie replied, and went from being able to say nothing to saying, perhaps, too much. "I have no money, no phone, and not a single friend in this whole city. I'm in big trouble. People I love are in big trouble."

The pastor unfolded her arms and lowered her eyebrow. "Sounds like prayer might be a good place to start."

"Yeah. Prayer. I think I'd like that." Jessie nodded, then gestured at the lock screen. "But I'm trying to get in touch with someone, and what I *really* need is your password."

It wasn't meant to be humorous, but the pastor laughed all the same. Her eyes grew big and were full of light.

"Okay," she said. "Okay."

"Okay?"

"Yes." The pastor stopped laughing, but her eyes were still big. "And water? You look like you could use a glass of water."

Jessie smiled gratefully.

The pastor turned and left the room, but took only one step before angling her body backward and peering around the door. She nodded toward the computer on her desk.

"Jesussaves," she said. "All one word."

HER NAME WAS PASTOR VIRGINIA DuPont, and her kindness was as cool and refreshing as the water she brought. She set the glass down without a word and left Jessie alone. Moments later, the sound of the piano rang out in the big room, accompanied by her voice—a barrelful of soul and tenderness—replicating note for note Mahalia Jackson's "How I Got Over." It lifted Jessie like the wind.

As she had on Todd's phone, Jessie first downloaded the Tor browser and from there accessed the Trace. She went through the usual security protocols (still nothing new) and was directed to the landing page. Her attention went immediately to the notification icon in the top right-hand corner of the screen. It was highlighted.

Two new messages.

Both were from 9-$tar. The first was sent at 1:53 on Saturday afternoon, three and a half hours after Jessie had sent her last message. It read: A setup? Pls clarify. The second came through late last night, at around the time Brea had held a knife to her own throat. Jessie read this second message at least a dozen times. She could barely breathe.

Call me if u can. 5055550178. (Burner phone–SAFE)

These last thirty-three hours—scratch that, this entire *week*, since being jumped by Chance's crew—had pummeled and emptied her. There'd been no respite, no haven. The previous ten minutes had followed a different script, however, first with Pastor Virginia, and now with 9-$tar. Jessie had hands to hold.

She looked from the number on the screen to a telephone—an old-school landline—on the desk. She reached for it, then stopped. This could be a trap, of course. Jessie could dial that number and Burl would answer. Or Chance.

Pastor Virginia sang and sang. The church's acoustics carried and shaped every note. Outside, the rain had picked up. It slapped the window, keeping a different beat.

Jessie drew her hand back, then looked at the screen again. "Five-oh-five," she said, reading the area code. She googled it. Albuquerque, New Mexico. This didn't mean it *wasn't* a trap. An area code could be masked as easily as an IP address, she supposed, but what good would doubt and fear do her now? Flo was dead, and Brea was determined to be next. Jessie had to do something.

She picked up the phone and punched in the number. She messed it up the first two times but nailed it on the third. The line buzzed and clicked as a connection was made to a burner phone somewhere—she hoped—in the Land of Enchantment. Jessie gripped the receiver, holding it close to her ear. She heard the droning dial tone. It rang five times . . . six . . . seven . . . then Jessie realized she was calling the mountain time zone, where it was only 6:33 A.M.

She was about to hang up when a sleepy voice answered.

"J.S.?"

They had only ever communicated through DMs—had never heard each other's voices—but in saying her initials (the only thing about Jessie he knew), 9-$tar sounded as familiar as a lifelong friend. The relief was staggering.

"How did you know it was me?" she asked, catching her breath.

"I only gave this number to one person."

Jessie nodded. A warmth spread through her chest. She closed her eyes and felt herself unfurling.

"I need your help," she said.

# TWENTY-THREE

Flo had been moving more fluidly, though not without pain, for several hours, keeping herself hydrated and sporadically checking Brea's and Jessie's locations on the cell phone that Burl had given her. She'd watched a murky sunrise from one of the upstairs office windows, enjoying a view of the acres of farmland, forests, and freedom east of Reedsville. Shortly afterward, while mentally preparing herself to leave the relatively safe confines of the office space and put an end to this nightmare, a grayness swept through her and she passed out. Maybe she'd overdone it. Maybe it was a reaction to the many painkillers she'd taken, combined with whatever Burl had injected her with. Maybe it was good old-fashioned anxiety. Either way, she reacted, lost herself for a while, and woke up covered in sweat.

She hadn't been out for long. The clock on her newly acquired phone read 7:42, so maybe an hour. On the plus side, she emerged feeling clearer headed. She tested her body with another three laps of the office complex and two sets of stairs. At 8:34, Flo shimmied into her stiff, uncomfortable jeans and—not without considerable effort—strapped on her boots. She refilled one of the empty water bottles from the bathroom faucet, slotted the balisong into her back pocket, and, after nineteen hours of fast-tracked recuperation, left the vacant building.

RAIN FELL, AND THE AIR smelled faintly of grit and heat. Flo drew her left arm inside her T-shirt to keep the splint dry. She crossed the bridge she'd been thrown off without looking over the side. Her progress was slow.

The Track-U-Gen app placed Jessie in Shovel Town, where she'd been all night. Flo estimated she was four miles away—an hour's walk, for a more able body. Brea was in Lower West, considerably closer.

*You can't go toe-to-toe with them*, Burl had mansplained. *You're not fast enough or strong enough. They'll cut you down.* Flo looked west toward Main and spoke yet more of Burl's redundant advice out loud.

"Use stealth."

She even groomed an invisible mustache, which raised the ghost of a smile.

FLO STOLE AN M-65 FIELD jacket from a coatrack in a restaurant waiting area and a patchouli-scented bandanna from the neck of a spaniel tethered to a hydrant. The former kept her dry. The latter lifted the hair out of her eyes; it tended to flop when it got wet. Both served as a partial disguise, should she need one.

She could monitor her erstwhile sisters and hide from them but could not hide from Burl. He rolled up in his shiny silver Yukon as she approached the intersection of Harper and Main. The pendant swinging from the rearview brought a flashback that rocked her.

"How you feeling?"

"Not good."

"You look better than you did yesterday." Burl winked. "I guess that $B_{12}$ did the trick."

"It did something."

"You know where your friends are?"

"You gave me the phone, didn't you?"

"Uh-huh. Looking out for us both."

"Some would call it cheating."

"Some would," Burl agreed. "But Chance won't be any the wiser, and his bookmaker is a corrupt dog with more money than I could ever spend."

Flo wiped rainwater from her face, taking care around her gashed cheekbone.

"Now . . ." Burl lifted his cell phone from the holder clamped to the air vent and pointed the back of it at Flo. "Chance wants a visual on you. Go ahead and give him a big smile."

Flo didn't give Chance a big smile. Burl shot ten seconds of video regardless.

"Ain't you a sourpuss," he said, appraising his camerawork. "How about you put your game face on instead? I'll have two corpses to ID by the end of the day, and I'd sooner yours wasn't one of them."

He drove away, and Flo spat onto the road where his SUV had idled. She held her fractured arm a moment, then caught a breath and moved on.

FLO SAW BREA AN HOUR later. She'd referenced the app every now and then, trying to get a read on her direction. It was not a question of getting to where Brea was but where she was going to be. There were few shadows at this time of day, even in Reedsville, but striking from a doorway or from behind a parked car would be just as effective.

It took time. Flo went wrong more than once, and Brea was a faster walker. The randomness of Brea's route didn't help, and she doubled back on occasion. Flo finally got ahead of her on Brooks Street and watched her approach through the windows of a parked van.

She had two immediate reactions. The first was one of surprise. Brea had shaved her beautiful blond hair, right down to the scalp. She looked more resolute and, despite the marks on her face, more impenetrable. She had rigidness and angles where before Flo had seen only smooth lines. It spoke to Brea's character, perhaps—a fierceness she'd so often depended on, now stripped of its pretty layers.

Flo's second reaction was fear. Their long fight flashed through her mind. It took only seconds, but she experienced every blow again, both given and received. Her legs threatened to fold beneath her. She leaned against the van and gasped.

Brea approached on the other side of Brooks Street. Flo remained out of sight and waited until she had passed, then staggered in the opposite direction. She ducked down a side street, cut through a deli, and hid in a back alley. Displaced rats scurried, complaining. Flo closed her eyes and breathed and waited for the tremendous anxiety in her chest to subside.

She hadn't realized how unprepared she was. A psychological wall had been constructed, one that Flo would need to knock down. Killing Jessie would be no easier. It would present different obstacles, but trauma was not one of them.

It took several minutes for her gunning heart to slow. One positive: the rain had stopped in that time and a strip of sunlight found the alleyway. Flo took the phone from her pocket and accessed Track-U-Gen. Brea's blip was ten blocks east already, approaching Main. Jessie had left Shovel Town and was now in Upper West, maybe three miles away.

"Okay," Flo said. "Jessie first."

She exited the alleyway onto Plantation Street. From here she had an uninhibited view northeast, toward the Wishbone Bridge and business district. Chance's skyscraper caught the sunlight like a blade. As Flo watched, its glowing digital clock switched from 10:59 to 11:00.

Eleven hours remaining.

BREA'S NIGHT HAD PASSED AS expected: long and cruelly. She'd walked circles for hours, rebuffed supplications for sex, drugs, and money, then tucked herself into a doorway and caught thin patches of sleep. She gave up somewhere around dawn and sat with sheets of newspaper wrapped around her upper body, watching puddles form on the sidewalk. An elderly woman who evidently believed Brea to be homeless handed her an apple, and she ate it as Eve might have, voraciously, as if it were the first apple she'd ever seen. She then ventured out into the rain, marveling—laughing, even—at the cool feel of the drops on her shaved head. It was a rare pleasure, and she was grateful to have experienced it on what would undoubtedly be the last morning of her life.

The next hours passed in a colorless stupor. Brea dragged her feet through the wet city streets, and although she felt hollow, there were times when she sensed the full weight of her guilt and burdens. Intermittently, she considered what Jessie had said: that there was another way—that they could use the Trace to get into Chance's computer and compromise his scheme. The idea was not without appeal, but Brea knew it was too dangerous a strategy. Chance's techies had already gotten their hooks into the Trace. Instigating a communication could end very badly.

The rain stopped. The sun edged higher, glimpsed through gray-tipped scraps of cloud. Carson's truck pulled alongside her as she trudged past a bus stop on Tallassee Avenue. He buzzed the passenger-side window down and announced—as if she needed reminding—that time was running out.

"I can end this quickly," Brea said, "if you tell me where my sister is."

Carson shook his head.

"What? No more clues?"

"No *nothing* without Mr. Kotter's say-so," Carson said, scratching his stubbly throat. "And Mr. Kotter is presently at church."

Brea had no response to that. She wiped dampness from the back of her neck and sighed.

"There'll be blood, though, in some fashion," Carson added. "Some of us are thinking now that it'll be your mama and that pregnant gal catching bullets."

Brea stopped walking, swaying in her boots as a sick feeling spread through her stomach. "Tell me where my sister is. Or where*abouts*. I just need a street name. Look at your phone and—"

"She's about halfway to hell," Carson interjected. A husky laugh rumbled from his chest. "I don't need my phone to tell you that. And you're a couple of steps ahead of her."

Brea's sick feeling turned to anger, but before it could manifest, Carson stepped on the gas and rejoined the flow of traffic. Brea sagged against the wall of the bus shelter and considered other ways she could end this *without* it looking like suicide. Would Chance determine that she'd broken the rules if she "accidentally" stepped in front of a freight train or a city bus? Or if she wandered into the hood and picked a fight with one of the gangs?

If there was a shred of consolation, it was in knowing that, one way or another, this would all be over soon.

SHE SPOTTED GOOSE OUTSIDE THE Wells Fargo on Main Street and again in Colonel Park. Just doing his job, probably, but Brea began to wonder if he had an alternative agenda. When she saw him an hour or so later, ogling her from the parking lot of the Waffle House on Franklin, she decided to confront him.

He was bouncing gum between his pearly whites, one elbow cocked on the open window.

"Goose, right?"

"That's what they call me."

"Why?"

"It's a *Top Gun* thing."

"Really?" Brea frowned, looking at his pale skin, smooth head, and boyish mustache. "You don't look anything like Goose from *Top Gun*."

Goose grinned and ran a hand over his head. "I wasn't always bald, you know. Speaking of which: I preferred *you* with long hair." He twirled a finger, gesturing at her getup. "This cue-ball thing isn't doing it for me."

"Like I give a fuck." Brea wrinkled her nose, then appraised him in a more curious fashion. "What's your deal? You're not like the others."

"What do you mean?"

"Chance's other minions watch me, but you *stare*."

"Is there a difference?"

"A big difference."

"Well, I wasn't aware I was staring." Goose swallowed hard. His Adam's apple bobbed in slow motion. "You look like someone I used to know. A *lot* like her—at least you used to, before you shaved your head."

"An old girlfriend?"

"Something like that," Goose said. "My wife, actually."

A herd of manic children, shepherded by one unfortunate adult, exited the Waffle House with the energy and furor of a drum solo. They twisted wildly between the parked cars, then saw Brea and stopped in their tracks. Brea—gaunt and tattooed, barely upright in her boots—flashed her teeth and sent them scattering. Elsewhere, a homeless woman on crutches canvassed drivers at a stoplight.

"I lived in Japan for three years," Goose continued, and Brea turned her attention back to him. "That's where I met Marit. She was Norwegian, a teacher, a sweetheart. We got married, then she got into a car accident and everything changed."

"She died?"

"Not right away. She was on a machine for seven weeks. Her parents wanted to hit the switch, but I held on to the crazy notion that she'd wake up and everything would go back the way it was." Goose gave his head a sad little shake. "Long story short: she didn't, and I decided to end her life support."

Brea wondered if Goose had been a decent man back in the day and had spiraled after this tragedy—a series of desperate moves and bad decisions, perhaps some jail time, culminating in him coming to Reedsville and landing a job with Chance Kotter, no moral compass required.

"Anyway, you are, or *were*"—Goose indicated Brea's new haircut by gesturing at his own head—"Marit's spitting image. What's the word? Her doppelgänger. It's disconcerting, is all, given what she meant to me."

"And here you are now, working for Chance Kotter, a worthless, corrupt piece of shit." Brea looked briefly at the heavens, then at Goose. "Marit would be so proud."

Goose spat his gum out the open window. "Every coin has two sides. In Chance's eyes, he's the good guy. He protects the people he loves and the things he's worked for."

"You believe that?"

"Let's just say I don't *question* it."

"This whole thing, you brainless fucking goons buying into Chance's methods, his *bullshit*—" Brea placed her hands on her hips and shook her head. "Jesus, this city. It's one big cult."

The homeless woman clopped forlornly along, her head held low and her raggedy clothes blowing. She looked like Brea felt: far less than a person, an unloved remnant.

"I'm just so tired," Brea said. Her fire had not quite gone out. A few smoldering embers remained. She peered through the Escalade's rear window—its backseat long and plush and dark—and one of those embers turned suddenly into a small flame. Her gaze flicked back to Goose. "Why don't you tell me where my sister is, and this'll all be over."

"No can do," Goose said.

Brea shrugged her shoulders. On the inside, she curled her hands around that flame and blew on it gently. "How about that backseat? I could do with resting my head somewhere comfortable for an hour."

"I'm sure you could, but Mr. Kotter says no help, no unfair advantages, at least not without his approval."

"Come on, man. I slept in a fucking doorway last night."

"Not my problem."

Brea took a step closer. She rested her forearm on Goose's open window and looked into his eyes. "Okay, listen. There's a better than average chance I'll be dead by the end of the day. I just . . . you know, want one last moment of comfort."

Goose shook his head. Two pink spots had bloomed high on his cheeks. He let out a wheezy breath and pressed the engine start button in the dash, perhaps meaning to drive away, take himself beyond the orbit of temptation. He was close to doing it, too—his right hand even grasped the shifter—then he screwed his eyes shut and gestured at the backseat.

"Get in," he said.

"Good decision," Brea said, curling her lip. She opened the rear passenger door and got inside.

# TWENTY-FOUR

Jessie asked for the time. The first four people she approached ignored her. The fifth—a teen wearing ratty Converse Chucks and black lipstick—fished a phone from his back pocket and monotoned that it was nearly one o'clock.

9-$tar was still an hour away, maybe a little longer, depending on traffic. Jessie thanked the teen and continued toward her destination, a repurposed warehouse in the industrial district.

SHE HAD TOLD 9-$TAR EVERYTHING. It took a while. Pastor Virginia had checked on her three times, and Jessie kept holding up her fingers. *Two more minutes . . . one more minute.* She was also aware that her red blip had been locked in this location for too long. Chance's band of brothers was no fan of Shovel Town, but if someone decided to investigate and found Jessie in front of a computer, talking on the phone, this whole thing would reach a miserable new high.

"Where are you now?" 9-$tar had asked after a long pause.

"I'm at a church in one of Reedsville's less desirable neighborhoods, and that's putting it kindly." Jessie looked out the window at the row of condemned houses. "I can't stay here for long, though."

"Okay," 9-$tar said. There was a snappy, decisive edge to his voice that Jessie liked. "TTPs: tactics, techniques, and procedures. I can probably link to Chance Kotter's computer through his cell phone. That's like finding the door, but we still have to unlock it."

"Right," Jessie said. Her heart fluttered. She wasn't sure, but she thought it might be hope.

"Then it's a matter of figuring out the best mode of attack from there."

"Yes." *Mode of attack.* She liked the sound of that.

"Very important: you and I need to keep a line of communication open, so I can tell you what's happening, and when I need further information," 9-$tar said. Jessie heard papers rustling in the background, a keyboard rattling. "How often can you get to a phone?"

"I . . . no, it's . . ." Jessie closed her eyes and drummed her fist lightly on the top of Pastor Virginia's desk. "I'm being watched. It's not easy."

"Gimme a sec." 9-$tar's keyboard rattled again. The sound lasted twenty seconds, but it felt much longer. "Yeah, thought so. That's good."

"What?"

"The Trace is made up of . . . I'm going to guess a hundred hackers, maybe a hundred and fifty, all of us working from home. We have hubs, though, in multiple cities across the country. You know, rendezvous points, places where we can meet up in person and brainstorm." His tone brightened briefly. He sounded like someone describing a scene from his favorite TV show. "Imagine a bunch of geeks with laptops, putting their heads together and getting the skinny on some real fucking dirtbags."

Jessie imagined it. That fluttering inside her grew more intense. It *was* hope.

"The big cities have multiple hubs," 9-$tar continued. "There are four in Los Angeles and New York. Chicago has three. You get the picture."

"Yeah," Jessie whispered.

"There's one in Reedsville."

Jessie switched the receiver to her other hand, unsurprised to feel the dampness on her palm and around her ear. Her heart rate had accelerated, a clear and constant drum.

"Let me see . . . it's in the southeast of the city. Emmaus Drive, close to the river." 9-$tar made a whistling sound through his teeth and rattled his keyboard. "I've never been. Looks like a refurbished warehouse. I can meet you there, but it won't be soon. I'll need—"

"Wait, *what*? You're in Albuquerque, right?" Jessie blinked, calculating the distance between the middle of New Mexico and Reedsville, Alabama. It had to be a thousand miles. "I mean, how . . . *what*?"

"Albuquerque?" 9-$tar said, the confusion evident in his voice. It took him a couple of seconds to clue in. "Oh, right . . . no, I applied an ABQ area code to this burner. An extra layer of protection. I'm actually in Louisiana, in the Florida Parishes. It's still five hours away, and that's if I boot it."

"Five," Jessie said, and winced. That was a big chunk of the day.

"Once I've got my ass into gear, sorted a few things out here, my ETA will be . . . let's say two o'clock." 9-$tar moved again. She heard his chair creak. "That gives us eight hours to get into Chance Kotter's shit and see what's happening behind the scenes."

"Yeah?" Jessie took a deep breath. "Can you find out where they're holding my mom and Imani?"

"I can try. I'll think of something, for sure."

"My god, thank you." She covered her eyes, quivering in her seat. "Thank you, Nine-Star. *Thank you.*"

"Call me Aaron."

"Aaron." She smiled. "And I'm Jessie. The *J* in J.S., that's what it . . . you know . . ."

"Jessie. Yeah. Got it." Aaron's soft laughter floated over the line. "Listen, I know you can't stay at the hub for long, so I'll give you a working burner. That way you can wander around the city, pretend to play their sick-ass game, and check in with me every hour or so. I'll keep you updated."

Jessie had always been quick to tears and made no apology for it. Tears were not a sign of weakness. Uncle Dog had always told her that tears were a sign of *heart*, and it was heart that made you fight. She remembered this now, wiping her eyes as her breath caught in her throat in a succession of shrill little jumps.

"Hey, don't cry, Jessie," 9-$tar said. "This is going to work out."

"Yeah."

"We've got this." His voice was full of care and reassurance. He said it again, reiterating these words, and Jessie soaked them up. She didn't dare believe. Not yet. But she wanted to. "We've got this."

EMMAUS DRIVE WAS A STRIP of commercial properties with an industrial aesthetic. There was a medical center, a sporting goods outlet, a large pet store, a U-Haul truck rental, various units selling goods ranging from wholesale meats to auto parts, and, of course, the building that accommodated one of the Trace's many hubs. It might have been a warehouse once—albeit a small one—but not anymore. Its bay doors had been bricked over, and windows had been built into its upper floor. Jessie thought it could function as office space, maybe even condos. There was a shared parking area in back with the Mary beyond.

Jessie walked past it at 1:34 and again at 1:52—the time clearly visible on the Kotter-Bryce Tower across the river. The first time, she scoped it casually. The second time, she looked for the signal that 9-$tar was there and waiting for her: a handwritten note on the front door reading NO SOLICITTING, deliberately misspelled. This had been Jessie's idea; she couldn't risk being seen outside with 9-$tar and walking into the warehouse together.

No note at 1:52, either. Jessie walked south for eight minutes, then cut west. She passed Cheap Spills, the dive bar where she'd left Todd the Pervert bleeding on the restroom floor. One good thing had come from that unpleasant exchange: Todd's cell phone, which she had used to establish a communication with 9-$tar. It was pretty fucked up to think that, without Todd, she'd be without even this sliver of hope.

North again, past a huge factory parking lot and more gray units. Chance's head of security, Burl, drove by in his shiny Yukon. He slowed down but didn't stop, just stared at her through his window. In keeping with her character, Jessie flipped him both middle fingers and mouthed, *Fuuuuck you*. She wanted him thinking that nothing had changed in her world.

Two thirteen. East on Emmaus. Jessie kept her eyes peeled for countrified fuckwits. She walked past the repurposed warehouse for a third time. Still no sign that 9-$tar was there. Frustration gathered inside her. She forced a steadying breath and reminded herself that the dude was driving all the way from Louisiana. As she crossed the street, walking away from the warehouse, Jessie glanced over her shoulder and noticed the front door swinging open. A dark-haired man appeared with a sheet of paper in his hand, which he taped to the door before going back inside. Jessie stopped. A cold flush ran through her body. She walked back toward the warehouse until she could read what was written on the sheet of paper. NO SOLICITTING. Jessie lifted a trembling hand to her mouth and surreptitiously checked her surroundings. There was plenty of activity—cars going both ways, customers shuffling in and out of the businesses—but no clear sign of anybody from Chance's crew.

Jessie's hope expanded, more than a sliver now. It felt like something she could hold and feel the weight of. She crossed the street and stepped onto the plain concrete lot outside the warehouse.

There was a window next to the door. She saw a light on inside.

"WHAT THE FUCK ARE YOU DOING?"

Flo gritted her teeth and sighed. "What do you mean?"

"Jessie is in the southeast of the city. I just saw the little bitch." Burl cleared his throat. Flo heard the tension in his chest and wondered how much of his kids' college fund he'd bet on her. Enough, she supposed. "She's been walking around the same goddamn neighborhood for thirty minutes, and you're what . . . a mile away?"

"Something like that," Flo replied.

"Jesus Christ. Get your fucking head in the game."

Flo was on Main Street, heading south. She'd spent the last three hours getting steadily closer to Jessie's blip, psyching herself up, occasionally stopping to rest her jangly limbs. When the phone in her pocket rang—it could only be Burl—she'd stepped into the dank stairway of a parking garage so she could answer in privacy.

"Cut me some slack," Flo hissed now, and lowered her voice another notch. "In case you didn't realize, it takes a lot of mental preparation to kill someone you love."

"Meanwhile, the clock is ticking."

"I still have time."

"What if I have to patch you up again?"

"You won't," Flo said. "She won't see me coming."

"Pray you're right." Burl breathed through his teeth, a sound like grit in a bag. "I'm heading out to Chance's now to set up some video feeds. You'd better be right on top of her by the time I get there."

He ended the call. Flo gripped the phone in her right hand, squeezing hard enough to glitch the screen. She took thirty seconds to get her shit together—as together as her shit could be, under the circumstances—and opened Track-U-Gen. Jessie's blip flashed in the industrial district, not far from the river. A mile, Burl had said, and he wasn't far off. Flo could cross Main, cut through Colonel Park, then continue south. Her aches and pains had numbed but not disappeared, and whatever Burl had injected her with couldn't cure her concussion. Still, one mile . . . she could do that in twenty minutes.

Maybe twenty-five.

JESSIE GLANCED THROUGH THE WINDOW and saw an unfinished entryway: a concrete floor, unpainted drywall, studs showing in places. It appeared the refurbishment was an ongoing process. She checked her surroundings again before entering. A few people walked in and out of the pet store across the street, but nobody looked twice at her.

It was just a matter of time before a pickup truck or SUV drove past this place, its driver checking it against his GPS app. He'd likely assume she was inside resting, maybe catching some z's before the final push. No rule against that. But Jessie didn't want to stay too long and provoke his curiosity. She would help 9-$tar get up and running, then she'd grab the burner and go.

Jessie opened the warehouse door and stepped inside. The entryway was L-shaped and smelled of wood, sawdust, and cement. She followed it around and came to a larger space with partially finished walls and neatly stacked building materials across the floor. A thin dust hung in the air. The ceiling was a maze of exposed wires and ductwork. It would make for an attractive complex of offices or apartments one day, but there was a lot of work to be done.

9-$tar sat on a stack of drywall panels, eating a sandwich, a laptop computer balanced on his knees. He was so absorbed in his work that he didn't notice Jessie until the tip of her boot kicked a small stone, sending it scuttling across the floor. 9-$tar jumped and looked up, the sandwich halfway to his mouth.

"Jessie?"

"Nine-Star?"

"Yeah." He closed his laptop and set the half-eaten sandwich down on top. "Wow, you *scared* me. And it's Aaron, remember?"

"Right, yeah. Sorry."

Aaron grinned and flapped his hand. He didn't look so different from the image that Jessie had conjured during their DMs over recent months, with his angular, geeky face and his hair standing in awkward quills. He had a chipped front tooth, she noticed, which gave him the look of a mischievous eight-year-old. Certainly, he could cause a lot of mischief with that computer.

"It's good to meet you, I guess," Jessie said, and pulled a face. "Okay, that didn't sound right. I'm sorry, it's just . . . I'd rather *not* be in this position, if you know what I mean."

Aaron gave her a comforting smile. "I understand. And just so you know, this is weird for me, too. The Trace is built on a foundation of anonymity. Meetups with operatives are extremely rare. I'm not sure it's ever happened before."

Jessie shuffled her feet. "I appreciate it, especially with you coming all this way."

"It's an exceptional set of circumstances," Aaron said. There was a childlike squeak to his voice. He coughed and thumped his chest. "Besides, we're all big fans of your work."

"I . . . I don't . . ." Jessie clicked her tongue.

Aaron ran a hand through his hair, raising more stiff quills. "We should, you know . . . make a start." He finished his sandwich in three bites and jammed his laptop into a backpack on the floor at his feet. Jessie used those few seconds to take in the environment, defining the basic layout: several rooms around a large, central space. It appeared to be more finished toward the rear of the building. Two of the rooms had complete walls. One even had a door.

"This is your hub?" she asked, inadvertently curling her lip. "It's not quite what I expected."

"I know, right?" Aaron threw his backpack over one shoulder. "You were probably thinking beanbags and foosball."

"An espresso machine at the very least."

"Yeah, I've been to the one in New Orleans a few times. It's *exactly* like that. Reedsville, however . . ." He spread his hands and sighed. "This is a fucking construction site."

"No kidding."

"Upstairs is finished, though." He pointed at the ceiling. "It's not exactly the Google headquarters, but it'll do."

He slipped off the stacked drywall panels and started across the warehouse floor. Jessie followed, navigating around the assorted materials, stepping between the framing studs of what would one day be a wall. There was a hallway on the other side leading to a wide set of stairs. Aaron and Jessie headed toward them, their footsteps echoing in the naked space. They were nearly there when Jessie faltered, suddenly consumed by the enormity of what they were trying to achieve, the risks involved, and her gratitude to Aaron. She stumbled, needing the wall for support.

"Hey, are you okay?" Aaron had stopped, looking over his shoulder with concern.

"Yeah, I'm . . . I'm . . ."

"You look like you're going to pass out."

Jessie shook her head and pushed herself off the wall. She wobbled on her feet for a moment, then took three steps forward and pulled Aaron into an inelegant but grateful embrace.

"I know I've already thanked you. It's just . . . I can't even."

"I get it," he replied, placing one tentative hand on the small of her back. "It's a lot."

"You don't get it. You couldn't possibly. But that's okay."

They parted. Jessie expressed her appreciation again, this time with her eyes, mustering all the feeling inside her. Aaron acknowledged her with a quivering smile and turned back toward the stairs. Now it was his turn to look unsteady on his feet. He managed several shaky steps and stopped.

"What is it?" Jessie asked.

"I'm . . . I'm fine." Aaron unshouldered his backpack and reached inside. Jessie heard a bright beep followed by a whirring sound. It sounded like a small fan. Aaron then removed a length of clear vinyl tubing—a nasal cannula—from inside the pack. He looped it over his ears and inserted the prongs into his nostrils. His eyes fluttered for a second, then snapped back into focus.

"Okay," he said. "Let's go."

# TWENTY-FIVE

Getting into strange men's vehicles was not something that Brea made a habit of. She had a plan, though, involving the santoku knife and Goose's throat. What she hadn't accounted for was actually falling asleep. Goose started driving, and the comfort of the backseat, coupled with the lulling motion of the ride and her fatigue, caused her eyes to grow heavy—or *heavier*, to be more accurate. Brea put her head back, then she was gone. She dreamed, too, a sequence of disturbing snapshots, most of them involving Flo, and woke up to find Goose had parked in the shady lot behind an auto repair shop. The touchscreen clock read 2:19, and he was jerking off in the driver's seat.

"Marit," he grunted, stealing glances at Brea over his shoulder. "Marit . . . *Maaa-rihhht* . . ."

Brea moved quickly. She whipped the knife from inside her boot, reached around Goose's seat from behind, and pressed the edge of the blade against his throat.

"You really miss your wife, huh?"

"Whuuffuck?" He was still jerking off.

"Put your dick away, boss."

"Hnnnh?"

Brea locked the blade tighter to Goose's throat. She drew a line of blood, and Goose put his dick away.

"Okay. Here's what's going to happen: you're going to open the GPS app on your phone and drive me to wherever my sister is." Brea leaned over the seat and tickled her breath against Goose's ear. "That's it. Your one instruction. Simple, right?"

"Ngggh. Fcckk."

"No, Goose, this is not open to negotiation. And I'd avoid bumpy roads, if I were you, because this knife is staying right where it is." Brea *did* lessen the tension, though, just a touch, so that Goose could breathe.

"We're not . . ." Goose hissed and swallowed, and Brea felt it through the blade. "We're not allowed to interfere. Everything . . . everything has to be fair. Mr. Kotter's rules."

"*Nothing* about this is fair," Brea said.

"Okay, but . . . he's not . . . not going to like this."

"He's not going to like that you were whacking off in his top-of-the-line Cadillac, either." Brea tickled Goose's ear again. "Now we both have a secret."

Goose nodded. He started the ignition and turned on his phone, mounted to the dash. "Which sister?" He clunked the transmission into drive and tapped the Track-U-Gen icon.

Brea narrowed her eyes. "What do you mean?"

"Which fucking sister?" Goose snarled, and jabbed a finger at the phone's screen. "Blue or red?"

"There's only one," Brea said. Her voice cracked with hesitation. She recalled throwing Flo off the Wishbone Bridge. It was the clearest, most dominant memory in her head. Flo had hit the water, gone down, and not come back up. "There should only be one."

Goose sneered and lifted his chin, perhaps getting the blade into a more comfortable position. He scrolled through the map on his phone, highlighting Jessie's red blip, then zoomed out to show Flo's blue blip. She was in Colonel Park, maybe half a mile from Jessie.

"Blue or red?" he asked again.

Brea's heart fell into the pit of her stomach with a wet, heavy splash. At the same time, it escalated in tempo and drummed tightly in her throat. Impossible, but there it was. Her legs flushed cold. Her upper body trembled. The blade jiggled against Goose's throat.

"You thought you'd killed her," he said. Their eyes met in the rearview.

Brea didn't want to respond, but her head moved loosely up and down.

"Afraid not." A smile crept onto Goose's face. "She dragged herself out of the river about half a mile from the bridge and laid low for the night. Recuperating, probably. Now she's back in the fight."

"Yeah," Brea gasped.

"So . . ." Goose lifted his foot off the brake and got the SUV rolling. He pulled out of the lot behind Bunny Digg's Auto and turned west on Franklin. "Which fucking sister?"

Brea closed her eyes. Her plan had been knocked on its ass, kicked through the dirt, and hauled back to the beginning. There was only one answer to that question.

She had to kill Flo all over again.

THE BOY WHO WOULD ONE day become the wren escaped the foster care system when he was seventeen, after his maternal grandfather (a wretched being) dropped dead of a stroke and his *nonna* invited him to live with her. The boy suspected it had more to do with her not wanting to be alone than any real kindness, but he was okay with that. The arrangement suited them both.

At age twenty-one, the boy, now the man, came into his inheritance: a college fund started by his parents in 1990, which, by 2006, was worth close to $100,000. It was not a life-changing sum of money, but it allowed the man to buy a powerful computer and a two-year course in advanced programming. It also gave him focus. An *identity*. Ever since the death of his parents, he'd felt soulless and isolated. He would spend long periods of time staring into a mirror and seeing nothing. With this new interest and education, the man began to take shape. In many ways, it felt like he was learning his own complex scripting language, understanding how his solitude worked and his hands and his pancreas and his limbic cortex. He had discovered a place in the world that was neither deep nor high but was all his own. His name was Aaron Gallo-Day.

He showed a remarkable proficiency with computers, quickly mastering Linux and other UNIX-like operating systems, becoming fluent in JavaScript and Python, eventually coding his own open-source materials. Through these, Aaron connected with a slew of like-minded creatives (some of whom would go on to form the network of gray hatters known as the Trace), developing social bonds, something he'd never managed to achieve in the real world. This was one of the many benefits of an online existence. He could explore, interact, and infiltrate without ever needing to leave his house. PTSD and agoraphobia did not exist in an environment of clients, servers, and protocols.

It was not enough, though. Coding provided purpose and escape, but not elevation. Aaron's first hack was for an Alabaman gubernatorial candidate, uncovering extremely sensitive data on a sworn rival. The clandestine nature of the work had sparked Aaron, but his feet never left the ground. His first kill was a seventeen-year-old autistic girl named Lucy Winthrop, and it had lifted him above the rooftops.

Aaron had hacked her life first, learning her routine. She was a keen swimmer and photographer and loved Mexican food and Lady Gaga. Every day, she posted a picture of her cat on Facebook. **PAWZ SAYZ HIYA!** Her mother had been killed in a train derailment in 2012. Her father worked at the Mary River Distillery and was known to imbibe. He bowled for the Reedsville Bronze Frogs every Friday and always came home drunk. One such Friday—the early hours of Saturday morning, in fact—he tottered through the back door, into the kitchen, and found Lucy dead on the tiles with a knife in her throat. It was ruled a suicide, but there were many who believed the old man responsible.

In Lucy, Aaron had recognized someone both fragile and limitless. Killing her had revealed an elevated perspective and a continued education of himself. He understood now how his breathing worked and his pineal gland and his scapulae and his dreams. He saw the freedoms he'd yearned for since being trapped in the wreckage with his dead parents, embodied by the small brown bird on the other side of the broken window.

He killed again seven months later and again a year after that. Both victims were homeless women, and he'd dragged their threadbare bodies down to the Mary and filled their chest cavities with rocks and tumbled them into deep water.

In 2020, his wren alter ego was born and as such claimed his first victim: Beverly Pickens, a fifty-two-year-old widow originally from Chicago. The final phrase of the haiku—written on a piece of yellow paper and placed in Beverly's left hand—read: *My song will be heard.* The wren had left her body in her garage beside the recycling bins and beneath a bicycle secured to the wall, blood and feathers everywhere, more feathers stuffed into Beverly's many wounds. He had achieved incredible altitude that night, breaking the iron bands that circled his chest, extricating himself from his crippling anxieties. The car in which he'd been trapped with his dead parents, and all the troubles that had arisen from it, were too small to see with the naked eye.

Beverly's killing was as dramatic and impactful as high art, which was exactly how Aaron viewed it. He'd created a display, an *exhibit*, to be shared and analyzed, that would incite a rush of emotion. The wren was a somebody now. A celebrity. He'd turned from an imprisoned, broken boy into a virtuoso with beautiful brown feathers and a clear, ringing voice.

All great artists sought their masterpiece, though, a defining work that would demand of them and pull from their souls, but reward in new and uplifting ways. Aaron recognized his from the moment he first set eyes on her, in a promo shot for the California-based cover band Crash the Moon. Such a sultry demeanor, but with a posture as sheer as a cliff face and shoulders he could build a nest between. And now here she was, desperate and scared and entirely—*entirely*—dependent on him.

He opened the door to his apartment and stepped to one side, letting Jessie enter ahead of him. As she did, he removed a stun gun from his pocket—it wasn't much larger than a cell phone—and locked the contacts to the side of her throat. She had no time to react, due in part to her mental and physical weariness, but mostly due to his birdlike speed. The wren triggered the device and sent 45,000 volts through her body. Jessie collapsed to the hallway floor with her limbs splayed, turning frightened, confused eyes up to him. The wren crouched and juiced her again, holding the contacts in place for five seconds. She stuttered and drooled and jerked.

His chest tightened with excited energy. He cranked the flow rate on his concentrator all the way up and breathed deeply for almost a minute. Jessie's eyes rolled, and there were twin black marks on her throat where he'd zapped her. The wren took flex-cuffs from his backpack and secured her wrists behind her back.

"I have two recurring dreams," he said, getting close enough to whisper in her ear. "In one, I'm locked in a box and the box sits on a cloud, and I feel both elevated and trapped. In the other, I'm being held—*cupped*, actually, because I'm a bird and a small one at that—and I look up to see a magnificent woman staring down at me. She's as big as God. Her eyes are the sun and moon, and her hands are the trees. That woman is you, Jessie."

There was a small pool of saliva on the floor next to Jessie's slack mouth. The wren dipped his tongue into it. It tasted much like his own.

This was about her. It had *always* been about her. On the surface, his plan had been simple: set a trap for the Bang-Bang Sisters, use Chance Kotter and his gang of Dixie assholes to debilitate them, then offer Jessie a lifeline. Deeper down, the machinery was more chaotic. Aaron had needed pinpoint judgment and a truckload of good fortune to utilize it. From the beginning—when he'd first approached Burl Rowan with information about the sisters—he'd been prepared for one of the many gears to slip. Destiny had been his companion, though, and for this reason, if no other, he'd remained optimistic.

"You are that woman," he said to Jessie again. He lifted her upper eyelid and looked at the curvature of her eyeball and the pale pink tissue around it, then sat crisscross applesauce and pulled his laptop from his backpack.

One thing Aaron had not accounted for was the type of GPS tracker Chance and Burl would employ. He'd expected a small device, similar to an AirTag, perhaps stitched into a pocket, which he could hit once with a hammer to remove Jessie from the map (and thus stop anybody from locating her). The durable, house-arrest-style cuff around Jessie's right ankle was a more challenging proposition. He could dig some tools out of the back of his closet and go to work on it, but a quicker and more effective method was to hack into Burl's Track-U-Gen account (everything computer-related went through Burl; Chance didn't have a fucking clue) and compromise the network. A tiny fly in the ointment was all it would take to knock—and *keep*—the entire account offline. It could be fixed, of course, but would require live support . . . which wasn't available until 9:00 A.M. Monday morning.

Aaron opened his laptop and worked his magic. After a minute, Jessie's eyes had cleared somewhat and she tried getting to her knees. Aaron zapped her again and down she went. He murmured contentedly and flapped his arms. Not a drop of blood as yet, and he was already airborne.

BREA KEPT LOW BEHIND THE driver's seat with the knife edge pressed to Goose's throat. He drove slowly, taking care not to hit any potholes or brake too hard. They moved south on Main, from one stoplight to the next.

"You can take the knife away," Goose said. "I'll still do what you want."

"Think I'll keep it right where it is," Brea said, and she didn't move it an inch.

They continued south. The tight-packed businesses that made up the heart of Main Street started to spread out, becoming strip malls, gas stations, outlets, and empty lots. Bulky gray factories smoked on the horizon. Goose took a left turn. They passed the back of the Roosters' ballpark and a Peterbilt dealership. Sun-faded billboards advertised divorce lawyers and injury lawyers and God. The road curved gently, paralleling the river for a hundred yards. Goose opened Track-U-Gen and scrolled to the blue blip. He took three turns, closing in.

"We're getting close," he said.

"Approach from behind. Make sure she doesn't see you."

They saw Flo twenty seconds later, dressed in a too-large field jacket with a red bandanna wrapped around her head. She moved stiffly. That she could move at all was something close to miraculous.

"Stop," Brea said, twenty yards away. Goose pulled over. Brea kept the knife to his throat and watched as Flo crossed a parking lot, then turned a corner out of sight. Brea opened the back door. "This is where we part ways."

"Good. Get the fuck out of here."

"First, show me where my other sister is." Brea didn't move the knife. "Jessie. She should be close."

Goose tried to scroll the map, but it didn't move. A loading circle appeared in the middle of the screen and kept spinning. Goose closed the app and tried again. This time he got a gray box and the message: **AN UNKNOWN ERROR HAS OCCURRED CHECK ONLINE HELP FOR SOLUTIONS.** He tried yet again and got the same thing.

"I don't know," he said.

Brea swallowed. Sweat trickled from behind her left ear and followed the curve of her jaw. "Okay, turn off the engine and give me the key fob."

"The fuck I will."

"I can't risk you driving ahead and telling Flo I'm right behind her."

She persuaded him by way of the knife, pulling it snug once again. "Give me the fucking key fob."

Goose turned off the engine, yanked the key fob from his pocket, and handed it back to her. She took it in her left hand, then removed the knife and got out of the Escalade. Goose wheezed and ran his fingers across his throat, smearing the blood. He looked at her through the open window.

"You're nothing like Marit," he said. There was anger in his voice, but mostly disappointment. "I've shamed her memory to think you were."

"That's on you, boss."

"I hope that Black bitch pulls your fucking guts out."

"Stay tuned, I guess." Brea turned and threw the key fob as far as she could. It flew through the air in a high arc and came down on a flat rooftop ninety feet away. She then inverted the knife, tucking the blade inside her wrist, and went after Flo.

FLO REACHED EMMAUS DRIVE. SHE saw no sign of Chance's posse but hid herself between two parked cars just in case. She pulled the cell phone from her pocket, turned it on, and opened the only app available to her. The Track-U-Gen logo appeared as usual, only to be replaced by the same unknown error message that Goose, unbeknownst to her, had received moments before. Like Goose (and like Burl, who was at Chance's house trying to access Track-U-Gen at around the same time), Flo closed the app and tried again.

Same result.

"What the hell?" Flo put the phone away, moved out from between the cars, and continued along Emmaus. She collated her memory of Track-U-Gen's 2D map with real-world information, recalling that Jessie's blip had been stationary for a while, somewhere between the U-Haul truck rental and G.O.A.T Sporting Goods. If Jessie was resting, she might still be in that location, but several minutes had passed since Flo had last checked the app. Jessie could have moved on.

One thing was certain: she wasn't far away.

Flo had needed the tracking app for her stealth approach, but now she had to increase her vigilance and rely on skills her beaten-up body was not ready for. If it came to a one-on-one fight, she would lose. And even if she *didn't*—if by some fluke or act of God she managed to defeat Jessie—she still had Brea to deal with. Brea, with her black tattoos and shaved head and tough bones. Just the *sight* of her had sent Flo into a tailspin. She could only hope that Track-U-Gen was up and running again before going down that hard road.

Flo braced her broken arm against her ribs to keep it steady. Every step sent painful vibrations through the damaged bones. She moved along Emmaus, keeping her eyes peeled. No sign of Jessie. No sign of Chance's men, either. Maybe Track-U-Gen was down for everyone. The possibility of this—the thought of being offline and unwatched, even temporarily—sent a cool and pleasing ripple through her. She checked the LED on her ankle cuff and it still flashed. The problem was more likely with the phone that Burl had given her.

She passed the U-Haul and an empty lot. Between it and G.O.A.T Sporting Goods were a redbrick warehouse with a gable roof and a flex building selling office supplies. Flo considered the warehouse. It had been given a recent facelift, with slider windows built into its upper story and its bay entrance bricked over. No goods in or out. Not anymore. Not unless they were small enough to carry by hand. Flo surmised the building functioned as something else these days.

This was close to where Flo had last seen Jessie's red blip. She might be inside the warehouse (the office supply store was closed) or in the parking lot at the back. If Jessie *was* still in the immediate area, Flo thought it more likely that she was down by the river, resting on the sloped bank and watching the water roll. That was a very Jessie thing to do.

Flo looked around again. Everything was normal, or as normal as it could ever be in this southern-fried shithole. She reached for her back pocket and felt the shape of the balisong there, then started along the side of the warehouse toward the parking lot and river beyond. Maybe it was her imagination, but she swore she could sense Jessie close by—that undeniable thing they shared, developed onstage and over tens of thousands of miles on the road. Their once depthless love.

# TWENTY-SIX

Jessie felt the floor sliding beneath her, as if the room had been tipped to an acute angle and gravity had taken over. Her eyes fluttered. She saw furniture scroll by: a small table, an ottoman, a painting that hadn't been hung. There were similar paintings on the walls depicting clouds and skies of variegated hues. She looked into a full-length mirror and saw 9-$tar dragging her by her boots.

Her disorientation gave way to panic. She twisted and kicked, but there were disconnects, delays. Her legs felt watery. She tried moving her arms, but they'd been tied behind her back.

9-$tar—*Aaron*, his name was Aaron, and he was supposed to be *helping* her—let go of her boots. Her legs flopped to the floor. He stepped around and crouched beside her. He had a stun gun in his right hand, and the sight of it cut through the dregs of her confusion. He'd blasted her with it already, of course—twice, maybe three times. Jessie tried to wriggle away from him, but he pressed down on the back of her head, holding her steady, then once again touched the stun gun's contacts to the side of her throat. There was a loud snap. Jessie's body curved as tight as a bow. Her brain filled with a riotous light and her nerve endings crackled. The last thing she was aware of before passing out was that she could smell her skin burning.

SHE OPENED HER EYES AND exhaled. Several feathers lifted in front of her eyes and spiraled lazily. They'd been scattered on the floor around her.

They were in her hair and along her body. That was when she realized who Aaron was—*what* Aaron was. A huge freight train carrying the worst of emotions screeched to a halt inside her. It shuddered and smoked. Jessie lifted her head, but every other part of her was paralyzed.

The wren had dragged her into a spacious room with a hardwood floor and the warehouse's original ceiling. She saw the exposed steel frame and the underside of the metal sheet roof. Thick cobwebs drooped. At floor level, it was remarkably modern. There was a long glass desk lined with computer equipment, a huge TV and gaming setup, a barrel chair that was big enough to sleep on. The walls were clean white, ornamented with more of those cloudscapes. One picture was different, though. It was of her—a rare shot of her wearing a bright summer dress (the opposite of .40-caliber goth), sitting on the Micheltorena Stairs in Silver Lake. The wren had lifted it directly from her Instagram account.

He stood at her feet, the stun gun in one hand, his cell phone in the other. He tapped the screen and music started to play. It was an operatic piece, sung in Italian. The wren kicked off his sneakers, peeled off his socks, and started to dance around her. Feathers lifted from the floor and swirled in accompaniment.

"My *nonna* used to play this all the time," he said. "From when I was just a little bird until I flew the nest a few years ago. Are you familiar with this piece of music?"

Jessie groaned and closed her eyes. She tested the restraints binding her wrists, but they were solid. Flex-cuffs, she guessed. Her right leg twitched.

"It's called 'La capinera.' It was composed by Julius Benedict, sometime in the 1800s. I don't know the exact year, but it's *old*." The wren stopped dancing and shrugged. His eyes were lamplights. "My *nonna* was an opera singer when she was a young woman. She traveled all over Europe. Then she married my *nonno*, moved to Alabama, and worked in a furniture store. How about *that* for a downgrade?"

The music filled the room, echoing in the exposed rafters. The staccato piano and flute perfectly replicated a small bird's flight, with the soprano adding color and depth. Jessie rested her head on the floor, and feathers swayed around her.

"This composition, though . . ." The wren cocked his head and listened. "Isn't it wonderful? So elegant, yet strong. *Capinera* is the Italian word for blackcap, a bird from the warbler family. But in the English language, this piece is known by a different title."

"The wren," Jessie rasped, not sure if she was responding to her captor or voicing the reason for her fear.

"That's right. The most sonorous and opportunistic of birds." The wren spread his arms and trilled, crudely mimicking the soprano's delicate voice. He pirouetted slowly, then sat in the feathers beside her. "I lived with Nonna for eighteen years, and she sang this every day. I *still* don't know what all the lyrics mean. My Italian isn't great. I just like the spirit of it, the way it makes me feel."

Jessie shifted her hips across the floor and moved her right leg maybe six inches. She looked at the stun gun in the wren's hand—she couldn't think of him as Aaron anymore, or even 9-$tar—then her gaze dropped to the GPS tracker attached to her ankle. The red light blinked dependably. She had hated it for so long, but now it seemed like a lifeline.

"I bought this old warehouse four years ago," the wren continued. "The Trace pays well. We have some incredibly generous donors. My plan was to convert it to office space and rent it out. That didn't happen. The world changed. COVID, right?"

"I don't . . . Whu-whu-what . . ." Jessie tried to form words. She gave up and clicked her tongue.

"Instead, I redesigned the upper level and turned it into one big apartment. I love it. Spacious, quiet, overlooking the river." He grinned and looked at the open ceiling. "It feels like a nest in a barn."

Jessie shifted again, angling her back to get her arms into a less painful position. Her heart galloped arrhythmically, a combination of crippling fear and the voltage that had blasted through her. She blinked and glanced at the winking red light again.

"You keep looking at this." The wren slotted the stun gun into his pocket, then tapped the tracker with the tip of one finger. "It won't help you, Jessie. I hacked into Burl's Track-U-Gen account and took the whole thing offline. No one will find you."

A sob gathered in her chest and escaped in a deep moan that disturbed the feathers closest to her mouth. She shuffled across the floor by inches, dragging her legs. What she would give for all her strength now and both arms free. Even *one* arm free. The wren grabbed her right hip and upper leg and pulled her back toward him.

The music hadn't stopped, and it was the same composition, she realized, played on a loop. Its high, frivolous energy sickened her. If only she could scream.

"I don't . . . don't understand . . ." She shook her head. "Why . . . *how* . . ."

"Shh, shh."

"Nine-Star . . . the *wren* . . ."

"My real name is Aaron Gallo-Day." He stood, perhaps to stretch his skinny little legs. That grin was still on his face. "Nine-Star is my hacker name. The wren . . . well, you know all about him. He's properly famous."

Jessie looked at her bright, sunshiny photograph on the wall. At the back of her mind, the pieces began to show themselves, too few and too vague to form a complete picture, but certainly the edges of something: 9-$tar establishing a communication with her, nurturing trust, then sending the sisters the wren contract, *enticing* them into his backyard. Jessie, alone and scared, would be easier prey.

"*You* did this," she said. "You used Chance's muscle, his resources, but you . . . you were behind it all."

"I had to have you. I *had* to find a way." The wren's eyes glazed momentarily. "You're not like the others, Jessie. I've dreamed about you—or a version of you—since I was a boy. That woman. That god-woman with trees for hands."

Jessie squirmed away from him again. He circled her, occasionally pausing to scoop feathers into his palms and sprinkle them onto her. She closed her eyes and *breathed*, remembering her training—the 4-7-8 technique that Uncle Dog had taught her, boosting oxygen to her muscles, inducing a calmer, more focused headspace. The music played maddeningly, building toward its finale. There was a second's perfect silence, then it started all over again.

The wren stopped close to her head. Jessie opened her eyes and saw his hairy little feet, his toes scrunching, toenails scratching the floorboards. He stooped and chirruped and touched his nose to her cheek.

"My god-woman."

She pulled away. Her boots scuffed limply across the floor.

The wren stood up straight. He had feathers in one hand. He licked his fingers and rubbed them over his face and stuck the feathers to the wet places. His thin chest expanded.

"I've been Burl's computer guy since 2014. Then, by extension, I became Chance's computer guy, which gave me access to his cloud, his hard drive—all his comings and goings." He stepped away from Jessie and sat in the deep round barrel chair. One of the feathers came unstuck and seesawed into his lap. "They say the eyes are the windows to the soul, but really, it's a person's computer. Five minutes inside someone's system, and you know everything about them you need to know."

Jessie breathed, 4-7-8.

"I knew from reading Chance's emails how damaged he was by his nephew's murder, then his sister's suicide. He was *broken*, Jessie. He probably didn't tell you that, but he was."

The music stopped and looped around again. It was the sound of mania. Peel back that obbligato flute and there would be deep gray spaces and misfiring neurons.

"I've been with the Trace for six years. It's *mostly* anonymous. I say 'mostly' because we know a little something about all of our operatives. There's always a digital footprint somewhere. With you, it was a backup email address provided by Brea. Very clumsy of her. Once I got to Brea, you and Flo were easy to find." The wren plucked the feather from his lap and twirled it by its shaft, momentarily transfixed by its dull colors. "I don't *usually* dig too deeply. I don't need to know everything about our operatives' personal lives. Most of them are boring anyway. Ex-cops. Ex-military. But when I saw *you* for the first time . . ."

His eyes suddenly brimmed with tears. He dragged a forearm across his face, smearing more of the feathers away. Jessie angled her hips and adjusted her right knee. The feeling was returning to her legs.

"I knew the Bang-Bang Sisters took out Johnny Rudd," the wren continued. "It wasn't a Trace job—a drunk driver would never make our shit list—but Flo had a motive that was worth exploring. So I put on my Nine-Star pants and went to work. As soon as I'd confirmed the hit, I approached Burl and told him that I could probably find information about Johnny's killer on the dark web. After a few months of cashing checks—making it look good—I handed him a picture of the Bang-Bang Sisters."

More music started to play, Wagner's "Ride of the Valkyries," layered over "La capinera." It took Jessie a few moments to realize that it was the wren's ringtone. He dug his phone out of his back pocket, looked at the screen, then showed it to Jessie. The caller ID was displayed: BURL.

"Talk of the devil."

The wren muted the opera music—a fragment of relief within this madness—and left the room to take the call. Jessie tried to muster a scream for help but managed only a dry hiss. She focused on her legs instead, bending and flexing them, waking the muscles.

"Poor Burl," the wren said, returning to the room a moment later. "Apparently, his favorite app isn't working. Go figure. I told him it was probably a server issue but that I'd look into it." His eyes danced in a sick, secretive way, and he pressed a finger to his lips. "*Shhhhh.*"

He started "La capinera" playing again. Jessie groaned and went back to her breathing. The wren watched her for a moment. All but two of the feathers had come unstuck from his face. He sat in his barrel chair again, his little legs crossed.

"In case you hadn't guessed, Chance and Burl do *not* have a crack squad of elite hackers. They *think* they do, but it's just little old me." He patted his chest proudly. "The Trace was never hacked. It was never furnished with false evidence. I worked with Chance and Burl on the setup and created a fake contract. Then I sent it to you directly, bypassing the Trace. They have no idea any of this went down."

A wheezy sigh leaked from the wren's chest. He really was birdlike, Jessie thought. Small, crushable. If she had her hands free—even if she could clamber to her feet without getting zapped by that damn stun gun—she'd have a chance.

"I'd already established a relationship with you through DM. I'd given you certain . . . *inside* information about America's new favorite boogeyman, so it was entirely credible that I would show favoritism and offer you and your sisters an exclusive window." The wren gathered feathers from the seat and stuck them to his face. "Then I sat back and watched it all play out."

"Quite the scheme," Jessie said. She looked at her picture on the wall again. "And all for me."

"All for you."

"How did you know Chance wouldn't kill us outright?"

"Because he's a fucking animal. He likes to play with his food. Besides, he's done this before, on a smaller scale. Four undocumented Mexicans who'd stolen from him, locked in a warehouse with one machete between them. It took sixteen hours for the lone survivor to finally emerge, and true to Chance's word, he let that man walk free."

The wren displayed his chipped grin, then got to his feet, spread his arms, and twirled. While he was distracted, Jessie rolled onto her butt and tried lifting herself to one knee. Her body would not cooperate.

"This game, this . . . *spectacle*. The rules, the city. *His* city." The wren still twirled. "Chance has been wanting to do this for years."

Jessie felt that freight train inside her, rumbling and smoking. She managed a husky cry for help. It sounded so small.

"I knew you'd take the contract," the wren said. "I knew Chance would implement his audacious plan. And I knew you'd get in contact with *me*, because what other choice did you have?"

Jessie tried getting up again. Sweat ran from her hairline. Spit dangled from her lower lip. With incredible effort, she tucked one leg beneath her and heaved herself into a sitting position.

"Some things were out of my control, of course. I didn't know if Brea or Flo would break one of Chance's rules and end the game. Likewise, I didn't know that they wouldn't kill you to save their own asses." The wren stopped twirling and stood over her, one hand on his pocket. "There was a lot of meticulous planning here, but I depended on a good amount of luck, too."

Jessie planted the sole of her right boot on the ground and pushed. Slowly, she rose to her feet.

"I guess someone is looking out for me," the wren said. He removed the stun gun from his pocket and whacked Jessie with it again. She hit the floor and shuddered. He hunkered next to her, pressed the contacts to the inside of her left thigh, and gave her another three seconds.

The music hit its vocal crescendo, ended with a flourish, and started again. The wren plucked a feather from the floor and ran it over Jessie's face.

"I wrote something for you," he said, and recited from memory: "*My songbird, my fate. Rapture, starlight beneath me. Your heart is mine now.*"

Jessie's eyes jerked in her skull. She saw everything in jagged flashes. The wren leaned over her, still stroking her face with the feather, and he seemed Goliathan now. From five-foot-zip to immeasurable.

"So many flights are glorious, Jessie, but end all too quickly." He licked the spit off her chin and made tasting sounds. "With no one to disturb us, it'll be a long time before my feet touch down."

Jessie stuttered and clicked her tongue. She imagined wings unfolding from the wren's back, their span so magnificent that they brushed the walls on either side of the room.

"Eventually, I'll return to earth. Then I'll float your pieces downriver. Little packages dressed in feathers, the haiku tucked into your womb. I'll cut your heart out of your chest, though, and keep it. I'll cherish it."

The music looped around again. She was in hell.

"It'll be something we share, like a pet or a child." He gently pecked her lips and the breath rushed out of him. "I'll hold it every day."

# TWENTY-SEVEN

The morning rain had cooled the air, but by early afternoon the temperature had risen into the low nineties. It was a lazy Sunday kind of heat, with everything moving slower than usual. A low mound of cloud rode the west, like white sheets strewn across the horizon, but otherwise the sky was a perfect, almost silvery blue. Brea remembered countless Sundays like this, sitting on patios or pool decks or rooftop bars, drinking cocktails and laughing with her sisters. Good memories, but she forced them away. Better to keep her mind like the sky: mostly empty, mostly blue.

Following Flo was not the problem—that red bandanna was as clear as a waving flag. It was finding the right moment to strike. Flo moved uncomfortably, but she was hypervigilant, scoping her surroundings at all times. This forced Brea to keep low and move by increments. She wanted to get as close as possible and strike quickly, giving Flo minimal time to react.

They edged along the side of the warehouse, Flo eighty yards ahead, then sixty-five, then forty-five. (Music played inside the building. It sounded like opera—not Brea's jam.) There were numerous places to take cover: behind a transformer box, a dilapidated shed, a portable storage unit. Brea moved from one to the next, slowly gaining on Flo. The cover was better still in the parking lot in back, which stretched behind the warehouse and the office supply store next door. It was only one-quarter full, but the vehicles were spaced so that Brea could move up without being seen. Flo cradled her left arm to her chest—clearly injured—and checked inside the vehicles. Brea got within twenty yards. She held the knife in the reverse grip and prepared to make her move. A dim part of her mind recalled deriding Flo for wielding a knife. Flo's response had been that she wanted to make it quick. *For me and for you*, she'd said, and now Brea knew exactly what she meant.

She watched Flo reach the back of the parking lot and step onto a strip of grass, separated from the river by a shallow embankment. She looked left and right along the river's edge. Brea inched out from behind the car. She was about to pounce when Flo turned around and started back across the lot toward the warehouse. Brea ducked and pressed herself to the side of the car just in time, then positioned herself so that she was behind Flo again. Her heart boomed, and she wasn't at all surprised. Their last fight had taken everything out of her. Flo was tough. Perhaps *too* tough. Staying low, Brea crept to the next car up.

Flo had undoubtedly been tipped off that Jessie was nearby, because she checked inside a few more vehicles, then headed to the door at the back of the warehouse. She rattled the handle, but it was locked. There were three windows. Two were new (still adorned with the manufacturer's labels) and the other was old and wood-framed, part of the original building. Flo tried them all. The new windows were sealed tight, but the old one had more give. It jerked open an inch, then two inches. With a touch more persuasion, Flo worked it wide enough. She hopped onto the sill, steadied herself with her one good arm, then scissored her legs through and dropped into the room on the other side.

Brea counted to fifteen and followed.

THE WHOLE BUILDING WAS HALF-ASSED, half finished. Brea climbed through the window into a drywalled room with no paint and no door. Beyond this, the warehouse's ground floor had a mazelike quality, with incomplete walls and building materials stacked shoulder-high. Fluorescent lighting burned at the front, casting long shadows across the floor. It was gloomier in back, where Brea moved furtively.

She couldn't see Flo, and this unnerved her. She couldn't hear her, either, because the operatic music playing upstairs was loud enough to envelop the small sounds at ground level. *Somebody* was home, evidently. Brea steadied her breathing and moved forward, slinking around the stacked materials. Sweat trickled down her back. The music upstairs ended, and she used that moment to *listen*, to focus on every minuscule sound. She heard something to her left, beyond the walls and shadows. A footstep? A gasp? It was too brief to be certain, and so was the silence. It lasted only a second, then the music started again. The same goddamn song.

Brea went left, in the direction the sound had come from. She placed her back flat to a wall, edged along it, and peeked around the side. No sign of Flo. Moving silently, Brea darted forward, tucked herself behind a pallet loaded with cinder blocks, then positioned herself against another wall. She heard a thump from upstairs, as if someone had dropped a heavy box on the floor. Her heart jumped with equal vigor. She breathed as evenly as she could and checked her surroundings. No movement. Nothing in the shadows. Brea sloped around the wall. She heard another noise from the upper level. It sounded like something being dragged across the floor.

Brea frowned at the distraction, took a moment to refocus, and pressed forward. She stepped into a narrow space filled with spools of electrical wiring and from there into a hallway. This appeared somewhat finished. The back wall was painted a clean white, and there was a new stairway leading to the upper floor. Brea looked to each side and over her shoulder. Flo was nowhere to be seen. She walked to the foot of the stairs and noted the dusty boot prints on the treads. Two sets.

Brea started up the stairs. She was halfway up when a sound on the ground floor froze her in her tracks: the shrill, insistent jangle of a cell phone ringing. It was quickly cut short, then Flo's voice drifted from beyond the half-built walls and shadows.

"What do you want?" she said.

"I WANT TO KNOW WHERE you are," Burl said.

"Check your phone, genius."

"When was the last time you checked *your* phone?" Burl retorted. There was a snap to his voice. He was agitated, then revealed the reason: "The app is . . . experiencing problems. It should be online again soon."

Flo chewed her lower lip and propped herself against a stack of drywall panels. She recalled the unknown error message that had graced the screen when she'd last opened Track-U-Gen. The issue wasn't with her phone, as she'd thought. The entire server was down. Flo looked at her flashing blue light and couldn't help but smile. Maybe the app *would* be online again soon, but then again, maybe not. Regardless, she liked Burl not knowing where she was and wanted to keep it that way.

"So?" he said.

"So?"

"Your *location*."

"Right. Yeah, I'm . . ." She looked around the warehouse. "I'm not exactly sure."

"What the fuck does that mean?"

"I mean this isn't my city. I don't know where the fuck I am."

"Give me a landmark," Burl snarled. "A store or business name. Walk your ass to the end of the block and give me the fucking intersection."

He was a blind shepherd trying to gather his flock of three, and the desperation in his voice pleased Flo very much.

"I see . . . factories," she offered vaguely.

"Factories. Okay." Burl took a deep breath. It hissed across the line. "Are you closer to the river or the railroad tracks?"

There was obviously no "find my device" functionality on the stripped-down phone Burl had given her, otherwise he'd be using it. It was also clear that some time had passed since he'd seen Flo's blip on the map—when he'd last called her, maybe, when she'd been on Main Street. He knew she'd been making her way to the industrial district, but that left a lot of real estate for one little sheep to get swallowed up in.

"The river or the railroad tracks?" Burl asked again, then switched lanes. "Wait. Is that music? Where's it coming from?"

Flo was about to give him another nebulous answer—yes, it was music, but she wasn't sure where it was coming from, maybe a parked car or somewhere on the next street—when the ability to speak deserted her. Her jaw dropped and her tongue flopped uselessly. The numbness spread through her chest and hips, down to her legs. If she hadn't been propped against the sheets of drywall, she'd have fallen on her ass.

Brea had stepped around one of the unfinished walls, flipping a knife—the santoku knife that Flo had stolen from Flavor Moon, by the look of it—in her right hand. With her shaved head, she looked both fierce and beautiful, although her expression reflected only the darkness she'd endured.

"Hi, Flo," she said.

BURL'S VOICE CAME THROUGH THE speaker. "Who's that? What's going on?"

Flo drew a tight breath, regaining some sensation in her upper body. "I can't speak right now," she said, and ended the call. She reached for her back pocket, swapping the phone for the balisong. With a flick of the wrist, the blade unfolded. The two women stared at each other with twelve feet of dusty concrete and their knives between them.

"Got your own phone, huh?" Brea said, stepping closer. Flo registered the readiness in her posture: her legs slightly bent, her weight more on the back foot. "Who were you talking to?"

"Burl," Flo replied. She pushed away from the drywall panels and also adopted a defensive stance, tucking her broken arm close and angling her body to shield it.

"Inside information?" Brea raised an eyebrow.

"Something like that," Flo said. She circled to her right, and Brea followed. "That son of a bitch has got money riding on me. A lot of money, by the sound of it."

The music upstairs ended and started again immediately. It was joined by the ringing of the cell phone in Flo's back pocket. Burl again, no doubt furious that she'd hung up on him. Flo let it ring.

"You going to answer that?" Brea asked.

Flo's turn to raise an eyebrow. Put the balisong away to answer the phone? Yeah . . . no. Not going to happen. She continued to circle. The debilitating fear she'd felt when she saw Brea earlier was present, but it had been engulfed by a surge of adrenaline.

"He patched me up after you threw me off the bridge, and gave me access to the tracking app," Flo explained. The phone stopped ringing. Now it was just the music from above and the sound of their boots on the floor. "I guess he needed to tip the scales in my favor."

"That dirty cheating bastard."

"Yeah, that's why I'm in this warehouse." Flo made a circling gesture with the tip of the balisong's blade. "I tracked Jessie to this approximate location, but I don't think she's here anymore."

"What's the app telling you?"

"Nothing. It's offline, and so are we."

Brea narrowed her eyes. She flipped the knife and caught it cleanly. "I hitched a ride with Chance's driver—put this knife to his throat and persuaded him to take me to you. His app went down, too."

"Like I said, we're offline. *Invisible.* That's why Burl called. He wanted my exact location." Flo shrugged with one shoulder. "I didn't give it to him."

"Good. It also explains why there are no fucking rednecks here, filming us on their cell phones." Brea stopped circling. She exhaled, and a smile crept onto her face. "Offline, Flo. Feels pretty damn good."

"I know, right?" Flo stopped circling, too. The air burned and buckled between them. How was it possible to love someone and want to kill her at the same time?

"I've half a mind to go after Chance," Brea said. She flipped the knife again. "He won't see us coming."

"His men will be on high alert, watching his property," Flo said. This was a scenario that had already played out in her mind. "We set foot anywhere close, and Burl will give the order to kill your mom and Imani. I like the way you think, but it's too big a risk."

"You're probably right," Brea said. She pursed her lips and swallowed awkwardly. "So . . . back to killing each other then."

The operatic piece looped around again. Brea and Flo looked at each other across the buckled space. Flo's breath snagged in her chest. Flashes of their last fight recurred: the river, the bridge, the barrage of kicks and punches. They were interspersed with better memories, equally affecting.

"I won't survive this day, either," Brea said.

"I know. We do what we have to for our little sisters."

Brea nodded. She started circling again. Flo matched her, maintaining the distance between them.

"Jessie will look after Imani," Brea said, trying to sift a reassuring nugget out of all the dirt. "You know that. She'll be a sister to her, too. An aunt to the baby."

Flo's eyes bloomed with tears and she blinked them away, momentarily lowering her guard to wipe the heel of her hand across her face. "She needs *me*, Brea. Our mom is dead. The baby's father is running some two-bit marijuana business up in Frisco. I'm all she's got. It would crush her to lose me, too."

"Yeah," Brea agreed with a sorrowful nod. Her new haircut accentuated her edges, but Flo wasn't the only sister with tears in her eyes.

They each took a deep breath, then moved at the same moment, perfectly in sync and aware of each other. Gazes locked, knives extended, they sprang out of their defensive stances and met in the middle.

# TWENTY-EIGHT

Jessie opened her eyes and blinked several times, absorbing her environment in frenetic bursts. The juxtaposition of the white walls and the blackened, original ceiling space chalked an analogical line through her mind, interpreting life and death, clearheadedness and delusion, an intelligent, soft-spoken computer programmer and a deranged psychopath. The cobwebs swayed in pockets of disturbed air. Jessie wondered if small birds nested up there, if they would return once the music had stopped and chirp ceaselessly to the wren.

He was nowhere to be seen. Several doors opened off this room, leading who knew where. The only one she was interested in was the exit. Jessie imagined the neighborhoods beyond, the hard streets, the muddy river. She thought of her sisters out there, still playing Chance's game. She thought of her mom and Imani.

"Breathe," she said.

In through the nose for four seconds, holding the breath in for seven, exhaling steadily through the mouth for eight. She repeated this. On the third cycle, she heard the wren in an adjacent room, tra-la-la-ing along to the music.

Breathe.

After five cycles, Jessie tried to move. Everything south of the waist was jittery. She stretched her legs and made circles with her feet, feeling her ankles grind and pop. She drew her knees as close to her torso as she could, then stretched her legs again. The soles of her feet tingled.

The wren entered the room. Jessie closed her eyes and lay motionless. He scattered more feathers across her body, upending them from a small bag, then continued through to another room. Jessie went back to her movements, rolling her shoulders and ankles, lifting her hips, flexing her legs. She kicked four times, and each one was snappier than the last. Soon, she'd be ready to try standing again.

She didn't get the opportunity. The wren returned and stood over her. He nudged her shoulder with his foot to gauge her liveliness. Jessie groaned and fluttered her eyelids.

"Jessie?"

"Hnnnh."

"Jessie?"

"Nnnn . . . fuck . . . fuck you."

"It's time to begin," he said.

He dug his hands into her armpits, lifted her upper body off the floor, and dragged her across the room. She left a trail of feathers. The wren had moved her maybe fifteen feet when he dropped her and gasped for breath. The emotion of the moment was getting to him. He grabbed his backpack from where he'd left it on the floor, activated the machine inside, and looped his arms through the straps. In one smooth but desperate move, he had the cannula laced over his ears with the prongs inserted in his nostrils. He appeared to grow several inches as the oxygen hissed into his lungs.

Jessie groaned. She pushed with her feet, shifting away from him, but he grabbed her again and dragged her toward a narrow door on the other side of the room. Jessie wanted to kick and struggle but resisted the urge. She needed to save—to *muster*—some energy, and she didn't want to provoke the wren into using his stun gun again. Another blast from that and she might not wake up for a long time. Perhaps ever. With immense control, she allowed her body to go limp, making it easy for the wren to drag her through the narrow door and into the room beyond.

A kill room. Also, a shrine. To *her*.

Plastic sheeting had been stapled to the walls, the floor, and the ceiling. When he finished with her, he would drag a mop through the pooled blood, then yank the sheeting down, roll it up, and burn it. He would probably need to burn the photographs, too, and there were a lot of them. They spanned her entire life, from when she was a baby to only moments ago; he'd snapped her while she was unconscious on the floor, hands tied behind her back, and had printed the shot off in glossy color. Other photos had been lifted from her socials, but not *all* of them. The baby pictures. Her fifth birthday party. Brandishing the silver medal she'd won at an under-ten gymnastics tournament. The wren—9-$tar—had been in her personal computer, too.

"I get to take my time with you," he said. He pulled Jessie into the middle of the room and set her on the floor. There were feathers in here, too, and they lifted when she sagged. "I may never come down."

A scream had been building in Jessie's chest, but it wouldn't come. She stared around the room with her throat making a leaking sound and her heart banging. The wren closed the door. He walked to a small table where more photos and feathers had been arranged, and from it he took a paring knife with a short, curved blade. He crouched next to Jessie, held her head steady, and sliced her cheek open—not a deep cut, but long, stretching from the corner of her mouth to the hinge of her jaw.

Her blood flowed. The wren dipped his fingers into it and smelled it and played with it. He grinned. Jessie saw the pale yellow staining on his chipped tooth and the moisture droplets inside his cannula. His machine whirred.

"*My songbird, my fate,*" he said. "*Rapture, starlight beneath me. Your heart is mine now.*"

Jessie's chest was locked tight, but her legs were not. She swiveled, bucked her hips, and swung her right leg around. Her goal, as always, was not power, but speed and precision—hitting her mark cleanly. The top of her boot connected with the cannula where it snaked into the backpack and detached it from the machine. The wren made an alarmed sound and pulled away from her. His free hand made panicky grabs for the end of the tubing.

She kicked again, aiming for the knife this time, a smaller target, which she missed by some distance. The wren spluttered breathlessly and retaliated. He brought the blade down three times—erratic, defensive attacks that weren't accurate. One shot grooved her calf, cutting through her jeans and the skin beneath. Jessie managed a rasping cry. She raised her right leg again, placed the sole of her boot against his chest, and shoved him backward. He rocked on his haunches and crashed into the table. It toppled to the floor, spilling feathers and photos.

Jessie sat up, rolled onto her knees, and got to her feet. She buckled and swayed and nearly went down. The wren—hissing like a broken pipe—lifted himself to one knee. Jessie knocked him down again with an unbalanced front kick. She reeled toward the door, turned her back to it, and grasped the knob in one hand. Without the freedom of her wrist, and with her palm lacquered with sweat, she couldn't open it. The doorknob slipped one way, then the other.

She uttered a croaking scream. The wren recited his haiku once again, singing it with the music, lifting his voice into a whistling falsetto. "*My songbird, my fate.*" He shook off his backpack and reattached the cannula. "*Rapture, starlight beneath me.*" He slipped the straps onto his shoulders again, inhaled, and boomed the final phrase. "*Your heart is mine now.*"

"Stay the *fuck* away from me."

"*Your heart is mine now.*"

The doorknob slipped and rattled in Jessie's hand.

The wren stood up and inhaled again. His little knife flashed in the stark light. He stepped toward her.

Jessie braced herself against the door and kicked, knocking the knife out of his hand. It skated across the floor. The wren went after it. Jessie followed with another kick, pushing herself off the door to increase her velocity. She struck the wren directly beneath his backpack, and he went down. He groaned and crawled toward the knife. Jessie kicked him again and again, aiming her boot at his ribs and stomach. It took all the strength out of her legs. She collapsed, another broken scream rumbling from her throat. Then she noticed that, when pushing off the door to attack the wren, she'd fortuitously twisted the knob just enough to release the latch. The door was six inches ajar.

It fueled her—*refueled* her. Jessie got to her feet and lurched toward the door. She booted it wide and stumbled out into the main room.

The wren picked up the knife and followed.

BREA AND FLO HAD BOTH trained with knives. They knew to position themselves defensively, drawing their shoulders in and tucking their heads low. They knew to stand behind their weapons and to use the knife to both parry and attack. In this regard, Flo's broken arm was less of a disadvantage, because she would keep her nondominant arm close anyway, to protect her chest and stomach. They knew not to slash wildly. For someone skilled in self-defense, such a move was easy to avoid and presented devastating counter opportunities. Knife fighting—as with any martial arts discipline—was all about movement, timing, and keeping a cool head.

They were tired, though, and not as sharp as the weapons they fought with. Both sisters attempted to strike first, meeting in the middle and aiming for their opponent's dominant hand. Cuts to the fingers or wrist would weaken their grip and potentially disarm them. Being in perfect sync, their blades clashed. The metal clanged and scraped. The sisters drew their weapons back and circled, waiting for another chance.

"I can't believe we're doing this again," Brea said. She wiped sweat off her brow.

"Me neither." Flo moved counterclockwise, keeping some distance from the half walls and stacks of materials, giving herself room to adjust to any situation. "We've been totally played."

"It comes with the territory, I guess. We've made a living out of confronting dangerous people." Brea feinted, using her footwork, not her attack hand. "I never expected to die of old age."

Flo didn't bite on the feint. She focused on Brea's weapon, ready to dodge or parry when necessary. Instead, Brea transitioned from reverse to hammer grip. It was a deft movement, as slick as a magician with a playing card, but Flo saw an opportunity to attack. She stepped forward and lashed out with the balisong—a short, sharp strike to Brea's knife hand. Brea partly deflected it, but the blade ran across her knuckles and drew blood. Flo followed with a downward lunge that Brea sidestepped, then a kick that she did not. It connected with Brea's chest and knocked her backward. She thudded into the stacked sheets of drywall. Her knife hand dropped. Flo moved forward again, thrusting the balisong like a bayonet, aiming for Brea's throat.

For a split second, Flo thought it was all over. Brea's defenses were down and her throat was exposed. Despite the disadvantage of having to fight one-handed, Flo had overcome the odds and beaten her sister—and *quickly*, too. But Brea was no ordinary opponent. Exhausted as she was, her mind resided one step ahead. She dodged left, lithe as a snake. The balisong's blade missed her throat by a millimeter. It slotted between two drywall panels and lodged there.

Brea countered, bringing her knife around in a flashing hook. There was no time to yank the balisong free, so Flo let go of its butterfly handles and ducked. As the weapon looped over her head, she directed a punch to Brea's exposed ribs. Brea winced and pulled back. Flo grabbed the balisong's handles and extracted the blade from between the drywall panels. In the same move, she sliced the air six inches from the tip of Brea's nose. It was meant as a distraction, giving her time to drive a front kick into Brea's solar plexus. Flo found the target, but the attack lacked power. Her lead foot came down too close to Brea, and she was suddenly vulnerable. Brea seized the opportunity. She swept Flo's leg perfectly, spilling her to the floor, then dropped to her knees and brought the knife down vertically. Flo rolled to her right, first over her good arm, then over her broken arm. The ends of her splintered bones ground together, sending a jolt of blinding pain through her. Brea's knife struck nothing but concrete. She tried the same vertical stabbing motion, forcing Flo into another grinding roll. Once again, the tip of the knife pinged off the concrete floor.

Flo was out of space. She drew herself to one knee, then slipped between the framing studs of an unfinished wall and into the area on the other side. Her head swayed as she got to her feet, and her vision tripled, reminding her that she was unquestionably concussed, despite whatever Burl had juiced her up with. Pain spiraled from her fractured bones, into her shoulder, down her spine. She wobbled and backed away as Brea— *three* Breas—stepped through the unfinished wall and into the same space.

There were more thumping sounds from upstairs. Dust sifted from between the exposed joists and ductwork. The music hadn't ended. It went around and around, a nightmarish carousel. Flo's gaze flicked briefly upward, then she held the balisong out again.

"Promise me Imani will be taken care of," she said, still backing away. "Not just occasional visits. She'll need time, care, and money. All the things I would have given her."

"Imani will be taken care of," Brea said. Blood ran off her knuckles, down the knife blade.

"*Promise* me, Brea."

"If Chance Kotter really is a man of his word, and Jessie walks free . . ." Brea fixed Flo with a wounded but sincere expression—the best she could muster, under the circumstances. "Yeah, I know Jessie well enough to promise on her behalf."

Flo nodded. That would have to do.

Brea opened her mouth, perhaps to say something else, only to realize that further conversation was redundant at best, inane at worst. She lunged forward instead, swiping twice with the knife. Flo avoided the first strike. The second slashed the front of her field jacket and opened it from shoulder to zipper. She stumbled backward, then set her feet and tried to counterattack. She jabbed, swiped, and kicked. Brea parried the knife strikes and drove her left hand down to block the kick. She retaliated with a kick of her own, extending her right leg and driving her boot into Flo's stomach. Flo hit the wall behind her, slid listlessly to its edge, and fell around it into the space beyond—the hallway with the single painted wall and new stairway. She bounced off the wrought-iron balusters, staggered, and collapsed to the floor.

Brea stepped into the hallway with her knife and her fist dripping red. She approached Flo but couldn't look her in the eye.

SO MANY DOORS. JESSIE COUNTED seven, but only one was an exit. She was disoriented, too. Blame it on the hits she'd taken from the stun gun, or the delirium-inducing music, or the constantly swirling feathers, or the bleak, intractable fear that had turned her soul into a chasm. She stood in the center of the main room and looked from one door to the next. The wren edged toward her, flapping his arms. *"Your heart is mine now. Your heart is mine now."* He had the paring knife in one hand and the stun gun in the other.

At full strength, she could beat him, no hands, no problem. Her battery was depleted, though. Every step was shaky. Every breath hurt. But what choice did she have? Even if she found the exit, she wouldn't be able to open the door before he got to her with either the stun gun or the knife or both. Jessie needed to put his ass *down* and buy herself some time.

*"Your heart is mine now."*

"Come get it, motherfucker," she said.

The wren swooped for her, crossing the distance between them in a blink. He aimed the stun gun at Jessie's chest, but she stepped to the side, leaving her raised knee where her body used to be. She twisted her hips as the wren ran into it. He gulped and folded. Jessie reset and aimed a kick at his lower leg. It was a solid shot. The wren cringed and backed away from her.

"*No,*" he cawed. His eyes expanded. He inhaled vigorously through the cannula and flapped his arms. "No . . . *no.*"

Jessie pressed forward. Two kicks. The first was to the wren's chest, knocking him backward. The second was to the tender spot just above his right kneecap. He howled and dropped. Jessie adjusted her stance, trying to generate as much stability as possible with her hands tied behind her back. One good kick to the temple would knock him unconscious.

He flailed with the knife, though, keeping her at bay while he regained his feet. Jessie took herself out of his range. His attacks were telegraphed and clumsy, but all it would take was for him to get lucky once. He lurched toward her, making big movements with the blade. Jessie stumbled backward. She watched the wren's hands—*both* of them. The knife flashed this way and that, but it was the stun gun that she was really afraid of.

He darted forward suddenly, switching his attack from a slash to a thrust. Jessie dodged left and lost her balance. She dropped to one knee. The wren chirped excitedly and thrust again. Jessie weaved, and the blade just missed the left side of her face. She drove forward, powering off one leg, and socked her shoulder into his stomach. They both went down, thumping to the floor with Jessie on top.

This was not a good place to be, in the wren's dangerous little arms. She had about one second before he pressed the stun gun's contacts to her ribs. He spluttered and wheezed, but his eyes—this close to her—were iridescent circles. She clamped her teeth onto his cannula and tugged, pulling it from his nostrils. *This* changed his expression. His eyes were still bright, but with panic now.

Jessie felt him shift his left arm, moving the stun gun into position. She rolled to *her* left—toward his knife hand—but not before he got off a quick shot. The voltage jolted her. She continued over his right arm, and he dragged the knife across her shoulder as she did. Jessie didn't feel the cut, only the warm blood trickling down her back.

The wren got to his feet. He reinserted his cannula, and again he appeared to grow. Jessie scuffed at the floor with her trembling legs, a last-ditch effort to get away from him. He mumbled something and careened toward her, kicking his feet through the feathers. So many feathers. They whirled and danced.

The music ended yet again, and Jessie filled the brief silence with a scream. It roared from the pit of her stomach, a long time in the making, born of fear but mostly rage. It echoed around the room and in the deep dark roof space. The wren cried and puffed out his chest and rose above her with his wings spread.

**FLO HAD SCRAMBLED AND GOT** to her feet, only to fall again, and harder. She managed to avoid falling on her broken arm. A small mercy. Not that it would have mattered. Her entire existence—including her pains—had been reduced to its final few seconds.

Brea moved with brutal smoothness and pounced on Flo knife-first. Flo managed to throw her right arm up and block the knife's descent, her wrist locked against Brea's, the business end of the blade six inches from her throat. Brea had the weight advantage, though, and those six inches quickly shrank to four, then two, then one. At the very moment Flo felt the tip of the knife on her throat, a scream rang out. It was penetrating and chilling and utterly familiar, to the point that all the strength drained from Brea's upper body. She sat up, the knife clasped loosely in her fist.

Flo had mentally transported to any one of the hundreds of gigs they'd played—specifically their version of "Piece of My Heart." They performed it with Erma Franklin's soul but Janis Joplin's raw emotion, and they closed out the song with Jessie giving everything she had—grasping the mic stand in both hands, building the vocal to a piercing, primal wail that never failed to elevate the roof. Take away the bass and drums, and it was the same sound Flo heard at that moment.

"That's Jessie," Brea said. She climbed off Flo and ran upstairs, taking them two at a time. Flo felt no reprieve, and all the fear she had for herself was transferred to Jessie. This wasn't in the least conflicting, even given their circumstances. She had tracked Jessie to this location with one thing in mind: to kill her. But whatever was happening to her now was far worse.

Brea was already at the top of the stairs. Flo picked herself up off the floor and followed.

# TWENTY-NINE

There was a broad landing at the top of the stairs with three doors leading off it. One was clearly a front door. It was sturdier, more ornamental, with a brass locking cylinder and doorknob. Dramatic ferns had been placed on either side in heavy clay planters. The incongruity was jarring—a tableau cut from some middle-class neighborhood and pasted into this incomplete renovation.

Brea hit the door at a run, shoulder first. It moved fractionally in its frame, but the lock held. Even at full strength, she wouldn't have gotten through. It was too solid. She took a step back and delivered a front kick to the lock, channeling power up through the floor, driving it into her hip and down to the bottom of her foot. The door shook but did not give.

There was no way of knowing that the wren was on the other side of this door, with his haikus and his feathers, except she *did* know—picking up bursts of her sister's terror, perhaps, a cross talk in the DNA they shared. She'd seen police photos of the wren's victims, their bodies emptied and mutilated, and it was all too easy to superimpose Jessie's face onto theirs. The images were so vivid, in fact, that Brea felt, on top of everything else, a bottomless and corrosive grief.

She threw her full weight into the door, then stepped back and kicked it again. No give, only an obdurate thud. Flo joined her. "Together," she said. Side by side, they attacked the door, twice with their shoulders, then with their feet—a barrage of kicks. Still no give. Brea groaned frantically, sucking in deep breaths. Her bruised face shone.

Flo yanked one of the ferns out of its pot, dragging its roots and a clump of moist soil. She tossed it away. "Help me, Brea," she said, attempting to lift the clay planter one-handed. Brea tucked her knife inside her belt, and together they hoisted the heavy vessel, backed up, and charged at the door. The bottom of the planter thumped against the wood, and this time there was a deep, loosening crack. They reset and charged again. The planter vibrated on impact, jarring their bones, but the cracking sound was louder. "One more," Brea said, but it was two more before the wood splintered and the door bowed. It was still locked, though. "One more," Brea said again. They rammed the door a fifth time. The wood splintered more, and the planter shattered, spilling big clay shards and sixty pounds of soil. Brea immediately grabbed the second planter and started to lift it, while Flo kicked the weakened part of the door—four, five, six, seven times. The seventh kick did it. The wood splintered inward, leaving a gap wide enough to reach through. Flo stumbled backward, breathing hard, and Brea took over. She dropped the planter, snaked her bleeding hand through the gap, and quickly found the thumb turn on the other side. She twisted it, pulled her hand back, and threw the door open.

THEY ENTERED A NEAT HALLWAY with cloudscape pictures on the walls and three more doors. The opera music came from behind the door directly ahead, although the sound carried oddly, circling through the open roof space that served as a ceiling. Brea and Flo stumbled forward, pushed the door open, and their hardwired awareness kicked in: simultaneously, they took cover on either side, ready for shots to ring out. None did. They entered the room, keeping low, assessing the environment. There was a puddle of blood on the floor, feathers everywhere. "Oh shit, oh no," Flo moaned. She'd just realized what—*who*—they were dealing with. Brea called Jessie's name, but her voice was broken, almost inaudible beneath the music. She rounded a large barrel chair and saw Jessie's right boot, then her left leg, then her waist, then her upper body. Her hands were tied behind her back and blood pooled from beneath her.

Brea dropped to her knees beside Jessie, whispering her name between jagged breaths.

"Is she alive?" Flo had the balisong in her hand again, still scoping their surroundings. Unless the wren had escaped via an upstairs window, he was somewhere close.

Blood ran from a shallow gash on Jessie's face. Her eyes flashed open and closed.

"Yeah," Brea said. She pulled the knife from her belt and cut the flex-cuffs binding Jessie's wrists. Her arms flopped to either side, but she couldn't really move them. "I'm here, Jess. *We're* here. Your sisters."

"Up," Jessie said.

"It's okay, Jess. We're here."

"Up . . . *up.*"

Brea followed Jessie's flashing eyes, craning her neck to peer into the exposed roof space. She saw nothing but cobwebs, then caught the merest movement: a feather, descending from the darkness, turning gently. Brea watched it spiral between the steel joists and lose itself among the other feathers on the floor. A coldness rolled through her. She looked up again, following the path the feather had taken, and saw him—his pale little hands, his pale little face. Brea straightened to her full height. Their eyes locked. The wren hopped birdlike across the joists and faded into the gloom.

"HE'S IN THE ROOF," BREA shouted. Her voice rose above the music. "Flo, cover the front door."

Flo nodded and shambled in that direction, visibly exhausted, but ready to head off the wren if he dropped into another room and attempted to slip past them. Without a fire escape—Brea couldn't recall seeing one latched to the outside of the building—the front door and stairway beyond were the only safe way out.

Brea was running on fumes, too, yet invigorated with purpose. She had gone from emotionally dead only hours ago to feeling more alive than she had for a long time. Her mind conjured the memory of her new daemon: the wild horse she'd glimpsed in a stroke of Arizona lightning, caught in the storm but full of terrified energy.

She clamped the knife between her teeth, launched herself off the back of the barrel chair, and grabbed one of the roof joists. Charged as she was, pulling herself up proved too demanding. Her arms trembled. She gasped and struggled.

Jessie came to her aid. She staggered to her feet, positioned her shoulders beneath the soles of Brea's boots, and boosted her upward. It wasn't much, but it was enough. Brea hooked her elbows over the joist, then lifted her lower body and looped one leg over. She flattened her palms against the steel, pressed down, and, with a big effort, heaved herself into the roof space.

"Kill that motherfucker," Jessie said. She collapsed onto the barrel chair and slipped to the floor.

Brea looked through the gloom and saw the small, hunched shape of the wren thirty feet away. He looked back at her—his eyes catching the light from below—then took off, flitting swiftly between the rafters with his arms spread.

SHE WENT AFTER HIM, CAREFULLY following one of the support beams and using the overhead purlins to maintain her balance. Cobwebs raked across her face. She steamed the knife blade with every quick breath.

The wren was nimbler, hopping between the beams and joists and expanding the distance between them. Brea briefly considered throwing her knife, but it was a tired, impatient notion (she could almost hear Uncle Dog screaming at her to never surrender her weapon). The santoku knife had a sharp point and a nicely weighted blade. It *could* be thrown, and she might get lucky, but she'd more likely lose it in the darkness.

Her only option was to hem the wren in and attack at close quarters. With this in mind, she proceeded through the roof space, passing over a kitchen, a bedroom, a closet, and another room that had been covered with plastic sheeting. Brea knew this was where the wren had planned to kill Jessie. This dire reality uncovered something else, a detail that had been submerged beneath the hoopla of Chance's game: that the wren was the reason the sisters were in Reedsville in the first place. Brea's hard-on for this sick motherfucker had brought them here, and now—together again, in their mad, beautiful triangle—they were going to finish what they'd started.

She stepped over the hallway and saw Flo posted by the front door. Flo acknowledged her with a nod. The look in her eyes told Brea that she knew this arrangement was temporary. Their situation was . . . *ongoing*.

Brea sidelined this thought and focused on the wren. Killing him would go some way toward making this shitshow worthwhile.

He scurried deeper into the roof. A proper ceiling had been installed beyond the apartment walls, with wooden joists placed at sixteen-inch intervals and drywall panels screwed into them from beneath. Brea edged forward. In low-light conditions, she'd always relied on her hearing, but here the music blanketed every small sound. *Almost.* Bats chittered in the depths of the pitched roof, and as Brea moved across the wooden joists, closer to the wren, she heard his hissing breaths.

"I can hear you," she said, trying to provoke a reaction, a *mistake.* She wanted him to respond. Or to move. "You sound scared. You should be."

He tried to hold his breath but only spluttered. Brea stalked toward the sound. He moved, as she hoped he would, bounding across the joists. His small gray shape was quick and ghostlike. He reached the front of the warehouse where the brickwork ascended in a triangle to the ridge. A pencil line of light from some fissure above bisected his face as he turned back toward her. He gasped and grunted and touched the wall, as if some exit would magic into existence. Brea closed in, thirty feet away, twenty, fifteen . . .

"Nowhere to go, fucker."

The wren screamed, the worst sound, a blistered, keening rush of steam-kettle noise. The bats Brea had heard dropped from their roosts and scattered. Brea ducked, instinctively covering hair she no longer had. The wren took this opportunity, not to run past her, but to attack.

The bats clouded the space above Brea's head. She looked up in time to see the wren moving toward her. He was crouched, fast and agile. She saw the blade in his hand. His face materialized behind it. He had small feathers stuck to his cheeks. A cannula ran from his nostrils, its tubing looped over his shoulder and into a pack on his back.

He struck with his knife, coming in low, aiming for Brea's legs. It opened him to a counterattack from above, but he was too quick and Brea was off-balance. He drew the blade across her left shin. She felt the sting of it—felt her skin and tissue separate to the bone. He was gone before she could retaliate, flitting past her, fading into the darkness.

The music ended suddenly. Someone—probably Jessie—had

located the speaker and cut the power to it. Thank God. The bats circled away, then found their exit and were gone. The near silence was sublime. Brea trained her ears and heard the wren's strange breathing. She followed the sound. After several wary steps, his hunkered outline appeared.

"I'm right here," she said. "Come at me."

"You're cut . . . bleeding." His voice was naturally high, but the tremor in it, and his shortness of breath, made him sound toylike. "Eventually, you'll weaken, then I'll come at you."

"Some strategy. You barely scratched me."

"Liar."

It was a lie. Brea felt the blood soaking her jeans, trickling into her left boot. The wound would coagulate before she bled out, but she was already weak. She wouldn't need to lose too much blood for her faculties to falter. The smart thing to do was to get Flo to call the police—she had a phone, after all, a little present from Burl—and let them know that they had the wren cornered. But Brea wasn't about to surrender the hit and give the credit to the Reedsville Police Department. She *wanted* this son of a bitch.

She stepped toward his outline. He moved accordingly, maintaining the space between them. Brea needed to put an end to this cat and mouse—this cat and *bird*—and close him down. If she could see him more clearly, she could anticipate his movements.

"I'm too quick for you," he said. "And you're only going to get slower."

Brea shook her head. She placed one foot on the drywall and let it take most of her weight. Before going all the way through, she lifted her foot, then stomped down three times. A jagged section of the drywall disappeared, hanging by a strip of surface paper before dropping to the floor ten feet below. A shaft of light penetrated the roof space.

The wren darted to his left, absorbed into the deeper dark. Brea followed, two or three steps behind. His machine-assisted breathing gave him away, but he moved again as Brea closed in.

She stomped a second hole through the drywall, then a third. The vertical shafts illuminated the darkness like searchlights at a Hollywood premiere. The wren tucked himself into the far shadows.

"What . . . you're doing . . ." he gasped. "It won't . . . won't work."

Brea's left boot squelched when she set it down. With her right, she kicked yet another hole through the drywall. A hefty piece fell away, dropping to the floor below with a dusty clap. A fourth shaft of bright light slanted through the darkness. The wren wasn't just an outline now. Brea could see the paleness of his face, his hair, the knife in his hand. She moved when he moved, gradually edging closer, penning him in.

He wheezed and jittered, truly birdlike now—a wren trapped in a hole, trying to retreat from the cat's reaching claw. Brea crossed two joists and positioned herself on a central support beam. She showed him the knife in her hand. Its blade was much larger than his. He started to cry. A small, scared thing.

His options had diminished. He could either attack again or throw down his knife and appeal for mercy. Brea could tell from the look in his eyes which way he'd go. An abrasive shriek—more crow than wren—ripped from his chest. He came at her low and fast, and this time she was ready.

HE WENT FOR HER LEGS again, slashing his little knife wildly as he swooped in. Brea twisted away from him. She hopped to the next joist, set her feet, and instinctively brought her knife down. The blade ran across the top of his backpack and sliced through his cannula as he passed beneath her. He straightened up and staggered over several joists, inhaling vigorously through the prongs still inserted into his nostrils. If he'd noticed that the line had been cut, he didn't show it.

He lunged with the knife, a pathetic, telegraphed attack. Brea dodged left and countered, whipping her blade across his knife hand. She severed his pinkie and ring fingers, but not completely. They dangled from the rest of his hand by thin, fleshy strings. The wren dropped the knife and screamed once again. Simultaneously, he noticed that his oxygen supply had been cut and pawed hopelessly at the cannula. Brea stabbed him in the forearm, the shoulder, and the side of his face. He tried to get away from her. Where he'd once been so light-footed through the roof space, he now floundered and reeled. He tripped twice and picked himself up. In that time, Brea stabbed him through his left thigh and upper left arm. Blood everywhere. He was a leaky bucket. A useless, disposable thing.

Brea let him get to his feet. He shuddered and looked at her, muttering unintelligibly. Brea heard something about wings and sky, maybe God.

She attempted to end it, thrusting forward with the knife, aiming for his sour, monstrous heart. Incredibly, he evaded the attack, hopping to one side, still birdlike in a way. He threw his bloody arms around her and tried to pull her down. Brea shook herself free, steadied herself, and attacked again—a kick this time. The sole of her right boot connected with his throat. He made a punctured sound and slumped. She followed up with a swift left hook that dropped him. He fell hard between the joists. The drywall sagged beneath him, but he was too light, too small, to break through.

He tried to get up but could only flail. Brea stood looking down at him, flipping the knife in her hand. This moment wasn't wasted on her. She'd killed lots of bad guys, and it never got old. But this kill, after everything they'd been through, and everything yet to come, would be all the sweeter.

"How many women have you killed?" she asked him.

"Including you?" Blood pumped from the hole in his face and ran into his eyes. He cackled and said something about wings again, then flapped his spindly arms.

"Reality check, motherfucker." Brea offered a bitter smile that he didn't see. "You didn't kill me."

"Who do you think brought you to Reedsville?" His teeth appeared in the mess of his face, something like a grin. "I *am* Nine-Star. I set you all up, and not one of you is leaving this city alive."

Something cold and slippery coiled through Brea's stomach. What he'd said seemed both logical and absurd, and Brea believed every word. She stared at him, the pieces spinning through her mind, some of them clicking together. The wren—9-$tar—struggled and bled and made broken sounds. A crack appeared in the drywall beneath him.

"If only I could kill you twice," Brea said. She stood over him, one foot on each of the joists he lay between. He made grabbing motions at her legs, but his arms had no strength. Brea flipped the knife a final time and caught it by the handle with the blade pointing down. She saw his victims in his eyes, counting herself and her sisters among them.

"Sky," he said.

Brea dropped to her knees and plunged the knife into the wren's stomach. It went deep, all the way to the handle. He jerked and shook. Brea twisted the blade, intending to cut upward through his guts, but the drywall finally broke beneath him. One moment he was there, writhing, in the next he was gone, not flying but falling. Light burst through the ragged hole he'd made, shining on Brea, still on her knees with the bloody knife clasped in her hands.

THE WREN FELL SIX FEET and landed back-first on the handrail around the stairway. His backpack broke the fall somewhat. It also bounced him over the handrail instead of spilling him to the floor. He fell another eight feet and landed midway down the stairs, breaking his hip and dislocating his spine on impact. Blood splashed the newly painted white wall. The wren toppled down the rest of the stairs, his limbs as loose as wet paper. He came to rest at the bottom, then started to crawl.

BREA CLASPED THE JOIST BENEATH her left foot, lowered herself, and dropped to the floor below. She staggered on landing, but it was a hell of a lot more graceful than the wren's descent from the roof space. She looked over the handrail and saw him, still alive, trying to crawl away.

"I don't . . . think so," Brea gasped. She rounded the handrail and stood at the top of the stairs. The knife in her hand dripped. She meant to go after him and finish the job, but had taken only one step down when a voice called out from behind her.

"*Noooo.*"

She turned to see Jessie and Flo teetering across the landing, both of them pale and damaged. It was Jessie who'd called out. She had Flo's balisong in her hand. She flipped the blade open and closed as she approached and shuffled past Brea without looking at her.

"He's mine," she said.

JESSIE TOOK THE STAIRS GRADUALLY, clasping the rail in her right hand, the balisong in her left. Her legs ached and jittered. It felt like she'd possessed someone else's body and couldn't make it move the way she wanted to. Her heart was entirely hers, though, full of grief and anger. Where there'd once been hope, there was now a deep, smoking hole.

As slowly as she moved, the wren was slower. He inched himself along the concrete floor, powered by one bleeding arm. His legs dragged behind him. A dark red trail marked his progress.

"Aaron," Jessie said, stepping down into the hallway. She'd wanted to say something to him. *I trusted you*, maybe, or some other bullshit phrase from that smoking hole in her heart. The words wouldn't come, though, and that was fine. The Bang-Bang Sisters had never addressed a target in the moments before killing him. Why should this lousy fucker be any different?

The wren garbled and spat. He looked back at her, but his eyes were so full of blood that he surely couldn't see much. Jessie made firmer strides and caught up. She dropped onto him from behind, straddling his backpack (she felt the purr of his oxygen machine between her legs), then grabbed him by the hair and pulled his head back. His throat bulged, the skin taut and thin over his Adam's apple.

"*Sssskkkkkuuuhhh . . .*" The beginning of a word he would never finish or a final hissing breath. Jessie didn't know, didn't care. She reached around with the balisong and drew its blade across the wren's throat, opening it from one exterior jugular to the other. She kept his head pulled back so that the wound gaped. It took only seconds for him to die. She rolled him over and stabbed him in the chest. He still had feathers stuck to his face. They were soaked with blood. Jessie had feathers in her hair and the folds of her clothes. She gathered them all—from him and from her—then opened the wren's slack mouth and pushed them inside.

THERE WAS AN INCREDIBLE STILLNESS in the warehouse. The sisters stood or sat with their heads low, not looking at one another, breathing stiffly. Before long, the silence was broken, but not by the sisters. The phone in Flo's back pocket rang, a bright and abrasive sound. Flo sighed. She did not answer.

Jessie got to her feet. She walked to the foot of the stairs and looked up at Brea and Flo. They hadn't moved. They stood close to each other, yet so far apart.

"I need to get his blood off me," Jessie said.

"Same," Brea said.

Jessie made her way upstairs, moving awkwardly, but each step was easier than the last. She, Brea, and Flo returned to the wren's apartment. They ate, drank, and showered. Not in that order. They downed painkillers and dressed one another's wounds. The wren had a robust first aid setup in his bathroom.

Five P.M. Five hours left in the game.

BREA SAT IN THE BARREL chair. Flo had thrown some pillows on the floor and she sat on them. She and Brea exchanged glances intermittently. There was no hate or anger in their expressions, only a mystified love—two people who had lost each other and didn't know how to find their way back. The santoku knife and balisong, both cleaned and gleaming, had been placed on the coffee table between them. This was where Jessie sat. Neutral ground.

"It all went exactly how he wanted," Jessie said. She'd relayed 9-$tar's scheme and everyone's part in it. "He played us, and he used Chance Kotter's muscle. Evil fucking genius."

"Not so much," Brea disagreed, plucking a loose strand from the clean white bandage wrapped around her right hand. "Last time I checked, he was lying at the bottom of the stairs with his throat cut."

"I thought he could help us," Jessie said.

She and Brea had towels wrapped around their bodies. Their clothes were heavy with blood—only some of it theirs—and they'd taken advantage of the wren's laundry facilities. They could hear the dryer tumbling behind one of the doors leading off the main room. Flo had avoided the worst of the bloodshed. She'd taken off the field jacket and bandanna and applied a clean dressing to the wound on her left cheekbone. She'd also reinforced the splint around her arm and wrapped it in duct tape.

"I hate to state the obvious, but the wren being dead doesn't change our situation," Brea said. She rolled some of the stiffness out of her neck and winced. "Mom and Imani are still in danger. We're running out of time."

"Are we still offline?" Jessie asked Flo.

Flo removed Burl's cell phone, opened Track-U-Gen, and showed her sisters the unknown error message. "Still offline," she confirmed. She flicked the phone off but kept looking at the screen, her brow creased, lost to her thoughts. Brea and Jessie thought she was going to say something else, but she remained in that silent, reflective space.

"It doesn't matter anyway," Brea said, flexing her fingers. "We can't stay here, not with the clock ticking. And as soon as we set foot outside, Chance's guys will find us."

"Eyes and ears everywhere. Friends on every corner." Jessie tucked her towel tighter, then touched the Steri-Strips Brea had applied to the cut on her face. "I thought I could find a way through this, but I can't. I just . . . I still don't know what to do."

"I have an idea," Flo said. Her eyes snapped into focus. They were lined with steel.

Brea and Jessie looked at each other, then turned to Flo. Both leaned forward, different in stature, identical in their intrigue.

"We're listening," Brea said. "What do we do?"

Flo curled her lip and nodded. She set the phone down on the coffee table and stared at it.

"First," she said, "we wait."

# THIRTY

It wasn't all about muscle, intimidation, and the ability to identify and eliminate threats. More often than not, subtler qualities were required, like coolness and mental fortitude. Being Chance Kotter's head of security called for strength both inside and out. When shit started to go sideways—as it was known to, with Chance's unconventional approach to problem-solving—Burl had to reestablish order and do so without so much as a hair out of place.

"*Burl?* Jesus goddamn Christ, where in the hell is Burl?"

Burl ran the cold-water faucet and splashed his face, his throat, and the back of his neck. He shut off the tap and counted to ten. Better. Somewhere between a five and a six on the "fuck this shit" scale. He grabbed a hand towel, dabbed himself dry, and checked his reflection in the bathroom mirror. There was too much color in his cheeks—rage tended to do that—and his throat was blotchy. His hair was all mussed up, and that wouldn't do. Burl removed a comb from his shirt pocket and fixed that. He groomed his mustache and eyebrows, too.

"*Burl?*"

He'd returned from Afghanistan in 2008 with a duffel bag full of nightmares and a prescription for Zoloft. The meds helped with the sleepless nights and the tremors and subdued the vividness of his memories—not just the bad ones. Burl's forty-three years were a collage of muted colors, a storyboard left in the sun. The meds also counterbalanced the stress of his day-to-day concerns, including his work life. He should have been a mailman. His daddy was a mailman, and that gangly, boss-eyed motherfucker had whistled his way home from work every day.

Burl returned the comb to his shirt pocket and took out his prescribed medication. He kept the box deep inside his jacket. Chance didn't know that Burl was on antidepressants, and Burl wanted to keep it that way. He likewise didn't know that Burl sat with a therapist once a month and that he often cried during the sessions.

"*Burl?* Goddammit!"

Burl pushed the Zoloft tab through the thin foil covering and swallowed it. He sighed, counted to ten again, and nodded at his reflection. Maybe a four on the "fuck this shit" scale. He straightened his tie and adjusted his jacket. There was still some redness north of the collar, but he otherwise appeared composed and strong—exactly what Chance needed to see.

He exited the bathroom and walked to the study, where he found Chance disheveled, scarlet faced. His boss had lost one of his shirt buttons and his belly poked through, like the head of a crowning baby.

"Jesus Christ," he snapped. "Where in the hell have you been?"

"Bathroom," Burl replied coolly.

"Yeah, well . . ." Chance threw up his hands. The sweat circles beneath his arms were as large as dinner plates. "What's the latest? What the fuck is going on out there?"

"Everything's in hand," Burl said, which was exactly what Chance wanted to hear, even if it wasn't strictly true. "The tracking app is still down, but we've got Aaron working on that. He thinks it's a server issue. If he can get it up and running, great. If he can't, it's no big deal. We just find the sisters and follow them. Keep them close."

"You found any of 'em yet?"

"No, but we've got fourteen guys out there looking. Nine vehicles. It's just a matter of time."

Chance raked his fat fingers through his hair and fastened his gaze on Burl. There was no fear in his eyes, but Burl noted a hint of concern. It was a rare thing for a man who usually had everything run his way.

"What if they come here?" he asked.

Burl had concerns of his own—hence the cooling-off period in the bathroom—but the sisters mounting a retaliatory attack was not one of them. "They won't. They know the consequences for breaking the rules. Besides, *they* don't know they're offline. Nothing's changed for them."

Burl said this with absolute confidence and his eyes didn't flicker at all. Lying was another of his many skills. *Flo* knew the servers were down. She might have told her sisters, but Burl didn't think so. She had too much on the line.

For Burl, the more distressing possibility—and the primary reason for his trip to the bathroom—was that Flo had been taken out of the game. She'd been tracking Jessie, heading toward the industrial district, but Goose had reported seeing Brea in that area, too. *I can't speak right now,* Flo had said when Burl called to get her location, and he'd detected the uneasiness in her voice. It was possible that she and Brea had come together again and that Brea had finished the job this time. Burl's distress was compounded by the fact that Flo hadn't answered the phone when he'd tried calling her back.

"You're probably right. They'd be out of their goddamn minds to come here." Chance stood at one of the study windows with his belly touching the glass, looking out at the horse arena, stables, and Aldrich Woods yonder. "They're as crazy as shithouse flies, though. What kind of security do we have in place?"

"Beyond the surveillance cams, motions sensors, and alarms?" Burl rubbed the back of his neck. His collar was wet through, but he didn't mind that at all. "We've got seventeen men on site, not including me. Two have been assigned to you. They're right outside that door, in fact, armed with AR-15s."

"Who?"

"Nash and Wilder."

Chance nodded his approval.

"Frank and Landry are at the main gate. Bobby Wallace is on the west balcony with a set of field glasses and a bolt-action .308. Just to remind you: Bobby's a retired Ranger. He spent six years in the sandpit and knows how to handle a precision rifle. That icy-veined son of a whore can hit a whitetail between the eyes at a thousand yards. There's no one better to scope out the back."

"Amen."

"I got Easton monitoring the surveillance feeds. I know, I know, there are tree stumps with higher IQs, but even Easton can sit at a laptop and flip between cams."

Chance shrugged as if he had his doubts.

"The others—that's eleven men, fully armed—are patrolling the grounds." Burl spread his hands and raised a smile that took all his face muscles to appear real. "And let's not forget about Errol."

"My boy," Chance said, and chuckled.

"He's in his enclosure right now," Burl continued, "but he can be sprung promptly."

Chance nodded and sighed, then stepped away from the window. He looked at Burl with tremendous gratitude. His throat was blotchy, too.

"This is all precautionary. Overkill, I'd say." Burl's voice was rock steady. His demeanor, too. Goddamn if he didn't deserve a pay raise. "Better to err on the side of caution, though, at least until we get eyes on the girls."

"No argument here."

Burl's phone chirruped. He removed it from his pants pocket and read a message from Tay Kelley: still no sign heading ovr 2 furnace st near the railyard Reid says someone blondies descripsion seen ther. Burl blew over his upper lip and texted back: Thx. Let me know what you find. His hand trembled just a bit, but he didn't think Chance noticed.

"Anything?" Chance asked.

"Maybe," Burl said, putting his phone away. "Tay says Brea may have been spotted out by the rail yard."

"The blonde?"

"Yeah. Well, until she shaved her head." Burl didn't know whether to feel relieved or not. The moment his phone had signaled a new message, he'd fully expected it to read that Flo's corpse had been found behind a shed or down by the river and that he should hightail it out to confirm. Only then would her name be crossed off the list, and those poor schlubs who'd bet money on her—including him—could begin the process of licking their wounds. It was good that they *hadn't* found a body, but they hadn't found Flo walking around, either.

Burl had always been an all-or-nothing man. Regularly, that attitude had resulted in success. A tireless practice ethic had led to him playing two seasons with the Montgomery Biscuits, where he'd won the Southern League title, and his discipline and stoic conduct had brought him back from Afghanistan—not without psychological baggage, but also not without a silver star and arrowhead device on his campaign ribbon. It had bitten him in the ass, too, like the time he'd entered a drinking contest with Boone "Keg" Merritt (so nicknamed because of the shape and swishy nature of his midsection) and had woken up two days later in a different city, dressed in women's clothes.

He'd been close to taking the "nothing" approach to betting on Chance's game. Why risk it, given his financial burdens? Then he saw a way that he could influence the outcome and decided to go all in. Burl had emptied his daughters' college education fund and placed it all—$38,600—on Flo. If she didn't win, it would break him, and he'd have some serious explaining to do to his wife. If Flo *did* win, he'd receive a payout of $154,400. After reinstating the girls' education savings (with a little more on top), there'd be enough money left over to cover Joanne's medication and psychotherapy sessions for a long time to come.

Burl's phone chirruped again. He looked at it with his heart thumping in his throat. It was from Mose Greene, saying that he and Micah were moving their search to Lower West. No mention of Flo, dead or alive.

"You think I should send the boys home?" Chance asked, spreading his hands across his belly. "You know, to be on the safe side?"

Chance's boys were currently in the man cave, watching football, tipping beers, waiting for the real action to begin. A few had already left, but the dedicated gamblers—Tucker Presley and Emmett Pound among them—had stuck around to see in which direction their money was headed.

"Everything's fine and everyone is safe here," Burl assured his boss. "You should join your friends and carry on as normal. I'll keep you updated. But as of right now, there's no reason to hit the panic button."

"God bless you, Burl."

Chance's trust in him was absolute. Still, Burl had used five beards to place that $38,600 bet, so as not to arouse attention or, even worse, suspicion.

"Besides, Emmett's as drunk as a boiled owl," Burl added with another fabricated smile. "I wouldn't let him anywhere near that goddamn helicopter."

"I hear *that*," Chance said, and chuckled again. He clapped Burl on the shoulder good and firm, then went down to join his boys.

Burl watched him leave. He took a full breath and placed both hands against his chest to try to ease the agitation there. His phone chirruped twice more: Carson and Strat, taking the search to Colonel Park and the business district, respectively. Burl thought he should get in his Yukon and hit the streets. Another set of eyes could only be a good thing. First, he flipped to his recent calls and tried his computer guy again. Aaron and his team had hacked into the Trace and found the Bang-Bang Sisters—had made this whole thing possible by luring them to town. Someone with that kind of tech savvy could *surely* get the Track-U-Gen app back online or figure some kind of work-around. Aaron's phone rang once and went to voicemail.

"Aaron, it's me again . . . Burl. I'm looking for an update on the tracking app situation. We're still offline here. Call me when you get this message."

Burl ended the call. He left Chance's study, stepped outside, and walked behind the toolshed where he wouldn't be overheard. He took his phone out again. Nausea swelled in his chest. He hacked and spat in the grass, then blinked bright spots out of his eyes and called Flo.

"Answer the goddamn phone. Come on, girl . . ." It rang twice . . . three times. His heart was on full auto, rattling away.

The phone rang twice more, then Flo answered.

BURL WAS SO RELIEVED THAT he couldn't speak. Fragments of words spilled from his lips. He took several seconds to recoup his composure and only then noticed that Flo was sobbing.

"Talk to me," he snapped.

"I duh-duh . . . I did it," Flo said around quick inhalations. She sniffed and said something he didn't catch.

"Okay. Take a deep breath." Burl leaned against the back of the shed. His legs were trembling. Appearing bulletproof was exhausting work. "What did you do?"

"I did it." More quick breaths, then Flo inhaled deeply. Burl sensed her fighting to get control of herself. "Jessie . . . Juh-Jessie. I . . . I killed her."

Burl closed his eyes. In seconds, he'd gone from remortgaging his house and consulting a divorce lawyer, to a brighter, warmer place where hope was a ripening crop.

"Where are you?" he asked.

"Jessie," Flo said again. "She . . . she was my friend. My *sister*."

"It's not over yet," Burl said coldly. "You're not free, and your *real* sister is still in danger. You need to get your shit together."

"I'm hurt—"

"Where *are* you?"

"In . . . I don't know . . . in a warehouse . . . some kind of warehouse. There's . . ."

"Flo . . . *Flo*." Burl stroked his mustache nervously. It was damp with sweat. "You can do this, Flo. Deep breaths."

She sniveled and inhaled, then made a sound like she was gritting her teeth. "It hurts to move. I can't . . . can't stand up."

"Flo, listen to me. I need to confirm the kill." Burl kept his voice low but looked around the side of the shed to make sure none of his patrolling guys had strolled within earshot. "I can help you when I get there, but I need to know where you are."

"South," Flo gasped. "Southeast."

"Good. Okay. A warehouse in the southeast." Burl nodded. "What else can you tell me?"

"It's . . . near the river."

"Do you remember the street name, or a street somewhere close?"

"No, I don't . . . don't . . ." Flo made that gritting-teeth sound again. "There's . . . I think it's a pet store . . . across the street. And there's a truck rental place, a U-Haul maybe, or a Penske. I can't remember, but it's close . . . close by."

Burl accessed the map in his mind, scrolling through streets in the industrial district. There was a U-Haul on Emmaus Drive, which backed onto the river. He didn't know if it was close to a pet store, but that wasn't the type of business he paid attention to. There *was* a G.O.A.T Sporting Goods, though, with a bright red sign and a Crimson Tide flag rippling in the parking lot.

"Do you remember seeing a sporting goods store?" he asked, fighting to keep the urgency out of his voice. "Goat. *Gee-oh-ay-tee.* Greatest of all time. It has a big red flag—"

"Yes," Flo said, and drew a long breath through her teeth. "Yeah, it's . . . it's close. Maybe two buildings away. Three. I don't know, but . . . but it's close."

"I know where you are," Burl said. Another profusion of relief opened inside him, as broad and colorful as a peacock's train. "Don't move. I'll be there in twenty minutes."

BURL MARCHED DIRECTLY TO HIS vehicle, the quickest he'd moved all day. He called Chance as he walked.

"Good news, boss. We've located Flo—"

"The Black one?"

"Yeah, the Black one. She's in the industrial district. Also, I've had it on good authority that Jessie—the little one—has been eliminated from the game."

"Hot shit."

"Heading down there now to confirm."

"We need photographic evidence."

"Yessir, I know."

"And Stoopy Joe'll wanna see bodies with his own eyes before he pays out. You can take her down to Pink's, but don't burn her up yet."

"Nossir, I won't."

"Good work, Burl."

"Thank you, boss."

"I'll go tell the boys."

Burl rang off, opened the door to his Yukon, and climbed behind the wheel. He was about to start the engine when the back of his neck tingled, just enough to raise the little hairs there. Christ knew, he wasn't at his best—his mind and his emotions had been put through their paces—but something felt a shade *off.* He couldn't say how or why, but this was the kind of intuition that had seen him through many hard situations, both in the military and working for Chance. He'd come to trust it over the years.

He got out of his vehicle and walked across the driveway to the front of the house, where Tanner Bowen and Matt Spencer were patrolling. Matt was forty-nine but mid-twenties fit, a former bodyguard and Hwa Rang Do champion. Tanner was six-six, a touch shy of three hundred pounds. He had an absence between the ears but the disposition of an industrial meat grinder. His party trick was busting cinder blocks with his skull.

"You. You," Burl said, pointing at both men with the index and middle fingers of one hand. "Grab a truck and follow me."

"Where we going?" Tanner asked.

"To ID a dead body," Burl replied, and then, echoing his intuition, "Even so, expect a fight."

# THIRTY-ONE

Brea and Jessie pulled their clean clothes out of the wren's dryer and got dressed. They looked at each other, their expressions dark with everything that had happened, their minds fixed on what lay ahead.

"Here we are again," Brea said. "Another job. Another performance."

"I'm ready," Jessie said.

Brea stripped a pale blue sheet from the wren's bed, sending feathers swirling through the air. She took it downstairs and draped it over the wren's body. The sheet covered him completely but didn't come close to covering all the blood, which had trickled out from beneath in a long tapering line.

"I think he'll come alone," Flo said, talking about Burl, "but he might not. We should prepare for that."

The stun gun was in the wren's pocket, out of juice. Flo found a charger in the kitchen, but there wasn't time to give the battery a sufficient boost. They briefly searched the apartment for other weapons and came up empty. Not even a baseball bat. Brea had her santoku knife tucked into her belt. Flo had her balisong. Jessie rifled through a meager cutlery drawer, eventually settling on an ice pick, a blunt pair of scissors, and a utility knife. She slotted the scissors into her back pocket and armed herself with the other two.

They shut off half the lights on the ground floor, creating pools of shadow, then unlocked the main door and took up position in sight of one another. Brea and Jessie hid behind stacked materials. Flo sat close to the wren's body, propped against the wall with one knee up and her forehead resting in her good right hand. She'd put the field jacket back on and had the balisong concealed in her left sleeve, blade ready.

THEY DIDN'T HAVE TO WAIT long. A vehicle roared up outside, its tires dragging across the gravel. Moments later, a second vehicle pulled up. Two engines were cut. Three doors opened and closed quickly. Brea was closest to the front of the warehouse. She motioned to her sisters and held up three fingers in case they hadn't heard. They both nodded.

Flo's plan was solid, but it came with immense risk. One slip, one wrong move, and everything would be lost. With a couple of hombres at Burl's side, that risk was three times greater. Flo had taken everything into account, though, and she'd been confident they could pull it off.

"We're all hurting, Flo," Jessie had said. "Are you sure about this?"

"One hundred percent," Flo had replied.

"If it goes wrong . . ." Brea hadn't sugarcoated it: "They'll kill us all. They'll kill Imani."

"It won't go wrong. It *can't.*" There'd been a look in Flo's eyes that Brea and Jessie had seen only once before: when Flo had decided to go after Johnny Rudd. That had been a reckless and emotional reaction, but they'd stood together then, and they'd do the same now. "I'm sick of these fucking men. I'm sick of being used . . . *demeaned.* We haven't had a move to make this whole time, but we've got one now. A good one. And we're absolutely taking it."

The main door hissed open on its pneumatic hinge. There was a pause, then footsteps, distinct in the stillness. They fell slowly, cautiously. Brea took silent sips of air, registering every sound. The footsteps edged closer.

"Stay alert," she heard Burl whisper.

Brea looked across at Jessie, tucked behind a stack of insulation batts. Despite her traumas—perhaps *because* of them—she was utterly focused, in the zone. They *all* were. As with any Bang-Bang Sisters gig, they knew their roles and understood that every note needed to be played with precision. This couldn't be a fight. It had to be an ambush. But *unlike* other

Bang-Bang Sisters gigs, their principal target could not be eliminated. No matter what, Burl had to live.

**THE THREE MEN HAD SPREAD** out. Brea approximated their locations from the sounds they made. One was a heavy breather, occasionally sniffing and clearing his throat. One had a habit of sucking through his teeth. One wore boots with hard, flat heels—Burl, probably, dressed somewhere between a cowboy and a mobster. He was the loudest, the *closest*, and steadily getting closer. Brea wrapped her fingers around the santoku knife's handle and drew it partway out of her belt. The heels tapped closer still.

Flo groaned, right on cue. There was a brief silence as the men stopped to listen. Flo helped them out with another suffering moan. This was followed by a cascade of footsteps, drawn toward the same location.

"Over here, boss," a voice said seconds later. It was deep and husky— the heavy breather, Brea thought—and not at all discreet. He obviously believed there was no threat, and that was a good thing. It meant he'd lowered his guard.

Brea shuffled to the edge of the lumber stack and peeked around the side. She saw Burl heading away from her, pistol drawn. His two compadres were just outside the hallway. They had their backs to her, looking in at Flo. One was silver-haired and, like Burl, clutched a semiauto in his right hand. The other had a deep crease at the base of his skull and a shoulder span as wide as a Coupe de Ville.

**THIS FUCKING PLACE, FULL OF** shadows, full of *cover*. The perfect location to stage an ambush. It was quiet, though, except for Tanner, breathing like a fucking horse. Burl was about to motion to the big dumb fuck to bring that shit down a notch, then somebody groaned—a pained, lamenting sound—and his thoughts switched track. Flo. That had to be Flo.

When he saw her, the alarm bells diminished enough for him to wonder if, this time, his intuition had been off. She sat against the wall with her head low and barely looked up when he elbowed past Tanner and stepped into the hallway. More than Flo, it was the bloodstained sheet and the humped shape beneath it, and the blood splashed down the stairs and across the walls and on the floor. Burl had seen enough killing in his life to know that this was the real deal.

"That stink, though," Tanner said, covering his mouth with the back of one intricately tattooed hand. "I think she done crapped her pants."

"Not *her*," Matt said, motioning from Flo to the covered body. "But there's a god-awful mess under that sheet."

Burl assessed the scene. His mind ran in such a way that it was hard to catch hold of anything. The relief was there, bold and flavorful. There were questions, too: So much love, yet so much blood? And where the hell did Flo find a bedsheet in a half-refurbished warehouse?

"You'd do well to get your shit together. By my count, there's still one sister out there." Burl kicked the sole of Flo's boot and extended his arm so that his watch popped out of his sleeve. "Three hours and . . . forty-four minutes until game over."

"Can't," Flo whined.

"The fuck you can't," Matt growled, and he kicked her sole, too. "Bitch, I got a fat stash on you."

Burl looked through the doorway to the main warehouse floor and saw no movement, heard no sound. He turned back to Flo. She'd said she was hurting, and that appeared to be true. There were no obvious new injuries, but who knew how many fractures, sprains, and hematomas were underneath those dirty clothes? Her chest palpitated with every ragged breath. Her hands were shaking. Burl yanked at his collar, catching a breath of his own. As soon as he'd confirmed that the environment was safe and had photographed Jessie's body, he would order Matt and Tanner back to Chance's house (there was a reason he'd asked them to follow in a separate vehicle). Only then would he be able to patch Flo up (again) and get her back in the game.

"Keep an eye on her," he said to Tanner, gesturing at Flo with the tip of his pistol. He scanned what he could see of the warehouse one more time—paying particular attention to the shadows—and said to Matt, "Watch our six. Something still feels off to me."

Matt raised his pistol and got into position. Burl wiped his mouth, stepped over the long runner of blood stretching across the floor, and approached the covered corpse. Tanner was right, the stink was insufferable. Burl didn't want to be in the vicinity of this death-and-feces cocktail any longer than he needed to be. He crouched next to the bedsheet, put his pistol away—Matt had them covered—and took out his phone. Three quick photos, maybe a couple of different angles. He tapped the camera icon and lifted the sheet.

There was too much blood to be able to tell who it was, but Burl knew who it *wasn't:* Jessie. This had been a man, with a timid, narrow jaw and at least a day's worth of chin stubble. His throat had been cut. He had puncture wounds through his face and chest. Burl thought he somewhat resembled his computer guy, Aaron—a runt of a man whom Burl had met only a few times—but it was difficult to be certain.

"What . . . what the hell?" Burl lowered his phone and tried to blink away the obfuscating mist that had settled in his mind. His confusion had drawn Matt and Tanner's attention, both of whom looked at him with questioning expressions. And if Matt was looking at *him*, it meant he wasn't watching their backs.

The loudest alarm bell yet chimed in Burl's skull and reverberated all the way down to the heels of his Justins. He dropped the phone and reached for his pistol, just as Flo whipped the butterfly knife he'd given her—the balisong, as she called it—from inside her sleeve and jammed it into Tanner's right foot.

The big guy roared—a throaty, howler-monkey sound. Burl freed his gun and, for a single, precious second, believed he was still in control, then everything turned to thunder. Everything went bang.

**JESSIE LACKED HER USUAL SMOOTHNESS** and speed, but her timing was perfect. She made her move the moment the silver-haired thug turned his back to her, weaving low through the shadows, rising up behind him, ramming the ice pick into the left side of his neck and the utility knife into the right. He stiffened. His gun hand snapped outward and—finger on the trigger—he squeezed off two booming shots, the first punching through the wall a foot above Flo's head, the second pinging off the wrought-iron balusters and into one of the wooden treads.

Silver Hair sagged at the knees, his blood squirting left and right. He gurled and flailed. Jessie tightened her grip on the ice pick and knife handle, lodged her knee under his ass, and used her elbows to hold him steady.

"*Brea*," she called, but her voice was lost in the rumbling echo of the gunshots. From the corner of her eye, she saw Burl swing his pistol toward her. He hesitated for half a second, trying to get a clear shot, then pulled the trigger anyway. Jessie felt the bullet thump into the center of Silver Hair's chest, killing him instantly. He flopped, an uncomfortable deadweight that she couldn't hold up. The knife slipped out of his neck. Jessie crouched, trying to remain shielded as he slumped.

All of this happened in a matter of loud, messy seconds—precisely as long as it took Brea to reach her.

IT CAME DOWN TO INSTINCT, that intangible, almost *supernatural* quality that so often meant the difference between success and failure. If Brea had tried to wrestle the pistol out of Silver Hair's dead grasp, Burl would have had time to pick out a target, steady his aim, and shoot either her or Jessie. Instead, she grabbed the middle-aged thug by the back of his shirt collar, helping Jessie lift him into a higher shield position. At the same time, she clamped her palm to the back of his right hand and looped her forefinger through the trigger guard, over his. She swung the gun—a Glock 29—toward Burl, looking over Silver Hair's shoulder, aiming down the length of his arm and through the pistol's sights. Burl fired a second or two ahead of her. His shot entered just below Silver Hair's left eye and exited the back of his skull in a shocking spray of mostly red. Brea blinked blood out of her eyes and fired back, squeezing Silver Hair's finger, which in turn pulled the Glock's trigger. The recoil was vicious. The 10mm round hit the wall but nothing else. She reset and fired again, everything so loud that only the muzzle flash at the tip of Burl's Walther PDP told her that he had fired, too. His follow-up shot went through Silver Hair's right shoulder, exiting at an upward angle and scuffing Brea's jaw. Her bullet hit Burl's gun hand, severing his thumb and forefinger and sending his pistol spinning. It was exactly the shot Brea wanted, but she barely had time to admire her aim before the big guy lumbered toward them, still screaming, still with the balisong in his foot.

**THEY COULDN'T HOLD SILVER HAIR** up any longer. He collapsed in a gory heap, sprawled on top of the sisters. Brea managed to squeeze off one more shot, aiming at the big guy. She hit him low, in his left thigh, but he kept coming. Jessie still had the utility knife in her hand—she'd lost her grip on the ice pick; too much blood—and managed to roll out from beneath Silver Hair and pop to her haunches. She leapt at the big guy and rammed the knife between his ribs. It looked small, protruding from his expansive side. He swatted her away with one enormous hand. Jessie staggered, hit the wall, and dropped to her knees. The big guy continued toward Brea. His screams had changed pitch, more like a shrieking goat than a howling monkey.

He lifted Silver Hair's corpse off Brea and tossed it into the hallway behind him. Brea got to one knee. She aimed a punch at the big guy's solar plexus. He woofed and backed up a step, giving her just enough time to rise to her feet and throw an elbow. The big guy absorbed it and countered with a windmill-slow haymaker. Brea ducked and attacked again—a right palm strike to the bullet hole in his thigh, then a left to his crotch. He doubled over, dragging voluminous breaths into his chest. Brea, finally with room to move, reached for the knife in her belt. She pulled it free, raised it high above her shoulder, and plunged it into the top of the big guy's skull.

His eyes rolled to whites, his jaw went slack, but he didn't go down. He swept blindly with his arms, caught hold of Brea's T-shirt, and began to shake her. She cried out, trying to kick and punch her way free. Jessie yanked the blunt scissors from the back pocket of her jeans and scuttled across the floor. She thrust them into the big guy's right knee, twisted, and popped the cap loose. He let go of Brea and teetered, still whirling his arms and screaming. During this time, Flo had crossed the hallway and liberated Silver Hair's Glock 29 from his hand. She took aim and pulled the trigger seven times. The first shot was directed toward Burl, who'd made a move for his pistol. The bullet struck the concrete an inch from his left hand, backing him up. The next four were spent on the big guy—three in the back and one in the skull. He dropped with an incredible thud and twitched for a time. The sixth and seventh trigger pulls fell on an empty chamber.

BURL PANTED AND BLED. HE hauled himself across the floor on his elbows and knees, making another move for his gun. Brea beat him to it. She picked it up and planted her boot on the back of his neck, holding him steady. Flo joined her, then Jessie. They looked at one another and nodded. Brea lifted her boot and rolled Burl onto his back. He looked up at the bloodstained sisters—all three, side by side—through furious, red-flecked eyes.

"The game's changed," Brea said, looking at Burl down the barrel of his pistol. "New rules. New stakes."

"New players," Flo added, and cracked a smile.

Burl screamed.

# THIRTY-TWO

Jessie cut a length of electrical wiring from one of the huge spools on the warehouse floor and used it to tie Burl's hands behind his back. Flo and Brea grabbed an arm each, dragged him across the floor, and sat him against the wall in sight of the three corpses.

"Whatever you're thinking," Burl said through gritted teeth, "it's a bad idea. Chance knows where I am. He'll send men to find me."

"You're a smart man," Flo said, tapping one finger against her temple. "Smarter than your average redneck, at any rate. I'd bet bullets to bubblegum you know *exactly* what we're thinking."

"I guess I do." Burl wrinkled his face and looked from one sister to the other. "But what you stupid bitches don't realize is that I had my SERE training before heading out to Afghanistan. Survival. Evasion. Resistance. Escape. Nothing you can do will break me."

"Nothing we can do to *you*, maybe," Flo said.

She kept an eye on Burl while Brea and Jessie rooted through pockets for truck keys, then moved the vehicles out front to the parking lot in back, where they wouldn't be seen from the road. It wouldn't do to have one of Burl's guys recognize his Yukon and come nosing around the warehouse. This was a private meeting. In the three or four minutes that her sisters were gone, Flo picked Burl's cell phone up off the floor and emptied his pockets of everything else. She found his wallet, a strip of Zoloft tablets, a spare mag (loaded) for the PDP, and a half-empty packet of breath mints. Flo placed all these things on the stairs, except for his cell phone, which she kept in her hand.

When Brea and Jessie returned, Flo turned the phone on and showed the lock screen to Burl.

"What's your passcode, Burl?"

Burl said nothing. He looked straight ahead.

"Come on. Let's do this the easy way."

Burl's skin was gray. Shock and blood loss. The ragged stumps on his right hand had stopped bleeding, at least, so he wasn't going to pass out on them. He wouldn't stay silent for long, either. Flo was sure of it.

"Passcode?" she said.

Nothing.

Flo looked at Jessie and shrugged, while Brea grinned through the blood on her face. A moment's stillness followed, interrupted by Burl's phone, which chirruped and buzzed in Flo's hand. She looked at it. A notification banner had appeared at the bottom of the screen, signaling a new message from Chance. It displayed only the first line, but seeing as Chance had written just five short words, she got all of it: **Where you at? Need news!!!**

Flo smirked and showed Burl. "I guess he doesn't know where you are after all."

Burl said nothing.

"Passcode?" Flo tried again.

Sweat ran off Burl's forehead, into his left eye. He blinked but was otherwise still.

"I thought you said he was smart," Jessie said.

Flo slipped the phone into her pocket. She crossed the hallway, stepping over the wren on her way to the stairs. "He's smart enough to know that we'll do whatever it takes to save our families."

"Right," Brea agreed. "I mean, Chance used that knowledge to manipulate us—back us into a corner. His whole scheme depended on it."

"Family is everything," Flo said. She removed Burl's wallet from the detritus on the stairs, flipped it open, and eased out his driver's license. "Burl Anthony Rowan. Sixteen twenty-four Willow Way, Reedsville, Alabammy."

Burl's lips peeled back over his gritted teeth.

"You know where Willow Way is, Brea?" Flo asked. "Do you recall seeing it while walking around this shithole city?"

"Nope," Brea replied. She pulled the chunky set of keys from her pocket and jangled them. "But I just drove that Yukon out back and it has GPS. A nice, big screen built into the dash."

Flo nodded. She vaguely recalled this from her brief ride in the vehicle. "Sixteen twenty-four. Will you remember that?"

"Uh-huh."

"Good. Have Burl's wife give him a call when you get there."

Burl made a deep sound and flexed his shoulders, maybe trying to tear through the wire that bound his wrists. He slipped halfway down the wall, and Jessie pushed him back into position with the sole of her boot. He sagged and lowered his head.

"You're wasting your time," he said. A runner of spit dangled from his lower lip. "I live alone. I'm not even married."

"The lies that come out of this man's mouth," Jessie said, and tutted.

"We *know* you're married, Burl." Flo looked at him, forcing a smile. The painkillers she'd taken were struggling to keep up. Her hips and arm throbbed, and there was a knifepoint feeling just above her left eyebrow. She showed none of this on her face, though. "According to Chance Kotter, your wife makes the *best* pear cobbler."

"We watched him filling his fat face with it just two nights ago," Jessie added.

"You remember that, Burl?" Flo asked.

Burl said nothing.

"What I *can't* remember," Flo said, still smiling, "is where she gets her pears . . ."

"Rhonda's," Brea said. "No, wait . . . Ruby's?"

"Rosalie's," Jessie said confidently.

"That's it." Flo flashed her teeth and winked. "Rosalie's. Right off the farm."

Burl lifted his head and looked at her hatefully, then flicked his eyes forward again.

"How many rounds in that PDP?" Flo asked Brea.

Brea yanked Burl's pistol out the back of her jeans. She knew exactly how many rounds remained—she'd already checked—but she made a show out of releasing the magazine and counting the cartridges through the little round windows.

"Fourteen in the mag," she said. "One in the chamber."

"Good," Flo said. She lifted her fingers to her cheekbone and stroked the wound that Burl had disinfected with iodine. He'd worked with such tenderness. "I've a feeling there are kids at home."

Brea clicked the mag into the grip and started to walk away. She'd taken only three steps when Burl spoke.

"Seven-five-five-eight." He swallowed hard. A tear flashed from his eye.

Flo took a deep, quivering breath. She tapped the numbers into Burl's phone and it unlocked.

"Attaboy," she said.

FLIES HAD GATHERED ON THE three corpses, most of them on the wren. Their insistent buzzing filled the stillness. Some of them droned around Burl, perhaps thinking he was dead, too. Flo, meanwhile, exchanged a brief communication with Chance, pretending to be Burl. She wrote that everything was hunky-dory and still on track. Chance asked if the little one was confirmed KIA, and Flo replied that she was. Chance wanted photographic proof. Jessie got down in a puddle of the big guy's blood with one eye half open and her jaw loose. There was enough blood on her face and clothes for it to look real. Flo took the snap and hit send. Ain't that the berries! Chance replied a few moments later.

Flo put the phone away and held her aching head for a moment. Beyond the flies' buzzing, she heard a freight train shuffling along the Waynesboro-Conecuh Southern Line, blowing its horn in long blasts. She vaguely wondered how something so noxious, so industrial, could sound so free. It felt like she'd been in this warehouse forever.

"Okay," she said to Burl, meeting his gaze across the hallway. "I've set Chance's mind at ease. Now he can go back to rolling in shit with the rest of his pig friends."

"We'll deal with him later," Brea put in.

Burl shook his head. His eyelids dropped heavily and inched open again. He looked from Brea to his fallen men, then followed the splashes and streaks of blood to the wren's body, partially covered by the sheet.

"You went after my computer guy," he said. A bitter, ugly sound escaped his throat, somewhere between a cough and a sigh. "Got him to hack into Track-U-Gen and take you offline. Smart. But did you really have to kill the poor son of a bitch?"

"Your computer guy came after *me*," Jessie said. The venom in her voice belied her fatigued demeanor.

"You knew him as Aaron Gallo-Day," Flo said. "We knew him as Nine-Star, our main contact at the Trace. One of his two secret identities."

"The other was the wren," Jessie said, growling the last two words.

"Bullshit," Burl retorted, but his eyebrows narrowed with uncertainty.

"He played you just like he played us." Brea nudged the wren's body with the tip of her boot. The flies took off and landed again. "He got you and your boys to do all the hard work, then swooped in to pick up the scraps."

"Not that it's important anymore," Flo added, "or that you need to know, but taking your tracking app offline was *his* idea. Nothing to do with us."

"He didn't want anybody to find me here," Jessie said. She swept a hand through her hair and looked down at the floor. "He wanted to take his time."

Burl stared at the wren, clearly not sure how to unpack this information. Flo removed the other phone from her pocket—the one Burl had given her. Light flashed off the screen as she held it up. "Thanks to you, I was able to approximate Jessie's location before the app went down. Brea followed me here." She and Brea locked eyes for an awkward second. "In a way, Burl, you saved Jessie's life. Inadvertently, of course, but still . . . kind of ironic, don't you think?"

He shrugged and made that bitter sound in his throat again. Flo looked at him with disdain, then woke the phone's screen and turned it toward her. The digits in the top left-hand corner read 6:51. They had Burl where they wanted him, but as long as Imani and Aubree were being held at gunpoint, time was a factor.

"Here's what happens now," Flo said. "We're going to call your associates, the ones holding Imani and Aubree hostage, and you're going to tell them that the game is over and that they can let our family members go free."

Burl sneered and shook his head. "I don't have their contact info on my phone."

"I swear, motherfucker," Brea hissed, "you tell *one* more lie, I'm paying your wife and kids a visit."

"We *watched* you call them," Flo said. There was a tremor in her voice, part pain, part exhaustion, mostly a deep and sour tension. She wiped her mouth with the back of her hand and lifted her shoulders. "Friday night, remember? In Chance's office? You had the one guy cut Imani's and Aubree's hands free so they could wave at the camera."

"This was right before Chance ate a bowlful of your wife's pear cobbler," Jessie added.

Burl lowered his head and was motionless for a long time. Flo kicked the sole of his boot—the same way he'd kicked hers—and he didn't move. They waited, sensing tiny breaks in his disposition. Finally, he exhaled with a rattling sound and looked up. He stared at Brea. She patted the keys in her pocket, and he nodded reluctantly.

Flo switched phones. She tapped in Burl's passcode and brought up his list of contacts, names like Micah and Dusty and Landry, a whole string of them, southern boys, and not the good ol' kind—the kind she could introduce to her mama, if she still had one. She blinked at the sharp pain in her forehead and crouched next to Burl.

"Who are we calling?" she asked.

"Lou."

Flo scrolled and found two Lous. "Lou T. or Lou W.?"

"W."

Flo's thumb hovered over Lou W. His contact picture was of a copperhead, fangs displayed, and Flo imagined an equally venomous man. She looked at her sisters, and they both nodded. This was it.

"Okay, Burl, I'm sure you don't need telling, but I'm going to tell you anyway: Be cool. Be convincing. I want an Oscar-worthy performance out of you." Flo leaned closer to Burl, making sure he saw the fire in her eyes. "If you try anything stupid or fuck this up, if any harm comes to our families, then it's going to end very badly for yours."

Burl's expression was as cold and somber as frost on a gravestone. Another thin tear slipped from his eye, though, suggesting the presence of a stoically concealed heart.

"One take, that's all you get," Flo said. "You need a moment to prepare yourself?"

"I'm ready."

Flo nodded. She made the call.

LOU'S PHONE RANG THREE TIMES before he answered. Flo had him on speakerphone. His voice came through so clearly he could have been sitting halfway up the stairs.

"Burl. What's the word, good buddy?"

"Word is the game's over," Burl said blankly. Flo gestured for him to add a dash of color and he did. "Everything went as planned. You can let the women go."

"It's over?" Lou asked, and Flo thought she heard a hint of relief in his voice. "Well, shit, who won? Tell me it was that long-leggedy blonde."

"You'll find out soon enough," Burl replied. His voice cracked. He closed his eyes, cleared his throat, and continued. "Cut the women loose, gather up your shit, and come on home."

"Yessir."

Flo ended the call. She dabbed the back of her hand to her eyes and exhaled. Behind her, Brea put her arm around Jessie and pulled her close. They were both fighting tears.

"You did good, Burl. Now we get to watch. Make sure." Flo returned to Burl's home screen and cast her mind back some twenty-four hours, when Burl had opened the live video on his phone and shown her what she was fighting—*killing*—for: Imani and Aubree tied up in that dank brick room. *Still alive, see?* Burl had said. *I assume you want to keep it that way.* Flo flipped through a couple of screens, looking for the right app.

"The live video feed," she said, and pointed at one of the icons. "This one, right? StreamSphere?"

Burl managed a vaguely affirmative grunt. Flo opened the app and got a login screen.

"Password?"

"Meganjoanne."

Flo raised an eyebrow. "Wife? Daughter?"

"Daughters."

"Good dad," Brea said. "Bad password."

Flo typed it in and connected to the video feed. She joined Brea and Jessie, and they crowded around the small screen, watching as Lou and another masked assailant cut Imani and Aubree loose. Both women got to their feet slowly. The men shouted at them, waving their arms. Aubree flinched, then curled her arm around the heavily pregnant Imani, and together they disappeared out of the shot.

Flo, Brea, and Jessie watched the screen for another minute, expecting one of the thugs to flout Burl's orders and drag their prisoners back into the frame. This didn't happen. The sisters stared at two empty chairs and a brick wall, until Lou—his black ski mask rolled up onto his head—approached the camera and killed the feed.

Flo lowered the phone. They looked at one another. Jessie broke first. The tears were already in her eyes, but now they fell in heavy drops that spilled over her fingers as she tried to wipe them away. Brea was next. She lowered her head onto Jessie's shoulder as big, breath-stealing sobs besieged her body. Her tears were copious and bright. Then it was Flo, who'd retreated a step, wanting to give Brea and Jessie a second together, but also wanting to dedicate a moment to her real sister. She closed her eyes and envisioned a future for Imani and her baby, one paved with the ups and downs of life but always filled with love. A shaky smile brightened Flo's face, then everything poured out of her. Jessie took her by the elbow and ushered her close, and the three sisters wept together, their recent histories set aside, their emotions in harmony.

Amid the pain and death, it was an instant of brilliant hope, a true win. They wanted the feeling to last but knew it couldn't. Chance's leverage had been negated, but the job was not yet done.

**"LET'S TALK SECURITY," BREA SAID,** rounding on Burl, who'd slipped down the wall again in a futile effort to tear through his restraints. "How many men at Chance's house?"

"A thousand," Burl replied, and cackled. "*Ten* thousand."

Brea hoisted him back into position and slapped his face hard. He looked at her with glimmering coals in his eyes and more red trickling from between his lips.

"The bargaining power is ours now," Brea said. "You better wise up, tell us what we need to know."

"What's the point?" Burl said. Brea's handprint was blooming on the left side of his face. "I could tell you the truth, or I could lie. You're not going to find out until . . . until you get there, by which time I'll be dead."

"He's right," Flo said.

"But I'll . . . I'll say this." Burl's words were slurred, like a drunk's. His left eyelid drooped. "You won't get close to Chance. He's too . . . too heavily protected. Your best bet is to quit while you're ahead. Leave town. If you let me live, I'll persuade Chance not to come after you. He won't . . . won't like it, but he's always listened to me."

"I don't think we've established enough trust to go that route," Jessie said.

"Then go on, get yourselves killed." Burl shrugged. "Like I give a fuck."

Brea ran the heel of one hand across her face and rejoined Jessie and Flo. "How do you want to play this?"

The sisters were silent for a moment, then Jessie said, "We can stage another death. We'll take a photo down by the river, send it to Chance. He'll think the game's over and lower his guard, and while he and the rest of his pals are celebrating, we'll make our move."

"Yeah, that's good." Brea nodded. "And I don't mind being the corpse. I get the feeling these fuckers will be very happy to see me dead."

"Don't be so sure," Flo said. "You're the big favorite, Brea. The celebrations will be louder and longer if they think you've won."

"Fucking idiots," Burl snapped. Blood sprayed from his mouth. "The first thing Chance will do is call his boys in off the street—the ones currently looking for you. Then you'll have twice as many men to kill. And even if he invites them in for a drink and a hoedown, there's still the cameras, the . . . the motion sensors . . . alarms . . ."

"And that goddamn dog," Jessie remembered.

"Right. Errol." Burl cackled again. "It's like I said: I'm your only hope of getting out of this. *Me*."

The sisters dropped into deep thought, their faces still wet with tears. The flies buzzed. Burl's phone chirped again, a message from someone called Mose, insisting that there was no sign of the "gals" in Lower West. We looked hi and lo, he'd written. KEEP LOOKING DAMMIT, Flo responded.

"What if . . . ?" Jessie pressed the tip of one thumb to her forehead, perhaps hoping to massage her half-formed idea into something more solid. "I don't know . . . what if we got Chance out of that house, away from all the security?"

"How?" Flo asked.

"Burl can tell him there's been a security breach," Jessie replied. "Maybe have his driver bring him here. Or somewhere else. Somewhere . . . secluded."

"Sounds like a surefire way to get all his alarm bells ringing," Burl said.

"I don't want to say he's right," Brea said on the back of a heavy sigh. "But he's right. Chance will double his security detail. Call in favors. Maybe bring his cop sister in, too."

"So what do we do?" Jessie asked, hooking the same thumb she'd pressed to her forehead toward Burl. "Let him live? Trust that he'll get Chance to back off."

"That's not happening, either," Flo said. "These men need to pay for what they've done."

Brea nodded in agreement. Her back was up, and she had a fire in her belly that burned despite her fatigue. "There's only one option here: Chance feels secure at his house. Or *more* secure, at least. It's the only place to hit him. If we go in quietly, we can take out a dozen guys before he knows we're there."

"We'll need weapons for that. The kind with suppressors." Jessie turned away from her sisters and approached Burl. His head was down, chin on his chest. She kicked him in the leg to rouse him. "You want to tell us what you did with our van?"

Burl looked up slowly. His skin was grayer. He didn't respond.

"Hey, our *van*." Jessie kicked him again. "What did you do with it?"

Burl rested his head against the wall. An ugly laugh rumbled from his chest.

"He won't tell us," Flo said. "We can threaten him, his family, but he'll just plead ignorant or tell us he sold it. And how do we prove he's not telling the truth?"

Brea put her hand out, looking at Flo. "Give me his phone," she said, and Flo did. Brea walked over to Burl and crouched beside him. She held the cell phone up to his face. "I think you know where our van is, and I think I'll find evidence of that on here. Maybe a message to one of your guys, telling him where to store it. Maybe an email receipt from a junkyard."

Burl's eyes rolled toward her. He licked blood off his lips and clenched his jaw.

"I don't care how long it takes. I'm going to check every DM, every message, every email. I'll check your trash cans and your spam." Brea turned the phone on and typed in Burl's passcode. "This is the tech equivalent of ransacking your office, going through your filing cabinets, emptying your drawers. How confident are you that I *won't* find any mention of our van?"

"Fuck you," Burl snarled.

"And hey, maybe I won't. And if I don't, you've got nothing to worry about. But if I *do* . . . well, I should warn you that the clock is ticking, and every minute you make me trawl through this phone is a minute I spend with your family."

Burl slammed the back of his head against the wall. "Fuck you." His teeth were stained red. "*Fuck you.*"

"This is not an idle threat, Burl. You terrorized *my* family, after all. You terrorized a pregnant woman."

Burl gasped and moaned. His throat darkened. Brea gave him a moment to catch his breath, then tapped the speech bubble icon at the bottom of the screen. A string of messages appeared.

"I can tell from your reaction that all the information I need is in here somewhere," she said, waving the screen in front of Burl again. "That SERE training doesn't count for much when your family is on the line. Or maybe you didn't really take it. Just another one of your lies."

Burl nodded, then shook his head, whatever that meant. His eyes dimmed woozily.

"You want to do this the easy way?" Brea asked. "Or should we start the clock?"

"Easy," Burl said. He pressed his lips together and swallowed with a loud click. "There's a two-car garage at Pink's Crematorium. It's across the river, on the edge of town, maybe twenty minutes from here. That's where you'll find your van."

"Good, Burl," Brea said. "Real good. The easy way is better, huh?"

"Go fuck yourself."

"Yeah. If only. What I'm actually going to do is drive out to Pink's Crematorium and see how accurate your information is. With that in mind, is there anything else I need to know?"

"Like?"

"Alarm systems? Attack dogs? Maybe Pink himself, with a shotgun?"

"Nothing like that," Burl said. "It's a no-questions-asked kind of place. And Ernie won't be there. He lives in Colton."

"Okay. And this garage . . . I'm assuming it's locked up tight." Brea dragged Burl's keys from her pocket and jangled them in front of his face. "Will I find the key on here?"

Burl made a grunting sound, not quite a yes, but close enough. "Your van keys are in Chance's desk drawer, though, with your phones and wallets, so you'll have to break . . . break a window if you want what's in the back."

"Speaking of which," Jessie said, stepping forward. "Our instruments, our weapons . . . is everything still there?"

"Maybe. Who knows?" Burl shrugged. "I don't know if Ernie's been nosing around, but it was all there when me and Goose dropped the van off last Tuesday."

Brea stood up and returned to her sisters. "I'll check it out. See if he's telling the truth."

"I think he is," Flo said.

"I think so, too," Brea said. "But I want to be sure before I put a bullet in his head."

BREA WAS GONE EXACTLY FORTY-SIX minutes. During that time, Flo dosed up on painkillers, then sat on the stairs, keeping an eye on Burl and answering the messages that came in on his phone. She had everyone chasing shadows. She also opened StreamSphere again, just in case. The feed was still dead.

Jessie, meanwhile, stumbled upstairs to the wren's apartment, clutching her thumping chest as she walked through the nightmarish space, with its open ceiling and cloudscape paintings, to the even more nightmarish kill room. Here, she removed every photograph of herself from the plastic-covered walls and the few that had fallen to the floor. There were seventy-three of them—seventy-four, including the large picture in the main room of her sitting on the Micheltorena Stairs in Silver Lake. Jessie broke the glass and pulled this picture from the frame, tore it into eight pieces, and threw them, along with the other photos, into the kitchen sink. She doused the pile with lighter fluid, which she'd found in a drawer, then added a lit match and watched it burn.

The high blue flames, the smell of the smoke, made Jessie feel better. She wasn't done yet, though. There were pools and splashes of her blood on the floor in the kill room and the main room. Jessie grabbed a cloth and a bottle of disinfectant and cleaned it away, scrubbing hard, making sure she removed every trace.

THE AUTHORITIES WOULD SPEND A long time putting these pieces together. (If everything went their way—probably too much to hope for— the sisters would be back in California before the carnage inside the warehouse was discovered.) They'd search, analyze, and interview, but would never get the whole picture. Jessie decided to help get them off on the right foot.

After killing Susan Orringer, the wren had written a haiku on her bedroom wall using black paint. Jessie found this paint—or a pot just like it—in a small closet off the main room. She took it downstairs, tugged the bedsheet back over the wren's face, and twisted the cap off the paint pot.

"What are you doing?" Flo asked.

"Giving the authorities a head start," Jessie replied. She crouched (not without discomfort), dipped her finger into the paint, and scrawled a message across the top of the sheet. It wasn't cryptic, imaginative, or clever.

It certainly wasn't a haiku, although there would have been something sweetly karmic about that. It was two concise words.

## DEAD WREN.

Poetry.

"WE'RE GOOD," BREA SAID, STEPPING into the corpse-strewn hallway. She tilted her chin at Burl. "The van's where he said it would be. I didn't check fully, but it looks like all our gear is still there."

"I guess the plan was to deal with us before picking our bones clean," Flo said.

"So it's on," Jessie said. "We're doing this."

"We have no choice," Brea said. "Burl isn't going to persuade Chance not to come after us. He said that to save his own ass. And Chance *will* come after us. Our families, too. We have to stop him."

"You're all going to die," Burl wheezed.

"Then we die," Brea said. "But I promise you this: even if he lives, Chance Kotter will know we were there. He'll be hurting for a long time to come."

"And it begins with you, his right-hand man." Flo stood up off the stairs and walked the few steps to where Burl was propped against the wall. He breathed raggedly, head down. Flo stooped and lifted the bottom of his chin so that their eyes met. "You brought me water. You brought me food. You eased my pain and dressed my wounds. But you said it yourself, Burl: You did none of those things for me. You did them for yourself."

"You're damn right," Burl said. His final words.

Flo nodded. She let go of Burl's chin. His head sank again. She stood up and gestured at Brea. There wasn't much in it. A slight nod, a twitch of the lips. Flo stepped backward as Brea moved in, drawing Burl's Walther PDP from the back of her jeans.

The last time she'd shot Burl, he'd walked away. He'd dug the fragmented bullet out of his ballistic vest, in fact, and placed it into her mouth. That wasn't going to happen this time. Brea placed the tip of the barrel an inch from the back of Burl's skull and pulled the trigger. The report was tremendous—a seismic boom that heralded the end of his life. He slid down the wall, his face gone, his jaw in his lap.

Brea looked at him through a swirl of pistol smoke. The fading report brought a sense of finality, which felt good even though it wasn't real.

Four dead now, and they were just getting started.

# THIRTY-THREE

They had mastered the art of efficiency, and not just when it came to dispatching bad guys. Mundane tasks were invariably handled with a precision that came only from years of being together, developing an understanding that bordered on telepathy. Whether they were setting up their gear for a show, cleaning their weapons, or changing a blown tire, the sisters got the job done with speed and thoroughness.

Removing themselves from a crime scene was no exception. In the past, they'd dealt with this by not placing themselves at the crime scene in the first place: no photographic evidence, no fingerprints, no DNA. This wasn't the case at the warehouse. The cleanup was significant. As ever, they worked in tandem and got the job done.

They began by washing the men's blood off their hands and faces, rinsing it out of their hair. They didn't have time for a complete head-to-toe scrub, but it was good enough. Again, Flo had avoided the worst of the mess. She finished first and went downstairs to take care of the weapons they'd handled, retrieving them from wherever they'd ended up, wiping the fingerprints off (or certainly obscuring them to the point where they couldn't be lifted), and placing them in the possession of the fallen men. She cut the electrical wire binding Burl's wrists and set the balisong in his good left hand. The big guy got the ice pick and the empty Glock 29. The wren got the utility knife. Silver Hair got the scissors and the santoku knife—a storied knife now, Flo mused, recalling how she had brazenly stolen it from Flavor Moon's kitchen what seemed like an age ago.

This restructuring of events lacked subtlety, but it would keep investigators guessing for the foreseeable future.

Brea and Jessie went to work on their other fingerprints. Using rags and disinfectant, they cleaned surfaces, doorknobs, drawer handles, light switches, faucets, the showerhead, the refrigerator, the washing machine and dryer, and anything else they had touched or *may* have touched, working upstairs and down. When they finished, they tossed the cleaning materials into a garbage bag, which they would drop into a random dumpster on their way to Chance Kotter's property.

Flo used the bottom of her T-shirt to lock the front door and shut off the lights, and the sisters left the warehouse via the back window. It was 8:37 now, full dark. Lights flickered on the other side of the river. A nearby factory steamed and banged, and they heard another freight train chugging south, its horn constant. On their way to Burl's SUV, Jessie plucked a used rag from the garbage bag and used it to remove her fingerprints from the truck she'd parked around back.

"Done," she said, rejoining her sisters.

"Good," Flo said. "Let's get the hell out of here."

They hadn't eradicated themselves from the scene completely—there were likely partial boot prints and certainly splashes of Brea's blood in the roof space—but they'd left nothing incriminating. In the unlikely event that they were ever questioned, and assuming they survived the night, they would simply claim to be victims.

JESSIE CLIMBED INTO THE BACK of the Yukon and splayed out across the seat. "Wake me up when we get to the van," she said. Flo took the passenger seat with a deep groan, her bruised and forlorn body responding to the soft leather and springs. Brea hoisted herself behind the wheel. It took two attempts. She started the engine and sat for a moment with her head on one shoulder, trying to blink the tiredness from her eyes.

"Can you drive?" Flo asked.

"Uh-huh."

"Shoot straight?"

"Always."

"I hope you're right," Flo said.

"I am." Brea turned her attention to the GPS, bringing up a list of recent locations. "I found my animal familiar—my daemon—on Interstate 40. A horse, caught in the storm."

Flo had started to slide deep into her seat but sat up instead, sparked by Brea's words—not the idea of her finding her daemon, but the image of a horse against the elements. A memory of Burl dropped into her mind, crouched beside her in the empty office and plunging a needle into a vial of clear liquid. *It's mostly vitamin B$_{12}$ with some Ritalin and* myo-*inositol,* he'd said to her. *They give this to horses to make them run faster.*

"Wait," Flo said. Brea had started to pull away but put her foot on the brake. Flo clicked on the interior light and opened the glove compartment. She didn't find what she was looking for in there, so hopped out of the SUV, stumbled around to the back, and popped the liftgate. There was nothing in the cargo space, either, except the garbage bag that Jessie had just thrown in. Flo checked the backseat area and the side pockets in the doors. No luck.

"Damn," she said, returning to the passenger seat, closing the door. "It was worth a shot."

"What were you looking for?" Brea asked. She was slouched on the armrest between them, her eyes heavy. Flo doubted she could shoot straight. She could barely *see* straight.

"A firm kick in the pants," Flo replied, recalling Burl's other description. She pressed her palm to her forehead and looked from Brea to the armrest. It was hinged, almost as large as a cooler. Flo reached across with her right hand and found the catch. "Move your arm," she said to Brea, and lifted the upholstered lid to reveal a deep storage compartment.

The leatherette case was inside, its zipper shining in the interior lights. Flo lifted it out, struggled one-handed with the zipper, and handed it to Brea.

"Can you . . . ?"

Brea unzipped the case, revealing four empty syringes, four new needles, and two bottles of a clear liquid. One was unmarked, half full. Flo wasn't touching *that*. The other was two-thirds full and had the brand name EquiAguante. Its red-and-white label was in Spanish, but it had a picture of a galloping horse, and Flo had no trouble picking "vitamina B$_{12}$" out of the long list of ingredients.

"This is it," she said, turning the bottle toward Brea. "I don't know about the long-term effects, but in the short term, I can tell you from personal experience that this really works."

"Works how?" Brea asked.

"It boosts energy . . . reduces pain. I guess it contains some kind of Ritalin, maybe morphine." Flo looked at the ingredients again. "I mean, it's mostly $B_{12}$. I *think*."

Jessie had sat up in the back. She reached between the seats, cupped Flo's hand, and turned the bottle toward her.

"This is a fucking *horse* stimulant," she said.

"Yeah," Flo said, and pulled a wry face. "It makes them run faster."

Brea was already offering her arm. "Shoot me up," she said.

THEY STARTED TO FEEL THE effects by the time they reached Pink's Crematorium. Their pupils were larger. Their heads were clearer. The aches and woes that weakened their bodies had been partially dulled. They were far from 100 percent, but they weren't walking dead by any means.

Pink's was an old chapel-like stone building with a chimney lost in the darkness. The Yukon's headlights passed over its broad shaft but not its crown. The garage was in back, along a gravel path that sounded beneath the tires like grinding teeth. Brea pulled up in front of the double doors. The sisters got out of the vehicle, moving more smoothly than when they got in. It took Brea a minute to find the right key and open the padlock. She rolled the door open and there was the van, dirty white, road tested, one of its back windows broken.

They changed into fresh, unbloodied clothes, then loaded up with semiautomatic pistols, suppressors, extra ammunition, and blades. Jessie slotted her nunchaku into her back pocket. Flo grabbed the customized case for her Fender Precision bass and flipped it open. The instrument was still there. Good. She removed it, then lifted the false bottom and saw that the Savage 10FP sniper rifle was still there, too. Even better. Flo snapped the case closed and put it in the back of the Yukon. Jessie was right behind her, carrying the nonlethal tools of their trade: ski masks, gloves, and the ÜberFlyte Series 2 drone.

"One more thing," Brea said. She'd uncovered their rudimentary toolbox and taken out a small hacksaw.

"I don't think we need to dismember him," Jessie said. "A bullet between the eyes will do."

"Silly," Brea said. She lifted her right boot onto the back of the van. The tracker on her ankle was still flashing, that cold green light announcing itself once a second. Brea started to saw through the solid band. It took a few seconds for the blade to catch, but when it did, she made quick work of it. The green light winked out and didn't come back on. Brea tore the device from her ankle and threw it away into the darkness.

"Damn, that feels good," she said, and looked at her sisters. "Who's next?"

BREA WAS CONFIDENT SHE COULD remember the route to Chance's house, but Flo found his address on Burl's phone, just in case. Brea entered it into the GPS and got moving. She decided to take the back roads, avoiding the traffic and stoplights of the city proper, not to mention the prospect of inadvertently pulling alongside any of Chance's men.

"How about some sounds?" Jessie suggested.

Brea turned the radio on. No shit-kicking stations for Burl. He'd been a yacht-rock fan, apparently. "Baby Come Back," by Player, filled the Yukon's interior with a melancholic silkiness that didn't fit the mood. Brea hit the tune button and kept hitting it until blood-thumping all-American rock blared through the speakers: "How I Could Just Kill a Man," the Rage Against the Machine version—a little *too* on the nose, maybe, but it elevated their pulses, got the adrenaline coursing. Jessie wasn't interested in sleeping anymore. She sat in the back, slapping her knees in time.

Flo took out Burl's phone and responded to numerous messages, all variations on a theme: We've driven top to tail through this goddamn city and we cannot find those gals. Flo's response was always the same: KEEP LOOKING!

Chance messaged, too. I want an update, face to face, he wrote, with a follow-up text moments later: Come on back to the house.

Flo looked at the speedometer: 50 mph. She looked at their headlights racing along the quiet back road. The GPS put them twelve minutes out. She smiled, typed in a one-word reply, and said it out loud as she hit send.

"Incoming."

# THIRTY-FOUR

*Sunday Night Football* was in full swing—the Steelers and the Raiders going at it with grunt and muscle—and there were a few boys sitting in front of the big screen. Most of them had gone home, though. They'd expected live video feeds of the sisters duking it out, spilling blood, until one of them emerged victorious. *That* was the plan, by Christ, and everything had been running so smoothly. Unfortunately, it had all fizzled out when the GPS went tits up. Burl had sent a photo of the little one lying dead on some cold concrete floor, and that had caused a flurry of excitement, but there'd been no video, no *action*. Chance's hopes of feeling like an emperor at the Colosseum—Titus, maybe, or one of those other toga-wearing sons of bitches—had taken a stark downward turn. There'd been a few side bets made on the football games, and Dylan Cobb had gone twenty-three seconds on El Toro Loco (winning Chance $5,000 in the process), but it hadn't been enough to raise the mood.

"I've seen wet fireworks with more pop," Tucker Presley had declared before leaving. The arrogant prick had narrowed his eyebrows at Chance—narrowed his goddamn eyebrows—and parked his ten-gallon hat atop his two-gallon noggin. "This was a big idea, Kott, and be damned if you didn't almost pull it off. Maybe you will yet, but my thumb enjoys fresh air and sunshine. It does *not* enjoy being jammed up my ass, which is where it's been for most of the day."

"I hear you, Tuck," Chance had countered. "But listen, as soon as we get that GPS—"

"Sorry, old friend, but this cowboy's hitting the trail," Tucker had said, and given Chance a look that was in some ways pitying and in others condescending. Chance wanted to punch him square in the nose. Actually, he wanted Burl here so that Burl could punch him square in the nose. "You let me know if Blondie comes through."

It wasn't just that they'd lost track of the sisters or that most of his friends had decided that the party had fallen flat on its ass; it was also Chance's growing sense of unease. Burl had assured him that everything was under control—they had men out looking, and security on the home front was amped—but Chance couldn't shake the feeling that something irrevocably bad had happened. He told himself it was just paranoia, but the truth was his stomach felt squirrelly in a way it hadn't for many years. The photo of the dead sister had helped, but not as much as it should have.

He'd feel better once Burl was back. *Maybe.* Because that was the other thing . . . the last few communications from Burl had seemed *off*, somehow. Chance had read those messages with a curious frown. Even the last one, Incoming, which should have been reassuring, had seemed decidedly un-Burl-like.

Chance turned his attention to the football game, if only to divert his thoughts for a moment. It didn't work. The Raiders' running back lost three yards on the play, which epitomized the last few hours for Chance. They had all the style, attitude, and muscle, but found themselves going backward. Things needed to change in a hurry.

"I'll be right back," Chance said to his compadres. "Need to make a call."

Only Mayor Austin Hasse acknowledged him, raising one hand in a *who gives a flying fuck* kind of way. Chance left the man cave with that feeling in his gut deepening.

Nash and Wilder were outside the door with their loaded AR-15s clutched to their chests. "Gentlemen," Chance said with mock cheeriness. They accompanied him to his study, one in front and one behind. "Precautionary" was the word Burl had used. He'd also called it "overkill." Whatever it was, needing an armed escort in your own goddamn house did not exactly set Chance's mind at ease.

He closed the study door behind him and walked over to the framed photograph on the wall that never failed to make him feel good: Harper Avenue, 1969, the year he was born. So much had changed since that photo had been taken, all for the better, and most of it because of *him*, Chance Kotter. He *was* the goddamn emperor of this town. He *was* Titus.

"And don't you forget it," he said to nobody at all. With a slight uptick in his spirits, he took out his phone and called Burl. Incoming, Burl had said, but what the fuck did *that* mean? Ten minutes? Three hours? He'd find out from the man himself. No more dumbass text messages. Burl's phone rang five times and clicked over to voicemail. "Fuck you, Burl, you whore's ass," Chance said after the beep. He hung up, then chastised himself. Burl was working hard, doing everything he could to rein this situation in.

"Cut the guy some slack," Chance said. He puffed out his cheeks, crossed to the west-facing windows, and looked out on the back of his property. It was too dark to see much of anything now except the blue of his swimming pool and a few ground lights around the patio. Emmett Pound's helicopter was out there somewhere, parked in the field some eighty yards yonder. The way Chance felt at that moment, he wouldn't mind getting on that whirlybird and having it take him someplace else. Arizona or Alaska or the fucking moon—anywhere this squirrelly feeling couldn't reach him.

The west view put Chance in mind of Bobby Wallace, who was up on the balcony with a hunting rifle and a pair of binoculars, much good would they do him in the dark. Chance found Bobby's number on his phone and gave him a call. Bobby answered on the first ring. Alert. Chance liked that.

"How's it going up there, Bobby?"

"Just fine, Mr. Kotter."

"All clear?"

"All clear."

"Glad to hear it," Chance said. "And the darkness ain't . . . you know, a problem?"

"No problem at all. I've got night-vision binoculars, infrared, good up to a thousand feet, and a thermal scope for the .308."

"Christ on a cracker. Ain't nothing getting past you."

"Nossir."

"Well, listen, Bobby, I appreciate your service. And do me a favor . . . gimme a call if you see anything out of the ordinary."

"Yessir."

Chance hung up. Speaking to Bobby—someone who knew what he was doing, by God—had lifted him just a touch. It had felt like positive yardage, not enough to move the chains, but it was better than going backward.

A MILE OUT, BREA TOOK the Yukon off-road, following an overgrown trail that led to an old pumping station. She drove slowly, bouncing over potholes and rocks. A gray fox crossed the path in front of them. It offered an evaluative stare before continuing down a shallow embankment into neighboring woodland. Fat bugs ticked in the headlights.

They arrived at a rusty chain-link gate that they could have rammed through without too much resistance, but Brea pulled to a stop in front of it and killed the engine. They were far enough along the trail to not be seen from the road.

Jessie had already entered Chance's address into the drone's GPS. She opened the back door, stepped outside, and launched it. Her sisters joined her, looking intently at the controller's screen.

The drone climbed three hundred feet into the night, then followed the fox's route, over the embankment and woodland beyond. They saw flashes of hot color where the trees were sparser: wildlife, most of it too small to recognize, but some deer, too, and a pack of sleek, wending creatures that could only be coyotes. It took three minutes to clear the woods, then they were over Chance's land, coming in from the south. The drone's thermal cam looked down on a barn, stables, and a horse arena. Jessie took over the controls. She dropped fifty feet and buzzed closer to the house. The first thing they spotted was Errol in his enclosure, sleeping now, but he wouldn't be for long.

"Any ideas?" Jessie asked, zooming in on the dozing dog.

"Gee, I left my favorite squeaky toy in the van," Brea said, and held up her .45. "Good thing I brought this."

"If we're as quick and quiet as we hope to be—as we *need* to be," Flo said soberly, "that dog won't even get sprung."

"Let's hope," Jessie said.

They flew over the front of Chance's property and followed a long driveway to the main gate. Two men were posted there, one of them sitting on a low brick wall, the other playing with his phone.

"We roll up in Burl's vehicle," Flo said, "and they'll probably open the gate for us."

"The old Trojan horse routine," Brea said with a tight smile, then pointed at the screen. "You see any security cams?"

"Nothing obvious," Jessie said. "I can zoom in closer, but we'll lose image quality."

"Maybe fly lower?" Flo suggested.

"Ambient noise," Jessie said, shaking her head. "As in there isn't any, or not much. We go any lower, there's a chance they'll hear."

She navigated the drone back toward the house, flying above an undulating frontage dotted with sweet gum trees and ground lights. They passed over a large, illuminated fountain, its water a phosphorescent orange in the drone's thermal cam. There were two more guys on the other side, guarding the front of the house, and another man patrolling the north-facing side. This was where the vehicles were parked, mostly pickup trucks. The sisters counted seventeen of them.

"That's a lot of traffic," Flo observed. "That means a lot of people to deal with."

Brea pointed out the shed she had been locked up in, where she'd been beaten and treated like an animal, made to eat out of a dog's bowl. Most of that had been Burl's doing, who, for all his potency and manliness, was now lying dead in a warehouse. He'd redeemed himself somewhat at the end, but Brea noted dryly that fewer bullets had been as satisfying as the one she had put through his skull.

Jessie guided the drone over the shed and along the west side, toward the pool. She stopped suddenly, her attention drawn to a splash of hot color at the top of the screen. It was a man, positioned on a balcony, clearly armed with a scoped rifle.

"Oh shit," Jessie said. "This dude's got the back of the house covered."

"And you can bet that scope is high-end," Flo added.

"We'll have to get at him from inside," Brea said, pointing at the double doors behind him. "Go through here. One shot. He'll be dead before he can swing that rifle around."

"Or . . ." Jessie directed the drone back toward the shed, wondering if she could climb onto its roof, or maybe into one of the trees, and get an elevated shot from there. Movement on the balcony caused her to pause, though. The man posted there had turned toward them. Jessie zoomed in and saw that he was looking through a set of binoculars, no doubt as good in the dark as the scope on his rifle. Brea and Flo noticed, too.

"Crap," Flo said. "We've been made."

They watched as the man lowered his field glasses and got behind his rifle. Jessie immediately lifted the drone up and away, ascending at forty-five feet per second. The ground scrolled beneath them at speed, the landmarks shrinking. They saw the shed and the parked trucks, then the screen glitched and went black.

"That son of a bitch shot us down," Jessie said.

They waited to hear the report. A mile away, in the stillness, it would take approximately five seconds to reach their ears. No report came. The shooter's rifle was suppressed, and his accuracy—hitting a small moving target from upwards of five hundred feet away—had not been compromised. The sisters looked at one another, thinking the same thing: this wasn't some redneck with a Saturday night special. This guy was a deadeye.

"At least now we know what we're up against," Flo said.

They climbed into the Yukon. Brea started the engine, shifted into reverse, and backed down the trail at speed. Emerging onto the road, she cranked the wheel and swept the front end around in a haze of dust, pointing north toward Chance's property.

STILL NO SIGN OF BURL. Chance tried calling him again but got the same voicemail response. He didn't leave a message this time, only hung up and shot daggers at the screen.

"Where in God's name are you, Burl?"

He'd known Burl since 1994, a skinny kid back then with a power mullet and buckteeth (he'd looked more like Freddie Mercury than Burt Reynolds), who'd spent most of his time on a shooting range or baseball diamond, and in Chance's opinion, it didn't get more American than that. He'd done a few small jobs for Chance back in the day but didn't join the payroll until his return from overseas, starting out as his driver and swiftly rising through the ranks as his skill set became apparent. It wasn't long before their personal relationship was as strong as their professional one. Chance had sat at the head table at Burl and Caroline's wedding in lieu of Burl's big brother, who'd been clobbered with the cancer stick eighteen months before. He'd been to both his daughters' christenings, to birthday parties, and to backyard barbecues. He and Burl had talked for hundreds of hours as confidants and friends. Together, they'd set the world to rights.

Chance *knew* Burl—knew him as well as or better than any man—and all his receptors, as employer and friend, told him that something wasn't right. Burl was conscientious and considerate. He answered the goddamn phone when Chance called. His job was to make Chance feel safe, and he was good at it.

"So what the fuck is going on here?" Chance asked under his breath. His gaze tracked to the photo on his desk of him and Ned Sargent, taken on a hunting trip to Alaska, and he searched Ned's eyes as if he—as well as being a musical godsend—had the answer to Chance's question. Ned did not. Chance switched to the photo of Bethany in her chief of police dress uniform, who did for his heart what that old photograph of Harper Avenue did for his soul. Bethany did not have an answer for him, either.

Chance sat down with a heavy sigh. His belly bumped his desk and woke his computer. A screen materialized, requesting his password. Chance entered it with agonizing slowness, speaking the word out loud as he did: "O . . . ba . . . ma . . . sucks." His desktop appeared, and Chance nodded in a self-congratulatory way.

"Okay, Mr. Computer. You wanna help me out here?"

Chance clicked on the GPS app (already open) and saw that it was still offline. Muttering a string of expletives, he X'd out of the program and opened StreamSphere, the live video app that Burl had installed only a few days before. It appeared Chance had signed out the last time he used it, because it, too, wanted his password.

He frowned deeply, drumming his fingers across his brow, as if this might summon the password to the surface in the same way that raindrops summon earthworms. He tried "obamasucks" and "ObamaSucks," but neither worked. He tried "chickenfried69" and "ChickenFried69" and, impatiently, "gofuckyourself," and the app told him that five attempts were too many and locked him out for ten minutes. Chance responded by hammering the keyboard with the fleshy side of his fist until the screen went black.

"Fuck you. *Fuck you!*"

Following several centering breaths, Chance realized that he didn't *need* the video app to get a read on the situation in California. He could simply call Lou Washerby. Lou was Burl's hire, one of his old military pals, but Chance had his number. He found it on his cell phone and hit the call button.

Like Bobby, Lou answered on the first ring.

"Mr. Kotter?"

"Lou Washerby, you old sumbitch. How's sunny California?" As if he gave one rat's ass about sunny California. Sunny California could disappear into a chasm in the earth for all Chance cared.

"Okay, I guess," Lou replied. "Rainy, actually."

"Huh. You don't say."

"I do."

"Well . . ." Chance's mind scratched around for something to add but came up empty. He smeared a gummy residue from the corners of his mouth and got down to business. "Listen, Lou, I won't use up too much of your time. I'm just calling to make sure that everything is good at your end."

"Sure is," Lou said. "Better than good, in fact. We got everything packed up inside of ten minutes and went out the back door. Nobody saw us leave."

Chance went stiff. It felt like a cat had clawed its way up the inside of his rib cage. "I'm sorry, Lou. Can you say that again?"

"After we let the women go," Lou said, speaking louder. "We cleared out in a hurry. Not so much as a doughnut crumb left behind."

"You let the women go?"

"Yessir." Lou paused, no doubt hearing the vibratory tension in Chance's voice. "Burl made the call."

The strength went out of Chance's legs. If he hadn't been sitting, he'd have collapsed to the floor. His mind filled with a vast, craterlike emptiness while simultaneously (and paradoxically) buckling beneath the weight of a thousand questions. Nothing made sense.

"Burl?" The word popped from between his lips on a strained whiff of air.

"Yessir."

"And you're . . . you're sure it was him?"

"I've known Burl more than twenty years. He saved my life in the sandpit—talked me through some dark places. I know the sound of his voice." A few seconds ticked by while Lou gave Chance a moment to respond. He didn't take it, so Lou cleared his throat and added, "Also, the call was from Burl's phone. His name was right there on the screen."

Chance started to shake. It began in his belly—that vibratory tension, like water building inside a pipe about to burst—and radiated out from there to all points of his body, even inside his mouth. His teeth rattled like bones in a jar.

"Mr. Kotter?"

Emptiness and chaos. If someone took a knife to his brain and sliced it like a piece of fruit, these were the things that would spill out. A clear thought occurred, though, within that contradictory space: that Burl had either betrayed him or been compromised. Both possibilities were unthinkable, but they gave Chance something to grab on to.

Lou started to say something else. Chance lowered the phone and hung up on him. With more coolness than he believed himself capable of, he brought up his recent calls and tried Burl again. Five rings, then voicemail. Chance left a message: "What the fuck is going on, Burl? Call me. Let's figure this out." He was amazed how steady his voice sounded, given the circumstances. He ended the call and put his phone down on the desk.

Then he screamed. The pipe burst and it all flowed out—a torrent of confusion, anger, embarrassment, frustration, and fear. Ripe color rose from inside his collar. He wondered if he was in danger.

Nash and Wilder stormed in with their AR-15s in the ready position. They assessed the study for threats and looked quite impressive doing so, like Secret Service agents . . . if Secret Service agents wore Wrangler jeans and John Deere ball caps. Seeing no imminent peril, they lowered their weapons and approached Chance's desk.

Chance took a spluttering breath and screamed again. Veins he didn't know he had bulged in his throat, and something small and quick pulsated at the back of his skull—another vein, perhaps, or an aneurysm in waiting. The sound out of his lungs was mighty while it lasted but petered off to a weak hiss.

"Christ and Moses," Wilder said, truly alarmed. "What in the hell, boss?"

"It's all gone plumb sideways," Chance said, and something between a groan and a sigh escaped him—a sad sound, in any case. He looked at the photograph of Bethany, and it occurred to him that he could pick up the phone and call her. She'd arrive with her lightbar flashing and a convoy of cruisers in tow. Chance quickly dismissed the idea. Having his sister fight his battles did not align with his manly pride. Besides, he'd promised not to ask more of her than he already had, and he was, above all else, a man of his word.

"Sideways?" Nash asked. "What do you mean?"

Chance's gaze dropped to the mean-looking semiautomatic rifle in Nash's hands, then switched to the exact same rifle in Wilder's hands.

"How many bullets in those guns?" Chance asked, flicking his finger toward them.

"Mag holds thirty rounds," Wilder said.

"Yup," Nash said, patting his rifle like a pet.

Chance nodded. Sixty bullets versus a couple of tired, kicked-around gals—maybe three gals, if that photo of the little one was a fake (and Chance was beginning to suspect it was). Either way, the betting man in him liked those odds, and he wasn't even taking Bobby Wallace into consideration, or the other men on site, or sweet baby Errol.

The sisters weren't blind to the odds, either. They were tough and they were pissed, but they weren't stupid. The best thing they could do was cut their losses and head for the hills. Because really . . . three *gals* attacking a highly fortified property?

Chance shook his head. He couldn't see it.

His phone rang. He leapt at it, thinking it might be Burl. It was Bobby.

"What is it?" Chance's voice was croaky from screaming.

"Well, Mr. Kotter, you asked me to call if I saw anything out of the ordinary," Bobby said matter-of-factly. "So I thought I'd let you know that I just shot an unmanned aerial vehicle out of the sky."

"A what now?"

"A drone." Bobby paused, then elaborated: "A surveillance drone, possibly gathering intel."

"Oh," Chance said. That quick little something continued to pulsate at the back of his skull. "Intel, you say?"

"Either that or just some kids fucking around. But to be on the safe side . . ." There was a sandpapery sound as Bobby scratched his whiskery jaw. "You might want to ready yourself for an attack."

BREA BROUGHT THE YUKON TO a halt twenty-five yards from Chance's front gate. Jessie and Flo hopped out. They were fully armed, wearing ski masks and gloves. Brea got rolling again, moving slowly, and her sisters followed close behind. Being outside the vehicle gave them a greater field of view and better angles. If the two men at the gate presented any problems—or even if they didn't—Jessie and Flo could pick them off from cover.

The brake lights flared as Brea pulled up to the high iron gate. She looked in the rearview and caught a glimpse of Flo's silhouette ducking behind a tree at the edge of the road. Eyes forward again, she noticed a camera on the wall to the left of the gate. Both men approached with hands on their sidearms. Unless they got up close, it was too dark for them to see through the front windshield. The plan—the *hope*—was that they would recognize Burl's vehicle and open the gate without needing to ID who was behind the wheel.

This was exactly what happened. "It's Burl," one of the fellas said. Brea recognized him from her time in the shed. Mr. Boot, she'd called him, because he'd taken his boot off and beaten her with it. Now, Mr. Boot pushed a button and the gate rolled open. The other fella—a small man with a big beard—stepped off to the side.

Brea edged the Yukon forward, buzzing her window down while curling her right hand around the grip of the suppressed SIG P226 in her lap. She shot the camera first, knocking it clean off its bracket, then put a bullet between Mr. Boot's eyes. He flew backward, over the low wall and out of sight. She didn't have an angle on the small man with the big beard, but one of her sisters did. He went from standing next to the open gate with a surprised expression on his face to lying in the driveway with a bullet in his neck. The force of the shot had lifted his beard like wind billowing a sheet on a clothesline.

He was still alive. Flo popped one into his skull. Jessie dragged his body off the driveway and rolled it into the bushes, then she and Flo closed the gate behind the Yukon. Flo got into the passenger seat. Jessie opened the liftgate, flipped the catches on the customized case, and took out the sniper rifle. From a smaller case, she removed an AAC Cyclone silencer, a Pulsar Trail 2 thermal optic, and a handful of ammunition.

"See you in five," she said. She closed the liftgate and disappeared into the darkness.

Brea thumbed the de-cock lever on the SIG and returned it to her lap. Her ski mask was already on her head. She rolled it down over her face, stepped off the brake, and purred along the driveway toward Chance's house.

"Trojan horse," she said.

They were in.

# THIRTY-FIVE

The drone had shown two men out front and a third pacing the north side of the house. As the Yukon advanced and its headlights picked out more details, Brea and Flo saw that the security had increased. There were now six guys out front. They all had their weapons drawn. One man was pointing histrionically, barking orders.

"I guess the recon drone tipped them off," Flo said.

Brea stopped the Yukon twenty yards from the nearest man, close enough for him to see that it was Burl's vehicle, close enough to read the quizzical expression on his face. His gun hand was at half-mast.

"*Burl*," he shouted. His voice had a kind of squeak to it, as if he'd swallowed a whistle. "Shit*fire*, Burl, that *you*?"

The other guys were looking their way. The one who'd been giving orders aimed his pistol at them. "Announce yourself, Burl, or me and the boys will have no option but to get trigger happy."

Brea shifted into park. "You ready, Flo?"

Flo's pistol—an SW1911—was tucked into the crook of her wounded left arm. She used her good hand to buzz the window down. "I'll take the three on the right."

"We go the moment I hit the high beams."

Three more guys came sprinting around the south side of the house. They took up position behind their firearms. One of them went prone, making himself a smaller target. A few of the other fellas had dropped to one knee.

"I'm counting to five, Burl," the order giver shouted.

He made it to two.

*TWO,"* HE YELLED, AND WAS hit in the chest by a high-caliber bullet. His boots left the ground, and he landed in a dead heap a good distance from where he'd been standing. The other men stood in stunned silence, as if they couldn't comprehend how a fella could go from vertical to horizontal so gosh darn quickly.

The shot came from between the trees along the north side of the driveway, fifty yards behind Brea and Flo's position. As Brea hit the high beams and opened her door—Flo mirroring her on the passenger side—a second suppressed shot punched the air, and a second man went down. He was a large hombre, maybe two-forty, but lifted by the .308 as if he weighed no more than an empty jacket. His big dead body crumpled to the ground and slid ten feet along the asphalt before stopping.

This scattered the remaining seven. Some ran blindly. Others went prone or sought cover. They didn't know where to point their weapons. Brea and Flo stepped out of the Yukon, keeping low behind the open doors, aiming through the open windows. Brea pumped two rounds into her first target—the man with the whistle in his voice. Down he went, triggering as he fell. Flo squeezed off a shot and hit her target center mass. He spun in his boots and tottered, and she dropped him outright with a bullet to the head.

Four down. Five to go. One made a run for the house and Jessie took care of him. The .308 tore his right arm off. He went down screaming. Jessie chambered a fourth round, found him through the scope, and put him out of his misery.

Now the bullets started to come back. The other men had jumped into cover, two behind the water fountain, one behind a planter at the foot of the front stairs, one behind the trunk of a black cherry tree. The shots ricocheted off the asphalt in front of the Yukon, knocked out its head-lights, and rattled the open doors. The sounds were blistering. Brea and Flo held their positions, being selective with their shots. Brea set her sights on one of the men behind the fountain: his muzzle flash, one shoulder, the top of his head. She squeezed her trigger twice and hit the inside edge of the fountain, sending up sprays of water and cement. The man dropped out of sight. Brea didn't move her sights an inch. She held her breath and waited. After a moment, he popped back up, overcompensating to take aim. Brea was ready. She fired and hit dead center, and the man, whoever he was, whatever his story, slumped to the ground with his life leaking from the hole in his head.

A CANNONADE OF SHOTS, MOST of them unsuppressed. The night shook.

So much for going in quietly.

Chance's house faced east. The shooter on the west balcony couldn't see the showdown out front, but he'd have no problem hearing it. Jessie put herself in his shoes. Would she continue to protect the rear of the property and trust that her comrades had the situation in hand, or would she abandon her post, take up position in one of the front windows, and assist?

"Assist," Jessie whispered, shielding herself behind a tree and detaching the 10FP's stock magazine. She'd taken four shots and needed to reload. Working in the dark, she pulled four .308 cartridges from her front pocket and slotted them into the box mag. One of the rounds slipped between her gloved fingers and fell to the ground. Rather than waste time searching for it, or even digging another from her pocket, she went with three. She locked the mag home and chambered, then swung out from behind the tree and scoped the upper windows. No movement. No sign of Mr. Deadeye, but Jessie had a feeling he was coming. She waited, moving the reticle from one window to the next, alert for any variance in heat signature. Nothing.

Jessie zoomed out and scoped the shoot-out between her sisters and Chance's men. Of the nine, only three remained, shooting from cover, the muzzle flash almost constant through the thermal optic. Jessie moved northwest, cutting through the foliage between the trees, until she had a line on the goon behind the black cherry tree. He bloomed in her sights, hot and white. Jessie placed the reticle between his shoulder blades and curled her finger around the trigger. She steadied her breathing, waiting for that stillness, that natural pause, between breaths. When it occurred, she completed the trigger pull and the round discharged. Jessie rode the recoil and watched her shot hit home. On a range, with a paper target, she'd have been low and to the left of the bull's-eye—a miss by her exacting standards. He was not a paper target, though, and she did not miss. The bullet tore through his midsection and sent him pirouetting in his boots. He died star shaped.

She worked the bolt, caught the spent casing as it ejected, and chambered another round. Returning to the scope, she noticed movement in one of the upstairs windows. She zoomed in and saw the curtain lift and the window slide open. The light in that room was out, but the emerging rifle barrel was easy to see. It rested on the sill for stability and had a suppressor threaded onto the muzzle.

From her position, Jessie saw only the barrel, not the man behind it. This meant that he—Mr. Deadeye, it *had* to be—couldn't see her, either. This wasn't her concern, though. It was the fact that the barrel was angled toward Brea and Flo. Through a premium scope, they would be magnified targets, as bright as flames, and their choice of cover would not help. At distance, the Yukon's doors offered reasonable protection against lower-velocity rounds, but they wouldn't stop a high-caliber bullet from a precision rifle.

With two shots, Mr. Deadeye could tear her sisters apart.

Jessie shouted at them to get *behind* the vehicle, but the constant gunfire drowned her voice. She then did the only thing she could think of: she raised her rifle, scoped the window, and fired a quick shot at the upper panes. In her haste, her aim was off. She hit the frame. Wood splintered. It had the desired effect, though. The barrel disappeared as Mr. Deadeye ducked for cover. Jessie had bought herself valuable seconds.

She moved toward her original position behind the tree, where she had a better sight line on the window. Of course, if Mr. Deadeye scoped along the driveway—and Jessie had to assume he would—he'd see her thermogram between the trees. She kept low, moving as quickly as she could (the EquiAguante was good, but it was no miracle cure), and tucked herself behind the trunk of a maple. Nearer to the house, shots rattled off the Yukon's bodywork. Its rear glass exploded as a bullet passed through the already broken front windshield. Jessie dropped to one knee. She chambered the third and final round in the 10FP's mag, then swiveled out of cover to scope Mr. Deadeye's window.

He was waiting for her. Jessie glimpsed him in the window and went prone just in time. The bullet fizzed over her head. If she'd still been kneeling, it would have ripped through her chest and killed her instantly.

Now he had to work the bolt, chamber another round, and reestablish his target. Jessie had two seconds. Still prone, her left elbow on the ground for support, she found him in the window, paused her breathing, and triggered.

Low miss. She hit the sill. Splinters flew and Mr. Deadeye flinched, but that was all.

Jessie rolled right, back into cover. A bullet thudded into the grass where she'd been lying. She kept tight to the tree and got to her feet. Her body trembled. Sweat ran into her eyes. She ejected the spent casing, detached the magazine, and reached into her pocket for more .308s.

Empty.

An ugly coldness washed through her. She tried her other pockets. There was nothing in her jacket, inside or out. The branches of her nunchaku were tucked into her right back pocket, she had a spare mag for her sidearm in her back left, and there were only a few spent shell casings in her front left.

"No . . . *no*." Jessie screwed her eyes shut. She recalled grabbing a handful of .308s when she'd lifted the 10FP out the back of the Yukon, but only enough for two full mags? Going back for more was out of the question—Jessie was seventy yards from the vehicle, give or take. She could follow the tree line for most of that distance, but she knew Mr. Deadeye would have multiple opportunities to cut her down.

On cue, another bullet scored the trunk of the tree to her left, shredding bark. Jessie shrank and dropped to her haunches. Out of bullets. Out of hope. Soon, Mr. Deadeye would give up on her and turn his attention back to Brea and Flo.

She cursed under her breath, recalling the cartridge that had slipped through her fingers when she'd reloaded the mag. A clumsy mistake. If she hadn't dropped it, that round would be chambered now, giving her one more shot at Mr. Deadeye.

"Have to . . . find it," she said between tight inhalations, looking at the ground around her feet. It was dark, twisty with roots, and this wasn't the tree she'd been standing behind anyway. It had been closer to the Yukon, an elm maybe, with a fork in the trunk and a sagging, splintered branch. The lights along the driveway had emphasized its clean white wound.

Jessie had no time to think about it. She broke from behind the maple—zigzagging, staying low, throwing herself at the next nearest tree. Mr. Deadeye took his shot and pumped a bullet into the ground beside her, lifting a hefty divot of dirt and grass. Jessie made another scrambling run in the short seconds it took him to reload and adjust his aim. She reached cover before he could squeeze off a shot. This was an elm, but not *the* elm. She chanced a quick look and saw her tree no more than ten yards away, its broken branch standing out in the scant light. Somewhere at the foot of that tree was a single .308 cartridge that could—if fate was on their side—save her and her sisters' lives.

The ground was uneven, and it was dark. One slip, one trip, and she was dead. To make matters worse, there was barely any cover between her and the elm. In the three or four seconds it would take Jessie to reach it, she would be exposed.

She considered the semiautomatic pistol on her hip, a Smith & Wesson M&P in .40 caliber. Chance's house was the length of a football field away. Jessie could hit a target at fifty yards, but anything beyond that was more luck than skill. The best she could do here was fire a succession of rounds toward Mr. Deadeye's window and hope to get close with a couple of them. It might just upset his accuracy enough.

Jessie nodded. She unholstered the .40 and racked the slide. A deep breath. Her heartbeat rivaled the gunfire in the air. She sensed Mr. Deadeye waiting for her to make a move.

A step to the left. Two shots at the darkened window, then she spun to her right and broke cover from the other side. It was a bad idea to run in a straight line toward a sniper. She had to deke, crisscross, change direction. Doing this increased the time and distance to her destination. She covered it behind the .40 in her right hand, triggering shots as rapidly as her finger would work. If any of them came close, Mr. Deadeye didn't let on. He fired and almost found his target. If Jessie had zigged instead of zagged, she'd be lying on the ground with a tunnel running through her chest.

The shot unbalanced her, though. Her feet tangled and she fell, her aching body thumping off a snarl of protruding roots. Still firing, Jessie pushed herself to one knee and lunged for the tree. She touched down a couple of feet short and scrabbled the rest of the way. As she slammed her back against the elm and dragged her legs in, the heel of her left boot scuffed over something that rolled too smoothly to be a stone or a stick.

Jessie drew a surprised, hopeful breath, placed the 10FP across her lap, and patted the ground with her left hand. Within seconds, her fingers closed around the .308's distinct, cylindrical cartridge case. She felt the angle of the shoulder and the bullet's hollow point. Her eyes widened, registering gratitude and a splash of disbelief. She'd needed some luck and she got it.

The gunfire dwindled but didn't stop. How many shooters were still standing? Were her sisters still alive? Jessie shook these distractions from her mind. She had one job and one shot to do it with.

"Okay," she said. In the dark, with her hands shaking, she loaded the solo round and rose to one knee. Her only advantage was that Mr. Deadeye didn't know which side of the tree she was going to pivot out from. He would probably gamble and adjust if necessary. If he guessed right, she would be killed. Even kneeling, she'd be too large a target to miss. If he guessed wrong, it might buy her a full second . . . but in that time she had to locate him through the scope, steady her aim, and pull the trigger.

Jessie nodded and blinked sweat out of her eyes.

"You've got this."

One shot.

She considered breaking left—a marginally better angle on the window—but broke right instead, raising the rifle's buttstock to her shoulder and bringing the scope smoothly to her eye. From this point, everything happened in the one full second Jessie had anticipated, although time, being relative, dilated for her. Epinephrine flooded her bloodstream. Her senses sharpened. She scrolled the reticle over the front of the house and settled on her target's window. Mr. Deadeye's thermogram was bright white and beautiful. Also, it was larger than Jessie had expected. The top half of his head was visible above the scope, a near-perfect semicircle. Perhaps she'd caught him during a rare lapse in concentration or while blowing a cool puff of air over his upper lip. It didn't matter. Jessie placed the crosshairs over his forehead. Her breathing steadied. Her hands were between tremors.

She pulled the trigger.

Recoil, tough and tight. Jessie rode it like a bump in the road. The bullet traveled at 2,800 feet per second, but she saw it in dilated time. The impact, too. The upper right portion of Mr. Deadeye's head disappeared as if a tiny stick of dynamite had been lodged into his ear. He remained crouched behind his rifle for a moment, then slumped out of view. His blood painted the back wall in a thick glowing stripe.

FLO TOOK OUT THE LAST two guys. She was patient with the one taking cover behind the planter, waiting for him to expose some small part of his body—and he did: his left foot. In the light streaming through the narrow windows on both sides of the double front doors, she saw it edge into the open. A tiny target and, at forty yards, tough to hit. Flo missed with her first shot. The bullet fell short and ricocheted in some wayward direction. Her second shot was on the money. The man screamed and went down clutching the top of his boot, his upper body fully exposed. Both she and Brea took aim, but Brea held off the trigger. "He's yours," she shouted. Flo killed him with a head shot.

She was less patient with the last man standing—or *crouching*, to be more accurate, hunkered behind the water fountain, blind-firing over the top. Some of his shots rattled off the Yukon, but most were not close.

"You want to wait for him to run out of ammo?" Brea asked.

"Hell no. He could have six full mags in his pockets. I want to get this shit done." Flo stayed low behind the door. She checked her own magazine, catching it in her swollen left palm and counting the rounds in the dim dashboard lights. "I'm down to three rounds. How many have you got?"

"I just reloaded, so I'm good."

"Cover me," Flo said, using her thigh to drive the mag home. She rolled out from behind the door and ran toward the front of the house, peeling out as she approached to get a better angle. Brea kept the target in cover by firing shots in his direction, sending water up in sprays and fizzing rounds over his head. Flo leveled her pistol as she closed in from the side. He came into view, tucked low, shuddering. He didn't see her at all.

She shot him in the kneecap. He went down screaming. He still had his pistol in his hand and swung it toward her. Flo shot him in the armpit. The gun flew from his hand. He flopped onto his side and started to crawl. The sounds he made were horrible. Flo stepped toward him, getting as close as she needed to. She put her final bullet into his head.

Silence, if only for a moment. It was wonderful.

Flo sighed, adjusting her left arm, rolling her hips to work the creaks out of them. Brea joined her. They exchanged tired looks. There was still so much between them—so much to work out, if they were ever given the opportunity. For now, Flo rolled her ski mask up over her mouth and almost smiled. She handed her pistol to Brea.

"I could use a reload."

"Sure."

Brea replaced the empty mag, using one of the two extras in her back right pocket. She racked the slide and gave the gun, grip-first, back to Flo.

"There," she said. Flo thought Brea was referring to the pistol, but her eyes were focused on something over Flo's shoulder. Flo turned and saw a figure emerging from the trees lining the north side of the driveway, illuminated in ghostly fashion by the ground lights. It was Jessie. She continued to scope the front of the house as she walked, then lowered her rifle and called out to them. Her voice was cracked, barely audible.

"Shooter's down," she said.

Brea pumped her fist in acknowledgment. Flo raised her .45 in a weary salute. Both women then turned back to face the house.

"Maybe there's only one man left to kill," Brea said.

Flo pulled her ski mask all the way down. "We can hope."

They mounted the front steps, got behind their pistols, and entered the house.

# THIRTY-SIX

**C**hance turned the football game off. He stood in front of the blank TV screen and addressed his friends: Emmett Pound (drunk off his ass), Dylan Cobb, Mayor Austin Hasse (also drunk off his ass), and Mason Nurll. They'd come for the festivities, to see some real blood sports and perhaps make a chunk of dough, but that wasn't going to happen now.

"Boys," Chance said heavily, holding up both hands. "I believe our good time has been turned on its tits. I declare this party over."

They stared at him blankly. They'd all heard the gunfire. It had died down, but there was an overwhelming sense that there was more to come.

"If you wanna leave . . ." Chance puffed out a breath and lowered his hands. "Well, I don't recommend it. I think we're safer down here, but I ain't gonna stop you."

"Leave?" Cobb squeaked, pointing at the ceiling. "That sounds like a frying pan and fire situation."

"Don't it?" Mason agreed.

Chance patted his big belly and forced a smile. He felt none of the emotions he wanted to feel and all the emotions he didn't. And what a miserable kick in the teeth *that* was, especially considering all the hard work and effort he'd put into this. "Listen, fellas, I got top-notch security in place. Good men, armed and such. There's a goddamn Army Ranger on the west balcony, for Christ's sake."

"Gobbless . . . America," Emmett slurred.

"And there are two men right outside that door"—Chance pointed—"with fully loaded AR-15s."

"I should have brought Bessie," the mayor grumbled. "Bessie" was his legally purchased M16 rifle. It cost him $21,000 back in 2007. He didn't fire it often, but he looked damn good holding it in campaign posters.

"You don't need Bessie," Chance tried to reassure the mayor, but there was a big lump in his throat that didn't feel good at all. "Just stay put. Let my security do its job. This'll be over in a wink."

Chance turned the game back on and walked across the man cave, thumbing his phone as he did. He called Bobby Wallace, hoping to get a read on whatever was happening outside. A *lot* of gunfire, that was for sure. Bobby didn't pick up, though, which Chance saw as an ominous sign, considering he'd answered right away the first time Chance had called. He scrolled through his contacts, saw Bethany's name, hovered over it for a few seconds, and kept scrolling. Chance didn't want to involve his sister—having her clean up (and *cover* up) his mess—unless there was no other choice.

He called Carson Withers instead.

"Listen up, Carson. We got a situation here. May be nothing, may be something, but I want you to round up as many fellas as you can and come on back to the house. Come armed. Every gun, every bullet you can find."

There was a lengthy pause, then Carson said, "I got a message from Burl a while ago. He wants us to keep looking for the gals."

"Don't you worry about that," Chance said. "Just get your asses back here."

"But Burl—"

"But Burl *nothing*," Chance snapped, and Emmett Pound looked over at him, frowning. Chance lowered his voice and continued. "I believe Burl has been compromised. You are my new number one. Congratulations on your promotion, Carson. Now get your fucking ass back to the house."

Carson didn't say anything, but Chance heard the anxiety and confusion in his breathing, which came across the line in jittery little gasps.

"I don't hear 'yessir,'" Chance said, wrinkling his upper lip. "Is there a problem, Carson? Is there something about my simple request you're failing to comprehend?"

"I understand well enough, boss. It's just . . . a few of the boys . . .

*most* of them, actually, in talking to them . . . they got a bad feeling about the way things are shaping up. Reid and Strat clocked out already. The last I heard, they were at Fat Fanny's, drinking up a storm. Goose left your Escalade somewhere in the industrial district and got a Uber home." Carson pronounced it *Yooba*. "The truth is, I ain't sure I could round up a posse, even if I'd a mind to."

"And have you a mind to?" Chance had to work hard to keep from growling.

"Nossir, I don't believe I do," Carson replied. He took a wobbly breath and continued. "As well as fellas, you're asking me to bring every gun and bullet I can find. Now, I may not be the brightest Crayola in the box, but that sounds like a volatile situation to me . . . and the *last* time we stepped into a volatile situation, we lost two men and Howie Chisolm got his Jesus balls blowed off."

Chance bubbled up inside, everything red. He could taste his emotions—a battery-like residue at the back of his throat. "Just so I got this straight . . . are you telling me you're scared of a buncha gals?"

"Sounds to me like *you* are," Carson answered.

"Goddamn you, Carson Withers. Goddamn you and your fucking children." Chance clutched his rapidly beating heart. "I don't know what the world record is for going from being promoted to being fired, but you hafta be pretty fucking close to it."

Carson started to say something, but Chance hung up on him. He didn't want his friends to see him lose control, but there was no way around it. Fully bubbled over, he threw his cell phone across the room. It hit the wall with a sound that could only be the screen shattering. "*Whorefuckers,*" he screamed. His face was closer to plum than red. "*Goddamn sons of bitching cocksuckers.*" He walked over to the shattered phone and brought his bootheel down on it, breaking something on the inside, too. "*Fuck you, Carson. Fuck you, Goose.* Top Gun, *my hairy southern ass.*"

His friends had turned away from the game and looked at him with stupid, empty faces. Chance ignored them. He stood up straight and ran his hands through his hair, always so neatly combed but now unkempt—wild, even. And be damned if there weren't smallish tears in his eyes. He thought of his daddy, who'd no doubt have a word or two to say about those tears before imparting some tough but valuable counsel. And Tusk Sauerland, his mentor, his *hero*. Tusk would know what to do in a situation like this, by Christ.

*Get a grip on yourself*, the great man would say, or something close to it. *Find out what's happening, then take control of the situation.*

Solid advice, Chance reasoned, even if Tusk was too damn dead to have offered it. He knuckled the tears from his eyes, crossed the room, and opened the door. Nash and Wilder snapped to attention.

"You," Chance said to Wilder, pointing first at Wilder's chest, then at the ceiling. "Get your ass up there and find out what in the hell is going on. There's been no gunfire for a minute, but that don't mean there won't be, so stay sharp."

"Yessir."

"And while you're up there . . ." Chance grinned, showing most of his teeth. "Open the door to Errol's enclosure. I think he'd appreciate the exercise."

Wilder nodded and took to his heels. Chance told Nash to stay put, be doubly watchful, and fire twice as quickly—if called upon to fire at all. Nash said he understood. Chance closed the door. The grin on his face grew impossibly larger. He clapped his hands once, briskly, and returned to his friends.

They regarded him with the same bewildered expressions, like four empty-headed goldfish.

"I got three thousand dollars says the Raiders score on this drive," Chance said, gesturing flamboyantly at the screen. "Any takers?"

There were none.

IT WAS A LOT OF house to cover. Brea guessed ten thousand square feet, but she could be two thousand out in either direction. She and Flo started clearing rooms together, but it would take too long, so they separated. Brea took upstairs. Flo took the rooms and hallways on the ground floor. Each would rush to help the other if she heard gunshots.

Brea threw open a bathroom door and moved in behind her .45. It appeared empty. Nobody in the shower. Nobody curled up at the bottom of the sunken bathtub. Nobody in the linen closet. She continued through to the adjoining bedroom (equally empty) and back out onto the landing. The next bedroom she checked was featureless and bare except for a desk with an old computer on it and several plastic totes stacked against the wall. There was a door on the far side. It opened on a small surveillance room. Brea noticed two things simultaneously: the three monitors looping video footage from around the property and the large, dull-looking man hiding beneath the desk.

His eyes flashed, frightened. He managed to put his hands up.

"Don't shoot," he said.

INFILTRATION WAS ONE THING, THE *easy* thing. Exfiltration—getting out quickly and cleanly—was something else altogether. The sisters had planned to depart in the vehicle they arrived in, return to their van at Pink's Crematorium (Burl had told them that the key, along with their phones and wallets, was in Chance's desk drawer), and drive as far west as they could before exhaustion overtook them. Burl's Yukon wasn't going anywhere, though. It was punctured with bullet holes. Its fluids were dripping. Its windshield and headlights were shattered. They needed a different vehicle.

Jessie would take care of that. There were seventeen vehicles lined up along the edge of the driveway. All she had to do was dig through the corpses' pockets (nine of them outside—eleven counting the two by the front gate) until she found a matching key fob. Simple work. First, she had to fulfill her primary objectives: secure the exterior of the property, and make sure Chance didn't exit via a side or back door while Brea and Flo went through the front.

The drone would have been perfect for this. She could have secluded herself and scanned the property from two hundred feet in the air. Thanks to Mr. Deadeye (now just Mr. Dead), the drone was out of commission. Jessie had her rifle and thermal scope, but she needed a clear field of view. The roof of the shed that Brea had been locked in offered sight lines of the north and west sides of the property, as well as the driveway. It wasn't as high as she'd like, but it would have to do. She also needed ammunition for the rifle. This time, she'd take as much as she could squeeze into her pockets.

Jessie reached the ruined Yukon. She holstered her pistol and opened the liftgate. Glass dropped in glittering, tinkling chunks. She took a moment to scope the front of the house again. All clear. Jessie rested the rifle against the rear bumper, swept broken glass off the ammo box, and was about to open it when something caught her eye. It rested on the floor of the cargo area, reflecting a faint bead of light.

"No safe travels for you," Jessie said, reaching to pick it up. It was the St. Christopher pendant that had been hanging from the rearview. There was a bullet lodged in its sterling silver center.

Jessie smiled, momentarily distracted—so much so that she didn't hear the purebred Doberman pinscher sprinting across the lawn toward her, panting gruffly and growling from the back of its throat. One moment she was standing in the driveway, thinking the pendant would make a good (suitably goth) memento. In the next she was lying on her back with Errol on top of her.

FLO WORKED HER WAY THROUGH the ground-floor rooms, clearing one, then the next, not ready to believe that there were no bad guys left to eliminate. There had to be at least two or three still in the house—a last line of defense between the sisters and Chance.

She moved from a walnut-paneled hallway into a room furnished with polished chesterfield chairs and cramped bookcases. Several titles caught her eye: *One-Shot Grizzly Hunting*; *The America We Left Behind*; *ALL Lives Matter, Dammit!* These were disturbing enough, but the painting hanging above the fireplace was even worse. It was of Chance, dressed like Johnny Cash, armed with a couple of six-guns instead of a six-string. Just looking at it filled Flo with nausea and anger. Unable to help herself, she raised her 1911 and fired two rounds into his bulging stomach. The suppressed reports pierced the silence. She felt better.

It had been a reckless reaction, though. Flo kept her finger on the trigger and waited to see if anyone would investigate the sounds. After a moment, she moved toward the door at the far end of the room, momentarily sliding the pistol into the crook of her left arm. As Flo reached for the handle, the door swung open from the other side, and she found herself face-to-face with one of Chance's men.

It was Wilder. She recognized him from their brief but woeful time in Chance's study. He'd been standing next to Errol, holding his leash, man and dog looking equally mean. He looked the same now—*meaner*, if anything, with dilated pupils (Flo had been around enough weekend rock stars to know they were cocaine induced) and an AR-15 in his left hand.

Flo moved first. She removed her pistol from its temporary holster and started to swing it toward him. He reacted deftly, grabbing her by the wrist, angling the gun away and twisting at the same time. Flo's fingers splayed. Her pistol fell to the floor. Wilder grinned. He switched his grip from her wrist to her throat. His teeth made hard clicking sounds as he spoke.

"Little Black sheep just found the wolf."

Flo threw a right hook that bounced off his jaw but didn't move him. His grin expanded. He pushed her backward and locked both hands on his semiautomatic rifle, lifting it into position.

HIS NAME WAS EASTON. HE had a man's whiskers but a boy's brain, and a young boy at that. His face was wet with tears.

Brea yanked a cable from one of the monitors (it promptly went blank) and used it to tie Easton's hands behind his back. He sniveled throughout and asked her not to make the knot too tight. Brea did not comply.

"Down on your knees," she snapped.

Easton got down on his knees.

Brea put the muzzle of her .45 to the back of his head. He cried louder and prayed to Jesus.

"Jesus can't help you now, Easton."

"Yes, ma'am, he rightly can."

"Well, let's put that to the test." Brea cocked the SIG's hammer. It made a deathly click. "When I leave this room, you'll either be shot dead or knocked unconscious. We'll leave that up to Jesus to decide, but you can make his job easier by answering a few questions."

"Yes, ma'am."

"Where's your boss?"

"Mr. Rowan or Mr. Kotter?"

"Kotter."

"Mr. Kotter. Yes, ma'am. I believe he's down in the basement. The *man* cave, he calls it. I sometimes call it the bat cave, though." Easton hawked a clump of snot into the back of his throat and swallowed it with a wet gulp. "Just my little joke."

Brea felt something in her chest. Resolve, she supposed, mixed with relief. She didn't think that Chance had given them the slip—this was his fortress, after all, where he felt safest—but all these empty rooms . . . she was beginning to wonder.

"And how do I get to the basement?" she asked.

"There's a door in the hallway off . . . off the kitchen," Easton whimpered. "Next to the portrait of Cotton Tom Heflin."

Brea didn't know who Cotton Tom Heflin was or what he looked like, but she'd find the door. She was about to ask Easton what kind of security she could expect in the basement when her eyes were drawn to one of the monitors. It had scrolled through various camera shots in and around the property. The swimming pool. The front door (a corpse on the steps). The four-car garage. Now, it displayed a room that Brea recognized. She flashed back to Friday night, being led from the shed and through the house—through this room with its bookcases, leather chairs, and Chance's ostentatious painting above the fireplace. Brea saw that painting on the monitor now. She also saw Flo tangling with one of Chance's men. As she watched, the man—it looked like Wilder—grabbed Flo by the throat, pushed her backward, and swung his AR-15 toward her.

"This room," Brea said urgently, twisting Easton's head toward the monitor. "What's the quickest way there?"

"That's the library," Easton said, still sniveling. "Mr. Kotter calls it his . . . his contemplation room."

"I don't give a *fuck* what he calls it. *What's the quickest way there?*"

On the screen, Flo stepped forward and aimed a kick at the tip of Wilder's rifle. There was a glimpse of muzzle flash, then the video feed switched to a view of the back patio. Brea heard the shots, though. They thundered around the large house, sending chills through the walls.

"Go left along the landing, then downstairs," Easton gasped. "Turn right at the bottom and right again at the elk's head. Look for the double doors."

Brea brought her pistol down and cracked the butt off the top of Easton's skull. He flopped to the dusty floor, out cold.

"I guess you were right about Jesus," she said, and blazed from the room.

# THIRTY-SEVEN

When it came to fighting dogs, Uncle Dog, perhaps ironically, didn't have much to offer. "Climb a tree," he'd said with a crooked smile. "If you can't do that, give up your nondominant arm, then go for its eyes. If you're lucky, the animal will back off. If not . . . well, try to protect your throat for as long as you can."

Jessie surrendered her left arm, and Errol clamped on. The power in his neck and jaws was terrifying. He shook his head, chomping, adjusting his grip. Jessie had put on a black leather jacket when she'd changed into fresh clothes. It was an old favorite, cracked by too many road miles and gigs. It offered some protection, but not enough. Jessie screamed as she felt Errol's canines sink through the worn leather and into her forearm.

She braced, trying to keep the animal from thrashing. His paws were on her chest, pushing her down. His breath smelled of wild things. Uncle Dog had told Jessie to go for its eyes, but she thought a .40-caliber attack would be more effective. She removed her right arm from where it covered her throat and reached for her pistol. For one horrible moment, she thought it wouldn't be there—that it had come unholstered when she'd tumbled to the ground—but her palm curled sweetly around the grip. Jessie drew in one smooth motion, pressed the muzzle point-blank to Errol's throat, and pulled the trigger.

*Click.*

She triggered again. *Click.* And again. *Click.* A deep moan rumbled from her chest. She had spent all her rounds shooting at Mr. Deadeye's window. There was a spare magazine in her back pocket, but she could hardly reload with her left arm locked between a Doberman's jaws.

Jessie pulled the trigger again, just in case.

*Click.*

Errol shook his head violently and established a tighter grip. Jessie—not forgetting that an unloaded firearm still had its uses—whipped her right hand around and cracked the pistol's polymer frame off the top of Errol's snout, not once but three times. With the first strike he dug in harder. With the second he yelped. With the third he yelped again and backed off. He looked at Jessie with his head low to the ground and his withers pumped. There was blood on his teeth.

Jessie started to her feet. She got most of the way up when Errol pounced again. He clamped onto the hem of her jacket, planted his paws on the ground, and dragged her backward. She fell to one knee and the pistol slipped from her hand. It bounced once off the asphalt and landed somewhere in the shadows. Jessie cried out as Errol shook and tugged. She looked desperately toward the house, hoping to see one of her sisters sprinting to her aid, partially illuminated by the ground lights.

All she saw were corpses. Nine dead men. Soon there'd be ten, she thought. A woman. Jessie still had a trick up her sleeve, though—or in her pocket, to be more precise. She unzipped her jacket, pulled it off her shoulders, and let Errol yank it the rest of the way. Her arms slipped out of the sleeves. She lunged forward, putting valuable distance between her and Errol as he shook her empty jacket in his jaws. It distracted him for two seconds. Maybe three.

He ran at her again, all bloodlust and muscle. Jessie pulled the nunchaku from her back pocket, clasping one branch as she whipped the other out in front of her. She planted her right foot and twisted at the hip, putting as much power as she could muster into the attack. The foremost branch drew a tight semicircle in the air. In the split second before it connected, Jessie recalled the countless hours she'd spent training, developing accuracy—*precision*—by knocking Ping-Pong balls off bamboo poles, having to repeat over and over if the bamboo trembled even a little.

Errol pounced, but the nunchaku halted his attack. The tip of the branch cracked off his jaw with incredible force. He landed on his rump, howling, then scrabbled back to all fours.

Jessie got the nunchaku under control, spinning the lead branch in a fast figure eight and catching it between her rib cage and arm. Errol snarled, planting his front paws as Jessie backed away, giving herself more space and response time. She closed out all distractions. Chance Kotter didn't matter. Her sisters were inconsequential. Her bleeding left arm wasn't a thing. She focused entirely on the attack dog. He was the world and the stars, the sunrise and the sunset—everything condensed into one beautiful, ferocious package.

She executed two cautionary swipes with the nunchaku. Errol hopped backward, then circled to his left, edged forward, and retreated again. Jessie called on her vocal range to make a booming, death-metal sound. This added to Errol's uncertainty. He lowered his shoulders and backed up a step. Jessie gave another warning bark. She buzzed Errol again with the nunchaku. He woofed, hesitated, and turned tail.

Jessie looked for the dull gleam of her pistol but couldn't see it. She glanced at the Yukon and noted the 10FP sniper rifle resting upright against the rear bumper. There was no time to load it and get off a shot. Errol had withdrawn to a less threatening distance, but he'd turned back toward her, still with his teeth showing and his cropped ears pinned to his skull. Jessie reasoned that being *inside* the vehicle with the liftgate closed would be infinitely safer. And if she could grab the sniper rifle on her way in, all the better.

She went for it. A desperate, stumbling dash to the Yukon. Errol gave chase the moment she turned her back. She heard him, *sensed* him, gaining on her. His low-end growl eclipsed her ragged breaths. Five feet out, Jessie threw herself into the SUV's cargo area. She landed clumsily, grabbed hold of the backseat, and pulled her legs in. The tip of her left boot clipped the rifle, and she turned in time to see it slide along the bumper and topple to the ground.

Errol closed in. Thirty-five feet away. Twenty-five. Fifteen.

Jessie lunged for the liftgate. She reached up with her bleeding left arm, curled her fingers into the recessed handle, and yanked down. It hadn't fully closed when Errol sprang from the ground. He collided with the liftgate's bottom edge, tumbled backward, then scrambled to his paws and pounced again. This time, the door was all the way down. Errol hit the metalwork with a solid thump.

He picked himself up, backed away, but didn't go far. This was a respite. That was all. Jessie knew this. She'd counted on it lasting longer, though.

Errol came through the broken rear windshield seconds later.

**FIVE ROUNDS HAD EXPLODED FROM** the barrel of the AR-15. They ripped through several books on the top shelf of the nearest case and punched holes into the ceiling. Shreds of paper, wood, and drywall rained down. Those shots were meant for Flo. They would have ravaged her body and thrown her from one end of the room to the other.

Kicking the tip of the barrel had been more judgment than luck. It had bought her a few seconds, but what Flo really needed was to either disarm Wilder or find a way past him and retrieve her own firearm. In her experience, it was better to be good than lucky, not the other way around. And she *was* good, despite having ninety-nine problems and only one functioning arm. Her body and soul were trained for adversity, but she couldn't dodge those bullets for long.

She followed the roundhouse kick with an elbow to Wilder's sternum, then changed the angle of her forearm and popped her fist into his throat. He staggered, already swinging the AR-15 toward her. Flo slapped the barrel away and drove her right boot into his solar plexus, a firm side kick that knocked him back a step or three. It was a good shot, not necessarily a *smart* shot. Flo needed him close. She couldn't give him space to maneuver his rifle into position. Anything beyond the length of the barrel was dangerous.

He recovered quickly—slightly off-center, maybe, and wheezing from the throat punch—but his finger was on the trigger. Flo gave him nothing stationary to aim at. She twisted to her left and wheeled a full three-sixty, bringing her arm around to complete the spinning attack. Her fist connected with Wilder's jaw. It didn't drop him, but it turned his head sideways. He squeezed the trigger three times and hit the opposite wall.

It was another good (not lucky) shot from Flo. It had also been instinctive, a gut reaction. If she'd had time to think about it, she wouldn't have used her left arm.

The pain was next level. Flo's fist vibrated on impact and sent tiny tremors along her forearm, causing the splintered ends of the bones to quiver and clash. Her nerve endings hoisted flags of varied, dramatic colors, not just in her arm but throughout her body. A sparkling fog temporarily blinded her.

She screamed. Her legs weakened, and she faltered, stumbling away from Wilder. Her vision returned in snapshots. She glimpsed her pistol on the floor, then Chance's Man in Black portrait, then Wilder bringing his rifle to his hip. He didn't bother lifting it to his shoulder and aiming along the barrel. This close, he didn't have to aim.

Flo did the only thing she could. She leapt through the air—gunfire followed her—and came down behind Chance's luxurious chesterfield sofa. Wilder didn't let up. Bullets tore through the upholstery, sending up scraps of leather and cushioning. Flo flattened herself to the floor and crawled on her belly.

The room was filled with monstrous sound. Soon, Wilder would bore of firing at the chesterfield and step around it. He'd have a clear shot at her. Flo needed to be ready. Her secondary weapon was a Japanese-made tanto with a seven-inch blade, secured in a drop-leg sheath. She unclipped it and rolled onto her back.

The gunfire stopped. Flo kept perfectly still. As the reports faded, she heard Wilder's aroused breathing (a big gun could do that for some men). It betrayed his position. Flo slid the tanto from its sheath, rotated it in her hand so that she was holding the blade, and raised it up over her shoulder.

"You're so fucking dead," Wilder said, his southern twang abnormally shrill. Some of that was adrenaline. The rest was cocaine. The dude was as high as the Kotter-Bryce Tower. "I don't know how many rounds I got left in this mag. Maybe eight. Maybe ten. However the fuck many, I'm spending them all on you."

The top of his head floated above the back of the chesterfield, then he jumped into view. He had a fiery smile on his face and the AR-15 at his shoulder. From Flo's position on the floor, she didn't have a clear shot at his chest or throat. His balls were exposed, though. His knees and stomach, too. They were all good targets, but she opted for the lethal shot—the most difficult shot.

She went for his head.

Flo whipped her right hand forward, and the tanto flew from between her fingers. It cut through the air on an upward trajectory, turning evenly. Flo believed from the moment the knife left her grasp that her shot was on target. She visualized the blade sinking in between Wilder's eyebrows and burying itself deep in his brain.

Not quite.

The blade zipped past the left side of Wilder's face and sliced his ear off—a clean cut that left it dangling from a strip of cartilage. He blinked, surprised, then removed his hand from the AR-15's handguard and inspected the raw spot on the side of his head. His fingers came away bloody. His severed ear swung back and forth. Wilder prodded it with a dark, disbelieving expression.

"Is that . . . is that my *ear*?"

Flo tried to get up. She scrabbled awkwardly to one knee but overbalanced and fell again. Wilder snarled and gave her his full attention, both hands on his rifle. Blood streamed down the side of his neck.

"Bitch," he said. "You took my goddamn ear."

Flo backed away, pushing at the floor with the heels of her boots and her one good arm. She bumped up against the wall and could go no farther. Wilder fixed the AR-15's sights on her. He hooked his finger around the trigger. Despite his injury, the adrenaline, the cocaine, his hands did not shake at all.

"Killing you just got better," he said.

The rifle's bore was narrow and endless. It should have been more chilling, but Flo had cast her mind elsewhere. She saw her mother's face, too young, too beautiful. She saw Brea hitting the drums and Jessie hitting power chords. And she saw Imani, of course, in all her radiance—Imani and an incandescent child emerging from a forest with nothing but openness ahead of them.

It was enough to know they were free.

**THE FIRST BULLET HIT THE** back of Wilder's neck and exited through his throat. He wasn't quite dead when the second bullet hit. This one stayed in his skull. He dropped to his knees and then onto his face. His mean heart pumped one last time and never again.

Flo didn't realize she was holding her breath until she exhaled. It came from deep in her lungs and made a low-pitched sound. Everything flowed out of her, except life, which flowed back in. She took another breath and lowered her head. That vision of Imani and her child still hovered in her mind, like the afterimage of a burning light.

"Flo?"

She blinked. The mother and child faded . . . replaced by another woman. Brea stepped around the bullet-riddled chesterfield, stood for a moment over Wilder's body, then slowly approached Flo. Her eyes appeared overly bright through the holes of her ski mask.

"Hey you," she said. She holstered her .45 and held out her hand.

Flo took it.

THEY LOOKED AT EACH OTHER through a mist of emotions. Tears gathered on Flo's lower lashes. She blinked them away and swallowed hard.

"Thanks," she said.

"Sure," Brea said.

A complicated silence fell between them. Brea broke it not with words, but by clearing her throat and turning away. She took two steps, then Flo stopped her. She placed her hand on Brea's shoulder and pulled her close. The sisters held each other tight and felt something inside that could be moved or thrown into shadow but never destroyed.

The embrace lasted longer than the silence. They separated. Their eyes glistened in a similar way. Flo nodded, then looked over Brea's shoulder at Chance's portrait on the wall, all hubris and wile, two holes in his belly. Brea followed her gaze.

"I know where he is," she said. "Come on."

"GIMME YOUR PHONE," CHANCE SAID to Emmett, leaning close enough to see the swollen blood vessels in his eyes. Emmett backed up a step and wiped bourbon-scented sweat from his jowls. It appeared his head bobbled even more when he got nervous. Sumbitch couldn't keep the damn thing still.

"Huh?" he said distantly.

"Your phone," Chance hissed. "Give it to me."

They were at the pool table, having hoped a game of eight-ball would divert their minds from everything that was happening. It had not. The gunfire outside had been one thing. It was the sweet music of home defense, after all, as American as Cracker Barrel or Willie Nelson's braids. But gunfire *inside* the house was a more ominous prospect. Chance could only conclude that his defenses had been compromised.

Enough was enough. It was time to call his big sister.

Emmett unlocked and handed over his phone. Chance all but snatched it out of his hand. He tossed his pool cue onto the table and walked to the other side of his man cave, dialing on the go. Bethany's phone rang twice and went to voicemail. Call declined, in other words. No surprise. Bethany wouldn't recognize Emmett's number, and she was too strident a woman to accept calls willy-nilly—especially not on Sunday nights, when they had the beer-and-wings special down at Fat Fanny's.

Chance tried again. Three rings this time, then she answered.

"Who is this?"

"Sister, it's me."

"Brother?"

"Uh-huh."

Bethany didn't respond right away. Chance heard barroom sounds in the background: clinking glasses, raised voices, the football game on NBC. He felt a sudden and overwhelming envy of everyone there. What he'd give to have his ass on one of Fat Fanny's barstools, just a regular southern man with a regular allotment of problems.

He sighed and his throat cracked—only a little, but Bethany heard.

"What's wrong, brother?"

It was Chance's turn to pause. His woes ran single file through his mind and there were enough of them. Finally, he said, "I gave you my word that I'd ask no more of you, but the wheels have fallen off the wagon, so to speak."

"Care to elaborate?"

"Burl's gone AWOL. He may be dead. And I don't think he's the only one." Chance swallowed, and the taste was as bitter as dandelion greens. "I'd say the situation is . . . hostile."

"Hostile, how?"

"Shots fired and such." A deep breath. "You might wanna send a fleet of cruisers out here. As many fine officers as you can spare. Just leave the Staties out of it."

"Jesus Christ, brother," Bethany snapped. "You and your games. I will despair of you, I swear, for as long as my asshole points south."

"I know, and I'm sorry."

"Are you safe?"

Chance didn't know what "safe" was anymore. He was supposed to have top-of-the-line security—armed guards, surveillance equipment, a vicious attack dog—yet here they were. He cupped his brow and looked over at his friends. They were shit-scared, to a man. Mason had prayed for them all, but he was a goddamn Episcopalian, so it barely counted. Mayor Austin Hasse had called his wife to tell her he loved her.

"Chance?" Bethany said.

"Just get your ass out here," Chance said, and hung up. He returned to Emmett and slapped the phone into his waiting palm.

"You call Beth?" his friend asked.

"I did."

"And?"

"Officers are en route. Or will be, soon enough." Chance raised a half-assed smile and borrowed from Burl: "A precautionary measure. Overkill, even."

"Horseshit," Emmett said. "I know you, Chance, and I can see how goddamn scared you are."

Chance shrugged. His feeble smile turned into a grand frown. Emmett hitched up his pants and sidled in close.

"How many ways out of this basement?" he asked, his voice low.

Chance tilted his chin. "Why do you wanna know?"

"Because I mean to get my narrow ass outta here." Emmett hissed out a boozy belch and stepped yet closer. "I ain't waiting for your sister to round up some wet-behind-the-ears weekend cops. We're outside of town. They'll be fifteen minutes, even if they drop everything and haul ass."

"Ten," Chance said gruffly.

"Ten then. It's still too long." The more perturbed Emmett got, the more his head wobbled. "My chopper is parked in yonder field. I could *walk* to it in five and be well on my way to *Ch-Ch*-Chattanooga before the first blue lights are heading along your driveway."

Chance gestured at the door. "Well, get then. I ain't stopping you."

"I know that, but I want two things," Emmett said, and counted on his fingers. "Number one: safe egress. By which I mean a way out of this basement that don't involve me running through gunfire."

Chance nodded. A fair request.

"Number two . . ." Emmett paused. His chin fluttered and a fondness softened his eyes. "I want *you* to come with me, you dumbass."

In the past few hours, Chance had felt mostly sour emotions, but these words elicited something sweeter. It wasn't much—a bright piss in a stormy ocean, truth be told—but by God, he'd take it.

"I don't know, Em. You been hard at the bottle." Chance flicked his gaze toward the ceiling. "Might be safer to take my chances with them gals."

Emmett flapped a hand and uttered a short, wheezy laugh. "I'm a point or two over the limit, no doubt about it, but I can walk a straight line. And didn't I just whup your ass at eight-ball?"

"We played one game, and I scratched on the black."

"Like I said, an ass-whupping!" Emmett dropped a bleary wink. "C'mon, Chance. You're my best friend. If I leave without you and something bad happens . . . well, that'd sure be tough for me to live with."

Chance gave a mighty sigh. Hadn't he just been thinking that he wouldn't mind hopping into Em's whirlybird and flying far away? Well, this was his chance. The idea of beating a hasty retreat didn't sit well with him, though. This was his home. His castle. The trouble was, it was beginning to feel more like an island, one that was eroding, its population dwindling, as the waves crashed in. Chance didn't think he'd ever felt this threatened.

"Even if the cops get here in record time," Emmett continued, picking up on Chance's concerns, "all they're gonna do is park in the driveway and shout through a bullhorn. Town clowns ain't paid enough to storm a hostile domicile. They ain't SWAT."

"He's right about that," the mayor said from across the room.

Chance ran a hand through his hair. Another red fog passed through his head, but this time he kept it on the inside. He was too weary—too *sad*—to lose his shit again. His heart felt like a beaten dog.

"What a goddamn train wreck," he said, and held up both hands. "Okay, fuck it. Let's skedaddle. We'll assess the situation from a safer distance. Somewhere closer to Tennessee."

"Now you're talking."

"There are two ways out of this basement, not including the windows." Chance hooked a thumb at the ceiling. "There's the stairs to the main floor—"

"Too dangerous," Emmett interjected.

"Agreed. There's also a bulkhead in the furnace room. It opens up out back, then it's a clear run to the chopper."

"Well, shit, that's the ticket," Emmett said, snapping his fingers.

Chance held his chest and nodded, then looked over Emmett's shoulder at his other friends. They stood with stooped spines and tense expressions. Mason Nurll had aged twenty years, the poor son of a bitch.

"What about them?" Chance asked through the side of his mouth, using his eyebrows to gesture.

"Hmm." Emmett glanced indiscreetly behind him, then turned his wobbly head back to Chance. "I don't much care for the peanut farmer. And the mayor's got that gimp leg. He'd only slow us down."

"Cobb?"

"Cobb's a decent enough fella, but shit . . . it wouldn't be Christian to take him and leave the others. It's fairer to just leave them all."

"I guess," Chance agreed, nodding. For all his shortcomings, Emmett Pound was a fine Christian man. "But I wanna take Nash. He's right outside that door and fully armed. He can provide cover, if we need it."

"Deal," Emmett said.

"Then let's go."

# THIRTY-EIGHT

Errol had gotten most of the way through the windshield. His front paws were on the floor of the cargo area and his rear paws clawed at the liftgate from outside. The sound was like a dozen fingernails on a dozen chalkboards. He snapped ferociously. Saliva whipped from his jaws in long strings. Jessie aimed a kick at his sleek head, but he caught hold of her boot and shook. She freed herself before his teeth could sink through the leather and kicked again, then remembered that she still had the nunchaku in her right hand. There wasn't enough room to swing it, but she clasped one branch like a nightstick and rapped it off Errol's snout. He yowled. She whapped him again, and he retreated.

"Fuck you," she gasped, then shouted: "*Fuck yoooooou!*"

Errol backed away from the Yukon with his sides pumping. He walked a tight circle and came again, leaping halfway through the rear windshield and clawing for more. Jessie greeted him with a hard strike to the jaw. He whined and lunged at the nunchaku. She took another swipe, and this time Errol caught the branch between his teeth. He pulled. Jessie pulled, too. She planted both feet, wrapped the four-inch chain around her wrist for leverage, and heaved with everything she had. Errol fought hard. If he'd had all fours on the ground, he would have snatched the nunchaku out of Jessie's grasp. As it was, she had the advantage. She yanked, twisted, and jerked and gradually worked the branch free. It emerged from Errol's jaws, slick with foam, indented with the pressure from his premolars.

She struck him a fourth time. He admonished her with a deep woof and slunk backward through the windshield.

"Get the *fuck* out of here."

A weapon. A *different* weapon. Not this nunchaku—Jesus Christ, dogs *loved* sticks. Jessie wanted a blade or, better yet, a gun. She looked around the cargo area and checked the shadowy corners with both hands (her left arm throbbed and bled, but she could still wiggle her fingers). There was nothing. They'd brought only the weapons they needed and left everything else back in the van, including Burl's Walther PDP.

"Burl," Jessie said. This was *his* vehicle, and a man so heavily committed to doing bad things surely had another gun stashed somewhere—a sawed-off under the dash or a snubbie in the glove box.

Errol barked twice, letting Jessie know that he wasn't done with her. She glanced briefly at her arm—not good—and wiped her bloody glove across the front of her tee. A grayness touched the edges of her vision. She blinked until it cleared, then twisted her upper body and looked toward the front of the Yukon. Errol began to pace, his nails clicking on the asphalt.

Jessie made her move. She bumbled over the backseat, squeezed into the front, and ran her right hand around the footwells on the driver and passenger sides, hoping to feel a fixed holster and the buttstock of something mean. There was nothing, but Jessie didn't give up hope. She opened the glove box and felt around inside. Nothing again, unless she planned on subduing Errol with an owner's manual.

"What the hell, Burl?" she said, thinking that maybe he didn't want to keep a firearm in the same vehicle that his wife and kids rode in. Then again, this was the South, where guns and families went together like apples and pies.

Errol barked again. Jessie turned to the rear windshield and saw the ridge of his black-and-tan back gliding fluidly from left to right, as ominous as a shark's fin through shallow water. She fanned her ski mask to get a little airflow inside it, then checked the last place she could think of.

There was no gun in the center storage compartment. No knife, either. But there was *something*, and it gave Jessie a faint thread of hope. She removed the leatherette case and unzipped it. Flo had thrown away the paraphernalia they'd used, but there was still—thank God—one needle, one syringe, and an unmarked bottle of clear liquid. Jessie wasn't sure, but she thought this was the same knockout drug that Burl had injected them with at the beginning of this nightmare. Ketamine, she suspected, although she'd had no hallucinogenic episodes while she was unconscious. Whatever it was, it *worked*.

Jessie checked behind her again but didn't see Errol. She looked through the side windows. He wasn't there, either. Her hands shaking, her left glove slick with blood, she managed to screw the needle onto the empty syringe. She picked up the unmarked bottle and gave it a shake. Half full.

"Good."

Errol erupted over the front of the SUV. He landed on the hood and skated over the broken glass, in through the front windshield. Jessie screamed and backed up against the passenger door. The little bottle slipped from between her fingers. She juggled it for a second, then it was gone, disappearing into the darkness of the footwell.

Momentum carried Errol over the dash. His hind quarters hit the steering wheel, and he flipped into the driver's seat. His paws worked the air as he twisted his body and corrected himself. He stared at her for a moment, his hackles lifted. All his teeth were on display. Jessie raised her legs defensively. She had the needle in her left hand. It was useless without the anesthetic. She could stab Errol in the eye until the needle broke, but it wouldn't stop those teeth. The nunchaku was in her lap. She grabbed one of the branches and lashed out. Errol took a snap at it and missed. At the same time, Jessie threw a kick with her left leg. She caught him firmly behind one ear. She kicked again, and this time he grabbed her boot and locked on. His canines punched through the leather, into her foot. Jessie put up just enough resistance to keep his attention right there. Better her foot than her throat.

Errol shook his head vigorously. Pain traveled the length of Jessie's left leg, into her hips. She gritted her teeth, let go of the nunchaku, and reached into the footwell with her right hand. Her fingers ran over the floor mat, brushing through chunks of broken glass. Another scream pealed from her throat, followed by a higher-pitched sound that was partly surprise, mostly relief. Her palm had fallen blindly on the bottle of anesthetic. She snatched it up, only to juggle and drop it again.

It was easy to believe that some higher power was fucking with her, but better to believe in *herself*. Strength, resourcefulness, and determination were in her fabric. Capitulation was not. "I haven't taught you anything," Uncle Dog once said to her. "I've only unlocked what's always been there." These words had settled in Jessie's soul and given her a limitless perspective. She'd never met a chain she hadn't broken.

The Yukon rocked back and forth as Errol thrashed his muscular neck. His eyes were blank and resolute. Jessie sank lower in the seat, pushing back with her boot, keeping him at a distance. Her right hand swept the footwell and again found only broken glass. She took a long, hissing breath and forced herself to slow down, to *feel* her way around. This more composed approach paid off. Within moments, her fingers brushed over the small bottle. She scooped it up.

Errol writhed in the driver's seat, his claws shredding the leather upholstery. Jessie felt her boot filling with blood but focused on the needle in her left hand and the anesthetic in her right. She used her teeth to unscrew the bottle cap and then remove the rubber cover from the needle. With her leg being tossed around and her hands anything but steady, filling the syringe was always going to be the toughest part. She faced the challenge head-on, though, because she *had* to—because she was Jessie fucking Steen, and she was born to break chains. It took several attempts, but she finally inserted the needle into the bottle. She pulled the plunger all the way and filled the barrel.

"Come on, you fucker."

Errol tore a strip off her boot. His head snapped backward, allowing Jessie to pull her foot free. She clamped the syringe between her teeth and grabbed both ends of a single nunchaku branch. Errol chomped at her boot again. Jessie kicked him in the mouth with her right foot, then drew her legs back over the center console. Errol followed. He was no longer interested in her foot, though. He wanted the real meat. He wanted her throat.

Jessie was ready. As Errol leapt on top of her, she lifted the nunchaku branch, and his jaws fastened around it. She wrestled with him to intensify his grip, then let go with her right hand and removed the syringe from her mouth. The shift in momentum dropped his head closer. Jessie jabbed the needle into the side of his neck and pressed the plunger.

It happened quickly. Errol had a lean body and a rapid heart, and whatever Jessie had injected him with raced through his bloodstream. She saw it in his eyes first. The ferocity in them dimmed. His legs were next. They trembled, then sagged. Finally, all the tension drained out of his jaws. His mouth slid loosely along the nunchaku and his head slumped.

He was sleeping on her chest ten seconds later.

Jessie stayed where she was, catching her breath, recalibrating her mind. The broken pieces inside her—and there were many—rattled with every frantic beat of her heart. Before long, she had collected enough remnants of herself to continue. Errol's inert weight was too heavy to lift, so she opened the passenger-side door and shimmied out from beneath him. Adding to her misery, she fell backward out of the seat and landed hard on the driveway. Something in her spine crunched.

"Okay," she said, and blinked. The stars were beautiful at least. Jessie could have stared up at them for a long time—lost herself among them and all their sweet wishes—but the job wasn't finished yet. She struggled to her feet. Everything hurt. Her body was a hateful, angry thing. Jessie plucked a chunk of broken glass out of her torn arm, then limped to the back of the vehicle and retrieved her weapons.

# THIRTY-NINE

ait," Brea said. "This way." She looped her left arm through Flo's right and led her gently toward a door at the end of the hallway. "In here."

Flo frowned beneath her ski mask but went with Brea. They swayed and bumped shoulders as they took the few steps along the short hallway. It was only when Brea opened the door that Flo got her bearings. She'd been here before. This was Chance's study.

Friday night felt like a lifetime ago, but being in this room again reduced the last forty-eight hours to a blur. Flo turned on her feet, looking at the ornamental furnishings and mounted animal heads, and absorbed the memories in a bewildering rush. In some ways they made her feel indomitable; in others, she felt smaller, frailer. Flo knew that if she was to have any kind of future, she would need to find the place where these two lines came together. And *this*, she realized, would be the hardest fight of all.

"What are we doing in here?" she asked, looking at Brea. "Chance? I thought . . ."

"He's in his man cave, in the basement," Brea said. She was on the other side of Chance's large, rustic desk. She set her pistol down next to his computer and started rifling through his drawers. "Burl said our belongings were in here, remember?"

"Right," Flo said, and nodded. "Our phones and wallets."

"And the van key," Brea said.

Flo holstered her pistol. She went around to help Brea, taking the drawers on the right. There was nothing of note in the top two. She found hunting magazines, a Bible, and a ledger with the words *MONEY OWED* scrawled across the front. The third drawer down was locked. So was the one on Brea's side. In unison, the sisters grabbed their pistols, aimed, and blew out the locks. Their belongings were in a cigar box that Brea pulled from beneath a stack of files. She gave Flo her phone and wallet. Just having them in her hand made Flo feel closer to her old self. Brea took her own and Jessie's, along with the van key, and put them safely in her jacket pocket.

"That'll save us some time later," she said. "Let's go."

They got behind their pistols and left Chance's study, moving quietly along the hallway and through the main floor. It was eerily still and silent. Brea took the lead, although she didn't quite know the way. "Kitchen," she said under her breath. "Hallway. Cotton Tom Heflin." They found the kitchen a minute later and passed through it into a wide, resplendent corridor. There were six doors opening off it and twice as many paintings. Some were of Alabama through the ages, others were of kingly deer and horses, and others still of rigid men. One of these depicted a doughy-headed individual dressed in fine clothes, his avuncular aspect offset by the coldness in his eyes. Flo suspected that the only thing missing from that head was a Klan hood.

Brea tapped the painting with the muzzle of her .45. "Cotton Tom." She opened the door immediately to its left. There was a small landing on the other side with wide steps leading down.

"This is it," she said. "The basement."

"I remember," Flo whispered. The memory of the days she'd spent handcuffed to a steel pipe emerged through the fog of everything else. She moved ahead of Brea. "I know the way from here."

They stepped onto the landing and took the stairs single file, staying close to the edge where the treads creaked less. The air smelled of booze, tobacco, and sweat. The only sound they heard was a low, bubbling hum.

The sisters darted down the last few steps, making more noise but not wanting to present as slow-moving targets to any threat-in-waiting. The area was empty. It was a vaguely diamond-shaped space with a green marble floor. The hum came from a vast aquarium. Flo glanced at the smooth-hounds moving through the water, then gestured at a door on the right. Brea nodded. They got low behind their firearms and approached indirectly, not wanting their shadows to appear in the crack of light underneath.

No sound from the other side. Both Brea and Flo took a deep breath. Brea motioned that she would go right. Flo nodded and flicked her head to the left. They breached by way of Brea's right boot. The door flew inward. They entered and scanned the area in seconds. This was the man cave, no doubt about it, with its mechanical bull, pool table, and vintage jukebox, but there was no sign of Chance Kotter. Three men stood in front of a silently playing TV. They all had their hands raised. One of them looked close to tears.

"*Where is he?*" Brea growled, an intimidating presence behind her ski mask and .45. She kicked over a small table with a bottle of bourbon on top and stepped closed to the men. "*Start talking or I start shooting.*"

The littlest man whimpered and pointed at a door on the other side of the man cave. "That dirty ol' sumbitch took to his heels. He and Emmett both. They're heading for the chopper."

"You'll catch up to his fat ass if you run," the man to his left said. He was sweaty, disheveled, and terrified. "They got Nash with 'em, though, and his gun is bigger than y'all's."

These corrupt assholes had thrown big money at Chance's game. They were *complicit*. Brea dropped each of them with a bullet to the right kneecap, then she and Flo bolted across the room. The door the little man had pointed at opened on a narrow hallway with five more doors leading off it. Flo knew there were cold, makeshift cells behind two of them. One of the remaining three doors stood ajar. They moved toward this first, threw it fully open, and moved in with their weapons ready. It was a utility room, dominated by a huge, rumbling furnace. Two dirty bulbs hung from strips of cord, emitting a brownish light. Other machines ticked, buzzed, and blinked. Brea and Flo checked the shadows as they swept through, fingers on their triggers.

It was an L-shaped space. The sisters turned the corner with due caution and saw concrete steps leading up to closed bulkhead doors. They ascended side by side, grabbed a door each, and lifted them open. There was a light directly overhead, illuminating the bulkhead and the steps below. Flo took aim and shot the light out, blanketing the immediate area in darkness. They advanced cautiously, emerging on the west side of the house. There was a broad patio and swimming pool to their right, a veranda to their left draped with clinging plants. Ground lights created a mood, but not the mood the sisters wanted. They shot the nearest ones and proceeded onto the lawn.

"I don't see a helicopter," Brea said.

"I don't *hear* one, either," Flo said. "Which means it's still on the ground."

"And where the hell is Jessie? She's supposed to be covering the exterior." Brea took a sudden breath. She and Flo exchanged dark looks.

"Jessie's fine," Flo said, but there was uncertainty in her voice. She swallowed hard and edged forward, sweeping her pistol from left to right. "I'm sure she—"

Gunfire ripped the silence apart. It came from directly ahead of them, a burst of muzzle flash in the darkness. Brea and Flo went prone, tucked behind their weapons. Flo cried out as her broken arm absorbed the brunt of her body weight. She blacked out for a few seconds but heard Brea returning fire. Bullets carved the ground around them.

CHANCE COULD LIST TWO HUNDRED strengths and sprinting would not be one of them. His body was simply not designed to move quickly. Notwithstanding, when gunfire broke out behind him, he picked 'em up and put 'em down.

Emmett kept pace for the first ten yards or so, then his drunk ass overbalanced and down he went. He hit the ground full of blasphemy. Every cowardly instinct inside Chance told him to keep running, but yonder whirlybird was just a big old lawn ornament without Emmett in the cockpit. Chance put the brakes on and went back for his pilot.

"Em, get *up*. Christ, we're under fire."

"My *ankle*."

"It'll be more than your ankle soon, you horse's ass."

Nash was on one knee, the rifle at his shoulder, spraying rounds toward the house. Empty shells somersaulted from the side of his AR-15. He looked like the lead character in a war movie. God love him.

"Jesus, Em, let's *go*."

There was grass in Emmett's mouth. "Urrgh."

"Gimme your hand."

Emmett offered his hand, and Chance hoisted him (*hoisting* was something else that wouldn't make Chance's list of two hundred strengths) to his knees, then oh-so-slowly to his feet. Emmett spat the grass from his mouth and went sideways at first, then forward. They ran together—still holding hands, by God—and made it to the chopper.

"We made it, Em." Chance pressed his lips to the fuselage and gave it a meaningful kiss. "Praise Jesus."

Emmett opened the door and climbed into the cockpit. Chance got in behind him, flopping across the backseat like he'd been rescued from the Battle of Khe Sanh. He closed his eyes and pressed both hands to his chest, feeling the manic pounding of his heart. Nash continued to trigger rounds into the darkness. Chance waited for the steady crack of the rifle to be enveloped by the roar of the rotor blades, then the weightless feel of the ground falling away as the helicopter gained altitude. When this didn't happen, he cracked an eye open and looked at Emmett in the cockpit. Had the son of a bitch suffered a heart attack?

He had not. Emmett sat in the pilot's seat, checking gauges and such, flipping a few switches here and there. "Landing lights off," he muttered. "Radio navigation . . . free air temp . . . all good."

"Em?"

"Rotor brake handle up."

"Em?" Chance gasped. "What the fuck are you doing?"

"Preflight checks," Emmett replied, and glanced over his shoulder at Chance. "You might wanna buckle up there, big buddy." He flipped a switch in the console over his head and something beeped. "Battery on."

"To hell with the preflight checks," Chance wheezed. He heaved himself upright and grabbed the shoulder harness but couldn't make head nor tail of it. "Just get this bastard in the sky."

As if to punctuate Chance's request, a bullet struck the fuselage. It didn't go through, but it made a sound like a rock falling on an aluminum roof. In the next moment, Nash went down screaming—leg shot, by the look of it.

"*Em!*"

"All right. Jesus Christ, *all right.*" Emmett pushed a button on a lever to the left of the pilot's seat. "Starter engaged," he yelled, and the chopper made the kind of sound that Chance wanted it to make. A fully operational *we're getting the fuck out of here* sound. "Applying throttle," Emmett cried a few seconds later, and the sound got louder.

"That's it," Chance cried. He wiped sweat off his throat and looked out the window. Nash was sprawled on the grass but still firing—putting up one hell of a fight. God love him. Better yet, the chopper's rotor blades were turning, getting faster and faster.

"Throttle is cranked," Emmett shouted.

"You're goddamn right it is," Chance agreed. He pumped his fist in the air and howled.

JESSIE HAD JUST FINISHED RELOADING when she heard unsuppressed gunfire from the back of the house. It had taken longer than it should have because of the teeth marks in her left arm. Her hand still worked, but her fingers were stiff, and the adrenaline—not just the pain—made everything shake. She hoped she could shoot straight.

Four in the 10FP's box max (and spares in her pocket), fifteen in the M&P .40. Jessie was as ready as she was going to be. She headed toward the house, but *slowly*, dragging her left leg. The gunfire continued. It being unsuppressed meant it wasn't Brea or Flo cycling the trigger, not unless one of them had appropriated a stray gun.

"Not good," Jessie said, limping faster. Her left foot splashed every time it came down. Her jaw clacked loosely. A new sound joined the gunfire: the distinct whir of a helicopter's rotor blades. Jessie envisioned Chance Kotter being bundled into the cabin by a couple of bodyguards, with a third thug following, walking backward while laying down suppressive fire.

Jessie shook her head. She couldn't let that happen. Chance *couldn't* get away.

There was a corpse on the lawn up ahead. He had two bullet holes in the center of his chest. Not Jessie's kill. The holes she'd made were bigger. She dropped to her knees and patted the corpse's pockets. There was a wallet or cell phone in the front left and a smaller, less symmetrical bulge in the front right. Coins, maybe, but probably keys. Jessie dug in and indeed pulled out a key chain with a Busch Light bottle opener attached and a tear-shaped fob with faded buttons.

"Thank you," she hissed. She pressed the red button on the fob, and an old Silverado parked thirty yards away honked once and flashed its lights invitingly. Jessie got to her feet and hobbled toward it.

THEIR TARGET—NASH, MORE THAN likely—had gone down screaming but didn't let up on the trigger. He was a hittable distance away, maybe forty yards, but Brea or Flo couldn't get a clean shot off. Nash compensated for his lack of movement with an increased rate of fire. The bullets zipped over the sisters' heads and thumped into the ground. Dirt and grass flew. The air was murky.

It didn't keep them from trying. They aimed at the telltale flash and pumped their triggers, their own muzzle blast contained by their suppressors. It was hard to tell how close they were getting. Maybe Nash was wrapped in Kevlar. Maybe he was bleeding from a dozen entry wounds. Either way, he returned every one of their bullets with six of his own. The only reprieve came in the three or four seconds it took him to reload.

The helicopter was another thirty yards beyond Nash, too far away to do anything more than dent the fuselage. Its blades turned with thunderous power. Its external lights winked mockingly. As Brea and Flo watched, it lifted slowly from the ground. Six feet. Ten feet. Twenty feet. It tilted forward, then balanced out and continued to climb.

"He's getting *away*," Brea screamed, and started to get to her feet. Flo reached across and pulled her back down. Bullets cut through the air above them. Brea was undeterred. She shook herself out of Flo's one-armed grasp, pushed herself to one knee, and unloaded manic shots at the sky. She didn't stop until her gun clicked empty.

The chopper kept rising.

# FORTY

And we have liftoff," Emmett cried triumphantly. He turned in his seat and gave Chance a radiant smile. "Jesus jumping Christ, I *told* you I'd get you out of there."

"That you did."

"I am the *man* with the *plan*. The goddamn *Em-Vee-Pee*."

Chance watched the ground fall away—not as rapidly as he'd like, but he'd sooner be fifty feet in the air and climbing than down on solid earth with those gals. He knew that one day he would make room in his heart for guilt (leaving his friends behind had been a shitty thing to do) and maybe some shame, too. But the overwhelming feeling in that moment—greater even than his anger—was *relief*. It was moon-sized and just as bright. Chance took it in his arms and let it crush him.

Emmett hooted and howled, wallowing in self-praise. Chance peered out the window (the ground wasn't much farther away than it was the last time he looked) and let out a long, chest-loosening sigh. Sweet mother-humping relief. In all reasonableness, he needed to be alive to feel those other things anyway. Guilt and such. And he for damn sure needed to be alive to put everything right. As God was his witness, he would find those gals and turn them inside out. No games. Just an ice-cold serving of revenge . . . and perhaps a little wager on the side.

He held his hands aloft and howled with Emmett. They tried out-howling each other and broke off laughing. Good Lord, they were like a couple of frat brothers slapping dicks.

"I am the bee's elbows," Emmett declared.

"I'd say."

"The rooster's strut."

"Hehe." Chance sighed again and wiped tears from his eyes. "That you are, Em. That you are."

JESSIE DROVE WITH THE HEADLIGHTS off but otherwise surrendered stealth for speed. She ripped along the south side of the house and around the shed, mowing down small trees and killing flowers. A sliding left turn took her across the patio (she missed the pool by about six feet but destroyed a handsome furniture set) and from there onto the west lawn. A muzzle flashed in the darkness ahead, and a helicopter ascended into the night sky. Jessie stomped on the brake. The Silverado slid twenty yards across the grass before stopping.

She got out from behind the wheel, staggered along the side of the truck, and boosted herself into the bed. Her rifle was back here. Jessie picked it up, chambering a .308 as she did. She rested her left elbow on the roof to stabilize her aim, then powered on the thermal scope. The darkness went away. Jessie saw her sisters. They were low to the ground, bullets cutting the grass and flying around them. Flo squeezed off hopeful shots while Brea reloaded her pistol. Jessie switched the sights to the man behind the muzzle flash. The range finder put him at sixty-eight yards. He was her priority.

She was shaking, though, even with the truck's roof providing support for her left arm. It was her right arm, too—her entire body, in fact, from her injured left foot to her gently whirling brain. Jessie blinked, took a breath, and placed the reticule over her target. He was firing from a prone position. There wasn't much of him to see. Jessie squeezed the trigger and missed right.

"*Fuck*," she gasped. "Come on, Jess. You've got this."

She ejected the spent casing and worked another cartridge into the chamber. Back to the sights. Back to her target. Everything shaking. The front of her ski mask was heavy with sweat. The shooter stopped firing to reload, pulling a fresh magazine from an attachment on his tac belt. He propped himself on one elbow to do this, presenting a wider target.

Jessie shot him through the chest and sent him flopping across the grass. She exhaled and worked the bolt. *"Shooter's down,"* she shouted. It was the second time she'd made that announcement. Her sisters owed her a drink.

*"The chopper!"* Brea screeched. There was a tone to her voice that Jessie had never heard before, like an old nail being yanked out of a post. *"Chance . . . the chopper . . . he's getting away!"*

Jessie adjusted her position, dragging her left arm across the roof—leaving a wet smear of blood on the paintwork—and pointing the rifle's barrel at the sky. She returned to the scope, zoomed out, found the helicopter, and zoomed back in. Ninety-six yards away and counting. It nosed up, yawed left, then yawed right again, as if the pilot were drunk or distracted. She saw his thermogram in the cockpit. He circled right, out of view. Jessie steadied her breathing—or *tried* to. It didn't translate to her aim, in any case. The reticule wavered unsteadily. When she managed to get a lock, the helicopter yawed again.

She found her target, hesitated for a fraction of a second, then triggered. Her shot missed low or maybe wide. In either case, the helicopter continued to pitch, yaw, and climb. It was more than high enough now to propel forward and zoom over the trees. That the pilot hadn't done so yet convinced Jessie that he was decently trashed.

One round remaining. Jessie had more in her pocket, but drunk pilot or not, that chopper would be out of range in the time it would take to reload. This one *had* to count. She expelled the empty casing. It glittered in the air and bounced off the bed of the pickup truck with a sound like a coin hitting the bottom of a jar. The bolt's smooth action eased the final cartridge into the chamber. Jessie pulled the buttstock into her shoulder and brought the sights toward her eye. She found the helicopter: 106 . . . 121 . . . 144 yards away. It had turned a half circle and was moving from left to right. Jessie followed it.

Her elbow slipped in the blood. She lost her target and had to reset. The range finder read 171 yards, but that number kept going up.

*"Jessie!"* Brea cried. *"Shoooooot!"*

One shot. This was it. Jessie closed her eyes and wiped the steam off her internal mirror. She saw who she was: a sister, a rainband, one part of a typhoon. She was also her own person, fiercely capable and unafraid. Like every other challenge she'd faced, this wasn't about size, power, or gender. Breaking it down, it amounted to no more than keeping her hands steady, finding the stillness between breaths, and applying a measly 1.5 pounds of trigger pull. It was about doing the small things right.

Jessie opened her eyes. She zoomed in on her target, 201 . . . 228 . . . 257 yards away.

"One shot," she whispered.

She curled her finger around the trigger.

"I AM THE MONKEY'S EYEBROWS. I am—"

One second everything was fine. Emmett's head was intact. It was right there and whole, wobbling stupidly on his shoulders, the same as always. In the next there was a tremendous bang, glass blew into the cockpit, and Emmett slumped to his left. One part of his skull was gone—it was just *gone*—and another part had flopped forward over his eyes like the peak of a baseball cap. Blood and other stuff coated everything.

Chance didn't scream right away. He was too stunned, too darn *confused*. Emmett had sagged over the collective—the lever to the left of the pilot's seat—and his weight pressed it down. The helicopter descended rapidly. It rolled gradually at first, then started to spin. Warning lights flashed and chimed. Centrifugal force pinned Chance into his seat (except for his stomach, which he'd left somewhere in the sky above him). His clothes and hair flapped in the wind rushing through the shattered windshield.

"Oh Jesus God, oh no, oh *please*."

That was when Chance screamed. It was not a sound becoming of a captain of industry, a leader of men. It was shrill and full of terror, rising in pitch until it matched the engine and rotor noise. He did not pray. His life did not flash before his eyes. There was no time for that. He thought of his sister and his dog, and that was all.

BREA AND FLO WERE ON their feet, their arms draped loosely around each other's shoulders. They watched the helicopter's anti-collision and navigation lights spiral in the darkness, dropping quickly. It took less than three seconds to hit the ground. There was no explosion, only a crumpling thud that Brea and Flo felt from two hundred yards away.

And then silence, as perfect as it was brief. Brea broke it.

"I want to see the body," she said.

They started walking, still with their arms around each other, more for support than anything else. If either one of them stepped away, the other would fall. After thirty seconds or so, they heard sirens wailing from the east. It was impossible to tell how far away they were.

"Those poor sons of bitches are in for a long night," Brea said.

"I know the feeling," Flo said.

A minute later—halfway to the crash site—Jessie pulled alongside them in an old Chevy Silverado with a broken headlight and a sapling stuck in its grille. She buzzed the passenger-side window down.

"Need a ride?" she said.

CHANCE HAD BEEN THROWN FROM the wreckage. He wasn't dead. His right arm was gone at the shoulder and a piece of the fuselage jutted from his left thigh. Everything else was either crooked or bleeding. He looked longingly at the stars.

The sisters stood over him, blocking his view, denying him that one final pleasure. They removed their ski masks and unholstered their guns. Chance's eyes grew big and ran with tears.

"Gals," he said.

When it came to Bang-Bang Sisters hits, only one of them would fire the killing shot. They did it quickly, without bravado. It was a job, that was all. *This*, though . . . this was different. Words like "revenge" and "personal" didn't begin to cut it. This man had violated, played with, and divided them—all while laying down money and laughing it up with his toxic friends. A single bullet would not be enough.

The sisters looked at one another, then leveled their pistols and fired simultaneously. One in the stomach. One in the heart. One in the head.

Game over.

THEY CLIMBED INTO THE SILVERADO, Brea behind the wheel, Flo riding shotgun, Jessie in the backseat. The sirens were getting closer. They looked back at the house and saw blue and red lights beating in the night sky.

Brea dropped the transmission into drive and pulled away. She steered around Chance's corpse and between pieces of the ruptured aircraft. A fire had started in the main wreckage. It would guide the police there.

They drove across the rear of Chance's property with the headlights out, invisible to all, gone like ghosts. They didn't talk. They didn't look at one another. Each sister was lost for a moment inside herself. It was the only place to be. Brea navigated the truck onto neighboring property, steering carefully between trees and through a shallow brook. On the other side, a safe distance from the house, she flipped a switch next to the steering column, and the one working headlight came on.

The way ahead was brighter.

# EPILOGUE

They had played every state in the Lower 48 and even nosed into Canada. Mostly in bars of the dive variety, but there'd been no shortage of juke joints, strip clubs, breweries, bingo halls, beaches, backyards, and festivals. Every show was a new experience, with its own unique energy, and every audience member was primed to be electrified. The sisters had put the miles in, and they had the stories (and the scars) to show for it. They were journeyed. They knew how to rock. But no matter how big the venue or how loud the crowd, there was no better feeling than playing a sold-out gig in your hometown.

Jessie strapped on her Les Paul and plugged in. She hit the tuner pedal and checked every string. All good. She flexed her left hand. There'd been extensive rehabilitation since the events in Reedsville: four operations (including the one on her left foot), two-hundred-plus hours of physical therapy. Errol had done a number on her. In those first weeks, she had barely been able to move her fingers. She had graduated in time to clutching a tennis ball, then squeezing a tennis ball, then finer motor skills like stacking coins and fastening buttons. Now, she could blaze up and down the neck of her guitar. Jessie still had trouble with some of the more technical solos, but she was getting a little better—a little faster—every day.

She stepped up to the mic and angled it toward her lips. "Feels good to be home," she said, and the crowd responded, ready to fuel and to *be* fueled. The perfect give-and-take. Rock and roll intercourse. Jessie felt it in her chest: butterflies with crackling wings. She looked at Flo, standing, as always, to her right, and knew that she felt it, too. It was in her flared eyes and the set of her shoulders. She cranked the volume knob on her bass and grinned. Jessie turned to look at Brea, who sat like a conqueror behind her kit. Her hair had grown out to punky quills, and she had a new tattoo on her left biceps that read PERFECTLY BROKEN. She twirled a stick in one hand and counted them in.

THEY STARTED WITH A NEW original—a fiery, up-tempo track with off-beat eighth notes and an emphatic bass line. Historically, the sisters hadn't written too much of their own stuff, but now they found they had things to say, demons to exorcise. This song was called "Not So Sweet." It was an anti-patriarchal commentary on narcissism and oppression: a rallying cry for being heard—being *seen*—in an environment where socially regressive behaviors were commonplace. They had played it for their stepcousin, Randy Vernier (who was continuing his uncle's legacy at Vernier Records). Randy had stopped the recording halfway through and critiqued, "It's too catchy to be angry, and it's too angry to be catchy. What in the hell is it even about?" The sisters looked at one another for a moment, then Brea and Flo said, "Womanhood," and Jessie said, "Togetherness," but they all knew it was mostly about fucking shit up.

They found writing music to be cathartic and therefore essential; only a small part of their rehabilitation was physical. They each had a deep and misty darkness inside. This wasn't a new thing, just a bigger thing, and too consuming to manage without help. Their therapists were in different parts of the city but charged the same extortionate rate. They were used to dealing with big personalities with big bank accounts. The sisters made them work for their money.

The therapy was not a solution, only a step in the right direction—one part of a rehabilitative process that included meditation, yoga, making music, and other self-care. Brea, Jessie, and Flo did not abandon their principles or about-face their characters, but they *did* allow more gentleness into their lives. There was space for both. They followed new paths and met new people. Their triangle remained intact, but creating distance helped make it stronger.

It helped, also, that the stories had fallen off the newsfeeds and social media platforms. For the first few weeks, Chance Kotter and Aaron Gallo-Day were everywhere, to the point where the sisters each found a suitably sized rock and crawled beneath it. When they finally emerged, the authorities were still trying to put the pieces together.

"It's an ongoing investigation," said Mart Millar, Reedsville's deputy chief of police. "We got a lot of bodies, and the only thing we got more of is questions. Rest assured, we will continue to work closely with federal agents and will do everything in our power to provide answers."

Those answers were not forthcoming, however, particularly regarding Chance Kotter's connection to the wren and why three of his employees—including Burl Rowan, his head of security—were found dead, along with Aaron Gallo-Day, at a warehouse in Reedsville's industrial district. There was a suggestion that the local authorities were *not* working closely with federal agents—that they were, in fact, withholding information and thwarting the investigation. Chief Bethany Kotter, speaking off duty but "on the goddamn record" at Fat Fanny's Ale House, said those claims were "outright horseshit."

One of the more outlandish theories purported that Chance Kotter—the Bruce Wayne of Reedsville, according to some—had assembled a crack team of vigilantes to hunt down and go after the wren, and the wren (who just happened to be Chance's computer guy) learned about this and put together his own hit squad. These opposing factions clashed at two locations, culminating in twenty dead. Beyond video evidence showing masked assailants on Chance's property, there was nothing to support this speculation.

The sisters were never mentioned as suspects or victims. They were never approached by investigators. There was a single post on Reddit in which a user called NAMST1RAM83 exposed the details of Chance Kotter's game. It was accurate enough that it could only have come from someone on the inside, revealing how Chance had captured the three vigilantes responsible for his nephew's murder and coerced them into a citywide hunt and fight to the death. There were a lot of gaps in the account, but it gained some traction and was upvoted to the top of the "Hate for Reedsville" subreddit. It read like a conspiracy theory, though, and the sisters were never named.

The conjecture outweighed the hard evidence. Certain people knew the truth, or at least more than they were letting on. Others—Caroline Rowan for instance, Burl's widow—demanded answers. She appeared on local TV and radio stations claiming that Chance Kotter was, for all intents and purposes, a mobster whose criminal interests had gotten her husband killed. These claims were quickly shot down by Reedsville's chief of police and other high-ranking officials. Ultimately, it became just another part of the drama—another question mark in a case that struggled to provide clarity.

The one definite was that the wren was dead. This glaring positive was jumped on by the Feds and local authorities alike and used to divert attention from the swirling, messy leaf pile of negatives. The events leading to his brutal downfall were shrouded in mystery and would likely remain that way. The important thing—emphasized repeatedly by those in charge—was that the wren was no longer a threat to the people of Reedsville and its surrounding communities. Substantial evidence found at Aaron Gallo-Day's warehouse apartment and on his personal computers (the haikus withheld from the press and therefore the public, among other things) confirmed beyond doubt that he was the notorious serial killer. It marked the end of an ugly chapter and offered closure to the families of the wren's victims.

The wren was dead. *Very.* Aaron Gallo-Day's celebrity, however, was in full flight. Media outlets across the country burrowed into his tragic backstory. They covered his parents' death in glorified detail and dwelled on his illnesses and solitude. A handful of people who'd known Aaron during his years in the child welfare system came forward, and they all described him the same way: intense, quiet, creepy. Solen Britt of WBRC FOX6 News asked a former caregiver if she ever believed Gallo-Day could be capable of murder.

"Well, he was just a boy. Maybe fourteen, fifteen years old. But yessir . . ." The elderly caregiver had trailed off, delivering an unintentional but wonderfully dramatic pause. "Some mornings I'd wake up surprised not to find a kitchen knife in this ol' bosom."

Slasherrama.com (Uploading PURE EVIL Since 1999) placed Aaron Gallo-Day at number four on its list of America's top ten serial killers, between John Wayne Gacy (holding on to that number three spot) and Dennis "the BTK Killer" Rader. Aaron's face graced the cover of every supermarket tabloid in the country. *Now That's NEWS!* alleged he ate fried worms for breakfast and was a descendant of Napoleon Bonaparte. A&E had already screened *Little Bird: The Aaron Gallo-Day Story* to mixed reviews.

Aaron was cremated at Pink's Crematorium on October 2, 2023. There were four people in attendance: Ernie Pink, Laura Regan (from the county coroner's office), Police Chief Bethany Kotter, and Aaron's only living relative—his grandmother, Francesca Gallo. The ashes were presented to the old lady afterward, who took them home, mixed them into a five-pound bag of Happy Whistler's Wild Bird Seed, and distributed them among the twenty-two feeders in her backyard.

This was the second funeral service for Bethany Kotter in as many days. The first was unspeakably more difficult. Her beautiful little brother was laid to rest at the Garden of Everlasting Light in a reserved plot between their father, Earl Kotter, and Chance's mentor, Amos "Tusk" Sauerland. The service was magnificently attended, despite the heavy rain. Seventies rock icon Ned Sargent delivered a heartbreaking eulogy, then saluted his fallen friend by firing a .375 H&H thunderstick into the sky.

Tributes were paid to the great townsman in the following weeks. There was even some talk of erecting a statue outside the Kotter-Bryce Tower or at least naming a street after him. Mayor Austin Hasse, speaking on crutches outside Reedsville City Hall, said he would float the idea at the next committee meeting, but he didn't appear overly enthusiastic about it. Indeed, the adoration for Chance Kotter was far from universal. He'd been cutthroat in his business dealings and had amassed quite the body count over the years. Many of those he'd overpowered on his way to the top made their voices heard. "It ain't Christian to speak ill of the dead," Pearl Gomer told the

*Reedsville and Colton Gazette.* Pearl had lost her small family-run business to Chance's predatory pricing strategies in 2010. "But Chance Kotter was a man so empty of heart you could argue he was never alive to begin with." Even Mason Nurll, speaking on crutches outside his peanut farm north of Reedsville, declared Chance a low-down son of a bee sting who got what was coming to him. "He claimed to be a man of God, but I've a notion he's boiling up crawdads in the devil's kitchen."

ONE SONG AFTER ANOTHER. THE crowd cheered and swayed, moving in sync with the band. It was beautiful to watch, to feel. Flo looked for Imani but couldn't see her in the haze of bodies beyond the stage lights. She was out there, though, and partying hard. This was her first night out since having the baby.

The sisters went seamlessly from their cover of Nirvana's "Come as You Are" to their take on the surf classic "Pipeline." All eyes were on Jessie, but the rhythm section, as usual, did the heavy lifting. Flo turned to Brea. They locked gazes and grinned, side by side in the pocket. The audience heard Jessie's guitar, but it *felt* the bass and drums.

After returning from Reedsville (by way of a no-questions-asked doctor they knew in Conway, Arkansas, who fixed them up enough to continue their journey west), the sisters moved into separate accommodations around the city. Jessie went back to the ranch in Chatsworth, Brea got the run of their shared house in NoHo, and Flo happily crashed on the sofa in Imani's tiny two-bedroom house in Panorama City. It was a temporary measure. Each needed distance from the others. Breathing room. *Healing* room.

There was no contact between them for nineteen days, then Flo got a text message from Brea. Join me for a drink? Three hours later, they were sitting in a bar on Lankershim Boulevard, clutching identical bottles of beer and listening to Django "the Vibes Man" Lopez play his saxophone onstage. They spent the first moments checking in with each other, but gently, wary of the things they'd done, even more so of the things they'd shared. One beer became two, and then three. The edge between them was as clear as the neon signs in the windows. Eventually, Brea addressed it. Flo knew it was the real reason she wanted to meet.

"It's the three of us. I know that. A triangle, right? But I've sometimes felt that it's more like three lines, and Jessie is the bridge. It's you, her, then me." Brea shrugged and swirled the beer in her bottle. "I mean, would we still be together if Jessie wasn't around?"

"Right," Flo said. Short of saying nothing, it was as noncommittal a response as she could manage. She tapped the bottom of her bottle against the cast on her left arm and watched the Vibes Man play.

"This might sound crazy, but after everything that happened . . ." Brea sat forward in her seat and waited for Flo to make eye contact. "I've felt something different between us. *Strong* different. We've done things, experienced things, that should have separated us completely, yet here we are."

"Here we are," Flo said.

"Can you travel that close to hell with someone and not come out of it newly bonded?"

"I don't know," Flo responded. "But if there is a new bond between us, a new bridge, it's made of . . . *complicated* pieces."

"Yeah." Brea nodded thoughtfully.

"And I think," Flo continued, "we'd both do well to tread carefully."

Brea raised her bottle to that. Flo did, too. They managed smiles that brightened their healing faces. It was a good start.

Flo had respected Brea's honesty and humility. What she hadn't told Brea was that she'd had similar thoughts and feelings but had not taken the time to meditate on them. She'd been too preoccupied with her own self-care. Every other moment was spent with Imani.

Four days. One hundred and two hours, in fact. That was how long Imani and Aubree were kept in that dank brick room—a maintenance building at a disused textile factory five miles south of LAX. They were given food, water, and access to bathroom facilities, but these things could not offset the mental trauma. Imani feared for her baby. She spent most of the time singing lullabies in as strong a voice as possible, hoping the thousands of tears she cried were not also dripping down inside her, where the baby would feel them. Aubree sang lullabies, too, and offered motherly reassurances that kept them both from breaking.

They never learned who their captors were or why they'd been taken.

After being released, they had crossed an empty parking lot and walked in a daze to Redondo Beach Avenue, where they flagged down help and called the police. Aubree had been reported missing by her husband, who'd told one of his caregivers by way of his eye-tracking software. Imani's disappearance had not been reported at all.

Investigators had nothing to go on. No eyewitnesses. No camera footage. No evidence left at the factory. There appeared to be no motive, and the only link between the two women was the sisters. Brea, Jessie, and Flo had all been called in for questioning on their return to Los Angeles, and they all pleaded ignorant.

"You have any enemies? Anybody who might want to use your family to hurt you?"

"Not that I know of?"

"Any overzealous fans?"

"We're not famous enough to have fans."

"And why are you all busted up? It looks like you got into a car accident."

"A fight, actually, after a gig in Waco. A few cowboy types who'd drank too much. It happens."

The police promised to continue looking into it, but in a city like Los Angeles, it wasn't likely to get to the top of anyone's list of priorities.

In those first weeks, Imani repeatedly told Flo how grateful she was to have her there. She was hurting inside. She was scared and confused, but her warmth and love could not be diminished. Flo felt the same way. She took as much healing from her little sister as she gave. They curled up on the sofa together and watched movies. They went shopping for baby things—and mummy things, too. Every time Flo sang to Imani's bump or rubbed her big fat swollen feet (as promised), something inside her moved closer to completeness.

LEON GEORGE BELLA WAS BORN at 2:03 A.M. on Saturday, November 4, 2023. It was a long labor—twenty-one hours—but the reward was eternal. Leon was healthy and strong. He was beautiful. Flo had stayed by Imani's side throughout, holding her hand, running a cold cloth over her brow. It was the best day of her life.

"I'll give you some time," Flo said to Imani after the fireworks had ended, and Leon was all burrito'd up in his bassinet with a soft little hat on his head.

"Don't go far," Imani mumbled, her eyes drooping.

Flo didn't go far. She walked to the hospital café and bought a cup of hot, strong coffee and drank it thinking about the future. There were a lot of question marks ahead, but everything suddenly seemed more possible. She returned to Imani's room forty minutes later to find her sister asleep with Leon curled up, tiny and precious, on her breast. Flo crossed to the window and looked out. Tears rolled brightly down her cheeks.

She watched the sun come up.

TWO HUNDRED AND FIFTY ON the floor. A capacity crowd. This was the sisters' first gig since everything went down. They'd rehearsed together, written together, but they hadn't played in front of an audience since September of last year. Brea remembered the gig: a rock club called Stray Bullets in some Podunk desert town not far from the Nevada state line. It had been an angry, messy show. The sisters were torn about turning around and going after the wren, and it had shown in their performance—the beginning of everything sliding downhill.

There was no divide tonight. They were tight and feeling it. They kept it moving, too, with minimal banter between songs, just enough to keep the people pumped. Brea ended "Sweet Soul Sister," by the Cult, with an impromptu solo, smashing her kit with manic rhythm and enthusiasm. The crowd exploded.

It felt great to have the band back together. When they played, when they were coordinated and on point, nothing could stop them. The sisters likened themselves to a triangle, even a typhoon, but really, they were three people with sublime chemistry. A rare and beautiful magic.

This wasn't the only band that Brea hoped to re-form. The Bang-Bang Sisters also hadn't performed for eight months, and Brea missed them. She regularly perused the Trace. There were plenty of well-paying gigs out there. America had become a nation bereft of many things, but bad guys wasn't one of them.

Brea had asked her sisters how they felt about taking their other band out on the road and was met with a muted response. Flo was too wrapped up with Imani and Leon. "I don't know . . . *maybe*. I'm just . . ." She had blown out her cheeks and flared her eyebrows. "It's like . . . my *life* right now. And hey, I meant to say: Leon just got his first tooth. It's the *cutest* thing." Jessie had said nothing, only shrugged, but Brea had seen the answer in her eyes: Sammy Manczarek. Jessie had met him at an L.A. Guns show at the Whisky in April, and they'd clicked immediately. Sammy was a chef and part-time tattoo artist. He enjoyed surfing, collecting vintage vinyl, and microdosing psychedelics. It was all still very new—they certainly hadn't hit the L-word stage yet—but from the way they were together, and the smitten look in Jessie's eyes, Brea suspected they were in it for the long haul.

"Okay, I'm picking up distinct *maybe* and *possibly* vibes here," Brea had said. They were enjoying post-rehearsal sushi at the ranch. The sun was shining, and she was feeling okay—more okay than she'd felt in a long time, in fact. "There's hope for a reunion yet."

"Stay tuned," Flo replied.

Brea would, but in the meantime, she was content to go solo. *This is my future*, she'd said to Jessie in that crummy motel room back in New Jersey. *I'll do this alone, if I have to.*

At the beginning of May, Brea had logged in to the Trace and checked the bulletin board, as she had so many times over the previous months. This time, she took it two steps further. First, by clicking and reading through one of the listed jobs, and then by accepting it.

Adam Filley had bludgeoned his wife of twelve years to death with a hammer and thrown her body into a ravine three miles from their home in Poway, California. No evidence linked him to the crime, except neighbors had heard Adam and Patricia Filley "kicking off like usual" the night before he'd reported her missing, and there were traces of an oxidizing detergent—no blood, though—in the trunk of his car. Adam was arrested on probable cause, brutally interrogated, and released forty-eight hours later.

Fast-forward six weeks. Adam, falling-over drunk, had blurted out to his brother that he was indeed responsible for killing Patricia, and that he would do it again if the bitch was still alive. Adam's brother had promptly shared this information with the on-duty homicide detective at their local police department. A drunken confession—which Adam vehemently denied making—would not hold up in a court of law, but it *was* enough to trigger the Trace's interest. Its hackers dug their clever little claws in and three days later recovered 112 deleted photographs of Patricia's bloodied corpse from a second phone owned by Adam, which he'd surreptitiously linked to a business account using a former employee's name. The Trace could have turned this information over to the police—anonymously, of course—but that wasn't what its donors paid the big bucks for.

Brea read all this with her fists clenched and her desire for vengeance rising.

She was on the road to Poway two hours later.

**SEVERAL MONTHS BEFORE THE ADAM** Filley job, just after Christmas, Brea had received a phone call. Her screen read **NO CALLER ID**. Brea didn't answer. It rang again two minutes later and again six minutes after that. That third time, Brea swiped the green button.

"Hello?"

"Good of you to finally answer." A female voice with a southern drawl. Brea's heart dropped and a sick feeling ran through her.

"Who is this?"

"The last person you wanna be hearing from, I'd say."

Brea had been hiking in Topanga, getting her mental and physical steps in, but now she sat down on a tree stump and lowered her head. She knew who this was, even though they'd never spoken before. A memory surfaced in her mind: Chance Kotter tapping a photo on his desk of a fiftysomething-year-old woman with blazing red hair. *Ain't she a button?* he'd said. Bethany Kotter, Reedsville's chief of police. This was confirmed with the next words out of her mouth.

"I buried my nephew almost four years ago and my sister not long after. You are responsible for both of those deaths. You and those little bitches you run around with."

Brea spat on the ground between her boots. "Yeah, listen, I think you've got the wrong—"

"Horseshit, missy, with a big fuck you on top." She even sounded like Chance, a female version of him, which, Brea supposed, she was. "Three months ago, it was my brother I buried, and that was your doing, too."

Brea sat up straight. It was a cool January day, sixty tops, but it suddenly felt like mid-July. Sweat beaded her nose, and that sick feeling had reached her head, where it revolved slowly. She breathed the fresh air and steadied herself.

"I know who you are, *Brea Steen* . . . and *you* should know that I can drop the hammer any time I choose." Bethany's voice wasn't all gravel. Brea heard tears in there, too. She imagined the police chief sitting behind the wheel of her cruiser with her phone in one hand and a balled-up Kleenex in the other. "I've got everything I need—witnesses and such—to put you and your bitch sisters away for a long time."

Brea believed there could be some truth to this but knew Bethany would never go that route. Incriminating the sisters meant exposing Chance's tortuous game and his many other corruptions, which included kidnapping two innocent women—one of them heavily pregnant—and holding them at gunpoint. It was an extremely damaging light to shine on the Kotter family name, and who knew how many other sins would come crawling out of the woodwork. This was the reason Brea, Jessie, and Flo had not been questioned about the violent events that had transpired in Reedsville last September. Key people were keeping schtum, evidence was either destroyed or covered up—all to protect Chance's memory, his estate, and the family he'd left behind. Likewise, the sisters were not about to implicate themselves in order to bring the evil empire down. In short, what they had here was what an old reactionary like Bethany Kotter would call a "Mexican standoff" and the sisters would call an "impasse."

"However," the police chief drawled now, and threaded more menace into her voice. "I'm a firm believer that the sentence should fit the crime . . . so maybe prison ain't the answer."

Brea tried swallowing, but her throat was dry. "I don't know who you are, lady, but I hope you find the help you need."

"You like to think you're some kind of angel of vengeance, huh?" Bethany let the question hang. Brea heard Reedsville in the background and it chilled her. "Yeah, so do I. My brother wasn't the only one with influence."

"I've heard enough," Brea said. Her voice cracked. "Hanging up now."

"I know where you are. You, your sisters, your families—"

Brea ended the call. She was breathing hard. Her T-shirt clung to the sweat on her back. It was a warning, that was all—Reedsville's chief of police flexing a little muscle—but it had crawled under Brea's skin. She got to her feet and screamed. The sound echoed around the canyon. After a moment, she took a long drink of water and waited for her legs to stop shaking. A breeze blew through her short hair. It rippled the toyon and the coastal sagebrush and hummed between the rocks where the king snakes lay hidden.

**THE FINAL NOTE GOT LOST** in a floor-lifting riot of applause. The Chrome on Sunset was a small venue, but it felt four times the size in that moment—a thousand drenched souls, not two hundred and fifty, pushing the walls beyond their limits, raising the roof, spilling copiously onto the sidewalk. Brea, Jessie, and Flo joined hands at the front of the stage. They drank it in. They could start fires with the way they felt inside.

And with that, it was over. The concertgoers finished their drinks and dispersed, leaving behind only echoes of themselves, vestiges of their separate but collective energies.

"That was a *rush*," Jessie said.

Brea pulled the van around front. They packed up their gear slowly, reluctant to relinquish that time and place and their part in it. They stood outside afterward, taking in the last of it, looking at one another with a wildness in their eyes they used to see more often. The Strip flowed around them, beautifully colored, perfectly alive.

"Before I forget," Brea said, "we have another show next Friday. E-Five in Santa Monica."

"I know that place," Flo said. "Great sound. Big crowds. That'll be chaotic."

"We've never had a problem with chaos," Jessie remarked with a smile. She held her hands out to her sisters. "Hey, bring it in."

They came together, their arms around one another, their foreheads touching, forming a shape they knew all too well. For one sweet instant, everything faded around them. They felt their bonds as women, sisters, and soulmates, and all the things they had in their hearts for one another. It was another kind of rhythm, another kind of rush. They separated at the same instant and the spell was broken.

There was power in knowing they could get it back.

The sisters climbed into their road-weary tour van and cruised home. City lights flashed across the dented bodywork. The engine blended with the noise. Brea flicked on the radio and tuned it to their favorite rock station. The DJ was spinning something restless that the sisters used to cover back in the day, when they were raw and dangerous.

"Remember this one?" Brea said.

"Yeah," Flo said. She turned it up.

# ACKNOWLEDGMENTS

*The Bang-Bang Sisters* was written to an up-tempo, hard-rockin' soundtrack, mainly all-female bands (for obvious reasons). There are too many to list them all, but I'd like to give a special mention to the Donnas, the Runaways, Babes in Toyland, the 5.6.7.8.'s, and L7 for driving up my energy levels when I most needed it. Music plays a big role in my work, whether I'm listening to it or writing about it, and I had some great bands on board for this one.

Huge thanks to the team at William Morrow, with a particularly bright spotlight on Nate Lanman, who edited this novel with professionalism and patience, and—as all great editors do—ultimately made it a better book. A big shout-out, also, to Jen Brehl, who worked her magic and secured me another swing at the tough-to-crack piñata that is the publishing industry. I'm incredibly grateful.

My agent, Howard Morhaim, is the reason this book is in your hands. As ever, he steered me with expertise and understanding, and told me the things I needed to hear. There's more to being an agent than selling books, and Howard is a cool, adept operator in every regard. I couldn't imagine a better person to have in my corner.

I'm a kid who grew up on the wrong side of the tracks, in a working-class neighborhood in a working-class town. The TV and movie industry seems utterly dreamlike to me, but Michael Prevett—my man in Hollywood—has a way of making me believe that anything is possible. He continues to show unbridled enthusiasm for my work, and who could ask for anything more? Thank you, Michael.

And how about some love for my beta readers? Being the first person to appraise a rough-around-the-edges manuscript is an unenviable task, and that's not lost on me. For *The Bang-Bang Sisters*, Shannon Kornelsen had that dubious honor. Shannon—as well as being an exceptional human being—is an incredible writer in her own right, who reliably floors me with her work. She understands the process and the business and gave me her feedback with all the care and attention I needed. Likewise, Chris Ryall, Tim Lebbon, and Christopher Golden (my second, third, and fourth readers, respectively) offered their praise and/or constructive criticism in all the right places. I'm so grateful to them all.

My mom, Lorraine Edgell, and her husband, Dave Edgell, have shown tremendous support for my work in recent years. This means so much to me. Dave passed away in September 2023 after a long battle with cancer. My mom sat by his bedside and read an early draft of *The Bang-Bang Sisters* to him during his final days. I understand this made him very happy, and this makes *me* very happy. Rest in peace, Dave. You were a good man.

Chris Myles and Mark Muralla keep my website looking fresh and professional and ask for very little in return. Thanks, guys. Olaf and Yuka Buchheim publish and support my work in Germany and are always the best, easiest people to work with. Vincent Sammy is a genius artist from South Africa who aligns himself with my vibe and re-creates my characters in a way that reliably leaves me awestruck. Sandra and Andrew Marsh remain stalwart standard-bearers who share in every high and low that this industry provides. Flavio Gomes is a dear friend and a generous spirit who provided invaluable help with the computing and hacking references in this novel, and I—not the most tech-savvy kid on the block—would have been lost without him. Big thanks, also, to Joseph Pace, who has shown a brilliant belief in me, and who always (and often unintentionally) keeps me entertained.

My Sunday night hangout is the open mic at the Elora Brewing Company, hosted by my good pal and musical mentor Adrian Jones. This is where I go to make music and to be with my friends. The EBC open mic crew is a kind, creative, uplifting group of people, with whom I had so many good laughs and great musical moments during the writing of this book. I love and appreciate them all.

Finally, thanks to my incredible family. Emily, I love you. Lily and Charlie, you are my life. I spend so much of my time in make-believe worlds, but you are the reality I will always return to.